Francis A Archibald

Methodism and Literature

A series of articles from several writers on the literary enterprise and achievements

of the Methodist Episcopal church.

Francis A Archibald

Methodism and Literature
*A series of articles from several writers on the literary enterprise and achievements of the
Methodist Episcopal church.*

ISBN/EAN: 9783337386283

Printed in Europe, USA, Canada, Australia, Japan

Cover: Foto ©Andreas Hilbeck / pixelio.de

More available books at **www.hansebooks.com**

METHODISM AND LITERATURE:

A

SERIES OF ARTICLES FROM SEVERAL WRITERS ON THE LITERARY ENTERPRISE AND ACHIEVEMENTS

OF THE

METHODIST EPISCOPAL CHURCH.

EDITED BY

F. A. ARCHIBALD, D. D.

WITH A

CATALOGUE OF SELECT BOOKS FOR THE HOME, THE CHURCH, AND THE SUNDAY-SCHOOL.

———•—•———

CINCINNATI:

WALDEN AND STOWE.

NEW YORK: PHILLIPS & HUNT.

1883.

PREFACE.

THIS book is believed to be a demand of the times, and especially in the denomination whence it emanates. Among the numerous agencies which Methodism has employed in her evangelizing labors, none has been more potent than the printing-press. This instrumentality was early recognized by the founders of the Church, who wisely took measures for its growth and perpetuity, and "builded better than they knew." With them a prime object was to create and foster a taste for reading, and to regulate the cost of literature, so that it might be brought within the reach of the great masses to whom they preached. Methodism was, indeed, the pioneer of cheap religious reading, organizing a system of colportage before the term *colporteur* had been engrafted upon our Saxon stock.

Mr. Wesley wrote books for the million, and sold them at rates which astonished the book-makers of his day. In 1782, seventeen years prior to the formation of the "Religious Tract Society of London," he organized, in connection with Dr. Coke, the "Society for the Distribution of Religious Tracts among the Poor;" but forty years before that, while prosecuting his evangelical work, he commenced printing and circulating tracts, and was the first to use, on an extensive scale, this means of popular information.

Asbury and his coadjutors brought the same spirit into America, and planted the germ of the present mammoth Book Concern, which has steadily grown from its earliest implantation, until now it has amassed a body of literature representing all phases of matured thought in the fields of systematic theology, moral philosophy, ecclesiastical history, religious biography, and Christian experience, and presenting to the world thoroughly digested systems, well-matured suggestions, and all needful appliances for the work of evangelization. The New York *Evangelist*, in referring to its purely Methodistic publications, says: "No religious body in this country can present, we believe, so various and extensive a collection of denominational literature as the Methodist Church."

That this work of the Church may be brought to the thoughtful notice of the public, and that its completeness, adaptation, and due importance may be presented in a befitting and permanent form, the papers that constitute the body of this book have been carefully prepared; and the reader who shall give them a proper consideration will doubtless arise from their perusal as fully convinced as the editor hereof that the publication is not only timely but necessary. Nearly every phase of Methodism in literature has here a comprehensive treatment, and the different fields have been so fully explored as to render a formal introduction almost unnecessary.

These papers begin, very appropriately, with the subject, "A Reading Church." The necessity for general information and mental culture is as true to-day as when Wesley, in his declining years, imbued

with deep solicitude for the permanence of the societies he had raised up, wrote these words: " It can not
be that the people should grow in grace, unless they
give themselves to reading. A reading people will
always be a knowing people. A people who talk
much will know little. Press this upon them with
your might, and you will soon see the fruit of your
labors." If Mr. Wesley regarded the neglect of
reading in his time a serious hinderance to Methodist
progress, how much greater does the impediment appear when viewed in the light of a reading age!

The " Book Concern " itself, the reservoir and the
conservator of the Church's best thoughts, as well as
the medium whence they flow out to vivify and serve
mankind, has its appropriate recognition in these
pages, and is immediately followed by subjects of
grave importance to the Church,—the methods for
the dissemination of our literature, and the duty of
the Church to our publishing interests. The time
was when every itinerant minister was *ex-officio* a
disseminator of the Church's literature ; but the immediate and pressing cares of the pastorate, which
have multiplied as the spheres of labor have become
contracted and the Churches have increased in membership, have been accepted, in many cases, as a
release from what the fathers deemed an obligation ;
but it must be admitted that the duty, in some form
or other, still remains. To the consideration of these
subjects the attention of the Church is now invited,
and a proper discussion of the duties of all interested
can not but result in good.

The three papers which follow direct the attention

to a vital issue now forced upon the attention of the Church in general, and which must be answered speedily if disastrous consequences are to be avoided. What we read, and what we should read, as well as the pernicious literature and novel-reading of the day, open up questions that concern the patriot as well as the moral philosopher; and the prospect that rises in the future, when a generation of youth fed upon the husks, and worse than husks, of much of the popular literature of the present, shall come upon the stage of action, is appalling to every philanthropist. Some of the fruit has already matured, as an examination of these papers and the criminal records of the country will amply show. Recent statistics disclose the alarming fact that not only in the large cities, but in the country places as well, nearly one-fourth of those arrested for crime of all grades are boys and girls between the ages of twelve and twenty. A secular newspaper, in discussing the subject, says: "That which has led many of these young persons into their unfortunate condition is the obscene literature so generally read by the young people of this country." This is the crying evil of modern society. It is sapping the foundations of virtuous liberty. There is no concealing the truth uttered by the papers in this book. If the Church is to grow up a healthful, influential, and permanent institution, with its membership fully equipped in the brain and heart, it must press out its literature everywhere, and seek to counteract the streams of death that are deluging the land.

The biographical and historical literature of Methodism, as will be seen by reference to the articles on these subjects, are by no means meager. It has been thought by some that our publishers have gone to an extreme in biographical publications; but these are the materials out of which history is made, and there seems to be a satisfactory and sufficient reason for every book of this character. The most ancient book in the possession of mankind, the Genesis of Moses, has recorded for all time a series of biographical memoirs, and upon the Christian Church the duty is enjoined by an express command to "remember them who have spoken to us the word of God," and to imitate their faith. A learned author of one of the biographies of Methodism says: "The providence and grace of God have, from age to age, raised up men whose lives should be a beacon of hope to them who come after. 'A true intellect stands like a watch-tower upon the shore.' The waves thunder against it, and vanish in spray. Its clear and steady lamp burns in the storm—a consolation and a guide, over the dark sea, to the haven of glory."

The paper on the "Literature of Bible Study" is not intended to be exhaustive of the subject. Such books as Wiseman's "Sketches from the Book of Judges," which Spurgeon places among the commentaries, and says is written "in a powerful style," have not always been introduced, although they might appropriately find a place in this department.

In the "Literature of Sacred Song" we reach a subject vital to the success of the Church in the past as well as the present. The first Wesleyan hymn-book was published in 1738. It contains seventy hymns, twenty-seven of which are by Dr. Watts.

A number of other hymn-books were issued by the two Wesleys up to the year 1779, when the standard hymn-book was published by subscription. Seven editions of it appeared in John Wesley's life-time. He had taken immense pains with it, selecting the materials with care, methodizing them with characteristic exactness, and transcribing it with his own hand. It was his last *great* work—a bequest of inestimable value to the Methodist societies and to the Christian Church at large, almost all the denominations in England and in this country, both in and out of the national establishment, having availed themselves of it in their various hymn-books to a greater or less extent. That acute and captious critic, Isaac Taylor, has said of the hymns of Methodism: "It may be affirmed that there is no principal element of Christianity, no main article of belief as expressed by Protestant Churches, that there is no moral or ethical sentiment peculiarly characteristic of the Gospel, no height or depth of feeling proper to the spiritual life, that does not find itself, emphatically and pointedly and clearly, stated in some stanza of Charles Wesley's hymns." This is the heritage which Methodism has had bequeathed to her, and which she is asked to cherish and sanctify to the glory of God.

In the field of books and benevolence we enter upon a subject which we do well to ponder. Our material resources, which have grown with our growth, are to be consecrated to the advancement of truth; and the issue is now upon us. A systematic method of giving the Church has always pleaded for; and something is now demanded which will not lessen our benefactions in the older directions, but will superadd to them the newer demands arising out of our altered circumstances. The establishment and endowment of libraries in our Churches are duties clearly pointed out by the requirements of the times.

No essential part of the cardinal doctrines of the Church has been overlooked by those who have had the care of the publishing interests. Even in regard to the teachings of the Church with respect to a higher Christian life, which some have thought required separate establishments for their exclusive publication, it will be seen that the literature on the subject is ample and of no uncertain sound. The authorized agents of the Book Concerns have done their work so thoroughly, and the doctrines of the Church have been so clearly enunciated, that the supplementary efforts resorted to appear, if not superfluous, certainly not so absolute a necessity as to demand a resort to such extraordinary measures.

But it is no part of our purpose to attempt an analysis of the book now in the reader's hands. That can only be had by its full perusal. That it is a unity in every minutia is not claimed. Writing on such kindred subjects, and without opportunity for previous consultation, if such a thing were desirable or possible, it is not to be wondered at that the writers should occasionally cross each other's paths, or even give utterance to some slight differences of opinion. But if the latter is true, it is true only in matters of non-essential import; while, on the other hand, the agreement is so hearty and emphatic as to furnish a proof that the Church is in essential harmony as to the baleful effects of much of the popular literature of the period, and that to counteract that influence a loud and urgent call is made for the diffusion of healthful spiritual reading matter, such as the publications which Methodism has always given to the world.

The extensive catalogue of books which follows these papers has been prepared with great care. The aim of the editor has been to assist our Christian people in making choice of the most safe and valuable books in the various departments of literature, from which libraries may be selected for the home, the Church, and the Sabbath-school.

CONTENTS.

METHODISM AND LITERATURE.

I.

A READING CHURCH.

CHRISTIANITY is a religion appealing to the reason. Wherever it goes, thought is quickened, literature is patronized, inventive genius wins victories, and brings its products to the world's help. Every other system of religion is overwhelmed by science and investigation. The inventions and discoveries that have been brought to light in the luminous pathway of Christ's kingdom, a kingdom that shines more and more unto the perfect day, would drive every other system to the wall.

But though the prophecy of doubt has assigned the religion of Jesus to the same doom, yet Christianity has taken, and continues to take, the results of genius and thought for her own benefit.

The Christian should never be afraid of truth; and to read and study should be as much a sacred duty as to pray and testify for his Master. To do this he must study economy both as to means and time; but he is the child of an economist who, though a king, suffers nothing to go to waste, and who, though he owns a universe, gathers and preserves every thing, so that not an atom is lost. He must practice self-denial both as to his appetites and his adornings, if he would fit himself for usefulness in the Christ-life. But he may remember, for his comfort, that he whose servant he is counted not his own life dear unto him, but whose joy was to do his Father's will; and then let him remember that the disciple is not above his Master or the servant above his Lord.

The Christian thus seeking for truth and usefulness will be prepared against surprises and bold assaults of the enemies of his Lord. Knowing the armory of truth, familiar with its weapons, he will be able to repel or hold in check every attempt of unbelief to shake his confidence. He will not be discouraged when ignorant followers become faint-hearted and ready to retreat. His well-supplied arsenal will, by the Spirit's help and the light of the Word, make him ready to endure hardness as a good soldier.

A well-informed Christian is not at all likely to desert his standard; for he has read of the triumphs of that vast army of whom the world was not worthy. He has marked the miracle of the Church's progress in the past; he has read of her triumphs in the last half century, and watches with a lively interest her victories to-day, as she plans broadly and intelligently for the conquest of the world.

In Christianity he sees a religion that unites in itself all that is of good report in the various systems of the ethnic religions, and, looking beyond the letter of the Word, he sees in its great and pure spirit, the manifested truth of God. Thus looking at the Bible, it is always for him a vase of most precious perfume, a casket of priceless pearls, a mine of inexhaustible wealth, a fountain of purest waters, a sun of surpassing brightness, an ocean of glory; indeed, a universe in itself; for all other treasures are indicated in it, and all other streams of thought and power and civilization flow to it and from it. There are many reasons why a gathered society of reading Christians may, indeed must, be a power. A reading Church will make an intelligent ministry. The time has passed when, if it ever did, the Church may boast of its inspired ignorance. It has ever been an error to defend Christianity and its supernatural character and divine origin by assuming ignorance and lack of mental power in the early disciples, apostles, and writers of the primitive Church. Who shall surpass Paul and John, Luke and Matthew, with Mark, in massive greatness, in beauty, sublimity, simplicity, and strength? They need no defense; they were worthy of any age. Their honesty, experience, and inspiration can be established without assuming that they were without ability or intelligence.

That God has used the unlettered and the ignorant is very true; but it does not prove that he would have his children or his heralds remain in ignorance. He can use any and all weapons, any and all kinds of material; but the order of his providence has, for the most part, chosen the best; and the book he has given to us is a very mine of literary and philosophic and mental wealth, quickening the thought, and stirring the heart of every student.

The greatest of thoughts, themes, and events are presented in the simple style of the narrative, or clothed in the glowing figures of poetry, or in the majesty of eloquence almost unequaled. And a man or woman who becomes a student of that Bible as he or she ought to study it, will soon want to know more of those other volumes of the great Author, the universe and the soul. The minister who would preach acceptably to a reading Church must be a reading minister.

While such a Church would not be captious or unkind, it would stimulate and appreciate its pastor, and would thus become the means and somewhat the occasion of his development and growth. To preach to such a Church the man of God would not need to preach philosophy or science. Such preaching would not meet their demands, while other lines of mere sensationalism would not answer. Having studied the Bible with such helps as they have, they recognize it as the all-containing book of their religion, and Jesus Christ as the Alpha and Omega of the book, and so they would have preached Christ and him crucified.

A reading Church will be a believing Church. There is a condition of soul that sometimes passes for faith, but it is simply enthusiasm. An abiding faith knows in what it believes, and is able to give a reason for its existence. An intelligent faith has nothing to fear from rationalism. It knows that the religion of the Gospels is no cunningly devised fable, and, founded upon the rock of experience, it remains after the storm is past.

A reading Church will, without doubt, be a benevolent Church. This needs only to be stated to gain the assent of every one whose observation includes such a Church. With breadth of information come breadth of sympathy, largeness of soul, a reaching out for the ignorant, needy, and unsaved.

So that we may safely make the statement that they who read largely give largely. But in all this we are supposing that the reading Church has a pure, strong, and helpful literature, adapted to the cultivation of both the intellectual and emotional in man, and that there is a purpose to use the knowledge for the glory of the great King.

A reading Church will be an enterprising and progressive Church. With eyes wide open, she will see the fields white, the gates ajar, the highways being cast up, and she will use her means wisely and at the fortunate time, entering fields of usefulness, and planting institutions of learning, missions for the saving of the masses, building churches for the needy, and scattering a pure literature where mental and moral blindness prevails.

J. S. BROADWELL.

II.

THE METHODIST BOOK CONCERN.

THE Methodist Book Concern had its origin in the theory that a Church must furnish a religious literature for its people. The Church must not only be devoted, but to secure its highest good and usefulness it must be intelligent. This intelligence is necessary in accomplishing the work assigned it by Providence, and where intelligence has been allied to vital godliness, Christianity has moved forward with the steps of certitude.

John Wesley early recognized the potency of the printing-press as an agency in the work of evangelization, and as early as 1739 began the work of publishing religious literature. From the beginning of his work in England, he was an author and a publisher; first the tract, then the magazine, and afterward the stately volume. Notwithstanding the constancy of his travels and the countless sermons he preached, he wrote thirty-two solid volumes—which have been published—and abridged and edited one hundred and twenty more. His preachers were pledged to circulate books as an essential part of their work. At the conference of 1749, arrangements were made by which every circuit was to be supplied with books by the assistant, and every society was to provide "a private room," and also books for the helper. A return was to be made quarterly of money for books from each society, and thus, says Dr. Stevens, "began that organized system of book and tract distribution which has secured to Methodism a more extensive use of the religious press than can be found in any other Protestant denomination of our day." To Wesley must not only be ascribed the impetus and methods in circulating religious literature, but to him also must be attributed the earliest recognition of the power of the press as an auxiliary to the work of preaching, and by his example, "the first to apply on any large scale this important means of usefulness to the reformation of the people."

The theory which brought into use the press in Mr. Wesley's day is the theory of the Methodist Episcopal Church to-day, and the inspiration of her publishing-houses. The mind needs instruction and fortification against evil every day and hour. Like all other things, it will become impaired; and spiritual truth must be its food and nourishment. As parents feed their children daily in order to secure growth and maintain health, so the Church must supply the reading which her children demand.

Under this conviction, the Methodist Episcopal Church in 1789, only five years after her organization, appointed Rev. John Dickins, then stationed in Philadelphia, a former student of the celebrated English school at Eton, as the book steward or agent. With a capital of six hundred dollars, which he loaned the Concern, he laid the foundations of our publishing-house. He managed the business for ten years, and died in Philadelphia, where the Book Concern was then located, leaving an enduring monument of his sagacity.

Previous to the establishment of the Book Concern, various works of Mr. Wesley had been republished in this country, chiefly by the ministers, among whom was Robert Williams, who realized some profits from the publication of a number of Wesley's sermons. Benjamin Franklin, whom Mirabeau called "the genius which had freed America," reprinted Mr. Wesley's Sermon on Free Grace, and gave it a wide circulation. But as these irregular publications were unsatisfactory to the preachers, a more thorough system was determined upon, which has developed into the present Book Concern. In the Discipline of 1787 the following record occurs: "As it has been frequently recommended by the preachers and people that such books as are wanted be printed in this country, we therefore propose: First, that the advice of the conference be desired concerning any valuable impression, and their consent be obtained before any steps be taken for the printing thereof. And, second, that the profits of the books, after all necessary expenses are defrayed, shall be applied, according to the direction of conference, toward the college, the preachers' fund, the deficiencies of our preachers, the district missions, or the debts of our Churches."

The first book printed by the Methodist Book Concern gave token of the breadth and catholicity of the spirit which actuated its founders. It was Thomas à Kempis's "Imitation of Christ," translated and published by Mr. Wesley in England, under the title of "The Christian's Pattern." This work which, next to the sacred Scriptures, has had the largest number of readers of which sacred literature, ancient or modern, can furnish an example, although written by a devout Catholic, had had an important influence on the mind of John Wesley and on the origin of Methodism, and is still not only in the catalogue of Methodist publications, but is urged upon its membership as a book eminently fitted to be "in the hands of every Methodist." Among the other works published the same year were Baxter's "Saints' Everlasting Rest," the "Methodist Discipline, a hymn-book, Mr. Wesley's "Primitive Physic," and the *Arminian Magazine.* The following was the imprint of the latter: "Printed in Philadelphia by Prichard & Hall, in Market Street, and sold by John Dickins, in Fourth Street (east side), near the corner of Race Street." The preface, which consists of an address to the "subscribers for the *Arminian Magazine,*" written in North Carolina April 10, 1789, and signed by Thomas Coke and

Francis Asbury, contains the following interesting declaration : " That the subscribers may not purchase polemical divinity at too great an expense, we shall insert in each number an original sermon on subjects curious, critical, interesting, and elegant, written by our well-known and much-respected friend JOHN WESLEY (all of them since he has passed the age of seventy, and some of them within the last year), which may convince those who are ignorant of him that he is not, as some have falsely advanced, in his second childhood ; and that his exercising the episcopal office for the forming of our Church in America was not the fruit of infancy in him or in us." The first sermon of Mr. Wesley's, perhaps, ever published by the Book Concern as such is found in this magazine, and is founded on 1 Tim., 6–9, the words being, " They that will be rich, fall into temptation and a snare," etc.

In 1799, Ezekiel Cooper was appointed editor and general book steward, and during his agency (in 1804) the business was removed to New York. He resigned in 1809, leaving the Concern with a capital of a hundred and forty-five thousand dollars, the net earnings of nineteen years. In 1808, John Wilson was elected principal agent, and the term of service in the agency was limited to eight years. Until this period the agents were regularly stationed as ministers, but from this time forward they were entirely released from pastoral labors. Mr. Wilson died in 1810, and the assistant agent, Daniel Hitt, assumed the entire control, and was elected principal agent in 1812. The *Methodist Magazine* was commenced in 1818, but after the establishment of the *Christian Advocate* in 1826, it was changed to the *Methodist Quarterly Review*, and both periodicals have been uninterruptedly issued ever since.

In 1820, Rev. Nathan Bangs, whose name was for many years intimately associated with Methodism in America, was called to the chief agency of the Book Concern, and infused into it a new vitality. He published " Benson's

Commentary," a work which has met with a large circulation, and also published a revised edition of the Methodist Hymn-book. Up to 1822 all the work of the Book Concern was done by outside parties, but during that year the first book was bound in the office on Crosby Street. In September, 1824, the agents also commenced printing in their own house.

In 1832 it became evident that the building on Crosby Street was too small for the increasing demands of business, and five lots were purchased on Mulberry Street. During the next year the front building was erected, and the business transferred to it. At this time Dr. John P. Durbin was editor of the *Christian Advocate and Journal*, and of Sunday-school books and tracts. Through his suggestion and wise foresight the Concern began the publication of a Sunday-school library, an enterprise which has been continued ever since, and which has resulted in a collection of books, which for variety, adaptation, and number is unsurpassed by any similar collection in the world.

In 1836 the entire building and stock of the Book Concern were destroyed by fire, the loss reaching the sum of a quarter of a million of dollars. The fact that the Church promptly contributed nearly ninety thousand dollars to rebuild is a proof that the Book Concern had won general confidence. Out of the ashes a new building sprang up, well adapted at that time to the purposes of a publishing-house. The separation of the Methodist Episcopal Church South, in 1845, gave rise to a law-suit in the United States Court, and the court ordered a *pro rata* division of the property, which gave to the Church South two hundred and seventy thousand dollars in cash and all the presses and papers belonging to the Concern in the South.

The Western Book Concern was established in 1820 by the General Conference of that year, and Dr. Martin Ruter, subsequently president of Alleghany College, was appointed to its charge, acting under the direction of the agents at New York. This branch has gone on steadily increasing, and has now become a great and independent center of publishing interests, with several depositories under its control. Although it has met with reverses, the chief of which was the Chicago fire in 1871, yet it reports a net capital of above three hundred and fifty-five thousand dollars, and sales during the year 1881 amounting to over seven hundred and fourteen thousand dollars.

In the Spring of 1869 the building on the corner of Eleventh Street and Broadway, New York, was purchased for the joint use of the Book Concern and the Missionary Society, at a cost of about one million dollars. It is conceded that for architectural beauty this structure is not surpassed on Broadway. Here are the offices of the editors, agents, and book-keepers. Here, too, are the wholesale and retail stores and mailing department. The manual labor of type-setting, stereotyping, printing, and binding is still done at 200 Mulberry Street.

Now, having looked at the outside of these buildings, let us step within, and see how the work is done. The book agents are appointed by the General Conference, but they are by no means independent. Whatever money they may see in a book, they can not bring that book out for the market without the indorsement of a censor appointed by the same high authority. The General Conference orders the publication of certain periodicals. Editors are also chosen to prepare the matter. The agents are obliged to print and circulate just what the editor provides. They have no right to dot an "i" or cross a "t." The two parties are independent of each other, though both are responsible to the same appointing body. In regard to books, the agents are at liberty to decline the publication of any one; but if they publish at all, the book must have the sanction of the book editor, or it never sees the light. Every manuscript of our Sunday-school books must pass the scrutiny of the corresponding secretary of the Sunday-school Union.

These editors have a keen scent for heresy, and if they find any thing dangerous to public morals they brand the paper, and it goes to the shades. In our markets there are inspectors of meats. Stale food is unhealthy, and the inspector stands as a guard to protect the public. So these editors are appointed to see that our children are not fed with dangerous and corrupting literature—a position vastly more important than that of the health officer. In our great ports are quarantine grounds and officers. Every ship must be boarded by the officer appointed, and it can not land its passengers until the certificate of the physician is obtained that there is no contagious disease on board. So all our books are quarantined until the guardians of the precious young souls in the care of the Church shall declare them healthful and saving. Here, we submit, the Methodist Episcopal Church has the advantage of those who have no official publishing-house. Independent publishers are irresponsible in the matter of public morals. The temptation will be strong for them to publish that which will sell best. If they cater to a depraved taste, which clamors after sensationalism, there is no one to call them to account. This independent censorship of the Methodist press is the safeguard of our children.

The guardianship of our press is not too rigid. As much as we sometimes feel the need of making books and papers that pay best, we do not desire to see the Methodist Book Concern spotted with the blood of young souls ruined by a pernicious literature.

Let us now call attention to *results.* Let it be understood that the prime object of the establishment and maintenance of the Book Concern was not, and is not, to make money. but to furnish religious reading for our people. And yet it is necessary to make money to secure the capital essential to the business.

3

As a result of work in our Sunday-school department of the Church, the conversions reported in the schools for twenty-five years past are fully equal to the increase of Church members. If, as Churches, we lose our hold of the children, our aggressive power is gone. We can hold them permanently only by solid doctrinal instruction in harmony with our pulpits.

The financial results have been remarkable. While money is not the primary object, we doubt if any other printing-house in the world can furnish a better financial record. There has been a constant drain upon the Book Concern for the general purposes of the Church. The theory has been, if no other provision is made for expenses, the Book Concern must foot the bill. During its existence, it has paid to the various interests of the Church, outside of its own business, a sum aggregating nearly two millions of dollars.

Other houses may add their profits to their capital for the purpose of increasing their facilities, or divide them among the proprietors; but the Book Concern has paid out its profits for Church interests from year to year. If the world has a parallel in the history of religious or benevolent publishing establishments, we have never seen the record.

The moral and religious results of a system which has sent out for nearly a century such a constant and full stream of devotional, instructive, and Christian literature can not be computed. The benefits are incalculable. Wielding the strongest arm of modern moral influence, laying a contribution on the best minds of our own and other Churches, and reaching the youth with a pure literature at the most plastic period of their existence, who can estimate its molding power, its edifying mission, its restraining influences, or its glorious benedictions?

The Book Concern is a child of Church necessities, in complete harmony with its spirit and discipline. In its wonderfully compact and comprehensive "Book of Discipline" all its preachers are enjoined, among other godly recommendations, to the "reading of the most useful books;" and, if any should lack taste in this direction, they are urged to "contract a taste for it by use, or to return to their former employment." And the laity, while prohibited the "reading of those books which do not tend to the knowledge or love of God," are expected to be a reading people; and to secure this end, it is made the duty of preachers "to take care that every society be duly supplied with books."

The work of the Book Concern has been in harmony with the highest spiritual interests of humanity, and its methods and objects are open to all. It invites and challenges examination. It aims to permeate society with its health-giving streams, and to reach all classes for their good. It asks the co-operation and friendly aid of all who labor for human weal. Shall the publishing interests not expect and receive it?

SANFORD HUNT.

III.

CIRCULATION OF OUR LITERATURE.

To supply Methodist people with Methodist literature is a Wesleyan idea; the means and methods by which this has been done for more than a century form a part of the connectional system of Methodism. During the early period of the United Societies in Great Britain Mr. Wesley resorted to the use of the press in defense of the evangelistic work to which he had been providentially called. Its utility as a means to extend as well as defend that work at once became apparent to his practical mind; he regarded it a providential agency, and employed it diligently in the production of a literature, the influence of which is manifest in both the doctrinal unity and connectional economy of Methodism. His "helpers"—the preachers— to whose loyal co-operation the success of the Methodistic movement is largely due, heartily joined him in his plans for the use of the press. With characteristic zeal they circulated the tracts, pamphlets, books, and magazine he published; and the supply of the people with good books was soon named in the conferences as one of the specified duties of preachers. The system thus developed was incorporated in the Wesleyan Church at the time of its organization, and has been carefully maintained and successfully operated by it for nearly a century.

The Methodist missionaries who came to America, having learned the utility of the religious press from its use by Mr. Wesley, soon began to sell (and some even to print) books that were helpful in their work. During the colonial period conference action was taken as to the republication and circulation of Mr. Wesley's books, and the whole matter became so interwoven with the operations of the young Church that five years after its formal organization the Conference (in 1789) assumed its control by appointing a book steward (the initial step in establishing the Book Concern), to superintend the circulation and sale of books through the preachers, and subsequently by appropriating the profits of the business to connectional purposes.

The Methodist publishing system comprehends and provides for both the *publication and circulation* of a Methodistic literature; *it is a connectional plan under which the Methodist Episcopal Church owns her press, supervises her publications, and* PRODUCES AND DISTRIBUTES *a literature that is in harmony with her doctrines, usages, economy, and mission.*

The capacity of the Book Concern to produce a literature should be mentioned in connection with the plans and means for its circulation. The value of the lands, buildings, machinery, material, etc., in 1881, exclusively devoted to and employed in publishing books and periodicals, was as follows: In the New York Book Concern, $359,880; in the Western Book Concern, $301,122; total, $661,002. The remainder of the capital is chiefly employed in the circulation of the literature, as will be shown further on. The $661,002 of the capital represents, in one way, the material and mechanical facilities of our Church for the production of books and periodicals.

Having had and now having in her ranks a large number of talented and scholarly men and women, she has successfully utilized her publishing facilities, and is still daily increasing the volume of Methodist literature. Fifteen editors, chosen by the General Conference, and eight assistant editors, are constantly employed; a large corps of writers with varied gifts are paid contributors to the periodicals; and besides these there are authors, many in number, preachers, laymen, and gifted women, Methodists, who devote time and talent to writing books. The present catalogue of the Book Concerns gives a list of about three thousand different books: nearly all of these, and many earlier volumes now out of print, are from the pens of Methodist authors. Our Church is rich in her corps of writers and authors, and strong in possessing the means to publish the productions of their consecrated talents.

The extent of the field she occupies and the diversity of her work, from that in the wealthy city church to that in the isolated frontier mission, requires a great variety in the form and kind of her literature. These wants have been fairly met with books, especially in the English, German, and Scandinavian languages, for the different classes of readers—for unawakened sinners, young converts, advancing Christians, and the closest students of the Scriptures—books for the preachers, books for the people, and books for home, Church, and Sunday-school libraries; and also with a periodical literature of great diversity in form and purpose. The money value of the books sold annually is nearly double that of the periodicals, yet a vast amount of reading matter from Methodist writers is furnished to the members of our congregations and Sunday-schools through the various periodicals published by the Church, ranging from the *Picture Lesson Paper*, for the youngest reader, to the scholarly *Methodist Quarterly Review*.

The circulation of the publications of the Book Concern, as already stated, has, from the first, been a part of the publishing system of our Church. It could not have been otherwise for the leading purpose of the Methodist preachers, in devising and projecting that system, was to furnish the people with a literature that would be helpful in the extension of Methodism; and in order to this it was as necessary to provide for the circulation as for the publication of that literature. These preachers, with the example of Mr. Wesley and his coadjutors before them, naturally and wisely adopted the Wesleyan plan, and became themselves the agents and representatives of the Book Concern to sell the publications approved by the Church.

The General Conference of 1792 made it the duty of the preacher in charge "*to take care that every society be duly supplied with books;*" that of 1880 added, "*and Methodist literature.*" (Discipline, ¶178, Sec. 7.) But for this plan and the zeal of the preachers in working it, it is quite certain the Book Concern could not have achieved its marked success. The circuit system carried Methodism to villages and sparsely settled rural districts, as well as to cities; hence a large proportion of our people could not have procured Methodist books had they not been brought to their homes by the Itinerant preachers. These devoted men were quick to perceive their opportunity of doing good by selling the books of their Church, and they engaged earnestly in this, as in every other pastoral and ministerial work. For many years after the publishing system was fully established, there were few Methodist pastors who did not carry the books into their charges; and as a result there were few Methodist homes, even in the remotest circuits, in which some Methodist books might not be found; and, in time, there were libraries in most Methodist Sunday-schools.

When, in 1826, the new era in our periodical literature was inaugurated by the publication of the *Christian Advocate*, the preachers brought it before the people; its circulation and that of the other *Advocates*, since established by the Church, to meet the wants of her ever-expanding field, has been chiefly secured and maintained through their efforts. From the first issue of the *Sunday-school Advocate* much has also been done by them to introduce and extend the circulation of our literature for the officers, teachers, and scholars in Methodist Sunday-schools.

DEPOSITORIES are a part of the system of our Church for the circulation of her books and periodicals. They are

distributing points rendered necessary by the growth of
the Church and the extent of the country. The first was
established at Cincinnati in 1820, and twenty years later
created a publishing-house under a distinct charter, and
entitled *The Western Methodist Book Concern.* Depositories have since been located at Boston, Buffalo, Pittsburg, Chicago, St. Louis, Atlanta, and San Francisco.
The stock of books, including those in process of binding,
in the Book Concerns and Depositories was worth, in
1881, at a low valuation, $484,294; add to this the value
of the buildings used for stores, stock-rooms, counting-
rooms, etc., and the capital employed by our Church in
carrying a necessary stock of her literature is at least a
million dollars. By authority of the General Conference,
special arrangements have also been made for the encouragement of Methodist book-stores in Philadelphia, Baltimore, Detroit, and a few other commercial centers. A
chief design of these depositories and stores was, and is,
to reduce the cost of transportation to the purchaser,
thereby enabling the preachers to supply their charges
with books on the most advantageous terms. The money
value of the literature sold through the seven Depositories
in 1881 was $549,694.15; namely, books, $375,023.72;
periodicals, $174,670.43.

The Sunday-school Union of the Methodist Episcopal Church was formed for the gratuitous circulation of
her Sunday-school literature. For many years its Corresponding Secretary has been the editor of Sunday-school library books, and more than two thousand volumes thus prepared for the press and published by the Book Concerns
are now found in their catalogue. The Sunday-school Union
is better known now through the Berean system of aids
for Bible study, the papers for the youth and children, and
various helpful requisites for officers, teachers, and scholars; but a very large number of books have been put
into circulation by its donations to needy schools, and it is

still doing this good work, especially in the pioneer and other mission fields of our Church.

THE TRACT SOCIETY OF THE METHODIST EPISCOPAL CHURCH was also organized for the circulation of Methodist literature in tract form. The tracts prepared by this society are published by the Book Concerns, and kept in stock, for donation by the several district committees, and for sale at a low price.

The Depositories are parts or branches of the Book Concerns; the Sunday-school Union and Tract Society are independent connectional societies. In the preparation and distribution of their special kinds and forms of literature they are intimately connected with the Book Concerns, but much of their work is distinct, of which a separate report is annually given to the Church.

Methodist preachers, by circulating Methodist literature, have made the Methodist press a most potent adjunct of the Methodist pulpit. It is well known, however, that they are not as diligent in all forms of this important work as aforetime. Many labor with zeal to circulate the weekly *Advocates* and the Sunday-school periodicals, and few (if any) entirely neglect this; but, on the other hand, they do not take so great care to supply their charges with the books. Where our people and Sunday-schools are convenient to the Book Concerns or depositories they, in many cases, supply themselves with books and Sunday-school periodicals, instead of ordering them through the preachers, as was formerly done. In many localities, particularly in the East, some part of our books can be secured through book-stores; so from one cause and another, it has come to pass within the past twenty or thirty years that a considerable portion of the book sales is direct to the people. It was formerly expected that the Sunday-school books would be ordered through the preachers; while this was generally done, a larger proportion of the schools was provided with libraries than at present. The multiplication of the kinds of Sunday-school periodicals may account, in part, for this change, but will not explain the fact that perhaps in not more than one-half of our schools is there the semblance of a library, and that in a smaller proportion of them is there a good supply of our books.

The number of our Sunday-schools having libraries is relatively less than twenty years ago, and the proportion of Methodist homes in which our new books, or even older standard works, are found is not increasing; as a consequence the youth in many of these Sunday-schools and homes are growing up, not only without the benefit of Methodist books, but also without even a knowledge of them. This fact is appalling, and considered in its rela-tions and bearings must occasion deep concern. Think of it! The field of Methodist literature has enlarged and the corps of Methodist authors augmented; the publishing facilities of the Book Concerns have been greatly improved, and the number and variety of Methodist books increased; our people have more means than ever before with which to purchase them, and yet there are hundreds of Meth-odist Sunday-schools without libraries, and thousands of Methodist homes in which there are no Methodist books!

Of course many of our people are able to buy but few books, and many of our schools are in poor communities, but this lamentable dearth of Methodist books is not con-fined to such homes and schools, but is too prevalent in the more favored sections and societies. For instance, a large conference, located within a well-improved part of the richest belt of the West, containing over two hundred pastoral charges and about five hundred Sunday-schools, with 39,806 scholars enrolled in 1881, reported one hun-dred and forty Sunday-school libraries in sixty-three of its charges, and no libraries in the remaining one hundred and forty-three charges embracing three hundred and sixty Sun-day-schools. After deducting the number in the infant classes, there were, by the report, about thirty-two thousand scholars, of whom less than nine thousand had access to Sunday-school libraries! Where the people are well-to-do, as they generally are in this section, the ratio of Methodist books in the homes is not likely to be much greater than it is found to be in the Sunday-schools. It is probable that in this as in other conferences many of the schools take our Sunday-school periodicals, and that some one of our weekly *Advocates* is found in many of the homes; but these are no proper substitute for useful and instructive books.

What can be done to increase the circulation of the books published by our Church? By what means can they be brought within the reach of our people, young and old? In a measure by Church libraries; also by Sunday-school libraries; and by collections in the home.

THE CHURCH LIBRARY.—To the writer it has seemed that in many places it would be practicable to establish such libraries, and they would be eminently serviceable; and during the past ten years the matter has been presented to most of the conferences in the West. The idea of a Methodist library is not new; the Sunday-school library has its recognized place, and years ago a " Methodist Family Library" was projected. The latter involved an expense that few families were disposed to incur ; the former, while valuable in its place, seems too limited in its scope to interest all classes; hence the question naturally came up, Why not combine what would have been the Family Library with the Sunday-school Library, and thereby create a Church Library, to meet the wants of all, old and young, in the Sunday-school and congregation? The suggestion has also been made that the books of such a library might be issued on a week-day evening, making it the occasion of an informal social meeting of the old and young in the Church. The influence of a good library, to which all would be drawn, would be beneficial in every way. In the congregation it would come to be "Our Library"—and through it all having any interest in the Church, whether in the congregation or Sunday-school, would be brought into pleasant association.

The Church Library would combine economy with utility. The Agents of the Western Book Concern presented this view several years ago, as follows:*

"We again emphasize the importance of so enlarging the Sunday-school Library that it shall contain reading matter adapted to all persons who *ought to be found in the Sunday-school*, either as teachers or students of the Scriptures; and certainly these classes comprehend a large portion of every congregation. We mention the following among the advantages resulting from such a library:

"(1.) Many of the best minds of the community will be attracted to our Churches and Sunday-schools, and be permanently benefited by the books such Libraries may contain.

"(2.) It would be a great economy. A few hundred dollars thus invested, which would require from each family but a small sum, will afford an amount of reading matter to a community that it would take thousands of dollars to purchase and place in each family.

"(3.) By thus timely putting suitable books within the reach of our more advanced Sunday-school scholars, we will save them from becoming ensnared by the ruinous productions of the irreligious press.

"(4.) The acquaintance thus formed with the useful literature of our press will induce the selection of many valuable books for our homes which would otherwise remain unknown to our people.

"Sunday-school workers will appreciate the further advantage of bringing the school and congregation nearer to each other, by alike interesting them in the Library as existing for their common use and mutual benefit. It would seem that contributions for a Library of such general interest could be readily secured, at least in every town

---
* Catalogue of 1873.

and village; and the Church that thus plans for the moral well-being of a community, and moves to meet so important a want, will strengthen its hold upon the people, and greatly increase its usefulness.

"It would not be difficult to so arrange for the weekly distribution of the books as to make it a pleasant occasion both for the members of the school and congregation, and thereby avoid the interruption of the worship and Bible study occasioned by distributing the Library-books during the session of the school.

"Why not make the Library the point in common about which the active workers in the Church and in the Sunday-school shall rally, that there may be unity and harmony in all those efforts that have in view but the one object of Christian work—the salvation of the people, both young and old?"

The necessity for the Church Library is not obviated by the existence of Public Libraries. These, as generally constituted, do not meet the wants for which the Church would provide a library. Certainly they do not foster a taste for the kind of reading that the Church should encourage. Usually, in the Public Library works of fiction, especially novels, form the largest class of books, and whether by American or foreign authors, they are selected without apparent reference to either their moral or political teaching. The official reports show this class of books to comprise from sixty to seventy-five per cent of the entire circulation of these libraries. They are, in the main, vehicles for the circulation of fiction at public expense. On the other hand, the Church Library would not only bring good books within reach, but its very existence, as well as its whole influence, would encourage the reading of a pure and wholesome literature. While publications of the Book Concerns would, of course, form an important part of such a library, it would also contain the best books of other publishing houses, selected with special reference to the intellectual and spiritual benefit of its patrons.

Several such libraries have already been formed in the West. Enough has been done to show that it is quite practicable for our Churches in many of the larger villages and towns to establish them. But this will rarely be done except under the leadership of the preachers. The people will not be found indifferent in regard to the profitable use of the press when their attention is earnestly directed to the matter. When the pastors become the advocates of well-appointed libraries, and urge their claims with the zeal their importance demands, the people will respond and make them one of the appointments of the Church.

THE SUNDAY-SCHOOL LIBRARY.—In many places it will not be deemed practicable to form Church Libraries, but there are few places where the people themselves, or aided by our Sunday-school Union, can not procure a Sunday-school Library. In many of our schools there are libraries, or the remnants of libraries, to which no new books have been added for years, and these must be replenished before an interest in the books can be awakened among the scholars. No argument is required to prove that a good library may be of incalculable value to a Sunday-school. Where this is recognized it is not difficult to enlist a community in a movement to purchase books. The preacher is the best leader in such a movement. If a school be without a good library because of a notion among officers and teachers that one is not needed, the pastor can do most to remove the fallacy; if it be from a feeling that many so-called Sunday-school books have a pernicious tendency, the Disciplinary Committee (Discipline, ¶ 257), of which the pastor is the head, can readily remove this objection; if from a general apathy toward the Sunday-school and its work, an interest among the people will only be awakened when a deeply interested pastor presses the matter upon their consciences and hearts.

Here the relation of our Sunday-school Union to the circulation of books is important. There are hundreds of schools in our Churches in the South and in the pioneer regions of the West which have never had a library book, and they are not able to purchase them. Books are not less needful in these schools than in the older and wealthier communities. It would be a great work, a truly missionary as well as connectional work, on the part of our Church to supply them. If, when the claims of the Sunday-school Union are presented, the extent and importance of this work were fully and earnestly set forth, would not our people furnish the means for so good a cause?

Books in the Home.—Whatever may be done in the way of Church and Sunday-school libraries, still some Methodist books should have a place in Methodist homes. They are unobtrusive witnesses of a cordial interest in the Church—a silent testimony in its behalf. The books belonging to the home are among the things which go, in some way, to make up its individuality—that character which distinguishes it from others and impresses itself on every member, especially the young. Methodist books in the Methodist home! Those old, familiar books—the biography, the history, the devotional, and even the doctrinal volume—how many remember them with a tender interest! Read there they became associated in memory with the sacred place, and their teaching was invested with an enduring charm. And there are lingering, grateful thoughts about the preachers who brought these books into the home. This Wesleyan plan put Methodist books into thousands of homes which otherwise would have been without them. What of the other thousands within the wide domain of the Church in which no one of the valuable publications of the Church is found!

Notwithstanding the improved facilities of transportation, and the development of trade in our country, there are large sections in the Western and many Eastern conferences in which there are no regular book-stores.; the same is true of entire conferences in the South; and, in all these sections our people can not buy Methodist books, not even Hymnals and Disciplines, through the trade. Post-routes reach every neighborhood and postage is cheap, but experience proves that only a few will order books by mail. It is out of the regular line; other things needed in the home are not secured in that way. Many are not advised as to what books are published; many who see them announced in the *Advocates* know little of their respective merits. So, in many ways, thousands of our people are as dependent upon the preachers in the matter of the best books for the home as was the great body of the Church half a century ago. In every pastoral charge in the connection there are some homes where Methodist books will not be found until they are introduced in some way by the pastors.

It does not follow that all former methods are to be uniformly pursued, that the saddle-bags are to be put into use again to circulate the books—though that might be done with great gain to the Church in not a few fields—but that, as the fathers supplied the people with books in the way best adapted to their circumstances, so now the same thing should be done in such ways as are most practicable and likely to secure directly and with the least labor and expense the best results. Slow and costly transportation made it necessary for them to order the books in quantity, and keep them on hand; but with railroads radiating in every direction from the cities in which the Book Concerns and Depositories are located, that necessity no longer exists, except it be in the remoter pioneer fields. The people are more likely to buy the books if they see them; but the preacher may readily meet this condition by sample copies of what he thinks will be of greatest value in his charge, and a dozen or a score of volumes, at most, would be all the samples needed at a time in either a circuit or a station.

A preacher may awaken some interest in the books by placing a Book Concern catalogue in every Methodist home, from the wealthiest to the humblest, within his charge. He can mention in his pastoral visits, at prayer, class, and official meetings, and sometimes from the pulpit, some of the books he may think would be most useful. During the past year a presiding elder, believing that the circulation of "The Class Leader," by Rev. John Atkinson, would do good, called attention to the book at his quarterly meetings, and sold copies to many of the class-leaders in his district. Revivals and other special meetings afford an occasion for the introduction of books especially adapted to them. Place in the hand of each convert and young Church member, at the beginning of a Christian life, either "Counsels to Converts," by Dr. George; "Elements of Methodism," by Dr. Stevenson; "At the Threshold," by Dr. Houghton; "Aspects of Christian Experience," by Bishop Merrill, or some other book of this general class published by our Church for the instruction and encouragement of the young Christian, and who can estimate the effect upon them and through them upon the Church and world! So there are times and seasons especially favorable for putting into the hands and homes of our people Methodist books adapted to almost every condition of the Church, every stage of Christian experience, every phase and form of Christian work.

To the pastor who purposes to benefit his people by furnishing them the books needful for spiritual culture there will be no lack of opportunity for their introduction. There are many preachers who, whatever be the character of their appointment, invariably increase the circulation of the Church papers, because they feel that the people need these papers, and that they ought to have them. The same feeling in regard to the books makes a preacher succeed in extending their circulation. Those who have a mind for this work never fail in it. The German books published by the Church are sold almost exclusively through the German preachers. In 1881 the sales of our German books averaged a fraction above ninety-eight cents to each member of the German Churches; of our English books a fraction under sixty cents to each member of the English-speaking Churches; the ratio of the circulation of the German periodicals quadruples that of the corresponding English periodicals. The circumstances and condition of the people does not account for this; the German preachers have Wesleyan notions of the importance of Methodist literature and of the advantage of conforming to the connectional plans; they have a mind for the work and it is done. Does not the wide circulation of our German books and periodicals have an important relation to the fact that the missionary collections in the seven German conferences in this country averaged in 1881 seventy cents a member, while the average throughout the other eighty-six conferences was only thirty-six cents a member?

WHAT HAS BEEN DONE. — While many Methodist Sunday-schools have never had libraries and many Methodist homes have been without Methodist books—many even without a Church paper—yet far more has been done in circulating Methodist literature than is generally known. It is not possible to ascertain how many books and periodicals have been printed and put among the people, but in the absence of exact data some idea may be formed from the financial results. The books and periodicals as compared with those of other denominations have been relatively cheap, and, a large proportion of them having been sold by the Book Concerns and Depositories at a discount from the retail or published price, the margin of profit has not been large, and yet the sales have been so great as to yield an aggregate profit of about three million dollars since the loss of the New York Book Concern by fire in 1836. During this forty-five years (notwithstanding the loss by fire in Chicago, in 1871, and the losses on non-paying periodicals and depositories established by General Conference, aggregating about four hundred thousand dollars) there has been an increase of $1,136,196.54 in the net capital of the two Book Concerns; and there has been paid out by order of General Conference, during the same period, above *fifteen hundred thousand dollars* for the benefit of the worn-out preachers, for the support of the bishops, and for other connectional purposes, including $366,909.62 to the Methodist Episcopal Church South under adjustment of the suit brought in the United States Supreme Court. The amount received for the books actually put into circulation in 1881 was $874,191, and for the periodicals $494,334; total, $1,368,525. During the past thirty years (since 1851) the sales of books and periodicals by the New York Book Concern and its Depositories have amounted to $16,997,331.28; of the Western Book Concern and its Depositories, $15,194,931.02; total in thirty years, $32,192,462.30.

While there are relatively more Methodist homes and Sunday-schools without Methodist books now than aforetime, yet the circulation of the Church and Sunday-school periodicals is relatively much greater. In 1851 the circulation of the three Church papers (two English and one German) was 44,374 copies, one copy for every fourteen Church members; in 1881, that of the eleven Church papers (nine English, one German, and one Swedish) was 170,000 copies, one copy for every nine members. In 1851, one Sunday-school paper, the *Sunday-school Advocate*, had a circulation of 90,000; in 1881 the circulation of the six Sunday-school papers (three English, two German, and one Swedish) was 447,546 copies, and the circulation of the three English and one German Berean Lesson Helps, which have superseded the old-time Question Books, was

1,437,122 copies (105,547 *Sunday-school Journals*, 1,081,775 *Lesson Leaves*, and 249,800 other Helps). This statement would not be complete without mention of the fact that all these periodicals have kept pace with the progress of the periodical press of the country; it should be particularly noted that while the circulation of our Church papers has quadrupled since 1851, their size has been doubled, thereby affording the readers a far greater variety of reading-matter while its volume is eight-fold, possibly ten-fold, greater than thirty years ago.

These facts, which indicate the progress of our periodical literature, gratifying as it has been, can not be separated from those which indicate that the circulation is below what it ought to be. Within the conferences in the Northern States and Territories our English Church papers average one copy for every eight members of the English-speaking Churches. No account can be taken here of the so-called independent papers; loyal as they may be to Methodist doctrines, they can hardly be loyal to the Methodist plan for a complete Church literature; and they can not be a fitting and profitable substitute for the official Church papers. The circulation of our English Church papers — one copy to eight members — compares favorably with that of similar papers of other denominations; but the *Christian Apologist* averages two copies for every five members of the German Churches. The official Methodist papers, the home-papers of the Church, are just as helpful to English-speaking Methodists as to German Methodists, and they are equally important in the home, whatever language be spoken there. Surely, in view of the number of subscribers to the *Apologist*, it is possible to double the aggregate circulation of the nine *Advocates*, and it will be done when all the preachers put their hand to the work. One hundred and fifty thousand Church papers making their weekly visit to homes that are now without any thoroughly Methodistic literature—who can estimate the result on the benevolent enterprises and spiritual life of our Church!

The circulation of the *Berean Lesson Leaves* compared with the average attendance of the scholars is relatively large; the *Sunday-school Journal* averages one copy for every two officers and teachers, and the Sunday-school papers one for every four scholars in our Sunday-schools. It is presumable that most Sunday-schools are supplied with lesson-helps and papers of some kind; hence, many have not those that are published under the careful supervision of the Church. If a Methodist Sunday-school should have Methodist teachers, it also should have Methodist lesson-helps and papers—not sectarian, but denominational — those that uniformly and faithfully present the Methodist doctrinal view wherever the lesson contains a doctrine about which the denominations hold different views. The whole influence of a Methodist Sunday-school should be in harmony with the teaching of the Methodist pulpit and with the Church-life of the congregation, and this will be entirely so only when the literature of the school—the lesson-helps, the papers, the library-books, and the songs—are Methodistic in matter and spirit. The thorough denominational equipment of our Sunday-schools depends in large measure upon the practical interest of the preachers in the matter. There are few Sunday-school boards that will persist in using lesson-helps and papers from an irresponsible press after the pastor has presented the important reasons in favor of the trustworthy and superior publications of the Church.

The *Tracts* of our Church have been carefully revised, new ones issued, and all put in attractive form, so the list furnishes what is needed to meet every kind of evangelistic and pastoral work. The Discipline provides for their use in every pastoral charge and for the collection of means for their gratuitous distribution wherever opportunity offers. They can reach those who seldom or never hear the Gospel, and tell the story of the cross in homes in which religious literature is unknown. Let pastors make their utility understood, and our people will provide means for their wider circulation.

The increase in the sale of our books has not kept pace with the increase in the circulation of our periodicals. This may arise in part from the fact that books are necessarily more costly; but is there not an opinion prevalent in many communities that the books may be dispensed with where there is a supply of papers? This is a capital, and too often a fatal, mistake; valuable as Methodist periodicals are, they can not fill the place of our books, whether in the home or Sunday-school. With all the progress made by the secular magazine and newspaper, they at best furnish only a fragmentary literature, transitory in character as well as form; numerous and popular as these have become, the press still teems with books, and public libraries are maintained, solely because periodicals alone can not supply the wants of a reading and thoughtful people. This fact is not less marked in the field of religious literature, as is evident from the number of books on religious and cognate subjects printed and sold, and as may be further seen by a comparison of religious books with religious periodicals, keeping in mind their respective scope, purpose, and possible benefits. Methodist periodicals exert a potent influence for good wherever they go, but every denominational interest requires that the books be circulated as well. Methodist books and periodicals together form the unit of Methodist literature; they each have their mission and should have their place in every Methodist home, society, and Sunday-school.

Why, then, is there a more active and general interest maintained among the preachers in the circulation of the periodicals than of the books? Some may underestimate the importance of religious books as means of edification; some may not consider how few persons are likely to procure such books unless their attention be directed to them, and how limited are the opportunities of most persons to purchase them; some may think that the periodicals are more directly helpful in the general work of the Church; but, really, in most cases, does not the indisposition to push the sale of the books arise chiefly from a feeling that it is purely a business transaction? Have not many who were once quite active in this work become inactive because of this notion? Have not many spent years in the ministry without offering to sell a book, because they have only thought of it as a secular matter, and have taken it for granted that the people regarded it in the same light?

It is not a mere secular matter; it involves some of the elements of business, just as does church building and the like in which the pastor usually is the most active person, and it is as eminently a Church-work. The Discipline discountenances every thing that tends toward secularizing the ministry, but it makes it the pastor's duty to see that his society is supplied with books, as well as other Methodist literature. The preacher who labors to secure a Church library or a Sunday-school library, or offers the books for sale to the people, does so through a desire to serve the highest interests of those concerned. His motive makes it a pastoral, not a secular work. His chief aim is to do good to the young and old by bringing them into companionship with the best men and women of the past and present—those whose lives have blessed the world, and whose thoughts, treasured in the books, are the richest legacy of the Church. He is moved in this by the spirit of the true pastor, and thereby, as the Church rightly expects him to do, brings into his own field of labor the undying inflence of what is strongest and best in the thoughts and deeds of the great and good.

The amount of books sold show that not a few preachers appreciate and improve their opportunity of doing great good by inducing the people to supply their Sunday-schools with libraries and their homes with good books. Other facts already stated show that not a few preachers are failing to do what might be done, and in their fields there is a dearth of Church literature. Experience has demonstrated that the extent to which the people purchase books for their homes and Sunday-schools is usually determined by the preachers' interest in the matter. What would be the result in a single decade should all the preachers give to the circulation of our books only a reasonable share of their time and attention? How much could and would be done in the organization of Church and Sunday-school libraries; how few Methodist homes would there be without some of the books of the Church; and as compared with the present, how much more securely would our people, young and old, be guarded against a pernicious literature by the presence of that which is pure and ennobling!

The Book Concerns in New York and Cincinnati, owned and controlled by the Methodist Episcopal Church, form the largest denominational publishing house in America, if not in the world; they are the direct result of the far-reaching plans of the founders of American Methodism for the production and circulation of a Methodist literature. The facts show that this, the oldest of our connectional agencies, has kept pace with the general progress of the Church. Here she has the capital and facilities to produce under her own supervision, all needful literature for her thirty-five hundred thousand communicants and Sunday-school scholars. This literature is being produced in all necessary forms and in many languages. The extent of its usefulness depends upon the extent to which the books and periodicals are put into circulation, and this the Church, by her time-honored Wesleyan plan, has committed to her preachers, those who are nearest to the people, who have their largest confidence and who may best understand their wants.

J. M. WALDEN.

IV.

WHY METHODISM PRINTS.

THERE is a providential reason why our Church is thoroughly equipped for service. We believe that Methodism has by no means completed her mission. She is just entering upon her grand world-work. Fifty years ago "the people called Methodists" were simply tolerated by fellow-workers. The Church was organized as if no other Church cared to co-operate with her. We were compelled to provide our own missionary, tract, Sunday-school, Church extension, and Bible societies. The conduct of these societies implied the printing-press. Inter-church toleration presently improved, so that the abolition of our Methodist Bible Society was expedient and safe; but the Church is so large and her plans are so comprehensive that our separate organization is as complete as if there were no other Church on the planet.

This is defensible and philosophical, because providential. Every Christian should thus hold himself prepared for all service, on the correct theory that God may at any moment call him to unanticipated duty in unforeseen directions. Consistent with the highest and frankest fraternity towards all the hosts of Christianity, each separate Church should be equipped, like co-operating *corps d'armée*, with infantry, cavalry, artillery, and munitions, and hold itself ready for instant independent yet related service.

We love to speak of our Church as a child of Providence. Nobody planned our body ecclesiastical in advance, as architects conceive a vast edifice before a stone is laid. Every one of our present vast departments of methodized

5

labor came as an original tentative hint to the men who asked God to give them generalship. Trial and experiment condemned some of our early devices, while the wiser items were approved by experience, and enlarged as God set his seal to the original conception. We boast not when we say that not even that huge engine of propagandism which gives coherence to Roman Catholicism in all lands is nearly so well organized as is our own Church machinery. Our comparative excellence lies in the fact that our system, as huge and commanding as it certainly is, has not a trace of absolutism in its genesis or later success. The entire organism is purely *voluntary*, and is indorsed and accepted by intelligent people because it succeeds on its merits. Those who doubt should look the facts over again before rendering a final adverse verdict. There is no manner of doubt that some people estimate their own Methodist Church too lightly, simply because they have not penetrated the providential theory of its rise and progress.

Methodism prints. There is no doubt of that fact. Why she prints is explained very naturally. John Wesley was a seer. When he was not praying or preaching, he was staring into the face of a printed page. Amid his prodigious labors for the Church, he did an immense amount of reading. Few men in literature have been such judges of books as was our founder. He knew the good by instinct, and repelled the bad book as an alert conscience rebukes advancing sin. The invented printing-press with its rude appliances came—but not by chance—in the very nick of time to make Luther's work possible. When God sent that greatest ecclesiastical event since the advent of Christ—Methodism—into the world, the improved printing-press and cheaper book made John Wesley's work practicable. Therefore, just as great railway magnates outfit their own "special cars," so Wesley fitted up his own private carriage that he might read comfort-

ably while he flew over the kingdom. Presently, dissatisfied with books as they were, he began to write and
re-write and edit books for his people. Next in order, he
began to own presses, which he employed to carry help,
suggestion, warning, and zeal to his rapidly multiplying
societies.

Some active minds then, as also in modern times, wondered why Methodism did not content itself with what
other people printed: When our Book Concern was in full
operation nearly fifty years ago, it was proposed to abolish
our Church presses and confine our reading to that which
others would contract to print for us. Even now it is occasionally said that our Church might as well operate railroads and conduct banks as to own and superintend print-
ing-offices. The suggestion would be valid if the financial
results of railroading and banking and printing were the
central thought and motive. We do print on the same
philosophy that occasionally moves a Church or Sunday-
school to charter a train for a specific excursion and for
definite results. When a Methodist party makes its plans
for a day, and wishes to control the hours of starting and
return, and particularly desires to determine who shall be
passengers and favored guests, it goes into the railway
business, induced by the same motives that sanction the
permanent existence of distinctive Methodist printing.

We get a suggestive· hint in the fact that two literary
institutions in this country possess a catalogue of over
seven hundred separate volumes of books written in opposition to Methodism. We happen to know that this large
list does not contain all extant anti-Wesleyan literature.
These volumes were written under the stimulus of men
who did not love our Church, and the physical fact of the
printing proves that the kingdom of printing-ink must
needs be taken by Methodist violence. Methodism was
young, and Methodists were too poor to buy dear books
written in their defense. A hundred considerations led

Wesley to supply books from his English presses for our people, and equally led our early workers to organize printing facilities for American Methodists long before they began to build and dedicate houses of worship. We can not forget that the Frenchy flavor that tainted English society and literature after the restoration of Charles compelled Wesley to provide cleaner things for his people. The entire tide was against evangelical Christianity. If society and the press have pure features in this country, the credit must be shared with the influence of the Wesleyan printing-presses which came to evangelize the New World.

Scrutiny will sanction this broad claim. While we thank God, as Lincoln did, for all the Churches, we believe that if Wesleyan influences were subtracted from the warp and woof of American civilization, the republic would be far less unlike the states of Europe, both in the instincts in its liberty and the tone of its society. Methodism came with the vanguard, and assisted quietly and almost unconsciously in shaping every campaign as the hosts flowed westward. Even then, as now, our power and influence were apparently more in the pulpit and on the platform; but we believe the paramount influence was in the tract, leaflet, biography, hymn-book, and Scripture, which came from Methodist presses, and were read and read again when the itinerant was absent or asleep. We make this point coolly and confidently. Men, if asked to nominate the greatest of silent powers over modern mind, are apt to name the daily press of the republic. We are sure that the paramount power is in the hands of the weekly press, and claim that the weekly religious press is the potentate which the enemies of good would first strike down. Our claim is based both upon the larger number of issues of the weekly press and upon the clear-cut, independent, and better-toned deliverances of that press.

In the interests of the very facts involved we make

this assertion. It is not true that the Church press is devoted to dogma and is useless as an element in journalism
for practical purposes. The average secular paper is con-
fessedly devoted to a secular and competing purpose. It
is the organ of a party or aspiring person. It seeks political votes for political and party ends. As Christian
citizens, we believe in God as the head of our nation, and,
as our Father, he is regarded as the head of a particular
family should be held by actual, loving children. If we
are entitled to any respect, if we are ordinarily honest
men and women, we dare not ask God to bless our national American household unless we propose to sanctify
his day, to make laws in harmony with his revelation, to
discourage Sunday travel and riot, to limit and defeat the
power of strong drink, to preserve the marriage relation,
and to prefer pure men for public office. The facts are,
while parties profess to respect the Churches, the whisky
ring is practically more potent in nearly all States than
is any single Church. Scarcely a single secular paper
openly opposes the power of the slums and of the corrupting saloon in party politics; Sunday observance is sneered
at by the average daily paper; the most successful journals and magazines dare not or care not expressly to defend evangelical doctrines, while the overshadowing universities in the land openly teach nothing save that which
discredits revelation.

We do thank God for all Churches, and we honor their
grand work; but it remains true that we discharge the
highest duties to catholic evangelicity by being sturdily
true to the body in which God has cast our lot. The
soldier serves best as artilleryman when he gives heart,
soul, body, and substance to that arm of the grand army.
The Church, as a Church, needs to fortify its schools and
pulpits and presses as preparatory to the national struggle
for truth and righteousness which is even now dawning
upon us.

Passing, with an honoring salute and a "Thank God," all the Churches and all the other grand appliances in our own Church, we earnestly exhort every member to give room and heart to the magnificent press system which is the admiration of all sister Churches. Methodism is connectional. It prefers to administer in every locality in relations to Wesleyan world-work. The strong everywhere aids the weak; the weakest man and the youngest Church are braced alike by relationship to the strongest and oldest.

As a part of our system, we have books pledged to our Church in the name of the common King. We have a system of *Christian Advocates* which represent the most independent, progressive, alert, aggressive, and successful in modern journalism. They are a unit as "Advocates" of every thing "Christian." Some persons too hastily conclude that, being "official," they are in bonds, and therefore not "free." On the contrary, their very plan and surroundings make them the freest on earth. It is argued that they must please and praise the powers that be, or the editors will be deposed, and that, consequently, the bread-and-butter argument is too potent. Not so. The individual nominally "independent" paper is immediately sensitive to its subscription-list, which so quickly resents adverse opinion. It is not conscious that it has a brotherhood of interlinked fellow-advocates to "strengthen weak knees." We know of not a single beneficent issue that has been carried in spite of the Church official press, or of a step in human progress that has not been grandly forwarded by our papers. In early days slavery was in some degree defended by the official papers; but that came of their small numbers and the absence of Northern competing thrift in that particular. As between the different official editors, no competition could be more thorough, and as between different systems the official editor can best afford to be personally independent. With respect to deference for the alleged powers that be, we make bold to doubt that "there be" any Methodist "powers" more powerful than the editors themselves.

Our papers are already supported and patronized beyond compare. It is no question whether, for the Church's rather than the papers' sake, there be not room for a new era of unprecedented *Advocate*-reading. We claim that no department of Methodist work is more successful than are our presses. Our papers keep pace with advancing population and national prosperity. Inferior prints cost a little less; but when panic and hard times wither other ventures, the official paper goes straight forward, without increase of price or abatement of valuable contents. Our papers are entitled to patronage and Methodist favor because they *are* *Methodist!* In a manly, fair sense, the Methodist organ has a claim in a Methodist family as legitimate and valid as that held by a Methodist family in a Methodist Church. We are members one of another. Organization is as vital to an army as is powder. Methodist efficiency depends on glad loyalty to every item in Methodist methods. The man who sneers at the claims of individual Churches, and shirks specific obligation on the plea of his enlightened "catholicity," has ceased to be valuable in any Christian work. As well might he desert his place in the organized line of battle, and go to shooting squirrels under pretense of serving his country. As well extinguish our light-house system on the sea-coast, and essay to save all mariners by burning tallow-candles held aloft by individual hands.

The most devout man is useful in proportion to his knowledge of his just relations to his brethren. The man who reads is conscious that God is working mightily through the related, fraternal, co-operating Churches. From books he will gain the regulating philosophy, and from the paper he notes the progress of the visible kingdom. The man or Church that sees how God favors the Church yonder notes the employed means of success, and takes heart again. Our grand army should feel the touch of individual marching elbows, and catch the inspiration of co-operating brotherhood.

The argument that sanctions the wise introduction of Church printing-presses remains to defend and explain their continued employment. No problem is more vital to our Church than that which relates to the replanting of the old-time interest in the scheme in the hearts of our people at large.

ARTHUR EDWARDS.

V.

WHAT WE READ, AND WHAT WE SHOULD READ.

WE can tell more easily what we read than what we should read.

Of making books and printing newspapers and other periodical literature, there is no end. The steam-press does its work speedily and well. It is a mighty agency for good and evil. Its leaves are not always for the healing of the nations. It, however, preaches, teaches, prays, and sings. It has a thousand tongues and hands. It toils on and on, and day and night and Summer and Winter are all the same to it.

The nations feed upon its words; kings and counselors fear it; and the tyrant trembles as he hears its fearful denunciations. It makes all professions, commerce, and labor contribute to its support. It reproduces for us the wisdom of the past, and lays by in store the results of the present for all future generations.

The people read. What do they read? Literature, science, art; they also read politics, theology, and even, a few, metaphysics. Most of the people read fiction.

All reading may be divided into two classes,—the solid and fictitious. Four-fifths, probably, read the latter. This conclusion is reached after considering the character of the books on sale in book-stores and the reports of custodians of public libraries. We do not here refer to school-books and reading in the line of the professions. The lawyer reads his text-books on law, the minister on theology, and the physician on medicine and surgery, while the merchant reads the daily reports of the markets, and the agricultu-rist the prices of farm and garden products and pub-lications giving specific information in regard to their production. We ask, What do we read for amusement, pleasure, and of habit? Only a few read the solid and the true, and not the ideal, fanciful, and imaginative. We call history, biography, geography, travels, works on art (such as painting, statuary, decorative, ceramic achieve-ments), and works on agriculture and science, solid. The-ology should also be included in this list. The publications of the Methodist Book Concern at New York and Cincin-nati, and those of other respectable publishers, may be found at prices within the reach of the poorest. All tastes are provided for, and may be accommodated in these rich depositories of wisdom.

What better enjoyment can we have for a few hours each week, of an intellectual character, than reading the records of the past as given in the works of Rollin, Gib-bon (revised), Froude, Macaulay, and other standard his-torians of Europe, and those written in our own land by Hildreth, Prescott, and Bancroft? what better pleasure than reading the history of the Christian Church by Black-burn, or of the Reformation by D'Aubigné?

Poetry comes under the head of solid reading when it is descriptive and instructive. What a list of acknowl-edged gifted ones could be given!—Horace, Homer, Virgil, Chaucer, Spenser, Shakespeare, Milton, Young, Cowper, Pope, Watts, Wesley, Montgomery, Bonar; and Bryant, Longfellow, Whittier, Holmes, and many others who have sung sweetly and grandly.

With the literary, scientific, religious, and artistic lore of the ages knocking for admission to our homes and hearts, we are guilty before God if we do not open to them. When we hear persons speak of history, travels, poetry, and the natural sciences as dry and uninteresting, we fail to understand the import of their words.

The daily and weekly newspaper should be in every home, due care being exercised that only the best enter. The world we live in is a great, active, progressive present, and only by reading a compendium of its doings can we keep pace with it. The Church is in the world, although not of it, and is moving forward, winning glorious conquests. Of its aggressive work, of its opposition, and of its successes, we may read reliable and interesting accounts in our Church papers.

The great majority of religious people read more or less fiction. A work is not always objectionable because it is "a novel," and we are not opposed to reading this class of literature as an amusement, provided the composition is good and a healthy moral tone pervades it.

Fancy and imagination have much to do with the happiness of the mind, and an appeal to these is not necessarily wrong. If the controlling interest of a novel is love, it should not be condemned, for God is the author of conjugal love; and if the narrations and descriptions of it are pure and rational, and the ideal of it within the limits of fact, its contemplation may not only be a pleasure, but lead to happy results. It always needs the shaping influence of Christian morals and restraints, and should be not only properly treated in literary productions, but in the pulpit and on the rostrum.

Without the moral moulding of these influences, love becomes a degrading passion, not far removed from blind instinct; with these, it gives dignity to the human form and elevation to the soul, creating an atmosphere of beauty in which to dwell.

With this recognition of a natural desire for novel-reading, we must protest against the practice and tendency of the incoming generation. How few youths voluntarily read history, science, biography, or poetry! If they read history at all, fact must be diluted and attenuated with fancy to an extent that even the youthful reader is compelled to ask, What is truth? Because of this style of history, the names of the great and good in Church and State, by the most of our young people are considered no more historical than those of Sinbad the sailor, Robinson Crusoe, or Captain Kidd, the pirate.

The young reader may ask, "Since you do not condemn novels, only those which are bad, how shall I know what is good or bad unless I read it?"

We do not find out what is poisonous in an apothecary's shop by tasting. This would be dangerous, and might prove to be a fatal mistake. It is not safe for a young person to select and read at will.

But since the book-stores abound with novels, and they are peddled on every street-corner and on every train, and are found in abundance in some of our libraries, it may be best to give a few rules, the observance of which will be of great benefit,

Do not read the cheap fiction which is known as dime and nickel novels. They are, without an exception, published by unprincipled and base men, who only seek gain. The books are full of slang phrases, representations of bloody deeds, murder, theft, perjury, homicide, suicide, and horrible recitals in low, vulgar, and often obscene and profane, language. An examination of a large number warrants this statement.

Ascertain from intelligent and cultured Christian men and women the names of good authors and of good books. A good man will not write a bad book. You can trust the opinions of our book agents and editors in the Methodist Episcopal Church. Not that we would limit to Methodist authors, but we would have our people receive the works that have gone under the review of 'the pure and cultured minds of the Church. We can not undertake in this chapter to give a list of the excellent authors whose interesting and often charming productions are on sale at the Methodist Book Concerns.

Works of fiction, even the best, are to be read as we take amusement. The rule should be to read solid literature. The importance of this is evident when we consider how much there is to be learned by reading the best authors, and the brevity of human life. At least a dozen solid books to one of fiction should be read. Even this is too large a percentage of fictitious literature, if it causes a distaste for the solid. To form the habit of reading even the best novels is to stand on dangerous ground. The desire for this class of stimulants increases as the demand is fully met, so that the reader of fiction may become the victim of a morbid literary taste. Thus time is wasted, means misused, and talent brought into bondage. We hardly know which is to be pitied the more, the slave of novel-reading or of alcohol. Both stand in the pathway of life, and will inevitably lead their victims to moral death, unless rescued and redeemed by the merits of Christ.

The persistent reader of novels is unfitted for the duties and realities of life. The leading desire is for more romance, more tragedy, deception, revenge, broken vows, and murder. Unless the cup is filled to the brim with these, it is not acceptable. The drinking of its contents never satisfies. This is excess, and brings sorrow.

This kind of reading familiarizes with crime; and, as a result, iniquity loses much that makes it repulsive. It weakens the sense of right and purity, so that temptation becomes formidable, and the power of resistance greatly weakened. Thus conditioned it is not unusual for individuals to become the subjects of unintentional imitation, and sin and ruin follow as results. We object to a very large proportion of light literature because it is written in a style that degrades the taste, and because it is usually illustrated by execrable art deformities, both in artistic execution and in the scenes described. Daggers, swords, guns, clubs, revolvers, fights, abductions, and all forms of crime are rudely portrayed. They often border on· the obscene, and would be so, were it not for the enforcement of the law. These pictures fasten themselves upon the youthful memory, and the regrets of after years will not erase them. They are specters haunting it through all the periods of life. They are demons of darkness, pestilential with moral death. They are the conceptions of minds steeped in the odors of Gehenna. Much of crime is instigated by this class of illustrated reading. The testimony of one young man near the gallows could truthfully be said of very many suffering for crime, "The impure novel brought me to this."

The approaches of evil, to be successful, must be gradual, and its true intention not apparent. It, like the cunning reptile hidden amid the beautiful foliage, first charms its innocent victim, and then devours. This serpent is in nine-tenths of the novels read by our youth.

But what shall we read? The best answer we can make to this query is, Read the Bible; read any religious literature, but above all, read the Bible.

The old poet well describes it:

> " If thou art merry, here are airs;
> If melancholy, here are prayers;
> If studious, here are those things writ
> Which may deserve the ablest wit.
> If hungry, here is food divine;
> If thirsty, nectar, heavenly wine.
> Read, then; but first thyself prepare
> To read with zeal, and mark with care;
> And when thou read'st what here is writ,
> Let thy practice second it.
> So twice each precept thine shall be,
> First in the book, and next in thee."

Read carefully that which is recognized by the Christian Church as the best in history, biography, science, art, and general and religious literature.

Is it not the duty of parents and guardians, with the strong hand of authority, if need be, to protect their children and wards from the poisonous literature which the sordid cunning of the enemies of virtue and religion thrust into our homes and schools? Let these retreats of our youth be cleansed as by fire; let the godless, vile stuff be given, whenever found, to the flames.

Children read, and they should; and interesting and wholesome productions should be furnished them. Much of their success in after life depends upon the selection made for them. Upon this foundation they build for the future, and the question must be settled by the parent whether the foundations of character and life shall be laid in the sand of low sensualism and skepticism or on the solid granite of purity and eternal truth.

N. B. C. LOVE.

VI.

PERNICIOUS LITERATURE.

It is as much the duty of parents to watch the books and papers read by their children as it is to be careful concerning the food they eat. No parent will knowingly give adulterated or poisonous food to his children; nor will any wise parent allow them indiscriminately to gormandize on all sorts of edibles. He prefers to select their food for them, and to train them in those habits of eating which distinguish the civilized man from the savage.

Yet many parents, wise in this, are not equally wise in selecting moral and intellectual nourishment. Their children are allowed to read whatever they can find, and it is sometimes boastingly said of them, "They read every thing they can get hold of." This is regarded as a mark of precocious intellect. It is rather evidence of extraordinary folly, as much so as if they were to eat every thing they could lay their hands on, wholesome or poisonous.

The country is flooded with books and papers for children and young people. They are to be found not only in book-stores, but on the news-stands in the streets, and are peddled in the railway-cars. They are made attractive, not so much by good paper, printing, and pictures—for many of them are very inferior in this respect—as by taking titles, bold head-lines, and representations of exciting scenes. They are filled with blood-curdling stories, which tell of adventures with Indians, cannibals, pirates, highwaymen, burglars, murderers, smugglers, and other vile personages. These stories are illustrated by pictures in which the rifle, the pistol, and the knife are prominent.

Lightning, storms, earthquakes, fires, water-spouts, wrecks, and every thing else horrible or grotesque in nature, are depicted. Ferocious beasts and still more ferocious human beings are seen in every possible position where hatred, revenge, or blood-thirstiness can place them.

These stories thus illustrated are educating thousands of the children of the present generation. They cultivate a vitiated taste, so that history and truthful narratives and ordinary travels have but little attraction, lacking, as they must, the highly spiced flavoring of these more popular stories. They prepare their readers for deeds of foolish adventure and of crime. Every now and then we read of youngsters from nine to twelve years old starting away from home, without parental knowledge, to hunt buffalo or to kill Indians. They have caught the fever from the popular and exciting stories they have read.

Of course, these little fellows soon come to grief, and are glad to get home again; but there are those a few years older and richer in resources who are not so easily discouraged. These have an ambition to imitate the bold burglars, smugglers, and pirates of whom they have read, and they do not hesitate to rob where they have the chance, and then retire to some recess in the woods, or some cave in the hill-side, to enjoy their ill-gotten booty. The police in New York City, a year or two ago, unearthed a nest of these young thieves, who had a hiding-place under one of the city wharves, where they deposited their booty and lived luxuriously. They were lads of from twelve to fifteen years of age, and were imitating the example of the older villains of whom they had read.

The story of the Arkansas Railway train-robbers is still fresh in the public mind. These robbers were young men from eighteen to twenty-three years old, and they admitted that this sort of literature had been their inspiration. They were tried, convicted, and sentenced to seventy years imprisonment. An Arkansas paper states that one

6

of them, not long after entering the prison, became demented, the severity of his sentence having produced despair. After speaking for awhile of his father, mother, and sisters, among whom he imagined himself to be, his face suddenly grew dark, and, waving his hands wildly, he began to mutter broken sentences. "Seizing the bridle-rein, he sprang upon his antagonist's horse, and dashed away," said he.

"He's reading one of those wild books that we used to steal away and devour," said one of his companions in crime.

The poor, crazy fellow continued his recitation as follows: "'Halt!' he exclaimed, drawing a revolver, and leveling it at the head of young Horace. Slowly and sadly they left the church, and walked along the worn path to the rude grave of Lawrence. Standing near the stone placed there by the Indian, Casper and his fair companion—" And he muttered incoherently, the sentence dying away with a deep groan. Suddenly he raised himself, looked intently toward the door, and slowly sank back, dead.

Thus, in the unconscious declarations of his dying hour, he bore witness to the nature of the mental stimulant which had gradually poisoned his soul and brought him to a felon's end.

There is a kind of vile literature, too infamous to be particularly described, the sale of which is forbidden by law, though the trade is carried on secretly, in spite of law. The sensational books and papers which are publicly exposed for sale create a morbid taste, which finds its gratification in these baser publications. They are advertised extensively, though secretly, sometimes by means of circulars sent by mail, sometimes by advertisements of an apparently innocent character inserted in the daily papers. Occasionally even the religious press is thus used, unknown by editors or publishers, as the following fact will show:

Several years ago a friend of the writer saw in a religious periodical an advertisement of a beautiful toy, which could be obtained by sending twenty-five cents to a certain Eastern city. He sent his money, and obtained the toy for his boy, a lad twelve years old. So far every thing was innocent and unsuspicious. But with the toy came a circular recommending a tobacco-pipe purporting to have certain advantages over ordinary pipes. As he did not care to have his boy use a pipe he kept the circular for himself, and began to wonder what would come if a pipe were sent for. He did not experiment in this direction; but having occasion, a few weeks after, to visit the city from whence the circular issued, he consulted a friend, a government official, who told him what his boy would have probably received if he had sent for a pipe. With the pipe would have come a circular recommending a book; and if this book had been ordered, a circular concerning another book would have been sent, until, by this gradual method of advertising, the vilest publications issued would have been brought to his attention. Some of these circulars were given to our friend by this officer, and were afterward shown to the writer. The immoral character of the publications they advertise would clearly appear if we should mention their titles.

This is only one of many means devised by the devil to scatter the seeds of vice, that they may one day grow up and produce a fearful harvest of desolation.

Parents should know what reading their children have. The question should not simply be, What will please? but, What will profit? If pleasure and profit can be combined, it is well; but pleasure without profit should be avoided. No sensible parent would permit his children to eat colored candies merely because they are pleased with the brilliant hues; for he knows that this brilliancy but conceals the subtle poison.

Even our Sunday-school libraries need close inspection.

There are such libraries where the great majority of the books will be found to consist of novels, and very many of them of the trashiest sort. The taste for unwholesome literature is created in the very place where, above all others, there ought to be none but the healthiest influences. Those who use such libraries have no taste for useful reading. Whatever of good they may get from the study of the Bible is neutralized, in part at least, by the books they take from the library.

There need be no danger feared from our Sunday-school libraries if the provisions of our Discipline are faithfully carried out. Its language is sufficiently clear: "It shall be the duty of the preacher in charge, aided by the superintendent and the committee on Sunday-schools, to decide as to what books shall be used in our Sunday-schools." (Discipline, ¶ 257.) Where this duty is faithfully discharged, there is very seldom any ground for complaint. In many instances, however, the selection of library-books is left to a committee, appointed without any regard to the above-named requirement of the Discipline. Very often this committee consists of persons who are no judges of books, who will buy any thing that is "cheap," who are attracted by bright bindings and pictures and taking titles, and who thus, with the best intentions, oft-times buy a lot of worthless books which ought to go back to the paper-mill, or be thrust into the fire.

Our families and our Sunday-schools should be provided with a literature of the best and purest kind, so that their taste shall be cultivated and their spiritual nature improved. Above all, special pains should be taken to keep out every book or paper of an immoral or a merely sensational character.

J. M. FREEMAN.

VII.

THE EVILS OF INDISCRIMINATE NOVEL-READING.

> " A novel was a book
> *Three-volumed* and *once read ;* and oft crammed full
> Of poisonous error, blackening every page;
> And oftener still of trifling, second-hand
> Remark, and old, diseased, putrid thought,
> And miserable incident; at war
> With nature, with itself and truth at war;
> Yet charming still the greedy reader on,
> Till *done* he tried to recollect his thoughts,
> And nothing found but *dreaming emptiness.*"

ALTHOUGH there are some noble exceptions, which I would by no means include in the following estimate, still the general tendency of novels is to evil.

The average novel deals largely in the marvelous, and so puts a false coloring upon human life. Every one knows, who knows any thing in regard to this class of books, that they are, for the most part, but a compilation of startling adventures, strange coincidences, and hair-breadth escapes. The common life of mortals is an every-day affair, dealing with sharply defined realities, and as far removed as can be from the "romantic." But this popular literature aims to throw as fine a web of fancy and romance around every thing and every character as is possible ; and those novels which are strictly true to life, whose heroes, like Miss Mulock's "John Halifax, Gentleman," meet with no strokes of fortune save such as are the legitimate results of virtue and industry, are pronounced insipid and dull by the mass of novel-readers, no matter who wrote them, or what the moral—no matter how masterly may be the delineation of life and character. An unnatural spice of the unaccountable, the strange, will alone meet the demands of this perverted taste; and he who is the most skillful in preparing this mixture is, of course, the most popular.

Writers of this class commonly represent every-day, good young men as dull and tiresome to a young woman of spirit, while *pirate heroes* are invariably frank, generous, attractive, and open-hearted; so our novel-reading girls come to prefer pirate heroes to good young men. The flat, pointless tales of *Peterson, Waverly,* etc., go to the other extreme of improbability, and delineate effortless lives, made up of love passages, picnics, parties, etc., inclining their young readers to be satisfied with such events, and to aim at nothing higher. In either case the young mind is unfitted for the common events and the practical duties of real life.

The habit of novel-reading will inevitably enervate the manhood and dwarf the mind of its victim, and give him a disrelish for the common, but really great and grand, responsibilities of our existence. The world wants *men* and *women*, not sickly sentimentalists; it wants those who can rise above childish pursuits, and live in regions of lofty thoughts and worthy deeds. But the habitual novel-reader can not be such a character. He lives, like the opium-eater, in a sort of dream-land, and the realities of life fail to call forth his energies. Many a young man, after becoming mentally narcotized by this kind of reading, imagines himself under the influence of a sort of *destiny*. He lives so completely in the atmosphere of romance that he imagines it to be somehow or other connected with his own history; and with a listless scorn he looks upon the common fortunes of men. He feels lifted above that dead level of life where industry and energy are necessary to success, and expects to be borne, by some sudden wave of good fortune, to the position he covets. So he comes to be, what the world least wants, a man of *dreams* rather than a man of *deeds.*

Or, if he escapes this mental Scylla, on the other side yawns a moral Charybdis which is sure to ingulf him. As he studies these false characters—that with, perhaps, one or two noble qualities combine so many that are ignoble—first he admires, then he copies.

Reading the adventures of men who are represented as having an extensive knowledge of the world, he gradually gets dissatisfied with his present surroundings, and begins to look for a change. Laboring under a sort of fascination, he ventures into the broad and beautiful road that invites him. He passes through scenes of revelry and vice, and, wild with the boyish notion that he is "learning the world," he rushes on from evil to evil, until he is ruined by the wine-cup, the gambling-table, and the house of her whose "*steps take hold on hell.*" Facts are our witnesses here. I well remember the thrill of horror that went through my young heart when I was told that a class-mate of mine had committed suicide by hanging himself to the limb of a forest-tree. He was a notorious novel-reader, of a brilliant but romantic turn of mind, and, as might have been expected, when his trunk was examined, on a pile of the worst kind of French and English novels was a note ascribing his rash act to disappointment in a love affair with a silly little coquette of sixteen.

A young man who was recently hanged for murder ascribed his downfall to the influence of the vilest kind of novels, which he was allowed to read when eight or nine years old. "If *good books* had been furnished me," he said, "and no *bad ones,* I should have read the good books with as great zest as I did the bad ones. Persuade all persons over whom you have any influence not to read novels," was the parting message of this young man to his brother.

The chaplain of Newgate prison, in London, in his annual report to the lord mayor, referring to many fine-looking young men of respectable parentage, in the city prison, says that he discovered " that all these young men, without one exception, had been in the habit of reading those cheap periodicals which are now published for the alleged instruction and amusement of the youth of both sexes."

Indiscriminate novel-reading hardens the heart and perverts the sympathies. The young woman who sobs over the sufferings of some imaginary character, which never had an existence save in the waste chambers of the author's brain, will spurn from her door the *real* hungry and naked—will gather her robes closely about her, lest they brush against the mean and wretched whom she meets. She will mourn over the death of some imaginary fair one, the fancied victim of lust and deceit, but will turn with horror and loathing from her who, the real victim of treachery,

> " Mad from life's history,
> Glad to death's mystery;
> Swift to be hurled
> Anywhere—anywhere
> Out of the world,"—

dies with a lacerated and broken heart—dies in shame and despair.

And why is this? Simply because *real* misery has not the charm of romance thrown around it. Self-abnegation and charity are literally ideal virtues, if, indeed, they are virtues at all. The morbid mind, accustomed to over-wrought scenes of misery, has no interest in that which comes with the chill of reality rather than the warmth of imagination. Such persons have so often befooled their emotive natures that they have become stupid, and do not respond to the common suffering of common humanity.

Novel-reading will greatly diminish, if not take away altogether, the horror which the virtuous feel against vice and crime. Almost all that is shocking in vice is combined in these books with some noble quality, so as to make the hero, on the whole, an attractive character. The thief, the fortune-hunter, and especially the *rake*, are often presented as successful, elegant, and happy. Novels abound in immodest and profane allusions or expressions. Wantonness, pride, anger, hatred, and *unholy love* are the elements of most of them.

Indiscriminate novel-reading cultivates bad passions. In this case,

" 'T is distance lends enchantment to the view."

And as the beauties of imagination and the semblance of refinement are thrown around sin, the inexperienced mind is captivated; by degrees the baser passions are aroused and become dominant, the heart is corrupted, and the whole life is defiled. Under pretense of illustrating social life *as it is*, the reader is made familiar with its worst and most exceptional developments. Under these favorable circumstances the poison works until the latent fires of sin begin to burn. Fuel is added to the flames; fiercely and more fiercely they rage, until reason and judgment and conscience are consumed, and the man himself is destroyed.

How many a young man, ruined by open and secret sin, and an outcast from virtuous society; how many a young woman, crushed and heart-broken with her burden of shame, spurned by those who should soothe, and cursed by those who should comfort,—could point to the false views of life given by indiscriminate novel-reading as the influence that led them astray, and the terrible power of such reading to arouse the passions as the influence that ruined them.

I tell you this is no fancy sketch. On every side of us the subtle fiend is touching and blasting immortal souls. Men teach their children the pure truths of Christ's Gospel, and with a father's watchfulness and love shield them from corrupting and immodest society; but, because parents are indifferent to this subject, at the same time the

7

loved daughter—the idol of the household—sits quietly at
the fireside, drawing her ideas of society from such novels,
and taking into her young heart falsehoods that shall
poison all her future life. Under a pretense of photo-
graphing real life, the young are let into the vile secrets
of police courts, and made familiar with the foul details
of every social sin. They gain a knowledge of human
frailties—a precocious wisdom, which " makes them *rotten*
before they are *ripe.*" And this evil is not confined to
second and third rate novelists. It sullies the otherwise
fair fame of many a first-class writer of romance. For
example, take Charles Reade, a man of noble genius,
who, at the first, gave us some works that were powerful,
pure, and healthy. In his later productions, through un-
worthy attempts to cater to this vile, popular taste, he has
descended to the lowest level of indecency. It needs but
a glance at his books called " Griffith Gaunt" and " A
Terrible Temptation" to show that they are not fit for circulation in virtuous homes. There is a grain of comfort
for us in the fact that not only religious periodicals, but
leading secular papers and magazines cry out against such
a prostitution of this author's great powers. Some of Victor Hugo's stories, so extensively circulated in this country, as well as some of Mr. Swinburne's poems, outrage
every principle of decency and humanity. And these are,
in most respects, writers of the highest order.

*Indiscriminate novel-reading tends to destroy the taste for
other and more substantial reading.* Familiarity with popular fiction gives a disrelish for simple truth, and engen-
ders the pernicious habit of reading merely for *amusement.*
This destroys the love of sober investigation; it renders
science, history, biography, critical essays, and books of
travel (in which the healthy mind takes so much delight),
tedious and unattractive; it dwarfs the memory and reasoning powers, and makes the imagination morbid and
unhealthy by constant excitement.

Let a young man or woman accustom the mind to this unnatural excitement, and it will soon be evident that, when it is not under the influence of that stimulant by *reaction*, it sinks to such an insensible state that solid reading can not arouse it to interest. The mind is very like the body in this respect. Let a man accustom himself to the use of stimulants (such as wine, brandy, or tobacco), and soon he will be utterly unable to arouse himself to great exertions, and to call out all the energies of his nature without the aid of such stimulants. On the contrary, if he accustoms himself to a strong, healthy diet, without unnatural stimulants, he can at any time command his entire energies, bringing them to bear upon the accomplishment of his object.

So the mind of the habitual novel-reader is debauched by the wine, the brandy, and the tobacco of literature; and it will take no interest in a book that does not contain these elements; it can not be aroused to activity in any other way. I have the proof of this in the experience of every confirmed novel-reader. The modern novel, with its false history (and how often we hear of history manufactured for the occasion by the novelist quoted as real history!), its false biography, and its false morals, is an enemy to true mental culture.

Most novel-reading is anti-religious in its tendencies. I know there is, among a certain class of literary or semi-literary minds, a sympathy for these moral defects, and they sneer at our demand for a respectable deference to religion in all literature as illiberal and puritanic.

If there is any thing detestable, it is this cant about "*orthodoxy*" and "*fanaticism*" on the part of those who sneer at the sublime faith of Paul, of Calvin, of Wesley, of Newton, and of Washington, as a mere superstition, and who applaud those flings which men of more genius than grace make at religion, in their books, as marks of smartness and spirit. Such sentiments, however, show a weakness of the head only equaled by the corruption of the heart.

Popular novelists seldom, if ever, represent the sublime triumphs of Christianity, its purity, its heavenly mission to men; but, on the contrary, if they notice it at all, they only show you its perversions, and in place of a really regenerate heart and sanctified life, they give you the hypocrite. Many of them use religion as a cloak, to impart the greater perfection of cunning to their vilest characters. If they wish to represent a deceitful, wily *villain*, they will endow him with great pretensions to piety as a finishing touch to the picture. Or, if they assume to give a true Christian character, they make him a sort of weak-headed "goody," who only excites your laughter or your pity.

I make these charges plainly and understandingly, and am fully prepared to substantiate them. Even the best romance-writers, whose works are *classics* in our language, are not entirely free from this charge. Charles Dickens, whose works of fiction are pronounced so healthful to morals, and who really displays a noble sympathy with the poor and oppressed, is an example. Take his story of "David Copperfield." In this, the step-father of David, aided and abetted by a maiden sister, is guilty of all manner of meanness. He breaks the hearts and destroys the lives of *two wives in succession*, and treats little David with the greatest cruelty. This step-father and his sister are described as professedly pious and careful in all their outward religious duties. David's schoolmaster, who combines all that is tyrannical to his scholars with unfaithfulness as a teacher, is also described as a pious man. In short, all the characters of the story who awaken the abhorrence or the contempt of the reader are described as professors of religion, while nearly every worthy and attractive character is represented as holding himself aloof from religion, with an assumed superiority, or, at least, is shown to be wholly indifferent to it.

What reader of Dickens does not recall with disgust the saintly, conscientious *villain* Pecksniff, or the punch-loving preacher, Stiggins?

In Scott's most popular tale of "Rob Roy," a stern, cruel, unreasonable parent is represented as being made so by his religion, and one of the most grasping, dishonest business characters ever represented is a zealous Presbyterian.

Now, although such writers as Scott and Dickens may, in general, be valuable, and, under proper circumstances, may be read with profit as literary masters, yet this charge of religious misrepresentation can be maintained against them, and is a blemish upon at least a part of their works. But the wrong does not end here. From such writers these contemptible third-rate scribblers take their tone, and, as imitators always reproduce the *defects* rather than the *excellencies* of their models, by a natural process this evil has multiplied itself in every direction, and has blossomed out, and gone to seed, in the periodical trash already referred to.

Now, what will be the tendency of all this? Inevitably the young reader will learn to despise religion and to shun the Christian. When the novelist associates religion with the lack of all genial affections, with avarice and meanness, and connects irreligion with all that is socially or intellectually attractive, the inexperienced youth will come to regard religion as at variance with a true literary taste and as a matter of no moment to a man or woman of culture.

Says an eminent writer, in speaking of three very popular novels: "There is little hazard in asserting that these three novels have done more to undermine the belief in a change of heart and spiritual communion with God, and to destroy reverence for the Bible, than has been done in the same time by Thomas Paine's 'Age of Reason.' We are reluctant to admit it. We know how many of the admirers of these authors (and what genial minds are not admirers of them?) will revolt at the charge. We can not help it. We acknowledge all their excellencies, but the charge of irreligion is a valid one. It is also a *fundamental one;* and, in the estimation of a right mind, it is a *fatal one.*"

Such, then, are the tendencies of this extravagant literature; and overrunning the reading world with such trash is only preparing the popular mind for worse forms of literary and moral corruptions. We begin already to reap the terrible consequences. A few years since such obscene illustrated papers as are now thrust in our faces at every railroad depot and every news-stand would have been impossible; but now the public mind has become so demoralized by these influences of which we have been speaking, that such *literary rottenness* is quietly tolerated. Unless men awake to this subject, soon the flood-gates of hell will be opened upon us, and Churches and schools and all good influences will be utterly powerless to stay the tide of destruction.

Solve the problem as you may, these evils of which I have spoken are the unequivocal result of indiscriminate novel-reading. Modify and evade the conclusion as you will, it is the same.

This is a serious, a fearful question, that urges itself upon our attention with an increasing importance. It is a question that will tax all our wisdom and all our piety.

How shall we read novels? Dr. Curry says: "While we are free to declare our conviction that, for the most part, fictitious literature is *miserably poor provender for the mind*, we can also attest the real value of *some* novels that we have read."

None of us, probably, are prepared to say that under no circumstances should a work of the better kind of fiction be read. It may sometimes be a recreation, and the delineations of manners and customs in romance are often helps to details in history. Many works of fiction may be read with safety, some even with profit. But the very greatest care is necessary, in reading even the *best* of novels, lest too great familiarity with such literature should relax the mind, pervert its powers, and disqualify the heart for the active virtues of life.

In attempting to give advice upon this point I am fully aware of the difficulties in the way, not the least of which is the disposition of the young to take advantage of a reasonable license in certain things, and decidedly overdo the matter. But I am impressed with the fact that an indiscriminate condemnation of novel-reading is not wise; such a course is too extreme. Such a course will cut off the ears of our young people, so that they will not listen to what we have to say upon this subject.

I am also impressed with the importance of careful advice to the young, by way of instructing their inexperience and leading them to a wise course as regards light literature ; and the end to be secured is at least worthy the prayerful, thoughtful attempt.

In offering some advice upon this subject, let me say :

1. Read no paper or magazine which is mainly devoted to stories and novelettes.

2. Never allow children to read novels.

3. Read works of fiction only as a *recreation* and *relaxation* from severe mental labor. If you have but little time for reading and study, spend none of it in novel-reading.

4. Read only classics—those works of fiction that are of acknowledged merit, and are legitimate in their conception and aim. Seek the advice of some person of good judgment, experience, and mental training in making your selections.

5. Read only such fiction as you feel is worth reading for its own sake, such as you feel you can read over again, at some future time, with both pleasure and profit.

6. When you find that your limited reading of fiction interferes in the least with your mental or moral duties, then let it alone altogether.

7. Finally, that we may be right and act right in this important matter, let us seek a consecration of mind and heart to the Master's work. Let us look for the baptism of spiritual power, that we may so lift up Christ before the world that the old and the young will be drawn from sin to holiness, from Satan to the Savior.

I would address those who are in the morning of life, especially those who have become addicted to this pernicious habit. Let me urge you to think earnestly upon this subject. It concerns you intellectually and morally. It concerns your success in life and your safety in eternity.

Beware, O beware of this evil! It will poison your mind; it will ruin your soul. God purposes better things for you. The Church and the world want cultivated minds as well as regenerate hearts; and, with all your opportunities, you have no time to spend on trifles, or in doing that which will have to be undone. All about you are the materials for a perfect intellectual temple. May you be so divinely directed in your choice that every stone you place in the walls may be worthy and enduring, while the whole shall constitute a fitting support for the top-stone, which shall be perfect love to God and men!

R. C. HOUGHTON.

VIII.

METHODIST BIOGRAPHICAL LIT-ERATURE.

PART I.

Two thousand years ago, Terence, the great Roman poet, in embodying counsel for one who desired his philosophy of life, said : "My advice is, to consult the lives of other men, as he would a looking-glass, and from thence fetch examples for his own imitation." The late Thomas Carlyle suggested that "history is the essence of innumerable biographies," and declared that "there is no heroic poem in the world but is at bottom a biography, the life of a man." The lives of those who have lived, not for themselves alone, but for humanity, unconsciously to ourselves influence our minds, govern our pursuits, and shape our destinies. No good or great man liveth to himself; his influence, not limited to a narrow sphere, circulates through all the great channels of society. The great biographer Plutarch wrote parallel lives. His biographies run in pairs, each pair placing before the reader two human characters, which, thrown upon different circumstances and a different age, had yet certain affinities. In Methodist biography, as the brief survey which we propose to present may demonstrate, there are closer affinities than the Plutarchian characters, and yet an almost infinite variety in one comprehensive unity.

"The biographies of the chief men of Methodism," says the Rev. Dr. Curry, "have the two great excellences of being valuable and trustworthy *repertoires* of our ecclesiastical history, and in presenting in concrete and living forms our peculiar doctrines of Christian experience." The chief office of biography, then, is to perpetuate what might otherwise pass away, to illustrate what might otherwise become uncertain, and ultimately fade into deep obscurity. It is to embalm the great and the good, so that they can not perish from the earth; to enable us to gather within a single room a large part of the illustrious spirits of the past, to commune with them at our own pleasure, and even to become companions of their lives. In our Methodist biographies we converse with the illustrious dead of our communion by means which they themselves have furnished to us, or by narratives which, to general ability of treatment and to minuteness of significant detail, have added the charm of sympathy with the departed and the power to awaken and diffuse it. These characters of exalted Christian worth constitute an impressive heritage of the Church and the world.

Until a comparatively recent period the Methodist Church in America did but little in this department of literature, and nearly all the works of biography published by the Book Concern were reprints of European productions. It was so in the early history of Methodism in England; and must necessarily be so. The earlier preachers of the heroic age of the Church have other demands upon their energies, and it is only when they have made history that they can afford to pause long enough to record it. How brief is the mention made by Mr. Wesley in the Minutes of the death of his helpers! The "Cyclopædia of Methodism" says: "The first references to the death of ministers were made by Mr. Wesley in 1777, and are remarkable for their brevity. They are as follows: ' John Slocomb, at Clones, an old laborer, worn out in the service. John Harrison, near Lisburn, a promising youth, serious, modest, and much devoted to God. William Lumley, in Huxham, a blessed young man, a happy witness of the full liberty of the children of God. William Minethorp, near Dunbar, an Israelite indeed, in whom there is no guile.' In succeeding years these notices were somewhat longer. But when the sainted Fletcher died, who was so remarkable for his personal piety, his intellectual power, and his force as a writer, the only notice is, ' John Fletcher, a pattern of all holiness, scarce to be paralleled in the century.' So fully had the example of Mr. Wesley influenced the preachers that, at the time of his death, in 1791, the only minute was the following: ' It may be expected that the conference make some observation on the death of Mr. Wesley; but they find themselves utterly inadequate to express their ideas on this awful and affecting event. Our souls do truly mourn for their great loss, and they trust they shall give the most substantial proofs of their veneration for the memory of their most esteemed father and friend by endeavoring with great humility and diffidence to follow and imitate him in doctrine, discipline, and life.'"

But, however " diffident" his brethren may have been in reference to these obituary notices, it was otherwise with the great masses beyond them, and subsequently even with themselves. It has been estimated that, until the year 1848, portraitures of Wesley and Methodism, and works on that subject, from the penny tract to the volume of high pretensions, appeared at the rate of about four productions a year, from the time of the organization of the society in 1739, and these publications have immensely exceeded that proportion during the last thirty years. It is almost impossible to refer to the ecclesiastical system without referring to its founder, and this, too, in more or less of a biographical sense. But the first distinctive biography of Mr. Wesley was written in 1791, and bore the following title: " Memoirs of the Late Rev. John Wesley, A. M., with a Review of his Life and Writings; and a History of Methodism, from its Commencement in 1729 to the Present Time. By John Hampson, A. B." (Sunderland. 3 vols., 12mo.) According to Myles's "History of the Methodists," the biographer entered the Wesleyan ministry in 1777, his father having become one of John Wesley's assistants twenty-two years previously, and they both left the connection in 1785, Mr. Wesley, in filling up the Deed of Declaration, having omitted both their names from that document. It was the author's intention to publish his work during Mr. Wesley's life-time; but this was not done. It has been said of this book, that "as a documentary Life it has no value; its incidents, manufactured for the occasion, are of a coarse character, and its criticisms are of the most petty kind."

The narrative of John Wesley's last days by Miss Elizabeth Ritchie, who was present at his death, was printed and circulated throughout the connection immediately after his decease, and is the chief source whence Wesley's biographers derive their information respecting the closing scenes of his life.

The second Life of Wesley appeared in 1792, an octavo of 642 pages, printed in London, with the title, "Life of the Rev. John Wesley, A. M., including An Account of the Great Revival of Religion in Europe and America, of which he was the First and Chief Instrument. By Dr. Coke and Mr. Moore." This volume was published under peculiar circumstances. Mr. Wesley had named these two of his brethren and Dr. Whitehead as his literary executors; but a misunderstanding arising between Dr. Whitehead and the conference, the volume was altogether written by the two whose names stand in connection with its authorship. Dr. Whitehead, who had been one of Wesley's itinerants for five years (1764–1769), and who had afterward rejoined the Methodists, and was a local preacher at the time of Mr. Wesley's death, had received the manuscripts and other documents necessary to the work, and had entered upon the work of preparing the biography. In an evil hour he determined to hold the copyright, for which it had been suggested to him he could receive two thousand pounds. The temptation proved too great, as he was only to receive two hundred guineas for his labor. He refused to give up what he had already written, amounting to 128 pages, and the other literary executors were compelled to proceed without all the data requisite for the work. But the book was prepared by them, was printed, and before the next conference was held ten thousand copies had been sold.

Coke and Moore's life of Wesley must be distinguished .from Moore's "Life of John and Charles Wesley, and Memoirs of the Family," as the latter was published in 1824. It is a valuable contribution to the history of Methodism; but it is, in some places, tinctured with his own peculiar views, and especially with those of them which affected his personal position.

The first volume of Dr. Whitehead's Life of Wesley appeared in 1793, and the second in 1796. As it was written during a period of alienation from his former friends, and at a time when his mind was engrossed in a desire to vindicate himself from the just suspicions his conduct had aroused, it was hardly to be expected that the book would be unbiased in its character. Dr. Curry says that, "having the rod in his own hands, he did fail not to apply it, thus making his Life of Wesley a scourge to both him and his followers." Several editions of the book have since been published: one in Dublin in 1805, another in Boston in 1844, and another in Philadelphia in 1846, to the last of which the Rev. Dr. T. H. Stockton furnished an Introduction; and a more recent one in New York (1881).

The next biographer of Mr. Wesley was Robert Southey, poet laureate of George III, whose work originally appeared in 1820 in two volumes, reached a second edition, and was reprinted in New York the same year. In the third edition Mr. Southey purposed to make some importànt changes in the tone of the work, having been convinced by Alexander Knox that he was in error in ascribing ambitious motives to Mr. Wesley; but the third edition did not appear until 1846, after Mr. Southey had been dead three years, when it was edited by his son, the Rev. C. C. Southey, and no specific mention is made of his father's altered views. The next year (1847) an American edition was published by Harper & Brothers, edited by the Rev. Daniel Curry, and several editions have since appeared, the latest and best of which, carefully edited by " E. W.," is that of Bohn's Standard Library, published in 1876. Mr. Southey was unfitted to be the biographer of such a man as Wesley; not from any literary inability, but from inability to sympathize with his wonderful spirit and undertaking. Southey looked at things from a Churchman's point of observation; he had no personal acquaintance with experimental godliness, if, indeed, he had any belief whatever in it, and all that Mr. Wesley deemed vital and saving in Christianity he coolly explains away on philosophical principles. It must be admitted, however, that in collecting material for his biography he explored every accessible source of information, that he does justice to Mr. Wesley's great abilities, to his attainments as a scholar and his fine temper as a man and as a controversialist, and that he acknowledges the extensive moral good effected by his instrumentality. In his private correspondence with Wilberforce he says: "I consider him (Wesley) as the most influential mind of the last century, the man who will have produced the greatest effects centuries, or perhaps millenniums, hence, if the present race of men should continue so long." Yet his book has been variously judged by those inside as well as outside the pale of Methodism. Dr. Stevens speaks of its " questionable purpose and total misapprehension of the providential design of Methodism." Samuel T. Coleridge, who was his brother-in-law, says the book is "unsafe for all of unsettled minds," notwithstanding he had found no book so unfailing a source of enjoyment. Bishop Heber, in the *Quarterly Review* for 1820, says that "few persons could have been found, we think, better qualified for the undertaking than Mr. Southey has shown himself to be;" and Lord Macaulay, in his Essays, says : " The Life of Wesley will probably live. Defective as it is, it contains the only popular account of a most remarkable moral revolution, and of a man whose eloquence and logical acuteness might have made him eminent in literature, whose genius for government was not inferior to that of Richelieu, and who, whatever his errors may have been, devoted all his powers, in defiance of obloquy and derision, to what he sincerely considered as the highest good of his species."

Mr. Southey's work was followed almost immediately by Richard Watson's " Observations on Southey's Life of Wesley," which is distinguished throughout by great force of reasoning, and contains many passages of superior beauty and eloquence.

In 1823 appeared Dr. Adam Clarke's " Memoirs of the Wesley Family." This work was written in the short space of four months, and after its publication the copyright was presented to the Wesleyan Book-room. Dr. Clarke had, however, long entertained the idea of writing a biography of the founder of Methodism himself, and at the conference of 1820 had been officially requested to do so. The widely read memoir of the poet-laureate was then making a great impression on the public mind, and a number of influential persons, who dissented from the worldly-minded and sinister views of the character of Mr. Wesley presented in that biography, urged him, by earnest solicitations, to acquiesce in the request. Among these, Mr. Butterworth offered him five hundred pounds for the copyright. Nor was Dr. Clarke averse to the task, but greatly inclined to undertake it. He had, indeed, a feeling, produced by some incidents in conversations with him while living, that such a thing would be agreeable to Mr. Wesley himself; and he had been for many years accumulating materials for that purpose. The project, however, issued not in a distinctive Life of the founder of Methodism, but in a memoir of the family from which he sprang. This was subsequently reprinted, with a large accession of matter, in two volumes. The London *Watchman* said of it: "To those who have read the Memoir of the Wesley Family, no recommendation of ours will enhance its value. To those, on the contrary, who have that pleasure in reserve, we can promise an exquisite treat." It is now published in a single volume at the Methodist Book Concern in a 12mo edition.

The Life of Wesley by Richard Watson appeared in London in 1831, and was republished in New York the same year. It reached its sixth edition in London in 1839. This book, says Dr. Stevens, "has been the popular memoir" of the great founder of Methodism. It was not merely a condensed review of Mr. Wesley's life, deduced from the works of his former biographers, but contained a large portion of original matter. The influence of Mr. Wesley's labors and plans upon public morals and happiness, and the conduct which he pursued in reference to the established Church, are largely and ably discussed in this volume, and the charges of inconsistency, of schism, and of other evils, so often urged against him, are effectually repelled, while due respect is shown to the national Church, for which Mr. Watson cherished a sincere regard. The book is impartial, genial, judicious, and a devout recognition of the hand of Providence in the great Wesleyan movement. It well supplies the place of a species of philosophizing, even if it were of less objectionable type than that which is furnished by Dr. Southey and Isaac Taylor. An edition of this Life was issued by the Southern Methodist publishing house in 1857, and an abridgment of Watson's Life of Wesley ("Ahwal i Padri Wasli Sahib") was prepared by Rev. H. Mansell, and published from the Methodist Episcopal press in India.

In 1851 appeared Isaac Taylor's "Wesley and Methodism," and was republished by the Harpers in 1852. Editions were also issued in England in 1863 and 1865, and the *North American Review* said of it that "in point of style and method it takes precedence of the entire series of Taylor's productions." The *Methodist Quarterly Review*, on its appearance, remarked : "In this work Mr. Taylor abandons the line of spiritual pathology, and takes to that of criticism and prophecy." It elicited "An Apology for Wesley and Methodism, in Reply to the Misrepresentations of Isaac Taylor and the *North British Review*," by Rev. R. Macbriar, the second edition of which was published at Edinburgh in 1852.

In 1856-7 a Life of John Wesley by J. Beecham was published in London in connection with the eleventh edition of Wesley's works, and in 1868 appeared in France, from the pen of Matthieu Lelievre, "*John Wesley, sa Vie et son Œuvre.*" The next year (1869) an article on "Wesley and Methodism" was published in the *Revue des Deux Mondes*, from the pen of the eminent French statesman, Charles de Rémusat, in which he says : "The temptation, and also the facility, for presenting the subject to the public were set before me by reading an excellent Life of Wesley by Pastor Matthieu Lelievre. The want of a popular Life of John Wesley had been expressed among the French Methodist Churches, and this work was written in obedience to an order of their conference."

In 1870–71 appeared in London, from the press of Hodder & Stoughton, "The Life and Times of the Rev. John Wesley, M. A., Founder of the Methodists," by the Rev. L. Tyerman, in three large volumes. This was republished by Harper & Brothers in 1872. The author says in his preface : "For seventeen years materials have been accumulating in my hands. My own mass of original manuscripts is large. Thousands of Methodist letters have been lent to me. Hundreds, almost thousands, of publications, issued in Wesley's life-time, and bearing on the great Methodist movement, have been consulted. Many of Wesley's letters, hitherto published only in periodicals, or in scarce books, have been used ; and not a few that, up to the present, have never yet appeared in print." He says he has tried to make Wesley his own biographer, and has not attempted what may be called a *philosophy* of his life. He adds: "The work has been arduous; but it has been a work of love. I have not done what I wished, but what I could." The *Methodist Quarterly Review* (Oct., 1871) said of this book: " By the power of accumulation, by the incorporation of characteristic extracts, and often of entire documents, by abundant details, animated by his own real interest in his subject, he has massed together, in lucid order, a body of materials to which the future historian will ever resort, and upon which a class of enthusiastic readers will dwell with interest. He has done upon the whole a great and good work, for which abundant thanks are due him. But the standard life of Wesley is still a *desideratum.*" Mr. Tyerman had previously (1866) written the " Life and Times of the Rev. Samuel Wesley, M. A.," and in 1873 the Harpers republished his" Oxford Methodists," being memoirs of Clayton, Ingham, Gambold, Hervey, and Broughton, with biographical notices of others.

In the same year (1870) appeared " John Wesley's Place in Church History," by R. Denny Urlin, and "John Wesley and the Evangelical Reaction of the Eighteenth Century," by Julia Wedgwood. Both books were written from the stand-point of the Established Church, but they add nothing to the biography of Mr. Wesley. In Miss Wedgwood's preface she thus refers to another of Mr. Wesley's biographers: " I can not include in this list the work of the Rev. Thomas Jackson—by far the most interesting Methodist biography of the Wesleys—without a brief allusion to an interview with this venerable man, from which I derived a sense of the vitality of the system of religion represented by him, which the following record, being wholly occupied with the past, could not attempt to embody."

In 1874 the Rev. Dr. J. H. Rigg, principal of the Wesleyan Training College, Westminster, published his work entitled, "The Living Wesley as he was in his Youth and in his Prime." Dr. Rigg had previously written "The Principles of Wesleyan Methodism" (1850), and in that work had exhibited a remarkable grasp of intellect. In 1851 appeared his "Wesleyan Connection and Congregational Independency Contrasted." In a review of the "Living Wesley," Dr. Whedon expresses regret that Tyerman could not have been the collector of facts, and Rigg the biographer of Wesley. He also instituted the following comparison between the two authors: "Tyerman gives facts as crude and uncouth as he finds them, without the slightest capacity for their interpretation. Few men ever undertook history with as little of genuine historical ability. Mr. Rigg understands the true import of facts; he portrays character with truth and life; his style is fresh and pictorial, and he would have given us the Wesley the world is longing to see. We have read nothing on the subject surpassing these graceful pages." Dr. Rigg is also author of "The Relations of John Wesley and Wesleyan Methodism to the Church of England."

Numerous other biographies of Wesley, or works bearing on his life, have been published from time to time. Many of these have been the offspring of controversies, ecclesiastical or religious, pertaining to some particular period, and have been, consequently, ephemeral. Among those worthy of mention are the following: Prof. W C. Larrabee's "Wesley and his Coadjutors," a series of graphic sketches of the prominent events in Wesley's wonderful career, with notices of the more remarkable of his co-laborers (1859); Rev. J. B. Wakeley's "Anecdotes of the Wesleys," a work of which Dr. M'Clintock, who wrote the introduction for it, said: "Mr. Wakeley was happily inspired in the conception of this book, and the execution of the task has been felicitous" (1869); Rev. Edwin L. Janes's "Wesley his own Historian: Illustrations of his Character, Labors, and Achievements, from his own Diaries," a volume which *Zion's Herald* declared to be "the best book of the season; the mightiest man of ten centuries lives over his own life in these animating pages" (1871); and in 1881 Rev. R. Green's "John Wesley" (London, Paris, and New York), "a very admirable popular biography of the great reformer of England."

George Whitefield was one of the original "Holy Club," at Oxford, co-operated with Wesley for a time in evangelical labors, and afterward became the founder of the Calvinistic branch of the Methodists. Numerous biographies have been written, the first being published in 1772, two years after his death. It was from the pen of the Rev. John Gillies, D. D., minister of the College Church at Glasgow. A second edition of this book, with large additions and improvements, was issued in London in 1813, and in 1854 it was published in Philadelphia. It was also reprinted at Lexington, Ky., in 1823, from the third London edition. The "Life of Rev. Cornelius Winter," by William Jay, was published in London in 1809, and Southey says, "this volume contains a much more interesting account of Whitefield than is to be found in any Life of him that has yet been published." Among other biographies of him are the following: "Life and Times of Rev. George Whitefield," by Robert Philip, D. D., (1838); by J. R. Andrews (1864); by Rev. D. A. Harsha (Albany, 1866); "The Prince of Pulpit Orators," by Rev. J. B. Wakeley (New York, 1871); and in 1876 the Rev. Luke Tyerman published "The Life and Times of the Rev. George Whitefield," a work of twelve hundred pages, published in two volumes, for the materials of which the author "spared neither time, toil, nor money." It is the best biography of Whitefield extant. Like Wesley, he has been variously regarded. Garrick, who delighted to hear him, said that he could make his audience weep or tremble merely by varying his pronunciation of the word Mesopotamia. Sir James Stephen, in the *Edinburgh Review*, thus sums up his character and abilities: "From the days of Paul of Tarsus and Martin Luther to our own, history records the career of no man who, with a less alloy of motives terminating in self, or of passions breaking loose from the control of reason, concentrated all the faculties of his soul with such intensity and perseverance for the accomplishment of one grand design. Whitefield was a great and a holy man; among the foremost of the heroes of philanthropy; and, as a preacher, without a superior or a rival." Lord Bolingbroke, in his life of the Countess of Huntingdon, says that he was "the most extraordinary man in our times. He has the most commanding eloquence I ever heard in any person; his abilities are very considerable; his zeal unquestionable; and his piety and excellence genuine—unquestionable." When preaching Whitefield's funeral sermon Mr. Wesley spoke of his Journals thus: "For their artless and unaffected simplicity they may vie with any writing of the kind. If Mr. Whitefield has left any papers of this kind, and his friends account me worthy, it will be my glory and joy to methodize, transcribe, and prepare them for the public view." This work has been done by Dr. Wakeley.

The Rev. John Fletcher, whose original name was De la Flechère, and whose first religious exercise after ordination was to assist Wesley in administering the sacrament at West Street Chapel, was afterward very closely identified with the Methodist movement, and his life is of the most exemplary character. Southey says that Wesley looked to him at one time as the fittest person to act as his coadjutor, and succeed to as much of his authority as could be deputed to any successor. "The Life of the Rev. John William De la Flechère," compiled from the Narrative of Mr. Wesley, and other authentic documents, particularly the "Biographical Notes" of the Rev. Mr. Gilpin, was published in London in 1817, and reached its eleventh edition in 1839. It was also published, edited by Dr. T. O. Summers, in Nashville, in 1857, and is now published at the Methodist Book Concern in a 12mo edition. In 1786 a Life of Fletcher was written by Archibald Maclaine, D. D., the translator of Mosheim's "Ecclesiastical History." Dr. E. Williams, in the *Christian Preacher*, says he was "one of the holiest men that the Christian Church has seen in modern times." A "Memoir of Rev. John Fletcher" was published by Rev. Joseph Benson, in 1830. Fletcher's works contain an unanswerable defense of the doctrine of original sin, and of the Godhead of Christ; with a "Portrait of St. Paul," which every minister should carefully study. "His writings are distinguished by uncommon clearness and strength of argument, an uninterrupted flow of sacred eloquence, and a benevolence of temper which has seldom been equaled."

In 1806 appeared the "Life and Writings of the late Rev. William Grimshaw, A. B., Minister of Haworth, in the West Riding of the County of York. By William Myles." There had previously (1799) been published his "Memoirs," by the Rev. John Newton, rector of St. Mary Wolnooth, but this work all but ignores Mr. Grimshaw's connection with the Methodists. In 1859 the biographer of Jabez Bunting, in speaking of Grimshaw, exclaimed: "Would that some Birks, Hamilton, or Arthur would collect, arrange, and publish the materials still available for the biography of this intrepid churchman and Methodist!" At that very time, the Rev. R. Spence Hardy was preparing a work entitled "William Grimshaw, Incumbent of Haworth, 1742–63," which was published in

1860. Mr. Hardy has rescued from oblivion the memory of this zealous laborer whom Dr. Stevens denominates "the catholic-minded Grimshaw, evangelically the archbishop of Yorkshire," and the volume forms a most captivating and instructive chapter in the history of early Methodism. Charlotte Bronté's biography has, in our time, made his dwelling a place of fashionable pilgrimage; but a greater attraction to devout minds of that lone stone village on the Yorkshire moors is that there dwelt one of the bravest and most humble spirits that ever graced the Christian Church.

In 1815 the "Life of the Rev. Dr. Coke," by Jonathan Crowther, was published. Two years afterward (1817) appeared another Life of Coke, by Samuel Drew, of St. Austell, Cornwall, which was republished in New York in 1837. In 1860 the Rev. Dr. Etheridge published his work on the same subject. Dr. Coke was unquestionably one of the most useful men of his eventful and stirring age. While he lived he commanded a large amount of public respect, and when he died it was felt that the world had lost one of its ornaments and benefactors; the consequence was, the two ample narratives of Crowther and Drew, the first of which consists mostly of official documents illustrative of Dr. Coke's public service, with the personal recollections of the author, and the other, prepared with great care, from the private papers of Dr. Coke, but written with the intent of producing an elegant and scholarly narrative, and lacking in deep sympathy with the burning ardor of Dr. Coke's missionary operations. In consequence of these two comparative failures, for nearly half a century there was a yearning in the Methodist mind for a volume that should exhibit Dr. Coke as he really was in intellect and feeling, and give a full detail of the vast amount of evangelical labors which he was called to accomplish. Such a volume came at last from the pen of J. W Etheridge, who produced a narrative worthy of being placed by the side of the admirable life of Adam Clarke, by the same author. Dr. Coke was originally a clergyman of the Church of England, and a member of the University of Oxford ; he resigned his curacy in 1776, and thenceforward connected himself with Mr. Wesley. Inheriting a considerable fortune, he gave more money to religion than any other man of his age, clergyman or layman ; voyaged and traveled more for the evangelization of the world than any other man of the last century, not excepting Whitefield or Wesley; the " greatest man of his century in ministerial labors," as Bishop Asbury, himself one of the greatest, declared ; the first Protestant bishop of the Western Hemisphere; the founder of powerful missions in England, Wales, the West Indies, Africa, Asia ; and died himself a missionary on the Indian Ocean, and was buried beneath its waters.

In 1816 the " Life of Samuel Bradburn," by his daughter, Eliz. W Bradburn, was published in London. Mr. Bradburn was for many years esteemed the Demosthenes of Methodism, and is placed by Dr. Wakeley among her "Heroes." A man of gigantic stature and of noble person, with an extraordinary amount of mingled humor and pathos, Dr. Adam Clarke said of him : " I have never heard his equal. I can furnish you with no adequate ideas of his power as an orator. We have not a man among us that will support any thing like a comparison with him. Another Bradburn must be created ; and you must hear him for yourself." The biographer of Jabez Bunting says: " The biography of this extraordinary man, attempted by a daughter immediately after his decease, under circumstances of great discouragemement, has yet to be written."

No name in the history of Methodism, after John Wesley's, is more widely and honorably known than that of Adam Clarke. " His Commentary on the Scriptures," says Allibone, " will carry his name to the remotest generation." A copious life of Dr. Clarke, including a curious and characteristic autobiography, appeared in London in 1832-34, in three volumes, 8vo, edited by his son, Rev. J. B. B. Clarke, and was republished by the Methodist Book Concern in New York in 1833. Various members of his family, as well as some of his most intimate friends, had frequently and urgently pressed Dr. Clarke to publish, or prepare for publication, a memoir of himself. This he steadily refused until he learned that a life of him was even then in preparation. This induced him to undertake its preparation, and in June, 1819, he writes from Liverpool: "And thus have I brought myself on in my journey through life to the ninth year of my age; and unless death do stop me, I shall not stop in it till this be finished. I have written it in the third person as to the subject, and in the first person as to the narrator." On the 3d of July he writes: "I go on but slowly with the Life; and yet I get on. A few pages more might terminate what may be called my initial and religious history; and here I might leave it, for all the purposes of illustrating either God's providence or his grace. My literary life, as it may be called, is another thing, and belongs more to the world than to the Church of God; and I question if ever I shall attempt it." The remainder of his life was written by his daughter, Mrs. Richard Smith, from data furnished her by Dr. Clarke himself. But the book never supplied the wants of the general public as a life of Dr. Clarke. Too bulky for general and cheap circulation, and too minute and prolix for easy reading, it affords a repository of facts for the biographer rather than a biography itself. "The Life and Labors of Adam Clarke, LL. D.," was also written by Rev. Edward Hare; and in 1843 appeared "Adam Clarke Portrayed," by Rev. James Everett. The Rev. Dr. Deems has also written his life. But Adam Clarke, the conscientious and pains-taking student; the various scholar; the preacher, careful, plain when most profound, and always evangelical, pointed, and earnest; the diligent pastor;

this great, colossal figure, whose bold outline and fine proportions can never be hid, has been placed by Dr. J. W.
Etheridge on a fitting pedestal, and fixed in its true position, conspicuous in the gallery of connectional heroes.
His Life of Adam Clarke appeared in London in 1858,
and was republished by Carlton and Porter in 1859. In
this work Dr. Etheridge evinces that first requisite of a
biographer, a true and hearty sympathy with the subject
of his work, in a high degree. He discriminates well amid
the vast mass of extant material, selecting the salient
points of Dr. Clarke's varied career, and presenting them
clearly and boldly. The American edition says: "Most
of all is the work valuable as the history of a true and
earnest Christian life, simple and modest in its profession,
but manly and robust to the highest degree in its realities."
The *Christian Preacher* said: "Dr. Adam Clarke has done
more to promote the popular study of the sacred books
in England than any other man whatever; and at the
same time he has carefully applied them to the advancement of personal godliness."

In 1820 was published a "Memoir of the Life and
Ministry of William Bramwell," written by Rev. James
Sigston, an old and valued friend, and a minister of the
United Methodist Free Churches. This book has had an
immense circulation both in England and America, and is
still a popular work of Methodist literature. For more
than thirty years Bramwell was one of the most successful
preachers of Methodism—a revivalist, in the best sense of
that term. Dr. Stevens says: "The records of Methodism are crowded with examples of saintly living; but from
among them all no instance of profounder piety can be
cited than that of William Bramwell." Another "Life
of William Bramwell," by Thomas Harris, was published
in 1855. The biographer of Jabez Bunting speaks of "his
deep piety and fervent zeal," and says: "A biography
might still be written of him which should exhibit his ex-

ample to the imitation of the Methodist people, without, on the one hand, any enthusiastic eulogy of his defects, or, on the other, too much effort to conceal them."

In 1822 the "Memoirs of the Rev. Joseph Benson," by James A. Macdonald, appeared in London, and afterward in New York (8vo), and in 1840 a Life by Richard Treffry, which was also republished in New York. Adam Clarke calls Mr. Benson "a sound scholar, a powerful and able preacher, and a profound theologian." Besides his useful and elaborate "Commentary on the Holy Scriptures" (sixth edition, 1848), he was the author of several works on Methodism, such as "A Defense of the Methodists" (1793); "A Farther Defense of the Methodists" (1793); "A Vindication of the People called Methodists" (1800); and "An Apology for the People called Methodists" (1801). His deep and matured piety, great usefulness, sanctified learning, and disinterested zeal in giving the whole of his literary labors to the connection of which he was a member, procured for him the profoundest respect and most cordial affection, which extended beyond his own denomination. Very few men have been better read in the Greek Testament, and few commentators have given so clear an exposition of it. But it was in the pulpit that Mr. Benson brought those gifts and graces to bear upon the great end of all, the salvation of souls. While he preached, the scholar and the peasant bowed in common before the majesty of truth, which, in plain, unadorned English phrases, awoke them as with the thunders of Sinai, or melted them as with the voice from the cross. His sermons were attended, not only by the common clergy, but by bishops of the established Church. That great and good man, the Rev. Richard Cecil, greatly delighted to to hear him. He said that Mr. Benson seemed like a messenger sent from the other world to call men to account. "Mr. Benson," says Robert Hall, "is irresistible, perfectly irresistible." A masterly delineation of his character, from the pen of the Rev. Dr. Bunting, appears in the *Wesleyan Magazine* for 1822. Mr. Benson was also the author of "Memoirs of Peard Dickinson," and several other biographical volumes.

In 1829 appeared a "Memoir of the Life and Ministry of Rev. John Summerfield," by John Holland (8vo, New York), with an Introductory Letter by the poet, James Montgomery. Mr. Summerfield was one of the most eloquent pulpit orators that has ever appeared in America; yet James Montgomery, who read some of his discourses in manuscript, observed, "The sermons are less calculated for instantaneous effect than for abiding usefulness." His Life was also written by Rev. W M. Willett, and published in Philadelphia in 1857. Such was his peculiar and chastened eloquence that persons of all denominations and of all classes and professions in society flocked in crowds to hear him, and his services were sought for on all popular religious occasions. He ran his race speedily, like the torch-bearer in the Grecian games, reaching the terminus with it still blazing. In the same year (1829) was published the Life of Rev. Freeborn Garrettson, written by Dr. N. Bangs. This is one of our best biographies, not only precious to the Church as a memoir of one of her noblest preachers, but also valuable as a contribution to the history of Methodism. Freeborn Garrettson, says the *North American Review*, was "one of the most prominent and successful of the first generation of Methodist preachers."

In 1834 was published the "Memoirs of the Life and Writings of the Rev. Richard Watson," by Rev. Thomas Jackson, which was republished by the Methodist Book Concern in New York in 1841. A generation has passed away since Richard Watson, author of the Theological Institutes, in the very prime of his strength, finished a course of honor and usefulness peculiarly his own, and which none who ever knew him aspired to emulate. But neither his own published works, nor the funeral discourse delivered by Jabez Bunting, nor even Mr. Jackson's comprehensive Memoir, convey to the reader unfamiliar with Watson an adequate conception of the majesty of his person, demeanor, speech, and entire intellectual and moral character. As a preacher, his genius soared as high as that of the great Chalmers, and with a steadier wing; he had more of profundity and breadth than the eloquent Robert Hall; and with his pulpit exercises was mingled a strain of solemn and often pensive sentiment, reminding one of John Foster's best compositions.

In 1838 appeared in London a "Life of Mrs. Mary Fletcher, of Madeley," wife of the Rev. John Fletcher, by Rev. Henry Moore. This work was subsequently published by the Book Concern, and has met with an extensive circulation. Samuel Burder, in his "Memoirs of Eminently Pious British Women" (1815), says: "Had she lived in the apostolic age she would have taken rank among the presbyteresses or female confessors of the primitive Church. Had she been born in a Roman Catholic country she would doubtless have been enrolled among the saints of the calendar." In the same year (1838) also appeared in London "The Life of the Rev. Alexander Kilham," formerly a preacher under John Wesley, but in 1797 the founder of the Methodist New Connection. The work appeared anonymously, but it is understood to have been written by Blackwell.

PART II.

In the year 1839 appeared "A Sketch of the Life and Travels of the Rev. Thomas Ware," of the Philadelphia Conference, elected Book Agent in 1812, and a "Memoir of William Carvosso," written by himself, and edited by his son, Benjamin Carvosso. In 1879 the Rev. Dr. Wise published at the Methodist Book Concern, "A Saintly and Successful Worker," suggested by the experience and labors of William Carvosso. He was sixty years a class-leader in the Wesleyan Connection, and his memoir is one of the Methodist classics. His whole life was a wonder-ful illustration of the power of Christian faith, and his visits, prayers, and exhortations were the means of hun-dreds of conversions. His own record is that of a simple, earnest, and devout Christian.

In 1840 was published the "Life of Bishop Emory," by his son, Rev. Robert Emory, author of the "History of the Discipline." Bishop Emory was characterized by "accuracy of scholarship, broad and comprehensive views, fertility of genius, and administrative ability." His writ-ings were mainly controversial, among them being a "De-fense of Our Fathers" (1827), and "The Episcopal Con-troversy Reviewed" (1838).

In 1840 also appeared the "Life and Times of the Countess of Huntingdon." The anonymous author of this work has abused the Wesleys in many false details in his sketch of the separation of Wesley and Whitefield. In 1857 the Methodist Book Concern printed "Lady Hunt-ingdon Portrayed," published anonymously, but now known to have been from the pen of Prof. Z. A. Mudge. He has clothed the narrative with no ordinary grace of style. The subject of it, though remotely connected with the royal family and moving in the highest circle of aristocratic life, frequented the Moravian societies in London, and at the separation of Wesley from them, co-operated with the Methodist party. "Her Calvinistic opinions led her to patronize Whitefield when he separated from Wesley, and her talents, wealth, and influence placed her at the head of Calvinistic Methodism."

The first distinctive biography of Charles Wesley, the hymnist of Methodism, was written by the Rev. Thomas Jackson, and published in London in 1841, and in 1844 it was republished in New York, slightly altered. Previous to that time his biographies were written in connection with his brother John, Whitehead having in 1793, and Moore in 1824, written the "Lives of John and Charles Wesley." These were followed, in 1849, by the "Journal of Charles Wesley," edited by Jackson, with selections from his correspondence and poetry, and an Introduction; "The Poet Preacher," by Charles Adams, D. D. (1859); Rev. John Kirk's "Charles Wesley, the Poet of Methodism" (1860); Rev. Frederick M. Bird's "Charles Wesley, Seen in his Finer and Less Familiar Poems" (1867); and George Stevenson's "Memorials of the Wesley Family" (1876), a work pronounced "invaluable," and made up of papers originally in the possession of Rev. Henry Moore, but never used by him. The Wesleys issued fifty-seven publications of hymns, of which Charles Wesley composed over four thousand. Bird calls him "the prince of English hymnists," and James Freeman Clarke says "for the union of love and light, spiritual insight and poetic freedom, there is nothing to be compared to the best hymns of Charles Wesley."

In 1842 was published "The Life of the Rev. Wilbur Fisk, D. D.," written by the Rev. Dr. Holdich, and in McClintock's "Lives of Methodist Ministers" there is a sketch of Fisk by the Rev. O. H. Tiffany. Dr. Holdich was his chosen biographer, and this Life "is a deeply interesting portraiture." Dr. Fisk may be pronounced the founder of the educational provisions of New England Methodism, and in the "Centenary Memories," published in *The Methodist*, it is said that when he entered the ministry in 1818, "there was not a single institution of any note under the patronage of the Church. The Northern and Eastern Conferences united to found the Wesleyan University at Middletown, and Dr. Fisk naturally, and without a rival, was chosen its president in 1830. . And when, in 1836, he was elected bishop, he declined the office." He had previously declined the episcopal office in the Canada Conference, to which he had been elected in

1828. "As a preacher," says McClintock and Strong's Encyclopædia, "few surpassed him in eloquence, none in fervor." Dr. Whedon says, "His friends have compared him for his gentle piety to Fénélon; but it is certain that when aroused he could assume something of the imperious type of Bossuet."

In 1847 the Rev. William Reilly published in London his "Memorial of the Ministerial Life of the Rev. Gideon Ouseley," which was republished by Lane & Tippett, in New York, in 1848. The author was requested by the Irish Wesleyan Methodist Conference, in 1839, to prepare these Memoirs, but the work did not appear for several years afterward. In 1876, Rev. Dr. Arthur, author of "The Tongue of Fire," wrote a Life of Ouseley, which was published in London and New York. The minutes of the conference characterize Ouseley as "the most distinguished, efficient, and successful Irish missionary ever employed by our religious community," and Dr. Stevens says he "will be forever recognized as the Protestant apostle of Ireland." Thousands among the Roman Catholics listened to his ministrations, and the fruit of his labors are still abundant.

In 1848 the Rev. David Dailey, of the Philadelphia Conference, published a book entitled "Experience and Ministerial Labors of the Rev. David Smith," which he compiled chiefly from a journal kept by Mr. Smith. It is a record of a wonderful series of Gospel triumphs. In the same year also appeared from the Southern Methodist press "The Life and Times of the Rev. Jesse Lee," the apostle of Methodism in New England. It was written by his nephew, the Rev. Leroy M. Lee, D. D. (recently deceased), who realized some difficulty in its preparation. Jesse Lee left a very copious journal of his life and ministerial labors, and these were given to the Virginia Conference, and by that body placed in the hands of a committee to be prepared for publication. In the burning of the

Methodist Book Concern in New York, in 1836, the manuscripts of Mr. Lee, which had been deposited there for safe keeping, were entirely destroyed. But the " History of the Methodists" (1809), written by Jesse Lee, contained many important passages of his own personal history, and the story of his labors and triumphs in New England, constituting one of the most interesting periods of his life, was detailed at length in Dr. Stevens's animated "Memorials of the Introduction of Methodism in the Eastern States." A brief and rather meager Memoir of Jesse Lee, by Rev. Minton Thrift, was published in 1823; but this work was not only unsatisfactory to the immediate friends of Mr. Lee, but it disappointed the expectations of the whole Church. At one period Mr. Lee filled the office of chaplain to Congress, and in 1800 he received a tie vote for bishop on the ballot preceding that which elected Whatcoat by a majority of two.

In 1850 Judge McLean, of the Supreme Court of the United States, published a " Sketch of the Life of Rev. John Collins, late of the Ohio Conference." Mr. Collins was one of the pioneer preachers of the West, and preached, in 1804, the first Methodist sermon that was ever preached in Cincinnati. In 1854 the same author, turning aside from the preparation of two large volumes of the "Statesman's Manual," wrote and caused to be published a "Sketch of Rev. Philip Gatch" (Cincinnati, 18mo). Dr. Sprague, the eminent Presbyterian minister, and author of the " Annals of the American Pulpit," says of the author of these books: " Judge McLean was, during his whole life, a Methodist; but a Christian of nobler type, or one who was more at home in heavenly places, than he you would have to search for a long time before you would find him."

In 1851 the Rev. John F. Wright, of the Ohio Conference, published " Sketches of the Life and Labors of the Rev. James Quinn," who was for nearly half a century a successful minister of the Gospel, and labored in connection with other early pioneers of Methodism on the American frontier, suffering and achieving in behalf of religion and civilization. And in that year also appeared the "Life of Rev. Orange Scott," by Rev. L. C. Matlack, printed at the Wesleyan Book-room, New York. Mr. Scott was the founder of the "Wesleyans" in America, having withdrawn from the Methodist Episcopal Church in 1842. The memoir characterizes him as a faithful pastor, a bold reformer, and a godly man.

In 1852 Dr. Arthur published his "Successful Merchant," an attractive biography of Samuel Budgett, a man who commenced trade at ten years of age by picking up a horse-shoe and selling it for a penny, and ended at the age of fifty-six as one of the largest merchants of the West of England ; and in 1851–2 the Rev. B. St. James Fry published the Lives of the three bishops, " Whatcoat, McKendree, and George." These men left such meager materials behind them that all previous attempting biographers were able only to produce sketches a little more detailed than are allotted to all deceased ministers in the minutes of the conferences. Dr. Fry used the materials very skillfully, and the three lives, bound in a single volume, form an interesting record. The " Life and Times of Bishop McKendree" has also been written by Rev. Robert Paine, one of the bishops of the Methodist Episcopal Church, South. Judge McLean says of McKendree: " He was in the highest sense an eloquent man. With great simplicity and grace of delivery he united a force and beauty of illustration that approached nearer to the Sermon on the Mount than I ever heard from any one else."

In 1853 Harper and Brothers published " The Life and Letters of Stephen Olin, D. D., LL. D.," in two volumes. The book was edited by Drs. McClintock, Holdich, and other friends of the deceased. The intellect of the subject of this book was of that imperial rank to which few only can lay claim. At once acute, penetrating, and profound, he lacked none of the elements of true greatness. In overmastering power in the pulpit it is doubted whether, living, he had a rival, or, dying, he has left his like among men. The late Bishop Wightman, of South Carolina, was deeply impressed with Olin's pulpit eloquence, and recorded his admiration in terms the most enthusiastic which the language affords. Rufus Choate said that "his preaching was characterized by. the same rare combination of forcible thought and deep feeling that gave the preaching of Chalmers its great power." The *North American Review* said "he was a great man in the best sense of the word."

In 1854 Morton and Griswold, of Louisville, Ky., published "The Life of Henry B. Bascom, D.D.," by Rev. M. M. Henkle, D. D., and a memoir was also written of Bascom by Bishop H. H. Kavanaugh. Although Dr. Bascom never went to school until he was twelve years of age, he became one of the most distinguished orators of the nation, was elected chaplain to Congress in 1823, called to the presidency of Madison College in 1827, became professor of morals in Augusta College in 1832, was president of Transylvania University in 1842, elected to the editorship of the *Quarterly Review* of the Methodist Episcopal Church South in 1846, and bishop of that Church in 1850. Henry Clay pronounced him to be the most eloquent man he had ever heard open his lips. In that year also (1854) was published at the Western Book Concern the "Sketches of Western Methodism," by Rev. James B. Finley, who had the year before published his "Autobiography; or, Pioneer Life in the West." The latter was edited by Dr. Strickland, and is a book full of the stirring incident that marks every truthful record of American pioneer life. Besides the history of Mr. Finley's early life and ministry, the work contains memorials of Asbury, McKendree, Young, John P. Finley, Christie, and the two Wyandot chiefs, Mononcue and Between-the-logs.

In 1855 the New York Book Concern issued "The Life and Times of Rev. Elijah Hedding, D. D.," written by Rev. D. W Clark, D. D. From an intimacy contracted during the last years of his life, Bishop Hedding requested Dr. (afterward Bishop) Clark to take his papers and prepare his biography, if any should be demanded; and this book is the result. The original intention of the biographer was to make a personal biography; but finding Hedding's life so intertwined and blended with the early history of Methodism in New England, he enlarged it, and the title was made to conform to this idea. Bishop Hedding, in his life and death, has left to the Church of Christ one of the richest legacies; his life was a triumph of goodness, his death a triumph of faith. It has been said of him that, as "a theologian and divine, his views were comprehensive, logical, and well-matured. Not only had they been elaborated with great care, but the analysis was very distinct; and the successive steps were not only clearly defined in the original analysis, but distinct even in the minutiæ of the detail." He was mainly instrumental in the establishment of *Zion's Herald* at Boston, the first journal published by the Methodist Church in the United States; and no minister in the Church labored more zealously and efficiently in promoting the cause of general and theological education than he.

In the same year (1855), John Mason, book steward of the Wesleyan Methodists in London, published "The Life of the Rev. Robert Newton, D. D. By Rev. Thomas Jackson." The story of that long, laborious, and triumphant course has been so admirably told, that any attempt to epitomize it would seem to be presumptuous. In 1839 he visited America as a delegate from the British Conference, and his popularity was so great that he attracted vast crowds wherever he preached. He was, indeed, one of the most eloquent ministers of Methodism, was four times president of the British Conference, and during his labor of forty years addressed, from year to year, a greater number of people, probably, than any other man of his time. The *London Review* (1856), in speaking of his "Sermons on Special and Ordinary Occasions" (edited by Dr. Rigg, 1853), says: "That Dr. Newton possessed, with other essential but inferior mental qualifications, great mental vigor we find ample evidence in nearly every page of this volume; and we are at no loss to comprehend the causes which enabled him, for nearly half a century, to gather around him, wherever he went, listening and admiring crowds, and which made him the greatest preacher among a body of ministers unequaled for the power and success of their ministry in any period of the Christian Church." "The Life, Labors, and Travels of Rev. R. Newton, D. D., by a Wesleyan Minister," was published in the same year (1855).

In 1856 Carlton and Porter published "The Life of Rev. John Clark, by Rev. B. M. Hall; with an Introduction by Bishop Morris." The subject of this biography was at first a poor apprentice-boy in a tan-yard, and after his conversion was dismissed by his master to become an itinerant preacher, which he did by entering the Troy Conference. He subsequently labored among the Indians in the Northwest Territory, became a missionary in Texas, and was the adviser of Mrs. Garrett in founding and endowing the "Garrett Biblical Institute."

In 1856, also, was published by the New York Book Concern the "Autobiography of Peter Cartwright, the Backwoods Preacher," edited by Rev. W P Strickland. The third London edition, from the twenty-first American edition, was published by Heylin in 1859, and reached its seventh thousand in 1862. The *Methodist Quarterly Review*, on its appearance, said: "Peter Cartwright, judging from his many re-elections to the General Conference, from the popular stories of which he is the hero, and from the laudatory notices of some of our editors, has many admirers.

Such will doubtless buy, read, and admire his self-drawn picture. We are not, and never have been, among that number of laudators." Notices of the work appeared in the *North American Review*, Dickens's *Household Words* and the *London Athenæum*; and Parton, in his "Life of Jackson," calls it "the wondrous autobiography of glorious old Peter Cartwright." In 1873 the *Methodist Quarterly Review* published two favorable articles on "Peter Cartwright," which were written by M. Cucheval-Clavigny, and published in the *Revue des Deux Mondes* of Paris. In those articles the French reviewer deplored that Peter Cartwright had abandoned the early practice of keeping a journal, and says: "It would have shown us the preacher in his every-day life, brought us to the scene of his labors, his joys and sorrows, and would, at the same time, have presented a picture, taken on the spot, of material and moral life of the West at the opening of the century." Of the book itself, the writer adds: "With the intent of moral edification, his pen abounds in anecdotes. He makes record of obdurate sinners suddenly converted, of wicked men stricken by the judgments of God, hypocrites unmasked, heretics or atheists confounded." When Peter Cartwright's "Fifty Years a Presiding Elder" appeared in 1871, the *Methodist Quarterly Review* had somewhat modified its opinion, saying: "Whatever differences of view a large share of the Church has entertained, all are, at the present hour, unanimous in kindly recollections of the great services rendered by Peter Cartwright to Methodism and to our country. His history and character, typical yet unique, have impressed the public mind, without as within our pale, in Europe as well as in America. Even the most eminent review of Paris some years since gave a full article upon his history, as a phenomenon worth the study of the present day." In the same year the New York Book Concern published Strickland's "Pioneers of the West."

In 1857 the Western Book Concern published four books of a biographical nature: "Brief Recollections of Rev. George W Walker," by Rev. M. P Gaddis; "Recollections of a Superannuate," by Rev. David Lewis, of the Ohio Conference, a book which can scarcely be called a biography, as eminent characters of Methodism, such as McKendree, George, Merwin, and Ostrander figure in its pages; "Biography of Samuel Lewis, First Superintendent of Common Schools for the State of Ohio," by William G. W Lewis—a noble memorial from a son to the character of a great, a good, and a heroic man; and the "Autobiography of a Pioneer," by Rev. Jacob Young, with an Introduction by Bishop Morris.

In 1858 Carlton and Porter published "The Pioneer Bishop: or, the Life and Times of Francis Asbury," by Rev. W. P. Strickland. Bishop Janes, who furnished a "Prefatory Letter" to the book, says: "In my early acquaintance with the history of our Church I was led involuntarily and frequently to inquire, Why has no biography of Bishop Asbury been furnished to the Church? I have heard brethren, both in the ministry and in the laity, express deep regret at this omission. My time did not permit me to examine the manuscript of this work sufficiently to justify me in analyzing and describing it; but I know that the author has the intellectual and literary ability, and I believe he has the persevering industry, the Christian candor, and the religious sympathy to execute the work with fidelity; and when thoroughly executed it will place another star of first magnitude and of richest effulgence in the biographical galaxy of the Church." Dr. Bangs, who wrote the Introduction, in referring to the practice which obtains with some biographers of padding their books with accounts of great men and other equally irrelevant and extraneous matter, says: "If an apology could rightfully be made for this kind of biography for any public man, it might be made for Bishop Asbury, for certainly he stood up before the community as a giant in intellect, and as a saint of the first magnitude, having professed and exemplified the 'heights and depths' of 'perfect love,' and displayed the zeal and diligence of an apostle in the work of the Christian ministry. Dr. Strickland, however, has not availed himself of this privilege, but has confined himself strictly to the life and labors of Bishop Asbury, calling him, very appropriately, the 'pioneer bishop.'" Dr. Whedon said of the execution of the work : "It had seemed a fatality for any one to undertake the task of portraying our founder bishop for history. Dr. Strickland has conquered the fatality, whether of death or failure, and he has with great industry and ability collected the scattered material, traced the mighty labors and triumphs of the hero, and delineated the lineaments of the man with a true and life-like pencil." The *American Theological Review* described it as an "interesting volume." The "Journals of the Rev. Francis Asbury" (3 vols., 8vo), appeared first in the *Arminian Magazine* in 1789, and one volume was published during his life-time. The remainder were not published until 1821, five years after his death, when the whole were issued by Bangs and Mason, then Agents of the Book Concern. But the edition was imperfect, and they were republished in 1854, with corrections. Until then, although Bishop Asbury had been dead thirty-seven years, a full memoir of his life had not been written. "Asbury and his Co-laborers," by Prof. W C. Larrabee (2 vols.), was published in 1853, and the Rev. F. W Briggs, about the same time that Strickland issued his work, published in England " A Study of Bishop Asbury." The *Revue des Deux Mondes* (Paris) calls Asbury "the real founder of American Methodism, and says: "Asbury, Lee, McKendree, by their truly evangelical works, by their perseverance through every trial, by their poverty and their sufferings, must have appeared to their contemporaries worthy successors of the apostles. In fact, it was impossible to carry to greater lengths the renouncement of self, and to devote themselves more completely to the salvation of their fellow-men." Of Asbury, McClintock and Strong's Cyclopædia says: "In diligent activity, no apostle, no missionary, no warrior ever surpassed him. He rivaled Melancthon and Luther in boldness. He combined the enthusiasm of Xavier with the far-reaching foresight and keen discrimination of Wesley."

In 1859 Derby and Jackson, New York, published "Ten Years of a Preacher's Life: Chapters from an Autobiography," by Rev. W H. Milburn, known as "the blind preacher." Mr. Milburn had published two years previously his "Rifle, Axe, and Saddle-bags," and in 1860 his "Pioneers, Ministers and People, of the Mississippi Valley." Mr. Milburn became a Methodist itinerant at the age of twenty, and his early ministry was spent chiefly in the Southern States. He became a popular and eloquent lecturer and chaplain to Congress, was subsequently ordained in the Protestant Episcopal Church, but returned in 1872 to Methodism.

In 1859 also appeared the "Life of Jabez Bunting, D. D., with Notices of Contemporary Persons and Events, by his son, Thomas Percival Bunting." The American edition was issued by the Harpers. The author says that his father, while in active service, felt a deep repugnance to having his biography written, but as old age crept on, other thoughts took possession of his mind. In his will, dated in 1852, he desired his two elder sons to examine his papers and destroy such portions as it might be expedient to dispose of, and he left his executors to exercise their discretion as to what use should be made of the remainder. The result was this book, the record of a man who, since the death of Wesley, has been more felt in the economy of British Methodism than any other. "He became," says Stevens, "the recognized leader of the Connection. Its most important measures were either conceived or

10

chiefly effected by his unrivaled ability and influence."
Dr. Leifchild, an eminent divine of another communion,
said at his grave, that "in the extent of his information,
the comprehensiveness of his views, the conclusiveness of
his reasoning, and the urbanity of his manners, I never
saw his equal and never expect to."

In 1860 at least four Methodist biographies were published—two of American, one of English, and one of Irish
Methodism. Dr. W P Strickland was the author of
"The Life of Jacob Gruber," a man whom the *North
American Review* characterized as "a devoted, laborious,
and successful minister, possessing much influence with the
ministry and the laity. His wit was of a satirical character, and not particularly palatable to the objects of it."
Wakeley puts him among the "Heroes of Methodism,"
and he was alike remarkable for "strength and originality
of mind, energy of character, depth of piety, prodigious
labors, power of endurance, extensive usefulness, and simplicity and regularity of life." The other book, edited by
Strickland, was "The Autobiography of Dan Young, a
New England Preacher of the Olden Time," who entered
the itinerant ministry in 1805, traveled a few years, then
removed to the West, where he subsequently entered upon
a legislative career in Ohio. The London biography of
1860 was "The Life of the Rev. John Hunt, Missionary
to the Cannibals of Fiji," by G. Stringer Rowe. Mr.
Hunt was one of the early missionaries to the Fiji Islands,
and translated the New and parts of the Old Testament
into their language. The book is worthy of the subject,
and tends to deepen the favorable impressions of the piety
and intellectual gifts of a man who was largely instrumental in the moral revolution of Fiji from a state of can-
nibalism to a state of Christianity. The Irish book of
contemporaneous publication is the "Life and Labors of
Rev. Fossey Tackaberry, with Notices of Methodism in
Ireland," by Rev. Robert Huston. For piety and zeal, for

vigor of mind and loftiness of purpose, the subject of this memoir was a man of whom Irish Methodism may well be proud.

In 1861 Robert Carter and Brothers published " Annals of the American Methodist Pulpit; or, Commemorative Notices of Distinguished Clergymen of the Methodist Denomination in the United States, from its Commencement to the Close of 1865. With an Historical Introduction. By William B. Sprague, D. D." (8vo. Pp. 848.) The *North American Review,* in reviewing this book, said: "That compiling the annals of the American pulpit was a work eminently proper to be done, none will deny. That no fitter man than Dr. Sprague could have been selected for its performance, will be scarcely less than unanimously conceded. The volume whose title is given above is the seventh in his series." The *Methodist Quarterly Review* said: "The best critics in Methodist history pronounce the work remarkably accurate, approving the faithfulness of Dr. Sprague in the performance of his arduous work."

The "Life and Times of the Rev. Dr. Nathan Bangs," by Rev. Abel Stevens, LL. D., bears date 1863, and in 1864 the *American Literary Gazette* said that "the author has performed his labor faithfully and zealously." No name was more fully identified with American Methodism for the sixty years of his ministerial life than that of Nathan Bangs. There was no department of labor in which he did not serve; and in them all, as missionary. preacher, editor, and author, his devotion, diligence, and success were alike conspicuous. His biography is, to a large extent, the history of the Church, and his unspotted life, his simplicity of character, and his earnest devotion to goodness and truth, gained him the love and esteem of all denominations.

In 1866 the New York Book Concern published "Reminiscences, Historical and Biographical, of Sixty-four Years in the Ministry. By Rev. Henry Boehm,

Bishop Asbury's Traveling Companion, and Executor of his Last Will and Testament. Edited by Rev. Joseph B. Wakeley." The author tells us that, in 1847, the New Jersey Conference appointed a committee to confer with him in respect to his journals and other papers, and aid in preparing them for publication. But the committee was too widely separated for any effectual result, and Dr. Wakeley and he, at intervals during a space of twelve years, revised his manuscript journal of two thousand pages, and produced this book. In 1876 Dr. Wakeley published a revised edition of the work entitled, "The Patriarch of One Hundred Years: Being Reminiscenes, Historical and Biographical, of Rev. Henry Boehm."

In 1866 appeared, from the New York and Cincinnati Book Concerns, the "Life and Letters of Leonidas L. Hamline, D. D., one of the Bishops of the Methodist Episcopal Church. By Walter C. Palmer, M. D. With Introductory Letters by Bishops Morris, Janes, and Thomson." In 1869 the Rev. F. G. Hibbard, D. D., edited the works of Bishop Hamline, the first volume of which was published at that time; but the second volume did not appear until 1871. Dr. Hibbard also wrote the biography of Bishop Hamline. Of him Henry Clay, himself a prince of orators, said: "I have never seen such dignity in human form before." This is the testimony of one fully capable of judging, and who was intimately associated with him, the Rev. Dr. Elliott: "As a preacher he was in the first rank in all respects that regard the finished pulpit orator. His style as a writer would compare favorably with the best writers in the English language. He had no superior for logic, argument, or oratory." Dr. Kidder, in reviewing the biographies of Palmer and Hibbard (January, 1881), says: "The Methodist Episcopal Church has always manifested a commendable interest in properly written memoirs of her deceased bishops. But, unfortunately, in several instances there has been either a lack of data attainable for the production of such memoirs, or a lack of interest or industry in preparing them. Bishop Hamline has had two excellent biographers, while of eight others of our deceased bishops no adequate memoirs have as yet been published." Bishop Hamline was one of the agents in the conversion of Dr. Nast, the apostle of German Methodism, and was in deep sympathy with the work of Methodism among the Germans in this country, rendering it great service. Dr. Nast says: " I have often tried to express my gratitude for what, under God, we Germans owe to that great man of God, Bishop Hamline." The *Church Review*, an organ of the Protestant Episcopal Church, pronounces Hamline to be "the most extraordinary man for exquisite culture, manly grace, impassioned eloquence, and saintly piety that Methodism has produced on this continent, and who, in grasp and brilliance of genius, has had scarcely a superior in America." In 1869 also appeared " The Bold Frontier Preacher. A Portraiture of Rev. William Cravens, of Virginia. By Rev. J. B. Wakeley." The subject of these sketches was a bold preacher in Virginia against slavery and intemperance. On his removal to Indiana he entered the traveling connection, and did effective work on the frontier settlements.

In 1871 Hitchcock and Walden published the "Life and Times of Rev. Thomas M. Hudson," written by himself. Rev. C. A. Holmes, D. D., who furnishes the introduction to the book, says: " For fifty years he has been a minister of the Methodist Episcopal Church. From the organization of the Pittsburg Conference, in 1825, he has been a member of the conference; and none will question that its present high position is as much due to him as to any one man. None has done harder work, been more abundant in labors, been wiser to plan, or gathered higher honors." The book is interesting and valuable.

In 1872 appeared the first volume of " The Western Pioneer; or, Incidents in the Life and Times of Alfred

Brunson." The second volume was published in 1880. Dr. Brunson preached, during the period of seventy years covered by the book, about ten thousand times, and was instrumental in the conversion of about six thousand souls and the erection of forty churches. The book is specially valuable as a picture of the past times in the progress of Methodism and of our country, as furnishing testimony in regard to some important characters and events, and as the record of the services of an able and faithful pioneer in our aggressive movements.

In 1872 also was published " Incidents and Anecdotes of the Rev. Edward T. Taylor, for over Forty Years Pastor of the Seamen's Bethel, Boston. By Rev. Gilbert Haven, editor of *Zion's Herald.*" This book, besides the graphic delineations of its author, embodies vivid descriptions of Father Taylor by Miss Harriet Martineau, Miss Hosmer, Charles Dickens, John Ross Dix, the Rev. Dr. Bellows, and the Rev. James Freeman Clarke, the latter of whom remarks of him, " He was a genuine Methodist, and no one wished him to be any thing else." The Rev. Dr. Whedon, that prince of book reviewers, says of this biography : " Our American Methodism is not poor in biography. It is rich, and will be richer, in a great variety of character. Men of statesmenlike capacity, like Asbury and Hedding ; men of rare eloquence, like Summerfield and Bascom ; men of rich accomplishments, like Fisk and McClintock,—have lived memorable lives, commemorated by competent hands. But no biography, in our whole catalogue of England or America, after Wesley and Fletcher, is more abounding in matter to touch both intellect and heart than Father Taylor portrayed by Gilbert Haven."

In 1873 there was issued from the Wesleyan Conference office, London, " Recollections of My Own Life and Times. By Thomas Jackson. Edited by the Rev. B. Frankland, B. A. With an Introduction by G. Osborn,

D. D." Mr. Jackson was twice elected president of the British Conference, was nineteen years connectional editor and nineteen theological tutor. The *London Quarterly Review* says that to him alone must be attributed the impetus among the Wesleyans which so much elevated their Sunday-school instruction, and threw a hedge of a more direct ministerial oversight around multitudes of their youth.

Harper and Brothers printed in the same year "The Life of the Rev. Alfred Cookman. With Some Account of his Father, the Rev. George G. Cookman. By Henry B. Ridgaway, D. D. With an Introduction by Bishop Foster." He was a man of unusual pulpit power, and "among the names which the Church, with humble, grateful joy, inscribes upon her tablets as examples of the purifying, elevating power of divine grace, there is a place for the name of Alfred Cookman." His father was an eminent pulpit orator and a preacher of great ability and success. In 1838–39 he was chaplain to the American Congress, and the "hall of representatives at Washington never echoed more eloquent tones than during his chaplaincy to Congress."

In 1874 was published in New York "The Life and Times of George Peck, D. D. Written by Himself." This is the book of a distinguished minister, editor for four years of the *Methodist Quarterly Review*, and for the same length of time editor of *The Christian Advocate*. One of his contemporaries, quoted by McClintock and Strong, wrote concerning him: "I view him as one of the most remarkable men of our times—one whose genius and piety are indelibly stamped on the ecclesiastical polity and wonderful growth of the Church—whose wise counsels and Herculean labors are interwoven in its development. For the past fifty years of his whole life he has been distinguished by a devoted love to the Church and unswerving loyalty to honest convictions of truth."

"A Life-story of Rev. D. W Clark, D. D., Bishop of the Methodist Episcopal Church. Compiled from Original Sources. By Rev. D. Curry, D. D.," was published also in 1874. Bishop E. O. Haven said of the fitness of the biographer for the work : "Of nearly all the great enterprises in which Bishop Clark participated as leader or associate, Dr. Curry could say, ' *Magna pars fui;*' and while generally he was so fully in accord with him as now in receiving them, so as to give the work much of the freshness of an autobiography, he is at the same time so individualistic as not to be in danger of laying aside the criticism and analysis of a genuine biographer."

"The Life of the Rev. James Dixon, D. D., by his Son, Rev. R. W Dixon," appeared also in 1874. Dr. Dixon was president of the British Conference in 1841, and in 1848 he visited America as the representative of the Wesleyan Methodist Church. "His ministry was practical, tender, and searching ; his eloquence sententious, racy, and epigrammatic, full of originality, and never failing to enchain his hearers."

In 1874 also appeared the "Memoir of the late Rev. Benj. G. Paddock, with Brief Notices of his Early Ministerial Associates," by his brother, the Rev. Z. Paddock, D. D. Besides the biography proper, the book contains an appendix, with extended sketches of George Gary, Abner Chase, Seth Mattison, Isaac Puffer, Charles Giles, and others. The book is called a Memoir, but it is rather the Life and Times of its subject, who was one of the pioneer Methodist preachers of Western New York.

In 1875 appeared "The Wesleyan Demosthenes. Comprising Select Sermons of the Rev. Joseph Beaumont. With a Sketch of his Character, by Rev. J. B. Wakeley." The sermons and record of a natural orator, which carried all before them in their delivery, the discourses being "characterized by brilliancy, earnestness, and impetuosity."

In 1875 also appeared the "Life of Rev. Thomas A.

Morris, D. D., late Senior Bishop of the Methodist Episcopal Church. By Rev. J. F. Marlay, D. D. With an Introduction by Bishop Janes." His biographer says it was the wish of Bishop. Morris that the story of his life should be written by his friend and colleague, the late lamented Bishop Clark, who not only consented to undertake the work, but had made considerable progress in gathering material for it, when failing health, together with the incessant and exacting duties of the episcopal office, compelled him to relinquish the engagement. "At his request, and under his appointment as literary executor of Bishop Morris, I have endeavored to carry out his original plan of the work as nearly as possible." Dr. Wentworth says the biographer "has done his work well, and the thanks of all good men are due to him for this edifying contribution to the ever-swelling volume of Christian biographical literature." As one of the last in the long line of Methodistic heroes, and as, perhaps, the very last of the pioneer bishops, Thomas A. Morris must ever hold a high place among the leading men of the Church. It has been said of him : " To the charming simplicity, both of taste and manners, which eminently characterized him in all the walks of life, he added the graces of a genuine nature and beautiful Christian character. As a preacher he was chaste, sincere, and many times greatly eloquent. As a bishop, he was considerate, careful, and judicious, never forgetful of the most humble of his brethren in the administration of his high office."

In 1876 the New York Book Concern published the "Life and Letters of the Rev. John McClintock, D. D., late President of Drew Theological Seminary," by George R. Crooks, D. D. This book has been called a labor of love and a tribute of reverence to a noble character. "The task was," says Dr. Whedon, "no doubt, easy, from the freshness of the writer's recollections, from the contributions of McClintock's friends, such as Longacre, Biglow,

11

and Mrs. Robinson, and from the habits of copious journalizing and epistolizing." Dr. McClintock was a profound scholar, a successful author, an influential patriot, and a preacher who swayed the minds of his hearers by his fervid eloquence, and satisfied the understanding by the clearness and scientific precision with which he arranged and set forth the stores of his varied learning.

In 1877 was published by W C. Palmer, Jr., "The Life and Letters of Mrs. Phœbe Palmer, by Rev. Richard Wheatley." This is the record of an active and fruitful life. The materials have been so arranged by the author as to present what he calls "an accurate portrait of Mrs. Palmer's inner life." Quite a different work is another, issued in that year by Nelson and Phillips, entitled, "Scenes in my Life, Occurring during a Ministry of nearly Half a Century in the Methodist Episcopal Church, by Rev. Mark Trafton, D. D." An entertaining glance at the Methodist itinerancy of the last fifty years. In that year, also, was published by the Southern Methodist Publishing House the "Life and Papers of A. L. P. Green, D. D.," by Rev. William M. Green, and edited by T. O. Summers, D. D., a very interesting book.

In 1879 appeared the "Life of the Rev. Thomas M. Eddy, D. D.," by Rev. Charles N. Sims, D. D., with an Introduction by Bishop Simpson. This is a deeply interesting and edifying narrative, and presents the character of Dr. Eddy in its most engaging and impressive traits. *Zion's Herald* calls it " the picture of a truly manly man, an earnest Christian, an eloquent pulpit orator, and a faithful and eminently successful minister of the Gospel." The *National Repository* says: " Dr. Eddy was a man of the present time, a real, living character, in fullest sympathy with his age and environments; active, earnest, and of sufficient abilities to make his career in life worthy to be recorded and studied. The author has honored himself in honoring his departed friend."

In 1880 appeared "Memorials of Gilbert Haven, one of the Bishops of the Methodist Episcopal Church," edited by W H. Daniels, with an Introduction by Rev. B. K. Peirce, D. D.; and "Gilbert Haven: A Monograph," by Rev. E. Wentworth, D. D. The latter is a 12mo., of forty-two pages, an address delivered before the Troy Conference in 1880, and published by request of that body. "The 'Monograph' is, perhaps," says the *Methodist Quarterly Review*, "the best of the many tributes that have been paid to the memory of our deceased bishop. No departed personage of our Church ever received so unanimous and loud a volume of eulogy and elegy at his decease." Of him it has been said that none of the men who have been identified with American Methodism combined in themselves greater powers, nobler sentiments, better purposes, wider judgments, or greater efficiency than Gilbert Haven. "The friend of the black man, the lover of his country, the devotee of his God and the Church, the advocate of all that is good and true and beautiful, he died too soon for the happiness of his fellows and the prosperity of the Church militant."

In 1882 appeared "The Life of the Rev. Edmund S. Janes, D. D., late Senior Bishop of the Methodist Episcopal Church," by Rev. H. B. Ridgaway, D. D. The author closes his book by saying: "It is yet too early in history to assign the comparative place of our bishop among his contemporaries, or among the holy worthies of the past. Nor is it important to do so. His position is somewhat unique. No man certainly since Asbury has made a stronger or more distinctive impress upon American Methodism; his wise sayings, holy example, heroic services, sweet charity, and self-denying piety, will be honored by generations to come."

Besides these, a great many memoirs, biographies, and autobiographies of the early preachers and others have been written, some of which gained only a limited local circulation and others have passed entirely out of print. Among others are: "The Life of Rev. Benjamin Abbott," by John Ffirth, the record of an extraordinary man (1809); "The Methodist Memorial," by Charles Atmore (1813); "Memorials of the Rev. John Henley," by John G. Avery" (1844); "Recollections of an Old Itinerant," by Rev. Henry Smith (1848); "Memoirs of Joseph Entwisle," by his son Rev. J. Entwisle, a truly edifying memoir (1848); "Memoir of Rev. S. B. Bangs," by Magruder (1853); "Footprints of an Itinerant," by Rev. Maxwell P Gaddis (1855); "Life of the Rev. Valentine Cook," by Rev. E. Stevenson, D. D. (1856); "Memoir of Rev. Wm. Gurley," by Rev. L. B. Gurley (1861); "Mother of the Wesleys," by Rev. John Kirk (1865); "The Boy Preacher; or, the Life and Labors of Rev. Thomas Harrison," by Rev. E. Davies (1881); "Life of Bishop Roberts," by Rev. C. Elliott; "Biography of Rev. W G. Caples," by Bishop E. M. Marvin; "Life of Bishop Capers," by Rev. W M. Wightman, D. D.; "Fifty Years a Presiding Elder," by Rev. W S. Hooper; "The Man of One Book," a Life of Rev. Wm. Marsh, of Maine, by his daughter; "Memoir of Rev. Isaac Smith," in 1822 missionary to the Cherokee Indians; Osburn's "H. C. Wooster;" Dr. Frazer's "Rev. John Lindsay;" Dr. Hibbard's "Abner Chase;" Vail's "Zenas Caldwell;" E. W Sehon's "Samuel A. Latta, M. D.;" Rev. John Lancaster's "Lady Maxwell;" "Memoir of Mrs. Mary A. Mason," with Introduction by Bishop Janes; "Life of Hester Ann Rogers," of which many thousands have been sold; "Memoir of Richard Williams;" and autobiographies of Thomas Rankin, George Shadford, Thomas Ware, Martin Ruter, and Billy Hibbard, the last an eccentric, but successful, early New England preacher.

W. B. WATKINS.

IX.

HISTORICAL LITERATURE OF METH-ODISM.

THE historical literature relating to Methodism in Europe and America is, considering the comparatively brief period since it had its origin, remarkably copious and of a remarkably varied character. This results from several causes.

1. The religious movement known as Methodism has, from the beginning, been one of great activity and intense earnestness. It has set in motion agencies that have had great influence throughout large portions of Christendom, and in many countries of the heathen world. The development and operation of these agencies have been, as was natural, reported and chronicled in various publications and to an extent which has greatly enriched the historical literature of Methodism. The deeds of heroic toil and patience have awakened admiration, and inspired the pens of ready writers to record them.

2. The evangelistic work of the Wesleys and of the preachers whom they employed and directed was from the beginning a startling innovation upon the methods and usages of the established Churches in England, Ireland, and Scotland, and of the dissenting denominations as well; and, as a consequence, they excited prejudices and opposition of the most determined and often of the most violent character. The new "sect" was everywhere spoken against, and, for a long time, everywhere persecuted. From a very early day in the movement the press began

to teem with publications of various kinds, having for their object to impede or to destroy the work carried on by the Wesleys and their coadjutors. The system of warfare thus inaugurated was kept up, with more or less pertinacity, against nearly every feature of Methodism, whether of government, doctrine, or usage, down to the middle of the present century. H. C. DeCanver, in 1846, printed a catalogue comprising a list of two hundred and seventy-seven such books, most of which have already been forgotten, and are wholly useless except to the mere antiquarian. As the publications in refutation of Methodism involved, to a greater or less extent, the history of Methodism, the replies to them, when replies were deemed necessary, partook of the same character. It is to this cause is due that very considerable portions of Methodist literature are of a historico-polemic cast.

3. It has been the misfortune of Methodism, up to within a recent date, to suffer from divisions and secessions in consequence of difference of opinion among its ministers and lay members upon questions of government and policy, or, as in the case of the Canadian separation, in consequence of considerations of expediency. The result of these divisions has been the formation of a very considerable number of organizations almost identical in doctrine and usage, and differing principally in government. Each of these bodies has its history, both of the causes which led to its organization and of its establishment and growth.

4. Methodism has not only had a large development in those countries in which it had its origin or an early planting, but, through emigration and the indefatigable labors of its missionaries, it has taken deep root and produced very important results in many other lands, as in France, Germany, Italy, Switzerland, India, China, Australia, Japan, New Zealand, Mexico, and South America. One of the most important, as it is one of the most interesting,

departments of our historical literature, and one which ere-long will be exceedingly prolific of publications, is that which will comprise the records of these aggressive movements in the most distant, and, not long since, the darkest portions of the earth, but now, thanks be to God, fast being irradiated with the light of the best Christian civilization.

5. The periodical literature of Methodism, begun at an early day, and fostered with sedulous care, chiefly as a means of defense and as a helpful advocate of its institutions and enterprises, has naturally become the chronicler of its doings, its plans, and its purposes, as well as the advocate and the helper of its growing undertakings. In this way it has done much to create as well as to record history.

6. The last, but not the least, of the sources of Methodist historical literature to which we will refer is the journals kept by Methodist official bodies of their own doings, and the journals kept by ministers who have occupied prominent positions in their respective organizations, and have recorded their experiences and observations. In a large degree these journals have been among the richest of the sources from which the historical writers of Methodism have gathered their most entertaining and most trustworthy information.

Until one has thoroughly explored all these departments, all these sources of knowledge, he can not justly claim to have made himself conversant with the field of the historical literature of Methodism.

Our limits will not allow us to speak minutely of all the works which Methodism and its antagonists have published in the various departments here named, and we must content ourselves with a brief survey of the principal ones which are accessible to the general student of our history.

I. The rapid progress of the evangelistic movement

begun by the Wesleys and Whitefield demanded not only apologetic tracts from the early Methodists, but, in process of time, historical narratives of the results attained. The first full account of that great movement was "A Chronological History of the People called Methodists, from their Rise in the Year 1729 to their Last Conference in 1802," by William Myles, London, 1803. One great excellence of the work is the many original documents which it contains. "The economy of Methodism," says the *Methodist Magazine*, "on account of the numbers and respectability of many of its adherents, becomes more and more a subject of inquiry. Many wish to know by what means the Methodists, in the course of about seventy years, have become so numerous a people. Some, unacquainted with their economy, are wont to attribute their rapid increase to either laxity in discipline or falsity in doctrine. A little attention to the contents of the volume before us will convince them that the growing prosperity of the Methodists can not possibly be attributed to either of these causes."

The earliest history in this country was Jesse Lee's " History of the Methodists," published in 1810. Mr. Lee issued a prospectus and took up subscriptions for this work before he put it to the press. The list of names at the close, of those who subscribed for it, shows the places visited by him personally, and the interest taken by the Church generally in the enterprise. "If Mr. Lee," says his nephew, Dr. L. M. Lee, recently deceased, who wrote a narrative of his life and times, "contributed nothing to the literary wealth or credit of Methodism, he has brought it under great and lasting obligations for his collection of facts; constituting, as they do, the *materials* out of which the early history of Methodism in America, if ever better written, must of necessity be composed. Every subsequent laborer in this department of the Church will be compelled to resort to Mr. Lee for authority as well as information; and in proportion to his fidelity here will his work be true and valuable. And while the credit of being the first historian of Methodism belongs to him, his industry in collecting facts, and his fidelity in recording them, will entitle him to the respect and gratitude of Methodism to the latest period of its history." In the year 1807 Joseph Nightingale published at London " A Portraiture of Methodism," which he claimed to be an impartial view of the rise, progress, doctrines, discipline, and manners of the Wesleyan Methodists. Nightingale had been a preacher among the Wesleyans, but had left them before writing this book, which is rather a caricature than a portraiture. It, however, suggested the preparation of another work, by Jonathan Crowther, which was issued at London in 1811, and reprinted in this country in 1813. It is entitled "A True and Complete Portraiture of Methodism; or, The History of the Wesleyan Methodists, including their Rise, Progress, and Present State." This work is altogether trustworthy.

In 1838 Nathan Bangs issued the first volume of his "History of the Methodist Episcopal Church," and completed it in four volumes in 1841. For many years this was the standard history of the Church, and must always be regarded as a monument of the diligent research and painstaking industry of the author. It is a repertory of facts, many of which fell under the author's own observation, and from which all subsequent writers have drawn. Dr. Robert Baird says of it in his "Religion in America," that "it is an invaluable work, written in a truly calm and Christian spirit, and displays a sincere desire to present every subject which it treats in an impartial manner." Nor is this praise undeserved, as any one may verify by examining the work itself.

A brief "History of the Rise and Progress of Methodism" in England and America, by James Youngs, A. M., was published in New Haven in 1830. It reached a second edition; but its circulation was confined mainly to the

New England States. A fuller account of our ecclesiastical work in England is "The History of the Religious
Movement in the Eighteenth Century, called Methodism,"
by Dr. Abel Stevens, in three volumes, 12mo. This work
was issued in New York in 1858–61. The style is picturesque
and the narrative deeply interesting. For this undertaking
Dr. Stevens collected ample materials—and the materials
are not scanty. His was already a practiced pen. He had
acquired an easy and correct style by his former publications, "Sketches and Incidents ; or, A Budget from the
Saddle-bags of a Superannuated Preacher" (2 vols., 18mo,
1843) ; "Memorials of the Introduction of Methodism
into the Eastern States" (first series, 1846; second series,
1849) ; "Sketches from the Study of an Itinerant"
(16mo, 1847) ; and "An Essay on Church Polity" (1847).
As editor (of *Zion's Herald, The National Magazine*, and
the *Christian Advocate and Journal*), he wrote much and
well, and Hon. Wm. McArthur (since lord-mayor of London) said of this work, which was reprinted in London, that
"what Macaulay has done for England, Stevens has done
for Methodism." His history of Methodism was followed
by a "History of the Methodist Episcopal Church in the
United States of America," in four vols., 12mo, 1864–67.
Of this history there is no end to the praise, both in the
Church and without. The *Atlantic Monthly* says: "As a
history, the work is not only creditable in a denominational and ecclesiastical point of view, but it is a valuable
contribution to our national literature. Any ordinary ability would have made a readable *story* out of such materials ; but to make a *history* worthy of the name required
the hand of a master." This work has been condensed
by the author into one volume, 8vo.

Dr. Stevens's histories were followed by "American
Methodism," by M. L. Scudder, D. D., in a portly 8vo
volume, published as a subscription book (1867) ; "A
Comprehensive History of Methodism, in one volume,"

(12mo), by James Porter, D. D. (1876) ; " A History of
Methodism, for Our Young People " [and a good one for
older persons, too], by Wm. W Bennett, D. D. (1878) ;
" Methodism, Old and New, with Sketches of Some of its
Early Preachers," by J. R. Flanigen (1880) ; and by a
" History of the Methodist Episcopal Church in the
United States," by Rev. P. Douglass Gorrie (1881). Rev.
Wm. H. Daniels also prepared for the Methodist Book
Concern, as a subscription book, an " Illustrated History
of Methodism," which is published in one large volume,
8vo. It has had a remarkable success, and several edi-
tions have already been printed.

In addition to the histories above mentioned there are
several of a character somewhat different, designed to show
rather the inside workings of the Methodist movement,
and to present its statistical results. Of this class we
name " A Compendium of the Laws and Regulations of
Wesleyan Methodism," by Edmund Grindrod (London,
1842) ; " A Compendium of Methodism, embracing the
History and Present Condition of its Various Branches in
all Countries," by James Porter, D. D. (Boston, 1852) ;
" Centenary of Wesleyan Methodism : a Brief Sketch of
the Rise, Progress, and Present State of the Wesleyan
Methodist Societies throughout the World," by Rev. Thos.
Jackson (1839) ; " Methodism in its Origin, Economy,
and Present Position," by J. Dixon, D. D., ex-president
of the British Conference (18mo, 1848) ; " Ireland and
the Centenary of American Methodism," by Rev. William
Crook (12mo, London, 1866) ; " Methodism and the Centennial of American Independence," by Rev. E. M. Wood
(12mo, 1876) ; " A Hundred Years of Methodism," by
Bishop M. Simpson (12mo, 1876) ; " Statistical History of
American Methodism during its First Century," by Rev.
C. C. Goss (16mo, 1866) ; " Centenary of American Methodism," by Abel Stevens, LL. D. (12mo, 1866) ; " Fox
and Hoyt's Quadrennial Register of the Methodist Epis-

copal Church," by Henry J. Fox and W B. Hoyt (1852); "History of the Discipline of the Methodist Episcopal Church," by Robert Emory, revised and brought down to 1856, by W P Strickland; "History of the Revisions of the Discipline," by David Sherman, D. D. (12mo, 1874); and the "Cyclopædia of Methodism, embracing Sketches of its Rise, Progress, and Present Condition," by Bishop M. Simpson (large 8vo, 1878).

Of local histories, or those relating to portions only of the territory occupied by Methodism, there is no lack. We name the more important of these in the order of their locality rather than of their date. "Memorials of the Introduction of Methodism into the Eastern States" has already been mentioned. Others relating to the Eastern and Central States are, "Troy Conference Miscellany, containing a Historical Sketch of Methodism within the Bounds of the Troy Conference," by Rev. Stephen Parks, (12mo, 1854); "Memorials of Methodism in New Jersey," by Rev. John Atkinson (12mo, 1860); "Reminiscences of Methodism in West Jersey," by G. A. Raybold (18mo, 1849); "History of the Wesley M. E. Church of Brooklyn, L. I.," by Gilbert E. Currie (12mo, 1876); "Early Methodism within the Bounds of the Old Genesee Conference, from 1788 to 1828," by George Peck, D. D. (12mo, 1860); "History of the Methodist Episcopal Church in Canada," by Thomas Webster (12mo, 1870); "Methodism within the Bounds of the Erie Conference," by Rev. S. Gregg (1865); "Sketches of Western Methodism, Biographical, Historical, and Miscellaneous, illustrative of Pioneer Life," by James B. Finley (12mo, 1854); "Pages from the Early History of the West and North-west, with Especial Reference to the History of Methodism," by Rev. S. R. Beggs (12mo, 1868); "Indiana Methodism: being an Account of the Introduction, Progress, and Present Position of Methodism in the State," by Rev. F. C. Holliday (8vo, 1873); "Reminiscences of Early Methodism in In-

diana," by Rev. J. C. Smith (12mo, 1879) ; "Protestantism
in Michigan : being a Special History of the Methodist
Episcopal Church, and Incidentally of Other Denominations," by Elijah H. Pilcher, D. D. (8vo, 1879) ; "History
of the Organization of the Methodist Episcopal Church
South," by A. H. Redford (8vo, 1845) ; "Memorials of
Methodism in Virginia, from its Introduction in 1772 to
the year 1829," by Rev. W W. Bennett (12mo, 1871);
"The History of Methodism in Kentucky," by Rev. A. H.
Redford (3 vols., 12mo, 1868) ; "Western Cavaliers," a
continuation of the history of Methodism in Kentucky to
1844, by the same (12mo, 1876) ; "History of Methodism
in Tennessee," by J. B. McFerrin, D. D. (3 vols., 12mo,
1875) ; "The History of Methodism in Georgia and Flor-
ida, from 1785 to 1865," by Rev. George G. Smith (12mo,
1877) ; "Annals of Southern Methodism for 1855," 1856,
and 1857; by Charles F. Deems, D. D. (3 vols., 12mo,
1856–58) ; "History of the Great Secession, eventuating in
the Formation of the Methodist Episcopal Church South,"
by Charles Elliott, D. D. (large 8vo, 1855).

II. The early controversies through which Methodism
passed were chiefly those of doctrine. Calvinism was the
dominant creed of the established Church and of the majority of the dissenters. When Mr. Wesley accepted and
began to preach Arminian theology, he was at once antag-
onized by such writers as Hervey, Toplady, Whitefield,
Warburton, and others ; hence the publication of his "Doctrinal Tracts" and "Sermons." These were followed by
other polemical and apologetic treatises, notably among
them those of Benson and Fletcher. Methodism attracted
to itself many strong minds. The founder of the Methodist
system was himself an acute dialectician, and Mr. Fletcher
is unsurpassed in the clearness of his statements and the
force of his arguments, as shown in his "Checks." Richard Watson's "Institutes of Theology" have never yet
been surpassed. Adam Clarke's "Commentaries" and

"Sermons" are strongholds of defense; and from the days of the first planting of Methodism at home and abroad, it has been compelled to give an account of itself.

In this country the early printed controversial works were more of a doctrinal than of an ecclesiastical character, though all along both have been necessary to maintain sound doctrine and establish the principles of Church government. After the organization of the Methodist Episcopal Church in 1784, it was called upon to defend itself from the attacks of high-church prelacy on the one hand and of the presbyterian economy on the other. The former were not so much, however, to be feared as the latter, as those came from without, these from within. The adherents of James O'Kelly were bitter and unscrupulous in their statements and reasonings, as he was himself. One of the fruits of the secession which he led was "A History of Episcopacy in four parts" (with special reference to American Methodism), by William Guirey (1796). Guirey was admitted on trial as a preacher in 1795, but soon withdrew. Other works, in opposition to the Church doctrines or economy, are, "Episcopal Methodism; or, Dagonism Exhibited," by Rev. Joshua L. Wilson (Cincinnati, 1812); "A Plain Exhibition of Methodist Episcopacy," by Rev. Asahel Bronson, an Episcopal minister (Burlington, Vt., 1844); "Difficulties of Arminian Methodism," by William Annan (fourth edition published in 1860); "The Government of the Methodist Episcopal Church Anti-republican and Despotic," by Rev. William McMichael (Pittsburg, 1855); "The Great Iron Wheel; or, Republicanism Backwards and Christianity Reversed," by Rev. J. R. Graves, Baptist (Nashville, 1855); "The Little Iron Wheel: a Declaration of Christian Rights and Articles, showing the Despotism of Episcopal Methodism," etc., by the same (1857).

When the lay movement and the mutual rights of pastors and people were first agitated, especially between 1820 and 1830, various publications, offensive and defensive, appeared. Those of the polemic character we name first: "The History and Mystery of the Methodist Episcopacy," by Alexander McCaine, elder in the Methodist Episcopal Church (1827); "An Exposition of the Late Controversy in the Methodist Episcopal Church," by Samuel K. Jennings, M. D. (Baltimore, 1831); "Essays on Lay Representation and Church Government," by Rev. Nicholas Snethen (Baltimore, 1835); "View of the Economy of Methodism," from the *Christian Spectator* (1829); "Brief View of the Government of the Methodist Episcopal Church," by Rev. W B. Evans (1829); "Essay on the Invalidity of Presbyterian Ordination," by John Esten Cooke, M. D. (1829); "Tribute to Our Fathers," by Rev. R. F. Shinn (1853); and "History of the Methodist Protestant Church," by A. H. Bassett (1882).

The works written in defense of our Church economy and government are more numerous and accessible to the reader. Among them are, "Defense of Our Fathers and of the Original Organization of the Methodist Episcopal Church," by Bishop John Emory (1827). This was written in answer to Alexander McCaine and others, and was followed by "The Episcopal Controversy Reviewed," written by the same pen. The latter treatise was published posthumously in 1838. "An Original Church of Christ," by Nathan Bangs, D. D., is in the same line, as also "Methodist Episcopacy," a tract by the same author. "Ecclesiastical Polity of Methodism Defended," by Rev. F Hodgson, D. D., was suggested by attacks made in the *Calvinistic Magazine* and other periodicals. "The Great Iron Wheel Examined," by Rev. W G. Brownlow, is a refutation of the work named above. "Methodism in its Origin, Economy, and Present Position," by J. Dixon, D. D., of the British Conference (1848); "Inside Views of Methodism," by Rev. W Reddy (1859); "Platform of Methodism," by Rev. M. M. Henkle (Louisville, 1851);

"Present State, Prospects, and Responsibilities of the Methodist Episcopal Church," by Nathan Bangs, D. D. (1850); "Essay on Church Polity," by Abel Stevens, LL. D. (1847); "Economy of Methodism Illustrated and Defended," by Thomas E. Bond, M. D. (1852), consisting of articles written during the "Radical" controversy from 1828 to 1830, and collected into book form; "Methodism Explained and Defended," by Rev. John S. Inskip (Cincinnati, 1851); "An Essay on Apostolical Succession," by Thomas Powell, Wesleyan minister (London, 1838); "Apostolic Succession," by Rev. Richard Tydings (Louisville, 1844),—are all valuable contributions to our doctrinal and governmental history.

The connection of the Church with slavery and its subsequent divorcement were the occasion of a protracted controversy. The abolition sentiment "would not down," and was productive of at least two schisms, one of great magnitude. The first, because the Church would not purge itself of all connection with slavery, took place in 1842, and eventuated in the formation of the "Wesleyan Connection;" the other, because the General Conference would not countenance slaveholding in its ministry, caused the withdrawal of all the Southern conferences and the organization of the Methodist Episcopal Church South. In this connection we can name only the larger or more important publications on this subject, in addition to those already given relating to the Church South: "Slavery and the Episcopacy," by George Peck, D. D. (1845); "Slavery in the Methodist Episcopal Church," by Rev. E. Bowen (1859); "Methodism and Slavery," by H. B. Bascom, D. D. (1845); "The Methodist Episcopal Church and Slavery," by Rev. Daniel DeVinne (1857); "An Appeal to the Methodist Episcopal Church on Slavery," by Abel Stevens, D. D.; "Stevens Answered in his Appeal," by J. K. Peck; "The Impending Crisis of 1860," by Hiram Mattison, D. D. (1858); "The Antislavery

Struggle and Triumph in the Methodist Episcopal Church," by L. C. Matlack, D. D. (1881). Several important works defending slavery were published in the South, and a number of transient publications on both sides of "Mason and Dixon's line."

III. The missions sustained by the Church have an interesting history. From the time when Dr. Coke urged the Wesleyan Conference to establish missions abroad, and especially the one in India, Methodism has been on the alert to enter every open door. As she was herself the child of Providence, so have her missions been. Now they occupy stations in every quarter of the globe. Through her agency

> "The Western empires own their Lord,
>   And savage tribes attend his word."

In the catalogue of books at the close of this volume a large list of works on the subject of missions is given. Though by no means complete, not even for those of our own Church, a careful study of any one section will give the reader a vast amount of information concerning the origin, history, and present condition of our foreign or domestic missionary work in the particular department comprehended.

IV The periodicals of Methodism are numerous. Mr. Wesley early recognized the importance of disseminating useful intelligence among his societies, and in 1778 established the *Arminian Magazine* (afterward called *The Methodist Magazine*, and now *The Wesleyan-Methodist Magazine*). It has been published uninterruptedly for one hundred and four years. In this country an *Arminian Magazine* (mainly a reprint of Mr. Wesley's) was undertaken, and one or two volumes were published about 1779 and 1780; but the time had not arrived for a successful venture in this line, and the undertaking was given up. In 1818 *The Methodist Magazine* was commenced, and eleven volumes were printed in monthly numbers. The work was then changed to a quarterly, and is still continued as *The Methodist Quarterly Review*. The *Ladies' Repository* was published from 1841 to 1876 inclusive (36 volumes); *The National Magazine*, from 1852 to 1858 (13 volumes); and *The National Repository* from 1877 to 1880 (eight volumes). The Church South has had its *Quarterly Review*, *Ladies' Home Companion* and *Home Circle*. The Methodist Reformers (Methodist Protestant Church) had their *Wesleyan Repository* and *Mutual Rights*, in answer to which *The Itinerant* was published under the editorship of Melville B. Cox. The papers established and issued by the Church are numerous, and we can not specify them. The oldest are *Zion's Herald*, *Christian Advocate* (New York), and the *Western Christian Advocate* (Cincinnati).

V. Lastly, among the sources of Methodist history are the general "Minutes of Conferences," the "Journals of the General Conference," "The Methodist Almanac and Year-book" (from 1834); and the published diaries of Methodist preachers. As these last are referred to under the head of "Methodist Biography," we need not name any of them here. The first separate "Minutes" printed of the individual conferences were those of the Pittsburg Conference in 1826. The same conference issued a second number of its minutes in 1836; and since the year 1850 the example thus set has been followed by nearly all the conferences in the connection. These are now recognized as the official records of their proceedings, when properly attested by the secretaries and presiding bishops; and as they contain the reports of conference committees, and many of them the memoirs of the deceased wives of the traveling preachers, they are important sources of information to the students and writers of our Church history.

F. S. HOYT.

X.

THE LITERATURE OF SACRED SONG.

I LIKE very much the anecdote, true or apocryphal—and I care little which—of an East Indian prince who came to England for the purpose of studying her people and her institutions. After some time spent in becoming acquainted with the most salient facts of our Western civilization—the shipping, the docks, and the wharves; the shops and the warehouses; the tramways and the railroads; the schools, libraries, museums, and churches; and, above all, the happy homes filled with comfortable and cultured people, he was finally admitted to an interview with England's Christian queen, when the question which had been shaping itself in all the months leaped forth into eager expression. "Tell me," said he, "if you can, what is the the secret of all this wonderful prosperity and power?" And it is said that the queen placed her hand on a Bible lying by, and replied: "This is the secret of England's greatness." Never was all that is worth knowing of political philosophy more successfully condensed into a single sentence. The fact that there are to-day in the English language alone probably not less than a hundred millions of copies of the Bible in whole or in part, is the one all-comprehending secret of the rapidly augmenting power of English-speaking peoples.

Now, wherever this Bible has gone, another book has gone too, waiting upon it as the moon upon the sun, and shining by its reflected light—

> "Leaving that beautiful which still was so,
> And making that which was not."

Of course I mean the hymn-book—a book which to-day waits for recognition, and intelligent and loving study almost as much as the Bible itself. The fatal ignorance by which men are "alienated from the life of God" is doubtless the ignorance of his Word and his Son; but closely related to this is the almost universal indifference to those voices of the Christian life which are heard in sacred song. Not that there is no delight in Christian hymns; on the contrary, they sometimes gather up in their history the sweetest and intensest experiences of the people of God. There are not a few into whose memories verses of hymns entered earlier than verses of Scripture, and they will be more likely to repeat them with their dying breath. And yet many of these hymns which are most precious wait for an intelligent recognition. They have never been made the subject of study. It has never been taken in hand to inquire as to their origin, their meaning, their character, their history, and their uses. Though the most articulate and adequate, as well as beautiful and harmonious, of all the utterances of the Christian life, they are not by the masses thoroughly understood. And it is because of this too general neglect and indifference that I select, for the few pages which I may here fill, the task of calling attention to some of the more important aspects of this subject.

1. As we contemplate lyric poetry in general the first thing which arrests our attention is its *antiquity.* The earliest of extant literature comes to us in this form. The oldest bit of literature in the Hebrew Bible, and in all probability the oldest in the world, is the song of Lamech, which is given in the fourth chapter of Genesis. This seems to have been preserved in its original form, and is a very perfect specimen of Hebrew and Oriental poetry, illustrating parallelism, assonance, and the strophical structure. Homer, the earliest of Greek writers whose works have come down to us, is scarcely more than half-way to the time of

this ancient song. It goes more than two thousand years beyond Moses, though he very greatly outranks every other known author in extant literature. And Moses is represented by several notable lyrical compositions; one of which, the ninetieth Psalm, has been the great funeral hymn in all the Christian centuries.

The oldest literature of the Hindoos is the collection of lyric poems known as the Vedas. Very extravagant claims have been made as to their antiquity; but it is quite impossible to fix with certainty, or even strong probability, their absolute date. The one thing which is certain is, that Hindoo literature, like Hebrew, is stratified, and that these Vedic hymns constitute the lowest stratum, and it is believed by those most competent to form an opinion that they may safely be set down as about three thousand years old.

Similar is the date of the Chinese "Book of Odes," also a collection of lyric poems. It is not only the oldest of the Chinese classics, but one of the very oldest books in all literature, probably ranking in this regard with the Vedas and the Davidic Psalms.

Nor is this form of literature obsolete. It is as well suited to an enlightened as a barbaric age, and is as much at home in the life of the cultured as in the tent of the nomad. In no previous period in the history of Christianity has lyric poetry been so multiplied as in the centuries of Protestantism. When Luther arose, it is estimated that there were in existence in all languages about one thousand Christian hymns; now there are probably one hundred and fifty thousand. Then, too, they were largely ecclesiastical in their character, the exclusive property of the priest, the choir, and the Church; now they constitute a liturgy of the people, so that wherever there is a worshiper there is likely to be a hymn.

2. This leads me to say that the *enormous volume of hymnic literature* claims attention. It is estimated that

there are in the German language alone not far from one hundred thousand hymns, and in the English language about one-half that number. As early as the year 1751 J. Jacob V Moser collected a register of fifty thousand printed hymns in the German language. One single author in the English language, Charles Wesley, wrote about eight thousand hymns; another, Watts, more than one thousand. Count Zinzendorf wrote about two thousand hymns, and Schmolke more than a thousand. The Moravian hymn-book, with its appendices and additions, as early as 1759, contained two thousand three hundred and fifty-seven hymns. Six years earlier Count Zinzendorf had published a collection of German hymns comprising two thousand one hundred and sixty-eight, to which in the following year he added a thousand more. In more recent years such men as Doddridge, Cowper, Newton, Stennett, Keble, Bonar, and a host of others, have made such large additions to the body of our hymnology as to be deserving of special mention. Now, when it is considered that among these one hundred and fifty thousand hymns there are some of the most exquisite gems in all literature, productions recording the deepest convictions of the human mind and the richest experiences of the human heart, and such, too, as have been admitted to the most sacred offices in human life, it will most certainly appear that here is a field of literature which no lover of God or of man can afford to be wholly ignorant of.

But all this is only a part, and the less important part, of the case. Aside from the Christian Scriptures, nothing in literature has been so multiplied as copies of Christian hymns. Nothing else is so familiar to human utterance, nothing so deeply engraven on the memory and on the heart; nothing so perfectly befits human experience in all its aspects and conditions. The multiplication of certain choice and popular books, such as the " *Imitatione*," the " Pilgrim's Progress," the " Thousand and One Nights," and others which will readily recur to our thought, in many languages and in every conceivable style of print and binding, cheap and popular as well as sumptuous and costly, is something wonderful, and attests most conclusively their vitality and their adaptation to the soil in which they have been planted. And yet in this very regard they fall immeasurably short of Christian hymns. Some of the most popular of these—such as "Rock of ages," "Jesus, lover of my soul," "Just as I am," etc.— have been multiplied and scattered, and engraven on human hearts and memories as nothing else has been. They have been multiplied literally by the million. They have become a part of the common life of the people, free and universal as air or water or light. It would be a hopeless task to attempt an enumeration of the copies of that precious hymn, "Rock of ages," which have been made in the last hundred years; but they have gone rapidly toward, if not actually beyond, a hundred million. Now, a literature which has become so wonderfully diffused must be a most potent and significant factor in human life, and fully commends itself to the attention and study of every Christian scholar.

3. This suggests *how important hymns may be as a means of influence.* A hymn is the most subtle and spiritual thing a man can create. It can go where nothing else can, and do what nothing else can. When re-enforced by harmonious and soul-stirring music, it is sometimes almost irresistible. Sung by thousands of human voices, and thus becoming a channel through which the full tide of human sympathy is made to flow, it is perhaps the best suggestion of the worship of heaven which we may ever receive in this earthly state. Many a soul has been borne aloft on the wings of holy song into an experience which, in all essential particulars, is identical with that of those who worship before the throne in heaven. And many a callous sinner has been reached and called back from his

apostasy and rebellion by Christian song when nothing else could have gained access to him.

In the time of the Wesleys the little Methodist society in Wexford, Ireland, was so persecuted by the Catholics that it was obliged to hold its meetings by stealth in a closed barn. One violent opposer, finding it out, arranged to conceal himself in a sack in the barn, so that he might open the door to his comrades so soon as the worship should begin. The singing began, and the man was so much charmed with the music that he waited to hear it through before he should begin his disturbance. And then he waited to hear the prayer, in the midst of which he was seized with remorse and trembling, so that he roared with fright, and emerged from his strange concealment a trembling penitent, and was soon genuinely converted. Southey calls this " the most comical case of instantaneous conversion that ever was recorded."

There is a familiar incident connected with one of Phœbe Cary's hymns which may well be taken as representative of a very large class of similar instances showing the power of sacred song. A few years since two men, Americans—one middle-aged and the other a young man—met in a gambling-house in Canton, China. They had been engaged in play together during the evening, and the young man had lost heavily. While the older one was shuffling the cards for a new deal, his companion leaned back in his chair and began mechanically humming Miss Cary's exquisite hymn, " One sweetly solemn thought." As these words, so tender and beautiful, fell on the ear of the man hardened in sin, dead memories in his heart came to life again. He sprang up excitedly, exclaiming, "Where did you learn that hymn? I can't stay here!" And, in spite of the remonstrances and taunts of his companion, he almost dragged him from the place, and poured into his ear the story of his long wanderings from a happy Christian home. He expressed his determination to lead a better life, and urged his companion in sin to join him. The resolution was kept; the man was reclaimed, and the story of his recovery came back to bless Miss Cary before she died. This hymn, God's sweet-voiced but invisible angel, had gone with the man through all these weary years of sin, and finally led him back to life and purity and salvation.

4. The function of song as an *instrument of expression* needs to be considered. This is by no means unimportant, though in this utilitarian age it may less engage attention. The realm of art is higher than that of mere instrumental efficiency. It is most intimately related to the noblest capacities and activities of the human spirit. These are essentially *creative*, and do not find their full scope in the mere adjustment of means to utilitarian ends. In the perfect life of the eternal future it is possible that these two forms of activity may blend in indissoluble unity; but in the life that now is, the question "*Cui bono?*" is sometimes allowed to crowd out the very best things in human experience. The highest exercise to which the soul can ever come—and it is one which shall occupy it in the ages of the eternal years—is that of *expression;* and in this will be embodied our proper selfhood, together with the impressions by which our individual natures have been developed and enriched.

Here, then, comes into view a function of song which allies it most intimately with the highest possibilities of human experience, even with those of the perfect life. When the soul comes to its divinest heights song is sure to be there. If it is not already in waiting it is created, as were the *Magnificat* and the *Nunc Dimittis.* Not that any expression may be adequate. He has had little of what should be called experience who has not known emotions "too deep for tears." There is a "peace that passeth understanding" and a "joy that is unspeakable and full of glory." But song and music go with the spirit to the

13

uttermost limit of rational expression, and so minister to
its highest needs. It used to be said of Luther that his
soul could never find full vent "except through his flute
amid tears." Good old George Herbert was wont to say
that "the time he spent in prayer and cathedral music
was his heaven upon earth;" and on the last Sunday of
his life he sprang from his couch, seized his violin, and
exclaimed:

> "My God! my God! my music shall find thee,
> And every string shall have its attribute to sing."

And then, after tuning his instrument, he sang a verse of
his own hymn:

> "The Sundays of man's life,
> Threaded together on Time's string,
> Make bracelets to adorn the wife
> Of the eternal, glorious King.
> On Sundays heaven's door stands ope;
> Blessings are plentiful and rife—
> More plentiful than hope."

5. Finally, we must recognize the function of song as
a *record of individual and national life.* This is involved in
its origin and nature, as well as in its uses and associations. That which most distinguishes lyric poetry is its
subjectivity. If genuine, it must bear the stamp of personal experience; and so it becomes one of the most important records of human life. The history which lies
imbedded in the poetry of the world is more comprehensive and more minute than any other written history.

The great hymn of Luther, "A strong tower is our
God," was written at the time of that grand historical protest in which the name "Protestant" originated, and so it is
monumental of this name as nothing else is. That precious
hymn of Christian trust translaced by John Wesley, "Commit thou all thy griefs," from Paul Gerhardt, was written
when its author, with his wife and little children, was making his toilsome journey on foot back to his native Saxony,

having been driven out from his church at Berlin because of his uncompromising adherence to the Lutheran doctrine. The lines were called forth by his wife's tears, though they were doubtless addressed as much to himself as to her. Anne Steele's best hymn, "Father, whate'er of earthly bliss," is the outcome of an experience of sorrow from bereavement and hopeless invalidism such as few are called to know. Very similar is the history of that most pathetic hymn of Schmolke, "My Jesus, as thou wilt." The one universally familiar hymn of John Fawcett, "Blest be the tie that binds," reflects the affectionate importunity of his little flock, by which he was led to forego London, to a church in which he had received a very flattering call, and thus, through this hymn, to become a citizen of the Christian world. That hymn of Charles Wesley which has, from the first, held the place of honor in all the leading Methodist hymn-books, "O for a thousand tongues," was written on the first anniversary of his spiritual birth; and its opening line is an echo of a remark of the good Peter Bohler, "Had I a thousand tongues I would use them all in celebrating the praises of Jesus, my Savior." Another hymn of his, which is pronounced by Southey "the finest lyric in the English language"—"Stand the omnipotent decree"—has for its historic background the Lisbon earthquake and the prevailing consternation produced by this appalling calamity. That most beautiful hymn of Henry Francis Lyte, and one of the most beautiful in our language, reflects the experience of a devoted pastor on the Sabbath of his final parting with his affectionate people, when the darkness of fatal disease and swiftly coming death was gathering fast about him. "Rock of Ages," as every body knows, is a monument of the thorough misunderstanding into which a belligerent Calvinist had come of the Methodist doctrine of Christian perfection; for it at first bore this controversial title, "A Living and Dying Prayer for the Holiest Believer in the World;" and the heartiness with which Methodists have taken up this hymn, written to refute one of their most cherished and most vital beliefs, proves most conclusively that in all matters of heart experience real Christians are one. And, to mention but one more—but that shall be the most ecumenical hymn of this century—"Just as I am," of Charlotte Elliott, stands in the very heart of evangelical Protestantism. The Haldanes, the great revival in Geneva, and especially that eminent man of God, Dr. Cæsar Malan, are all commemorated in this hymn. Miss Elliott had come to a spiritual awakening, and realized her need of a positive religious experience. For months her one prayer was that she might *know* Christ as her personal Savior. But for some reason she felt herself unable to lay hold of him by faith, and so this sense of spiritual comfort was denied her. Her sister, who had been in a similar state of mind, had come to the comfortable assurance of sins forgiven, and this served to deepen Charlotte's despondency. At this time (May, 1827) Dr. Malan visited at Miss Elliott's home, and became acquainted with her spiritual state. One day he suddenly turned to her and said: "Cut the cable, dear Charlotte. It will take too long to unloose it. Cut it; it is a small loss;" and then exhorted her to "give one look, silent but continuous, to the cross of Jesus." Challenged thus abruptly, she was driven from herself into Christ; and the result was that she found the assurance she had so long been seeking. All this is reflected in this most intensely and felicitously evangelical hymn:

> "Just as I am, without one plea,
>   But that thy blood was shed for me,
>   And that thou bidst me come to thee,
>   O Lamb of God, I come!"

F. D. HEMENWAY.

XI.

THE LITERATURE OF BIBLE STUDY

Throughout its entire history the Methodist Church has given "attendance to reading." On that very passage of Scripture its founder made this comment in his "Notes on the New Testament:" "Give thyself to reading, both publicly and privately. Enthusiasts," he exclaims, "observe this! Expect no end without the means." With this principle announced as a fundamental truth in Christian economics, and realizing the potency and value of Christian literature, Mr. Wesley at once inaugurated a system of comprehensive and extensive publication, the chief object of which was to aid in the study and understanding of the Sacred Scriptures, and to promote the spiritual life and growth of the soul. He practiced upon his own precepts, and was a most voluminous reader and writer.

As early as 1754, when Methodism as an organization had been only fifteen years in existence, Mr. Wesley commenced writing his "Notes on the New Testament," in the hope of employing them as an evangelical agency, and designing them, as he says, "chiefly for plain, unlettered men, who understand only their mother tongue, and yet reverence and love the Word of God, and have a desire to save their souls." In the Preface he tells us that for many years he had contemplated such a work as this; and, as evidence of his preparation for such a task, it may be stated that in ten weeks after he began the work the *rough draft* of the translation and notes of the four Gospels was completed.

In 1755 it was published in quarto form, entitled, "Explanatory Notes on the New Testament." Two years afterward a second edition appeared, and in 1760, in connection with his brother, he carefully compared the translation with the original, and corrected and improved the Notes, and published the whole in a new and enlarged edition. The translation used in the Notes, and on which he makes his comments, is one that Mr. Wesley himself made; and, as an evidence of his advanced scholarship, even at that early period, it may be stated as a remarkable fact that many of the verbal changes made in the Revised Version of 1881, and which are claimed by its friends to give it a special excellence, were anticipated and published by John Wesley one hundred and twenty-seven years ago. It was also published in paragraphs, and no improvement on Mr. Wesley's paragraphing has been made by the committee of the Jerusalem Chamber. He says that he did not alter the authorized version for altering's sake, but only where the sense was made better, stronger, clearer, or more consistent with the context, or where the sense being equally good, the phrase was better or nearer the original.

These Notes won approval from many eminent scholars for their conciseness, spirituality, acuteness, and soundness of opinion, and it is a question with many even yet whether their value has really been superseded by the productions of later scholarship. Dr. Etheridge, a modern scholar, says that "Wesley expresses more in a sentence than many writers in whole pages," and Dr. Adam Clarke wrote that, "though short, the notes are always judicious, accurate, spiritual, terse, and impressive, and possess the happy and rare property of leading the reader immediately to God and his own heart."

In 1765 Mr. Wesley published his "Explanatory Notes on the Old Testament," in three quarto volumes, in which he gave the pith of Matthew Henry's Exposition, with selections from Poole's Annotations, to which were added copious observations of his own.

The next important undertaking in this department of literature among the Methodists was not published until 1801. In that year Dr. Thomas Coke issued the first volume of his "Commentary on the Old and New Testaments," and this was followed by five other volumes, the last of which appeared in 1803. In the preparation of this work Dr. Coke was assisted by Samuel Drew, well known as the author of a work on the "Immortality of the Human Soul," and the subsequent biographer of Dr. Coke. Although this work drew largely upon a previous one by Dr. Dodd, it was nevertheless a thoroughly good and useful exposition of the sacred text. The plan of the work varied from the usual order. After the exposition, which was rather practical than exegetical, there followed what he called *inferences*, and, last of all, *reflections*.

In 1810 appeared the first volume of Adam Clarke's *magnum opus*, the "Commentary on the Bible," a bequest to the race. The eighth and last volume was not issued from the press until 1826. Concerning the preparation of this work the author says: "I have labored alone for twenty-five years previously to the work being sent to the press, and fifteen years have been employed in bringing it through the press; so that nearly forty years of my life have been so consumed." This was one of the greatest literary achievements of that age, and it has since become the most widely circulated commentary, perhaps, ever written. It is permeated throughout with the living spirit of our holy religion. By its luminous expositions of divine truth it presents to the masses a book adapted to their instruction, while to the scholar it offers the mature fruitage of critical sagacity and philological learning. Dr. Etheridge, the scholarly biographer of Dr. Clarke, says that the Commentary is "one of the noblest works of the class in the whole domain of sacred literature. It is a thesaurus

of general learning; and, as the exposition of an Eastern
book, it abounds, very properly, with a great variety of
Oriental illustrations, philological, ethnic, and antiquarian.　　　When we consider that this great undertaking was begun, continued, and ended by one man, and
that man engaged in the zealous and faithful discharge of
so many public duties, instead of reasonably complaining
that here and there it has a blemish, or that its general
plan is not in all respects filled up as completely as could
be desired, our wonder is rather excited that he should
have brought it so far as he did toward perfection.

The man who accomplished it achieved immortality, his
name having become identified with an indestructible monument of learning and religion." The last edition of the
" Encyclopædia Britannica" characterizes it as "a work
of much learning and ability, and it still possesses value,
though it is in great part superseded by the results of later
scholarship."

In 1811–18 the Rev. Joseph Benson published his Commentary, under the direction and patronage of the Wesleyan Methodist Conference.　It took rank at once as a
sound and learned exposition of Holy Scripture; and, in
the opinion of those competent to judge, this work still
perpetuates the usefulness of its author.　The Rev. Dr.
Bunting, who stood for years at the head of Methodism in
England, frequently and strongly expressed the high estimation in which he held this work, combining, as he said,
more largely than any other, and in better harmony, all
the excellences of a sober and thoroughly Wesleyan exposition of the sacred volume.　This opinion represents very
largely the general estimate in which Benson's work is at
present held by the Methodists of Great Britain.　Outside
the denomination the book has met with considerable favor.
The Rev. Dr. Horne, author of the " Introduction," says
of it: " An elaborate and very useful commentary on the
Sacred Scriptures, which, independently of its practical

tendency, possesses the merit of compressing into a comparatively small compass the substance of what the piety and learning of former ages have advanced, in order to facilitate the study of the Bible. Its late learned author was particularly distinguished for his critical and exact acquaintance with the Greek Testament."

In 1833 was published Richard Watson's "Exposition of the Gospels of Matthew and Mark, and of Some Other Detached Parts of Holy Scripture." This work was written during the sickness of its author, was cut short by his lamented death, and published posthumously, first in London, and in 1837 in New York. It is a work of masterly disquisitions, and evinces a deep and comprehensive knowledge of divine truth. Dr. Horne says: "The sole object of this learned and original work is the elucidation of the Scriptures, and by this means to lay the foundation rather than suggest those practical and pious uses to which they must be applied if they make us wise unto salvation." And another eminent critic of a different communion, the Rev. Dr. Williams, author of the "Christian Preacher," speaks of Watson's exposition as "an admirable specimen of sacred interpretation, replete with sound divinity, and well adapted to promote the piety of the reader."

In 1834 the Rev. Joseph Sutcliffe, A. M., published a Commentary on the Old and New Testaments, in two volumes, a work abounding in reflections of the greatest unction and beauty. The text of the authorized version is not given, and the Commentary is equally adapted for the family and the study, embodying, as it does, the results of the author's labors for about forty years. Horne says of it: "Many valuable elucidations of difficult passages will be found in this work, which are passed over in larger commentaries. The reflections at the end of each chapter are characterized by simplicity of diction combined with earnest piety."

The Rev. Joseph Roberts was sent as a missionary to

the East in 1818, and remained there nearly fourteen years. In 1835 he published "Oriental Illustrations of the Sacred Scriptures," collected from the customs, etc., of the Hindoos. This work not only serves to show the truth of Scripture, but it is eminently adapted to the elucidation of its meaning. On its appearance the *British Critic* declared it to be "replete with instructive matter," and Dr. Horne said it supplied "a most important desideratum in Biblical literature." In 1831 the Rev. James Wood had published a "Treatise on the Nature and Use of the Tropes of Holy Scripture."

In 1840 the Rev. George Cubitt, for fourteen years connectional editor of the Wesleyan publications, published his "Parables," and in 1844 his "Scriptural Expositions." In 1863 the Rev. W J. Shrewsbury's "Notes on Ezekiel" were published, edited by his son; and in 1865 appeared his "Notes on Daniel and the Minor Prophets." In 1869 the Rev. W H. Rule, D. D., published an "Historical Exposition of the Book of Daniel the Prophet," and in the same year appeared the "Exposition of Paul's Epistle to the Romans," by H. W Williams, D. D., who also published, in 1871, an "Exposition of the Epistle to the Hebrews." In 1877 the Rev. Joseph A. Beet printed his "Commentary on the Romans," intended for popular use, the author being an eminent Wesleyan scholar.

The Methodists of England have published numerous instructive and valuable works in the department of Bible dictionaries. As early as 1804 the Rev. James Wood published his "New Dictionary of the Holy Bible," in two volumes, which has since passed through numerous editions, the latest being published by Tegg, in 1863. In 1831 the Biblical and Theological Dictionary of Richard Watson appeared, a work that reached its tenth edition in England in 1850, and has been republished in this country at the Methodist Book Concern in New York, and at the Southern Methodist Publishing-house.

The Rev. John Farrar was a voluminous author in the line of Bible dictionaries. In 1844 he published his "Proper Names of the Bible;" in 1852, his "Biblical and Theological Dictionary;" in 1853, an "Ecclesiastical Dictionary;" in 1857, "A Key to the Pronunciation of Scripture Names;" and in the same year, "A Manual of Biblical Geography." Samuel Dunn was also the author of a "Dictionary of the Gospels," and James Creighton of a "Dictionary of Scripture Proper Names." The Primitive Methodist Book-room published, in 1854, a "Biblical Dictionary," by J. A. Bastow, a member of the Syro-Egyptian Society.

The American Methodists have emulated the example of their Wesleyan brethren, and have published numerous valuable works, which invite and contribute to the better understanding of the divine Word. For a long time they relied almost exclusively upon their English republications, and Clarke's and Benson's Commentaries were to be found in almost every Methodist library, the circulation of these works being far greater here than in England. Among the earliest books of an exegetical and practical nature was Joseph Longking's "Notes on the Gospels." This work was largely introduced into the Sunday-schools, and met the wants of the Church at the time, so far as the Gospels were concerned. In 1848 the "Notes on the Acts of the Apostles," designed for Sunday-schools, Bible-classes, and private reading, was published by Rev. Bradford K. Peirce, now editor of *Zion's Herald.*

In 1851 the Rev. Dr. McClintock, in commenting, in the *Methodist Quarterly Review,* on the Rev Andrew Carroll's "Critical and Exegetical Notes and Discourses on the Gospels," which appeared in that year, said: "A commentary upon the Scriptures is the great *want* of our Church in these times. Those that we have, however excellent they may be in many respects, are so far behind the present state of knowledge, especially with regard to the geography of Palestine, as to be useless, or even worse, so far as the illustration of Scripture is concerned."

The next year (1852) appeared Dr. James Strong's "New Harmony and Exposition of the Gospels," which consisted of a parallel and combined arrangement, on a new plan, of the narratives of the four evangelists, according to the authorized version, and a continuous commentary, with brief notes subjoined. It also possessed a supplement, containing extended chronological and topographical dissertations, and a complete analytical index. Every page gave evidence of unsparing labor, and the expositions were terse, vigorous, and eminently suggestive. The *Quarterly*, which had previously complained of the defectiveness of our commentaries, now pronounced this book, as a whole, an honor, not merely to Methodist denominational literature, but to the Biblical literature of the age. Dr. Whedon, in his Preface to his Commentary on Matthew and Mark, says that several of his most valuable illustrations were appropriated from this work. This was subsequently abridged, and followed, in 1854, by a Harmony of the Gospels in Greek.

In 1856 the Rev. Dr. F. G. Hibbard published at the New York Book Concern his "Psalms Chronologically Arranged, with Historical Introductions, and a General Introduction to the Whole Book." The author, by the learning and ability evinced in this work, rendered a great service to the Church. It brings this part of the Scriptures before the people in an attractive form, and is, as the author asserts, an attempt to place the reader in exact sympathy with the author of each Psalm at the time of writing. Four years before (1852), the Book Concern published Clement Moody's "New Testament Expounded and Illustrated, according to the Usual Marginal References, in the Very Words of Holy Scripture," together with notes and translations, and a complete marginal harmony of the Gospels.

In 1860 the Western Book Concern published a Commentary on the New Testament, by Rev. William Nast, D. D., the apostle of German Methodism in America. This work, which first appeared in the German language, was commenced at the instance of the General Conference of 1852, for the use of the German Methodists. It was originally issued in numbers, but is now altogether furnished in bound volumes. The English translation, the first volume of which appeared in 1864, from the pen of the author, has the following comprehensive title: " A Commentary on the Gospels of Matthew and Mark, Critical, Doctrinal, and Homiletical; embodying for Popular Use and Edification the Results of German and English Exegetical Literature, and designed to meet the Difficulties of Modern Skepticism. With a General Introduction, treating of the Genuineness, Authenticity, Historic Verity, and Inspiration of the Gospel Records, and of the Harmony and Chronology of the Gospel History."

The most considerable and scholarly of American Methodist enterprises in this direction is Dr. Whedon's Commentary, the first volume of which appeared in 1860. The project of a brief commentary was first suggested to the learned editor of the *Quarterly Review* by the Rev. Dr. Stevens, the historian of Methodism, and at his urgent request it was undertaken. Dr. Whedon himself thus explains its origin in his Preface to the first volume: " The preparing of a commentary on the New Testament was first suggested to the author in behalf of the tract department of the Methodist Episcopal Church. Its extent was then limited to a single volume, and its object to the tract circulation. When, however, that volume was completed as far as the Apocalypse, it was on all hands concluded that a work of a larger extent was more desirable, so as to be brought within the requisition of a resolution of the General Conference of 1856, directing a commentary suitable for general popular use to be prepared. The task of reconstructing was immediately commenced, and the present volume is thus far the result."

When the second volume (on Luke and John) appeared in 1866, the *Bibliotheca Sacra*, the judicious and scholarly Congregational review, said: "This Commentary, not less than the previous volume on Matthew and Mark, evinces the acuteness and perspicacity of the author." On the appearance of the next volume (Acts—Romans), in 1871, the same authority said: "Dr. Whedon writes in a perspicuous, precise, and forcible style. His thoughts in this volume are closely condensed. His views of the Epistle to the Romans, as they are here presented, are particularly deserving of study. He must have made special exertion to crowd so much matter in so brief a space." In 1875 this volume was translated into the Hindustani language by Rev. T. J. Scott, D. D., and published by the American Methodist Mission press. When the fourth volume (Corinthians—2 Timothy) was published, the *Canadian Methodist Magazine* said: "By this invaluable Commentary on the New Testament, Dr. Whedon worthily crowns the labors of a useful life. He brings to his task a ripe scholarship, a cultured critical faculty, and a keen insight into the meaning of sacred truth. The present volume is every way worthy of its predecessors, which have already achieved so distinguished a reputation both in the Old World and the New." The fifth volume is from Titus to Revelation.

In the meantime the idea of the work expanded into a Commentary on the entire Bible, and Dr. Whedon called to his assistance several of the most erudite men of the Church to aid him in its further prosecution. When Joseph Benson was appointed editor of the connectional publications in London, he was allowed three assistants in his office, so that he might pursue the preparation of his Commentary with as little interruption as possible. But Dr. Whedon, having the care and editorship of the *Quarterly*

Review, besides the editing of the denominational publications at New York, had prepared the whole of the New Testament Commentary alone, with the single exception of the Notes on Philippians and Colossians, which were furnished by his nephew, the Rev. D. A. Whedon, D. D., and was henceforth to occupy more the position of an editor than an author.

The first two volumes on the Old Testament have not, as yet, appeared. One of these, on Genesis and Exodus, will be from the pen of Dr. F. H. Newhall; the remainder of the Pentateuch is in the hands of Drs. Newhall, Steele, and. Lindsay. The third volume includes Joshua, from the pen of the Rev. Dr. Steele, and the Books of Judges to Second Samuel by Rev. M. S. Terry, D. D. Volume fourth, from Kings to Esther, is also by Dr. Terry; and the fifth volume, on the Psalms, is by Rev. F. G. Hibbard, D. D. This is an entirely different work from the "Psalms Chronologically Arranged." The sixth volume includes Job, by the Rev. J. K. Burr, D. D.; Proverbs, by the Rev. William Hunter, D. D.; and Ecclesiastes and Song of Solomon, by Rev. A. B. Hyde, D. D. The remainder of the book is in the hands of able and learned expositors, one of whom, the Rev. J. Horner, D. D., who is to write on Daniel and the Minor Prophets, is known to be one of the most scholarly and critical writers of the Church. When completed, this Commentary will form a repertory of the latest and most thorough scholarship, fully abreast of the demands of the age, and will doubtless amply justify the declaration of the *Wesleyan Methodist Magazine*, of London, when it says: "Of the numerous popular and portable commentaries which have appeared, this is undoubtedly the best."

In 1876 Dr. Henry A. Buttz, now president of Drew Theological Seminary, published the "Epistle to the Romans in Greek," in which the text of Robert Stephens, third edition, is compared with the texts of the Elzevirs,

Lachmann, Alford, Tregelles, Tischendorf, and Westcott, and with the chief uncial and cursive manuscripts. On this work the editor of the *Quarterly Review* made these interesting observations: " This, the first-fruits of Professor Buttz's scholarly labors in New Testament Greek, is also the first production of a Greek text from any of our three leading theological seminaries, and the first specimen of a Greek book ever, we believe, issued from a Methodist press in England or America. It is a noble, if not a large, commencement." It is also published by the Book Concern in an interleaved edition.

In 1878 the Methodist Book Concerns published " The People's Commentary," including brief notes on the New Testament, with copious references. The *National Repository* characterized it as a " very concise, very clear, and truly evangelical Commentary." The author, the Rev. Amos Binney, of the Providence Conference, had previously published a " Theological Compend," a work which has had an extensive circulation, reaching in its old edition to over forty thousand, and has also been translated into Urdu, Chinese, German, Swedish, Arabic, and other languages. A new and improved edition, with the Rev. Dr. Steele as co-author, appeared in 1875.

The Methodist Book Agents at New York announced, several years ago, their purpose to issue in original treatises a comprehensive " Library of Theological and Biblical Literature," under the editorial supervision of Drs. Crooks and Hurst, to which, beside the editors, who also undertake a part of the work, Dr. Harman, of Dickinson College; Dr. Bannister, of Garrett Biblical Institute; Drs. Bennett, of Syracuse, and Whitney, of Hackettstown (conjointly); Bishop Foster (two volumes); Dr. Ridgaway and Dr. Winchell, were to contribute each a treatise on his designated subject or department. The first volume, Dr. Harman's " Introduction to the Study of the Holy Scriptures," appeared in 1879. This work is not a compilation, but a composition. Its matter, in its entirety, has passed through the author's mind, and so become his own, thus securing its originality and freshness, and rendering all its parts harmonious among themselves. "The vast and varied erudition which he brings to his task makes him master of the situation, while his indomitable patience and perseverance never tire in exposing error and in tracking truth to its source."

Methodist authors have in a number of instances rendered material help in the publication of commentaries with which the Church has not been connected. In the preparation of Dr. Schaff's "Popular Commentary on the New Testament" (Edinburgh, 1879), Drs. Pope and Moulton, of the English Wesleyan Church, had committed to their joint labors the epistles of John, and Dr. Moulton, in connection with Professor Milligan, had charge of Revelation. In Lange's Commentary (1864) Bishop Hurst translated the Epistle to the Romans, on which the labors of both editors and translator were very great. "Upon no other book," says Dr. Schaff, "except Matthew and Genesis, has so much original labor been bestowed." In that Commentary, also, Dr. Strong translated the Book of Esther. He translated the frequent Latin citations, added the textual and grammatical notes, enlarged the list of exegetical helps, and furnished an excursus of the apocryphal additions to Esther, and another on the use of the book among the Jews.

In the department of Biblical dictionaries and handbooks on Bible instruction the issues from the Methodist press have been numerous, and a few only can be noticed. Rev. James Covel's "Bible Dictionary" appeared in 1839; a Concordance was published by Rev. George Coles in 1847; Dr. Hibbard's "Palestine, its Geography and Bible History," in 1851; the Rev. Dr. Akers' Chronology in 1855, and C. Munger's book on the same subject at a later period; Dr. Buck's "Closing Scenes in the Life of Christ," being a harmonized combination of the four Gospel histories of the last year of the Savior's life, in 1869; Holliday's Bible "Hand-book," in the same year; Whitney's "Hand-book of Bible Geography," in 1871; and Dr. J. M. Freeman's "Hand-book of Bible Manners and Customs," a scholarly and exhaustive work.

The most thorough and extensive of modern works of this kind—McClintock and Strong's "Biblical, Ecclesiastical, and Theological Cyclopædia"—though not a distinctive Methodist publication, was issued under the direction of Methodist editors. The work was commenced in 1853. From that time the editors were engaged, with the aid of several regular collaborators and of numerous contributors of special articles, in its preparation. The aim of the work, the editors say, is to furnish a book of reference on all the topics of the science of theology, in its widest sense, under one alphabet. There is no dictionary in the English language which seeks to cover the same ground, except upon a comparatively small scale. For the treatment of all the topics in systematic, historical, and practical theology, Dr. McClintock was responsible. But his death occurred previous to the publication of the fourth volume in 1872; yet he left numerous articles, which were used by Dr. Strong as far as they were practicable. The first volume was issued from the press of Harper and Brothers in 1867, and the tenth volume, completing the alphabet, in 1881. A supplement is to follow. This work is not only a Bible dictionary, but a universal reference-book on all subjects of religious interest. On the appearance of the second volume the *Bibliotheca Sacra* said: "Although this work is published under the patronage of the Methodist denomination, it is by no means a sectarian cyclopædia. It is instructive to scholars of all denominations. Many of its articles are written with great care, and evince a multifarious scholarship."

The Rev. Dr. J. H. Vincent is the author of numerous

minor books, which have been successfully employed as
aids in the study of the Bible. Among these are his
"Pictorial Bible Geography" and "Berean Lessons," to
the latter of which must be ascribed much of the impulse
to the modern study of the Bible in Methodist Sunday-
schools. To him, also, are we indebted for the germinal
concept which resulted in the adoption of the uniform
international lesson system, an arrangement that gives us
regularly, in almost every species of periodical, whole columns of Scriptural commentaries and religious instruction,
a system that finds its culmination in the development of
the "Chautauqua idea," which seeks as its object the universal diffusion of a wholesome literature, a God-enthroned
science, and a pure, sound, and stalwart evangelism.

EDITOR.

XII.

THEOLOGICAL AND DOCTRINAL LITER-ATURE.

METHODISM claims to be a faithful teacher of the whole compass of theological science. As has been shown by the Rev. Dr. Rigg, in the *London Quarterly Review*, it has its system of theology complete in all its parts, basing its existence and its work in the world, not upon any one or two specific doctrines, but upon the one broad foundation of Christian truth. Methodism, whether in England and her dominions or in America, has never given birth to a heresy; her annual conferences in various parts of the world exhibit the spectacle of thousands of pastors who are of one accord and of one mind as to the fundamental doctrines of Christianity.

But there are doctrines which she has specially emphasized: and the extent of their influence on the success which has attended Methodist preaching has been a matter of grave speculation among many thoughtful and philosophic observers of moral and mental developments beyond her pale. A few of these authorities we refer to. In the *North American Review* for January, 1876, the Rev. Dr. Diman, a professor in Brown University, thus accounts for what he calls "the enormous growth of Methodism" in this country: "The vital power of Methodism must be sought, not in its form, but in its spirit. It is impossible to account for its rapid growth save on the hypothesis that it met a great popular want. And it is equally impossible not to recognize the fact that this adaptation lay in the sharp contrast which it presented to the prevailing faith.

The immense popular influence of Methodism lay in its bold appeal from 'the theology of the intellect' to 'the theology of the feelings.' Calvinism, throughout all its camps, 'lay intrenched in the outworks of the understanding;' but to souls sated with theological formulas Methodism, with its direct intuitions of divine truth, came like springs of water in a dry and thirsty land."

In a notice of a sermon preached before the Old-school Presbyterian Assembly in 1851, by the Rev. Dr. Humphrey, the *New Englander* for January, 1852, says that Dr. Humphrey thus accounts for the growth of Methodism : " It might be clearly shown, as I humbly conceive, that its past success is to be referred, not to those doctrines which are peculiar to itself, but to those which are common to both theologies." Whereupon the reviewer remarks : " But will Dr. Humphrey deny that one of the chief causes of the spread of Methodism is the antagonism of its preachers to a notion of predestination, which served in the popular mind to cast doubt on the sincerity of God in the Gospel invitations ? Is not their success very much due to the emphasis with which they have insisted on the truth of God's unwillingness that any should perish—on the truth that none who will seek God are cut off from the hope of salvation, and that all *may* seek him ; nay, that all are commanded and entreated to do so ? The vitality of Methodism sprang from its assertion of these truths of the Gospel. So far, its power is the power of the Gospel."

The *British Quarterly* for August, 1852, in discussing this subject, says : " Methodism was evidently a reaction against the influence and authority of the high-and-dry people in the established Church. It seized on the orthodox doctrines ; but it did so that they might be made to produce their proper spiritual fruit. The Methodist element soon diffused itself freely through other religious bodies. The pulpits both of the established Church and of the Nonconformists came very perceptibly under its influence.' The *Contemporary Review* for January, 1880, in an article by Hillebrand on " T. e Eighteenth Century," makes this influence greater, perhaps, than is claimed by Methodist writers themselves. He asserts that "the High and Low Church of to-day are the outgrowth respectively of the Wesleyan movement of the last century," and adds: "Wesleyanism as a historical fact was abundantly fruitful. It gave new life to the State Church, roused it to resistance, and discovered to it its own weak points."

At first the influence of these doctrines was not recognized and admitted by the higher literary and ecclesiastical authorities of England; but in later times due credit, in many instances, has been awarded to the Wesleys and their coadjutors even by those who do not adopt their theological views. The *Westminster Review*, long in reaching its conclusions, in its issue for January, 1851, in speaking of Wesley, gives utterance to the following: "The sequel is well known: how he took up the labors, while others boasted of the privileges, of apostleship; civilized whole counties; lifted brutal populations into communities of orderly citizens and consistent Christians; and in grandeur of missionary achievement rivaled the most splendid successes of Christendom." In speaking of the influence of Wesleyan doctrines on Devon and Cornwall, the wildest and most ferocious people of England in Wesley's time, the *Edinburgh Review* of the same date as the one just quoted said: "No partiality for old-world investigations, no distrust of the self-opinion of modern times, will tempt us to affirm that the history of former ages affords any thing comparable to the phenomena of an existing society such as this, the last achievement of political progress." And Lord Mahon, afterward Earl Stanhope, in his History of England, in speaking of the improved character and usefulness of the Anglican Church, says: "Nor let any false shame hinder us from owning that, though other causes were at work, it is to the Methodists that great part of the merit is due."

It has been said that the doctrines of the founder of Methodism were drawn from Scripture, and that to it every article of the Methodist creed points and submits. Among the earliest of the controversies that Wesley participated in was that in reference to the doctrine of predestination. In this he was long and earnestly engaged. The secession of Mr. Whitefield from Arminianism to Calvinism gave rise to the controversy, and the war was begun by Mr. Wesley preaching, and afterward printing, his remarkable sermon on Free Grace, at Bristol, in 1740. In this publication he declares that he abhors the doctrine of predestination. To this sermon Mr. Whitefield replied, and the polemic war was thereafter waged for fifty years. Mr. Wesley's next publication on the subject was, "Predestination Calmly Considered;" and this was followed, among others, by "Serious Thoughts on the Perseverance of the Saints," "What is an Arminian?" "Thoughts upon God's Sovereignty," "Some Remarks on Mr. Hill's Review of all the Doctrines Taught by Mr. John Wesley" (1772), and "Some Remarks on Mr. Hill's Farrago Double Distilled" (1773).

Mr. Wesley wrote on all the doctrines of the Bible, and more particularly on those distinctive doctrines of Methodism which were assailed by the theology of the period. The list of the separate publications of John and Charles Wesley occupies sixty pages of Osborn's "Wesleyan Bibliography," and can not, of course, be recorded here. The principal works of John Wesley on practical divinity, however, may be mentioned as: 1. "An Address to the Clergy" (1756); 2. "A Plain Account of Christian Perfection" (1777); 3. "An Earnest Appeal to Men of Reason and Religion" (1744); 4. "A Further Appeal to Men of Reason and Religion" (1745); and, 5. His Sermons (one hundred and forty-one in number).

John Fletcher's works were principally directed against Antinomianism and Calvinism, and stand to-day unanswered and unanswerable. They justify the remark that "Methodism has been the standing advocate of the doctrine of free-will as a subjective and immutable attribute of the human soul." His works were originally published in eight volumes in 1803, but new editions have frequently since appeared. The *Christian Preacher* (English publication) says that "his works contain an unanswerable defense of the doctrine of original sin and of the Godhead of Christ, several pieces in vindication of general redemption and other points with which it is connected, and are distinguished by uncommon clearness and strength of argument."

Besides the works of Dr. Adam Clarke, Bishop Coke, Richard Watson, Joseph Benson, and others, all of whom entered *con amore* into the Calvinistic discussion, in 1817 the Rev. Edward Hare published three works of a controversial nature, namely : "A Preservative against the Errors of Socinianism," "A Caveat against Antinomianism," and a "Treatise on Justification." In 1824 appeared Nicholls's "Calvinism and Arminianism Compared." The controversy was carried to this side the Atlantic, where Calvinism had deeply intrenched itself, and where, perhaps, Mr. Whitefield's preaching had largely served to confirm its teachings. In the Eastern States Dr. Wilbur Fisk entered into the conflict with all the wealth of his noble intellect, and became an heroic and able defender of Arminianism. In 1837 he published "The Calvinistic Controversy," and at another date his "Reply to Pierpont on the Atonement." He had been preceded by Dr. Nathan Bangs, who, as early as 1809, began his career as an author by a volume against "Christianism," an heretical sect of New England. In 1815 he published his "Errors of Hopkinsianism," in 1817 his "Predestination Examined," and subsequently a "Life of Arminius" (1843).

In the Middle States the Rev. Francis Hodgson, D. D.,

entered the controversy by publishing his "New System of Divinity Examined," and subsequently, in 1855, "The Calvinistic Doctrine of Predestination Examined and Refuted." In 1813 the Rev. Asa Shinn, a controversial writer of considerable power, published his "Essay on the Plan of Salvation" (republished in 1831), and in 1840 his "Benevolence and Rectitude of the Supreme Being." Bishop Foster also published "Objections to Calvinism as It Is." In the South, where the doctrinal differences related chiefly to other phases of theology, the pulpit gave forth no uncertain sound on the subject, and the press sent forth such works as Dr. L. M. Lee's "Great Supper not Calvinistic," "Methodism and Calvinism Compared," by Rev. C. Collins, D. D., and Rev. J. E. Cobb's "Philosoophy of Faith" (1853), which treats rather of the nature, fruits, and relations of faith.

In 1853 there was published at the Methodist Book Concern at New York, a work written by Dr. Albert T. Bledsoe. It was entitled, "A Theodicy ; or, Vindication of the Divine Glory as Manifested in the Constitution and Government of the Moral World." It was divided into two parts, the first showing that the existence of *moral* evil is consistent with the holiness of God, and the second that the existence of *natural* evil, or suffering, is consistent with the goodness of God. At the time of its appearance the *Methodist Quarterly Review*, then under the direction of Dr. McClintock, commended it "as one of the clearest and ablest expositions of the moral government of God that has ever appeared." Seven years later, Dr. Whedon, who had in the meantime succeeded to the editorship of the *Quarterly Review*, in noticing an article in the *New Englander* reviewing Dr. Taylor on Moral Government, in which Dr. Bledsoe is said to sympathize with the views of Mr. Wesley, says: "As to Mr. Bledsoe, he 'sympathizes with Wesley' just so far as he agrees with Wesley, and no further; but, agreeing or not, he is no

Wesleyan authority." And Dr. Curry, in an article in the *Methodist Quarterly Review* for April, 1854: " The fact that this volume [Bledsoe's Theodicy] bears the imprint of the principal Arminian publishing-house of the country may lead some to suspect that it is but a re-statement, in a new form perhaps, of that side of the interminable controversy of the 'Five Points.' Such a conclusion, however, would be not only premature, but unjust to both the author and the publishers; for while he holds himself quite independent of all previous systems, whether theological or philosophical, the publishers are not to be held accountable for the opinions he advances." In 1845 Dr. Bledsoe published his "Examination of President Edwards's Inquiry into the Freedom of the Will," which is "a full, direct, and incontrovertible refutation."

In 1864 the Rev. Dr. Whedon, editor of the *Methodist Quarterly Review*, published his " Freedom of the Will as a Basis of Human Responsibility," etc. From the well-known ability of the author, but more especially from the character of the book itself, it was at once accepted as a standard authority, which rank it is likely to maintain. Dr. Whedon has also written able and elaborate articles on the Calvinistic controversy, contributing to the *Bibliotheca Sacra* a discriminating and scholarly paper on " The Doctrines of Methodism," and is the author of the article on " Arminianism" in Johnson's Cyclopedia, from which the following extract is taken: " Arminian Methodism has, in little more than a century of her existence, apparently demonstrated that the Augustinian 'systematic theology' is unnecessary, and what it deems the primitive theology amply sufficient for a production of a profound depth of piety, a free ecclesiastical system, an energetic missionary enterprise, and a rapid evangelical success.   .   The problems she has thus wrought suggest the thought that the free, simple theology of the earliest age may be the universal theology of the latest."

In 1853 the "Complete Works of James Arminius, D. D.," were published by Derby, Orton, and Mulligan, partly from Nichols's translation, and partly in a new translation by the Rev. W R. Bagnall, A. M., of the New England Conference of the Methodist Episcopal Church. The *Methodist Quarterly Review* said of these three volumes: "Our denomination, whose creed accords so completely with the teachings of this learned and accomplished and holy man is bound to maintain the freshness of his precious memory." "The Reformation needed to be reformed, and that work was performed by James Arminius doctrinally, and by John Wesley spiritually."

Of the larger systematic works on Methodist theology the first place is accorded to Watson's "Theological Institutes." They originally appeared in 1824, and have been since issued in many editions. They are, says Dr. Stevens, "an elaborate body of divinity, and have elevated the theological character of Methodism, which has everywhere recognized them as standards in its ministerial course of study." The elder Hodge speaks of this work as "excellent, and well worthy of its high repute among Methodists." In 1852 Dr. John Brown, of Edinburgh, characterized Watson as "a prince in theology, and the 'Institutes' as the noblest work in Methodism, and truly valuable." Drs. Bangs and Cocker reviewed the apologetics of the "Institutes" in the *Methodist Quarterly Review*, which called forth Levington's "Watson's Theological Institutes Defended" (1863). Dr. McClintock prepared an elaborate "Analysis" of the "Institutes."

In 1847 appeared the "Elements of Divinity; or, A Course of Lectures comprising a Clear and Concise View of the System of Theology as Taught in the Holy Scriptures," by Thomas N. Ralston, D. D. The author says that the design of the work is to present a clear and comprehensive outline of the general system of Bible theology in a smaller compass and a form less intricate and per-

plexing to private members, young ministers, and students
in divinity than the more critical and voluminous works
heretofore published on the subject admit.

In 1853 the Rev. Asbury Lowrey published his "Positive Theology: being a Series of Dissertations on the
Fundamental Doctrines of the Bible." This work, also,
was designed to set forth the leading doctrines of Christianity in plain and untechnical language.

In 1853 the Rev. Luther Lee, D. D., then a minister
of the American Wesleyans, published his "Elements of
Theology," and five years later appeared "A Complete System of Christian Theology; or, A Concise, Comprehensive,
and Systematic View of the Evidences, Doctrines, Morals,
and Institutions of Christianity," by the Rev. Samuel
Wakefield, D. D. This work has since been republished
in a somewhat altered edition, and can justly lay claim to
the praise accorded it by the *Methodist Quarterly Review*,
which said: "As a whole, as to the main outlines of our
Arminian Christian theology, we know of no work which
can be pronounced better than the volume before us."

In 1874 the Rev. Dr. L. T. Townsend, of the Boston
Theological Seminary, issued his "Outlines of Theology,"
the first part treating of general, and the second of Christian, theology. Dr. Townsend is the author also of
"Credo" (1869), "The Controversy between True and
Pretended Christianity" (1869), "God-Man" (1872), and
"Lost Forever" (1875).

In 1875 appeared "A Compendium of Christian Theology, being Analytical Outlines of a Course of Theological Study, Biblical, Dogmatic, Historical," by W B.
Pope, D. D., theological tutor in Didsbury College, Manchester; and two years afterward was published "Systematic Theology," by Miner Raymond, D. D., professor in
Garrett Biblical Institute. Both these works at once took
high ground as theological standards, and have been incorporated into the ministerial course of study. McClintock.

and Strong's Cyclopædia, in referring to Watson's "Institutes," says: "Although the works of Professors Pope and Raymond fill a niche in the temple of more recent literature which, of course, the 'Institutes' can not fill, the latter work can never be superseded." R. Treffry, Jr., issued his "Lectures on the Evidences of Christianity" in 1839; in 1872 the Rev. Edward Thomson, D. D., his work on the "Evidences of Revealed Religion," and in 1880 the Rev. Dr. Curry his "Fragments, Religious and Theological." In 1848 William Cooke, of the English Wesleyan New Connection, sent forth his "Christian Theology Explained and Defended," and afterward his "Theiotes," an antidote to Atheism, Pantheism, Unitarianism, etc. The Rev. B. F. Cocker, D. D., was the author of "Lectures on the Truth of the Christian Religion," published in 1873. They were originally delivered before the students of the Michigan University, the author filling the chair of mental and moral philosophy. He was the author, also, of "Christianity and Greek Philosophy" (1870), of the "Theistic Conception of the World," and of several other valuable works. In 1869 John Locke, English Wesleyan, published "A System of Theology." Dr. Adam Clarke was author of a work on "Christian Theology;" Dr. Hurst, of a work entitled "Our Theological Century," and Dr. John Hannah, "Lectures on the Study of Christian Theology."

The doctrine of the atonement has been a source of great controversy, the Methodist Church having combated from the beginning the limitedness assigned to it by Calvinistic denominations. In 1848 the Rev. George W Clarke published a work entitled, "Christ Crucified; or, A Plain Scriptural Vindication of the Divinity and Redeeming Acts of Christ." In 1857 the Rev. Dr. J. H. Rigg, of England, issued a work called "Modern Anglican Theology," a contribution on the doctrine of sacrifice and atonement against the laxity of the Broad Church theology of the day. The *British Standard* said of this book:

"It may be doubted whether any other man in Great Britain has so complete and strong a grasp of the entire theme." Dr. Pope also published works on "The Kingdom of Christ" (1869), and "The Person of Christ" (1877). In 1858 the Rev. Dr. Whedon delivered a discourse at the annual commencement of the Biblical Institute at Concord, which was published in accordance with a resolution of the corporation, and entitled, "Substitutional Atonement, Admissible by Reason, Demonstrable by Scripture." In 1878 was published Dr. D. Dorchester's "Concessions of 'Liberalists' to Orthodoxy," a work that treats of the Deity of Christ, the atonement, and endless punishment. In 1879 the Rev. Dr. J. Miley, professor of systematic theology in Drew Theological Seminary, published "The Atonement in Christ." Bishop E. M. Marvin, of the Methodist Episcopal Church, South, was the author, also, of a work on "Christ's Atonement."

Numerous works on Justification, the Witness of the Spirit, Sanctification, and other distinctive doctrines have been published from time to time. The "literature of the higher life" will be found treated in a distinct chapter. John Wesley was early led to believe that it was the privilege of a real Christian to have a comfortable persuasion of being in a state of salvation, through the influence of the Holy Spirit. In modern times the doctrine of the direct witness of the Spirit may be considered as peculiar to the Wesleyans and Moravians, as Churches; yet it has been distinctly stated and enforced by distinguished theologians of different countries, periods, and denominations. Several of Mr. Wesley's sermons are clear exponents of the doctrine. Among the works published on this theme are: "The Witness of the Spirit: A Treatise on the Evidence of the Believer's Adoption" (1847), by Rev. Daniel Walton; "The Witness of the Spirit" (1848), by Rev. Charles Prest; "The Mission of the Spirit; or, The Office and Work of the Comforter in Human Redemption" (1871), by the Rev. L. R. Dunn, and "Aspects of Christian Experience," by Bishop Merrill.

Among the works pertaining to the resurrection, immortality, annihilationism, and Universalism, we have the following, among others: Samuel Drew on "The Immortality of the Soul" and "Resurrection of the Body;" Dr. Wilbur Fisk's "Sermons and Lectures on Universalism;" "Resurrection of the Dead: a Vindication of the Literal Resurrection of the Human Body; in Opposition to the Work of Prof. Bush" (1847), by Calvin Kingsley, afterward one of the bishops of the Methodist Episcopal Church; "The Human Body at the Resurrection of the Dead" (1853), by George Hodgson; "Spirit Life and its Relations" (1859), by Rev. T. Spicer, D. D.; "The Resurrection of the Body" (1859), by Rev. H. Mattison, D. D., also author of "The Bible Doctrine of Immortality;" "Man all Immortal; or, The Nature and Destination of Man as Taught by Reason and Revelation" (1864), by Bishop D. W Clark; "Battle of Calvary; or, Universalism and Cognate Theories against Jesus of Nazareth" (1873), by Rev. J. W Chaffin, A. M.; "Universalism not of the Bible" (1873), by Rev. N. D. George, author of "Annihilationism not of the Bible" (1870); "Annihilation of the Wicked," by Rev. W McDonald; "The Separate and Continued Existence of the Soul after Death," by Rev. Eli M. H. Fleming, of the DesMoines Conference; and "Beyond the Grave" (1879), by Bishop R. S. Foster. This book is composed of three lectures delivered before the Chautauqua Assembly in 1878, with papers on recognition in the future state, and other addenda. This book created considerable comment, and called forth a volume entitled, "The Resurrection Life; or, 'Beyond the Grave' Examined" (1881), by Rev. I. Villars, of the Illinois Conference of the Methodist Episcopal Church.

Among other Methodist works that may be mentioned are: The "Catechisms, Nos. 1 and 2" (1852), by Rev.

D. P. Kidder, D. D.; "Studies in Theism" (1879), by
Borden P. Bowne, professor of philosophy in Boston Uni-
versity; "The Doctrine of the Trinity" (1846), by Rev.
Dr. Mattison; "An Exposition of the Articles of Religion
of the Methodist Episcopal Church" (1847), by Rev. S.
Comfort; "Letters on the Eternal Sonship of Christ"
(1849), by Rev. William Beauchamp; "Philosophy and
Practice of Faith" (1853), by Lewis P. Olds; "Saving
Faith: its Rationale," by Rev. I. Chamberlayne, D. D.;
"The Eternal Sonship of Christ" (1865), by Rev. R.
Treffry, Jr.; and "The Foreknowledge of God, and Cognate Themes" (1878), by Rev. L. D. McCabe, D. D. In
this work the author argues that foreknowledge leads to
foreordination, and hence he proposes to revolutionize Wesleyan theology by the introduction of the denial of God's
foreknowledge of future contingent events. Against the
doctrine that foreknowledge necessitates foreordination, says
the *Methodist Quarterly*, "John Wesley fought all over England with every Calvinist and fatalist in pulpit and philosophy, with Whitefield no less than with Toplady. Against
that Fletcher wrote his brilliant pamphlets. Against that
Watson rolled out his great sermons and treatise."

Among those who have written controversial and spe-
cial works on the subject of baptism may be mentioned the
following: Rev. C. Elliott, D. D., N. H. Lee, Rev. F. G.
Hibbard, D. D., Bishop S. M. Merrill, William Phillips,
L. Rosser, D. D., Rev. H. M. Shaffer, H. Slicer, D. D.,
Joseph Travis, Moses Hill, D. D., Rev. Wesley Smith,
Rev. N. Doane, and Rev. T. O. Summers, D. D. The last
is the author of "Baptism: a Treatise on the Nature,
Perpetuity, etc., of the Initiatory Ordinance of the Christian Church" (1853). This work argues, while discussing
the subject of baptism as a whole, that baptism is not regeneration nor its necessary condition or instrument; and
it rejects the Calvinistic theory that only the children of
believing parents are to be baptized.

Having thus, as briefly as possible, taken a general survey of the "theological and doctrinal literature of Methodism," we close the chapter with a sense of gratitude that while, in times past, our fathers were compelled to meet and combat heresies in multiplied forms, to expose errors, and save the Church from imbibing false notions, these controversies were nevertheless conducted in a Christian spirit, and have ever been, as a centripetal force, drawing all Churches and all Christians toward Christ, their common center. So that to-day, as never before, Christians see eye to eye, and, gathering around the common cross, they join in singing,

> "Blest be the tie that binds
> Our hearts in Christian love."

EDITOR.

XIII.

BOOKS AND BENEVÓLENCE.

A BOOK is the outside spot for which Archimedes searched so anxiously. There is no measuring its power. Throw the spelling-book and a New Testament into a country, and revolution is only a question of time. They will lift up the roofs of the cabins, and add stories on stories, till the cabins are mansions. They will push the jail aside for the school-house, and hide the gallows behind the church. They will widen the six-foot streets of China into the Broadways of commerce. They will patch up all the rents, and rend all the "patches." They will elevate every home, and envelop every inhabitant. They will leave their transfiguring power upon all the community. There is no measuring the power of books.

A book is a condensed and revised author. The author puts himself at his best. He is out for a purpose. He prepares his presence for a given result. Thus attired in his best, he has access to our inner selves. He has admission to our most secret hearts. In the form of a book he does not awaken antagonism as a person who seeks to instruct or correct us.

We take up the ideas and suggestions of a book a little as if they were our own discoveries. We have been searching for them, and when found we pass judgment upon them, adopting or rejecting them according to our sweet will, without any feeling that we are yielding to the superior strength or knowledge of another.

Books take us in our solitude. The difficult thing in making a case with most business and public men is to get an undisturbed audience, sufficiently protracted to present the whole matter. This a book can secure by coming when there is no one to interfere. We are at leisure; we look över the matter, and feel the argument and see the presentations.

Thus books furnish our *convictions.* We do not adopt the conclusions of the book, but we accept the information of the book, and this becomes a part of our opinion, and finally crystallizes into a conviction.

The benevolent causes of the Church depend upon *conviction.* The money to save the world must be conscience money. Impulse dies out like the flame from a wisp of straw. The boilers that feed the world's engines must be heated over stone-coal fires to make the world move. The aggressive power of a Church is in proportion to the consecrated brain of the Church. The people that keep abreast with the great movements in popular thought or in the public mind are the people to plan and execute campaigns against actual foes. Put into a family a well-selected library touching the great fields of the Church's labors and triumphs, and that family will grow into the first rank in the Church. This solid information is found in the books. A smattering may be picked up from the conversation of well-informed people. Outlines may be borrowed from the weekly papers, but accurate and instructive knowledge can be found only in the books.

Thus it happens that one does not find the most intelligent audiences in the great cities. Some men, the most intelligent in their departments of labor, may be found; but the mass do not average up with country audiences. In the country home, where the daily seldom finds its way, the family is trained on the books distributed by the pastor or through the Sunday-school. These become the staple for doctrine and for opinion. These make up the ground of conviction.

When we furnish books that master and unfold the

ground and work of our benevolences and secure their wide circulation, we shall raise a generation that will stand by the great Church benevolences. Given intelligence, and benevolence will be limited only by ability and piety. Put the mission-fields upon the mind of the Church, and the Spirit will press them upon the heart and pocket-book. In great organizations, as well as in individual accountability, *knowledge* is conviction.

C. H. FOWLER.

XIV

CHURCH LITERATURE AND EDUCATIONAL WORK.

METHODIST education begins in the family, and is continued in the Sunday-school and the Church. Besides the more formal work of instruction, a large and varied element of social influence permeates all these. It is carried on in seminaries, academies, colleges, and universities. Of late annual assemblies, having this largely in view, have been inaugurated; while, from the beginning, the mighty influence of the press has been employed to strengthen, direct, and supplement all other agencies. The work of education has a most intimate relation to the evangelization of the world. It goes hand-in-hand with the preaching of the Gospel. The evils of ignorance are, in number and magnitude, beyond estimation. In all its dispensations the Church has made earnest efforts for their removal. God complains, "My people are destroyed for lack of knowledge." "O that they were wise, that they did understand!" embodies the desire of his heart. To obviate these evils kings were required to write out copies of his law, and parents and teachers to inculcate its truth on the hearts and minds of the young. The apostles enjoyed for years intimate fellowship with the Great Teacher, and the Holy Ghost was given to bring all his sayings to their remembrance. Thus they were led to commit to writing the things most surely believed, and in which they would have the world instructed. The translation of the Bible and the writings of Luther and his coadjutors were mainly instrumental in the great Reformation. Wesley and his

followers used the press on a large scale as a most efficient
auxiliary "in spreading Scriptural holiness over the
world."

In God's good providence the Methodist Episcopal
Church has been led to employ ample means in promoting
education, and in always elevating the character and condition of its members and friends. The fathers made it
abundantly evident that they desired the improvement of
the people in intelligence as well as in religion, in knowledge as well as in holiness. They well knew that as men
were able to acquaint themselves with God, his character
and government, the wreck of their own nature by sin and
rebellion, and the fatal consequences arising therefrom,
with the marvelous provision for recovery from this state
of pollution and guilt, and the blessed results secured by
those who, with penitent and grateful hearts, accept the
overtures of divine grace,—in short, that as they enjoyed
and illustrated the presence and power of the Holy Spirit
as the revealer of truth and sanctifier of the soul, in that
proportion would they be joyous and stable in their own
profession and active and successful in more firmly establishing and more widely extending the triumphs of the
Redeemer's kingdom around them. They knew that religion is a wonderful awakener of the human faculties, and
that to a growing Church our schools and literature, rightly
conducted, would furnish in large degree the food required
for mental and moral health and strength. So various
institutions of learning sprang up, and under their fostering care increased in usefulness and strength. The *Methodist Year-book* for 1882 gives an aggregate of at least
thirty-three classical seminaries, thirty-eight colleges and
universities, eleven female colleges, and eight theological
schools connected with the Methodist Episcopal Church.
These ninety or more institutions had not less than $6,652,-
200 invested in grounds and buildings, and $5,019,388 in
their endowments. They employed a staff of 850 professors

and teachers, and supplied the means of study and instruction to 18,516 young men and women. The number of students taught in their halls from the beginning reach a grand aggregate of 342,311. It will require the unfoldings of eternity to reveal the aggregate of good accomplished through the educational department of our Church work.

If we turn to our literature, as represented by the products of the press, we find a magnificent supply in the way of weekly, monthly, and quarterly publications, and of books and book establishments rivaling the largest publishing interests in the world. The number, character, and influence of these, and their claims, will be more fully discussed by another hand. It is enough here to observe the wonderful providence which led the fathers of Methodism to enter on this field of labor, and the invaluable blessings which have been secured to the Church and the world. There is nothing more truly sublime in the history of the American Church than that presented by our pioneer preachers. Believing that people should search the Scriptures for themselves, they loaded their saddle-bags with Bibles, tracts, hymn-books, and works of religious biography, devotion, and doctrine. The literature of the Church as it then was, was scattered freely among the people as a matter not merely of propriety, but of principle and binding obligation. They firmly believed that for "the soul to be without knowledge is not good;" and so, while yet the Church had a hard struggle against ignorance, prejudice, and every form of opposition, they not only planted schools, but, by the circulation of good books and of all wholesome literature, cultivated a taste for reading. They secured among many thousands of the people that lived in humble cabins a much deeper acquaintance with the real master minds of the world and with the pure fountain of all learning than is now to be found in some lordly palaces. That more books may be found on the shelves of the latter is no proof that their owners are better acquainted with the Bible doctrines of the Church, or with its apostolic polity, or that they have any deeper love for that which constitutes the essence of its spiritual life.

Indeed, the fear is that the Church is in danger not more from laxity of doctrinal statement in its pulpits and from a mere formal and worldly spirit in its pews than from the flood of un-Methodist literature that has, of late years, crowded itself in every way into our families and Sunday-schools and Church libraries. Seduced by boastful and often untruthful representations as to cost and quality, and by promises of liberal rewards—promises often made only to be broken—Sunday-school officers, and even pastors sometimes, lend themselves to the work of introducing a literature that ignores, if, indeed, it does not directly antagonize, the pure truth of God as held by the Methodist Church. In such cases our children grow up, to a large extent, ignorant of the distinctive doctrines of the Church. The spirit and usages that characterized its heroic days are laid aside as obsolete or something to be ashamed of. The life of the Church is enfeebled and exposed to serious inroads of evil in every form. That this humiliating state of affairs is not more general is cause of profound gratitude. That in some places, through negligence or something worse, it does obtain, is cause of sincere sorrow, and calls for prayerful consideration.

In an age characterized by so many and such successful efforts to extend knowledge among all classes, on every subject and in all directions, the Church should see to it that in these two great lines of work—the planting and nurture of Christian schools ot the highest and widest learning, and the preparation and dissemination of a sound Christian and Methodist literature—she not only keeps pace with, but marches in advance of, other agencies and organizations. Her ardent zeal and perseverance in these directions mark her past history with an almost marvelous success, and enable her to point to a long and honored line of men and women distinguished as scholars, speakers, and writers among her ministers and laity. Their productions in daily, weekly, monthly, and quarterly publications, in lightest tracts and weighty volumes, have gone out, and still continue to go, benefiting and blessing the Church and the world. Other denominations have been, by her example, provoked to love and good works in this direction. As a consequence, many run to and fro, and knowledge, even the highest and best, is increased. Is it not pitiful that any in her pale should be ignorant of her noble record in this regard, and, of course, have no practical sympathy or desire to co-operate with her? In such houses no papers published by the Church are found. Good books are extremely rare. Their place is occupied by vulgar and pernicious literature, tending to lower the tone of the mind and to defile the soul. Any miserable pretense, inspired by ignorance or short-sighted selfishness, serves to excuse their owners from spending money or from taking interest in such things as are of real value. If circumstances seem to force them to do so, they listen eagerly to claims of pretended cheapness or superior advantage of institutions or publications entirely foreign, if not directly hostile; to those of their own Church. Their sons and daughters know little of what Methodism has done or is doing, or about the venerable men and women who, under God, have made and are making it what it is. The holy, zealous, self-denying, faithful lives of saints on earth and in heaven are but little known, and the inspiration of their teaching and example is scarcely felt. No wonder such are wavering, halting, unreliable, and bring forth no fruit to perfection in any line of Christian effort. No wonder their children have no tender regard for or attachment to the Church of their fathers, and are easily led or driven in other directions. They live, and die, and are forgotten.

They have no inheritance among those who find God's covenant blessings descend, entailed upon them and their children. By availing themselves of the advantages within their reach, and by the reasonable encouragement of their own Church schools and the publications of their own Book Concern, so superior in most valuable respects, they might have been enrolled among those who have their memory and their virtues fondly cherished and their lives of pure and elevated piety embalmed among the benefactors of mankind, and reproduced in their children's children to the latest generations.

In this discussion it is assumed that the relation of literature and education is one of reciprocity. They act and react each on the other, and both lie at the foundation of and pervade all our civilization, and enter every department of modern thought, activity, and influence. No branch of the Church can perpetuate itself and do its own proper work if it does not assiduously conserve and cultivate these two great interests. To depend on outside parties, and to let others attempt to do this important part of its work for it, is to manifest not only indifference to its own well-being, but to pursue a course that will certainly end in its destruction. Especially is this true in the higher walks of Christian literature and education. And if so now, it is destined to be even more so in the not remote future. The age is one of books, reviews, magazines, and tracts and newspapers. These are destined more and more to mold the vital forces of humanity, and to give them strength and direction. To do this wisely and well requires the ripest thought and the best possible culture. Conjoined with divine grace, these are destined to wield the destinies of our world. Error and falsehood, in diverse and often insidious forms, are diligently at work to mislead the mind, corrupt the heart, and keep mankind away from God. Can the Methodist Church dare to neglect the potent influence of truth and purity and love—in short, the power of literature and education in their best forms— and yet be innocent before God? Can any member be a true follower of Christ, and at the same time be indifferent as to the pleasure and the power these may supply in personal experience, and their marvelous formative and controlling power over others?

Grateful for the good accomplished and the still greater good within reach, let Methodists everywhere rally to the support of these interests. Let every man, woman, and child among us feel themselves to be co-partners in the great work of fostering and extending their influence far and wide in blessing humanity, and in making manifest the glory of God. No Church has a richer heritage in these respects, and never was it more worthy of support and more likely to be productive of good. Let our able authors be encouraged to write. Let all foster and strengthen our educational institutions. Let the Church not only be kept abreast with all that is best in the spirit of the age, but let her take her appropriate place in the very front of those who lead Immanuel's hosts, and then may we, with confidence, hope for the most blessed and glorious results.

MRS. ALEXANDER MARTIN.

XV

THE TRACT SOCIETY.

ITS ORIGIN, AIMS, LITERATURE, AND POSSIBILITIES.

THE Christian religion is essentially and pre-eminently a missionary religion. It is a vast missionary scheme that aims at the subjugation of the world to the dominion of right, truth, and purity. But for this fact it never would have left Palestine to seek and save the lost in other lands. Its great Founder, after having announced himself the Light of the world, then died for its redemption, commissioned his apostles to "go and teach all nations," to preach his "gospel to *every* creature." In this "great commission" we see the present duty of the Christians of to-day, and in its spirit we have the germ of Methodism with all its Christianizing agencies. Methodism was, and is, a necessity as an agency for the regeneration of the world. It is essentially missionary in its spirit, methods, and aims. The missionary spirit is bound up in its unique and magnificent economy. We wonder not, therefore, that John Wesley and his colaborers were much given to tract distribution. We wonder not that Mr. Wesley not only prayed and studied to find out the *wants* of the world, but planned, wrote, and labored to supply them. He lived and breathed and had his being in an atmosphere of culture and religion; hence, all his time and energies were consumed in bringing souls to Christ and helping them to develop into intelligent and useful Christians. He manifested an utter abhorrence of that old, fanatical, unphilosophical, and unbiblical adage that "ignorance is the mother of devotion" by instituting schools, writing tracts and books, circulating them through his preachers and in other ways. Gladly do we recognize that one of the grandest facts connected with the origin and growth of Methodism is its efforts to diffuse the blessings of education, and thus aid in establishing an intelligent and solid Christian civilization. From the beginning its ministers have been solemnly obligated to circulate tract and books among the people.

To aid them in this much-needed work the Tract Society was organized. The germ of its existence is in Christianity. The development of this germ into its present form can not be given in detail. A few facts only can be named. The Society was formed to meet a felt want, to aid in solving the problem, "How can the Church reach the thousands of non-church-goers, and bring them under the influence of the Gospel?" It was clearly seen that as they would not come near the Church, the Church must in some way draw nearer to them. To aid in accomplishing this work a Tract Society was organized in New York in 1817, which, after a few changes, resulted, in 1833, in the formation of a Society that undertook the management of three benevolent enterprises of the Church; namely, "The Bible, Sunday-school, and Tract Society." In 1836, however, the work of the Bible Society was turned over to the American Bible Society; and, after some other changes, the General Conference of 1872 brought all the benevolent societies of the Methodist Episcopal Church into organic unity. The Tract Society in its present form is, therefore, the growth of years, and is one of the grandest products of the missionary spirit of the Church.

The sublime aim of the Tract Society now is "to diffuse religious knowledge by the circulation of the publications of the Methodist Episcopal Church in the English and other languages, in our own and foreign countries." It will be seen that the field of its operations is as wide as its aim is Christly and grand. Were these facts studied by the ministers and members of our Church with that careful and prayerful spirit which their importance and relations demand, the results would be increased collections and a persistent purpose to make this agency effective in the accomplishment of its mission. The world's great *want* is correct religious knowledge. Its present state of degradation and ruin, its barbarisms and defective civilizations, with their tyrannies, cruelties, intellectual and moral darkness, and vile abominations, are largely owing to its false views of God and man. The object of our Tract Society is to diffuse the kind of knowledge that it most needs. That is, our Church proposes to send books, papers, and tracts to every mission-field, as well as to furnish books and tracts to supply the necessities of our work at home. Here is certainly a vast and momentous work—a work that is positively overwhelming in its magnitude and import, and one that demands much thought, wisdom, energy, sympathy, and money for its accomplishment. And we verily believe that all these would be forthcoming if our membership only saw the nature, grandeur, and Christly character of the work. The printing-press, if rightly used, can greatly aid the Church in saving the world. Of the work already done by it we can form no adequate conception.

The reports of our Tract Society tell us that our own press, during the past twenty-eight years, has issued about 700,000,000 pages of tracts, besides publishing for the benefit of the freedmen "a beautiful little weekly paper called *Good Tidings.*" This work has been done by the Tract Society, except as it has been aided by the Sunday-school Union in the publication of the above-named paper. Then, in addition to this, it has published a large number of pamphlets, weekly papers, and books for our foreign fields of labor. Since 1854 it has expended over $50,000 in our foreign fields. The vast aggregate of work done at **home and abroad** is simply amazing. Tracts, papers, **and** books published in foreign languages, to aid missionaries in their work, constitute one of the grandest monuments of the Church's foresight, wisdom, and energy, to say nothing about the work done at home. Foundations have been laid for building purer and loftier civilizations in many pagan lands. Then think of the many that this agency has brought to Christ, directly and indirectly; of the drunkards that have been saved, backsliders reclaimed, wavering ones confirmed, despairing and doubting ones inspired with faith and courage, sorrowing ones comforted, and inactive ones stirred and aroused to live earnest, useful lives, through the visitations of those little evangels called tracts. Many of those silent messengers have histories which, could they be seen and read, would thrill our souls and fire them with zeal to make their visits to unsaved souls and prayerless homes more frequent and powerful for good. Looking at past achievements, ought we not to keep before the minds of the people the very palpable fact that, without the aid of the Tract Society, neither the Church at home nor the Church in foreign lands can do its work as it needs to be done? Whence could come the books, tracts, and papers needed by the missionaries? And how can the non-church-going part of our home population be brought to Christ?

Let us not forget that, in other departments of thought and labor, the tract is a recognized power. Its power in the skeptical, educational, and political world is simply marvelous. Nearly fifty years ago Macaulay said, "Men are not converted or perverted by quartos." There is a prodigious power in a well-written, attractively got-up tract. Our Baptist friends have used it to make converts to their peculiar views, with marvelous success. Adventism could not have grown to its present proportions without it. Skepticism in all its forms has proved its power. Who does not know that worldlings, doubters, skeptics, sensualists, lovers of pleasure and worldly amusements, are greedy after books and tracts that condemn the Bible, the Sabbath, the Church, and all those who love them, as fanatics and old fogies, who are foolishly clinging to a worn-out delusion. Now, how can we counteract the mischief done by skeptical and semi-skeptical publications except by the publication and circulation of tracts?

Then, is there not a cheap and pernicious literature that can not here be described or characterized, that is scattered broadcast over the land? No mind but the mind of the Infinite can see the subtle and insidious workings of this poison in the minds of the youth of our land; and no mind but his can see how it pollutes their imagination and inflames their lowest passions, and thus ruins them for time and eternity. How, then, can these streams of a poisonous literature be stemmed? Not by our quarterlies, monthlies, and weeklies alone, nor by our Sabbath-schools and pulpits. These have their work; but they do not reach the thousands who never, or seldom, attend our churches. There is but one way to reach them, and that is *by tract distribution*. If the kingdom of evil sends out its poisonous missives, the kingdom of God must send out its millions of little evangels to counteract their destructive work. To write such tracts as the times need demands the very best talent of the Church. We have some, but there are not enough of *first-class tracts*. When we survey the battle-field, we see that in this country, Europe, and Asia there is a great conflict of thought, a great battle, raging between the forces of a spiritualistic and materialistic philosophy. The very foundations of revealed religion are threatened. "God or no God," mind or no mind, a personal immortality or an impersonal one among the gases of the universe, are the great questions now agitating the great sea of human thought. In view of these facts, is there not work for the Tract Society to do?—a work that no other agency can accomplish? Is it not true now, as in the past, that the children of this world are wiser in their generation than the children of light? O, if the Church would but use her agencies as she might, she could speak to the stormy seas of human thought and feeling, and there would be a great calm.

For it does seem, when we simply glance at her agencies, as if she possessed almost measureless possibilities. Her moral forces are simply vast, grand, and mighty. Her pulpits, press, Sabbath-schools, missionary, and tract societies furnish an equipment that can not be paralleled. It is the marvelous outcome of eighteen centuries of planning, suffering, and working. But mere *possession* accomplishes.nothing. It is of no use publishing to the world that we have grand machinery unless we set it in motion. It is of no use saying that we have "tracts for the masses" unless we circulate them among the masses. These talents must be *used*, or they will be taken away. They are used by our missionaries in India, China, Mexico, Germany, and other foreign lands, with good results. What Dr. Vernon says with regard to the benefits of tract distribution in Rome and other parts of Italy is true of other mission-fields. The missionaries of *all* lands can unite with him in saying that "tracts, papers, and books are immensely important to us." The tracts which they distribute "in public places, railroads, steamboats, and at the homes of the people," reach thousands that no other agency could reach so effectually. Many, through the earnest warnings, exhortations, and invitations of those little angels of light and salvation, are brought to the public service of God's house. They visit not only the homes of poverty, crime, and want, but the homes of the rich and the mansions of the great.

Now, if tracts can do such a glorious work for God and his cause in other lands, why may they not accomplish a similar work at home? The conditions are widely different, no doubt; but ignorant, debased, sinful, and suffering humanity is in as much need of the Gospel at home as abroad.   If, therefore, tracts can aid missionaries in bringing souls to Christ, and laying the foundations of a Christian civilization in other lands, why may they not aid in the work of soul-saving at home, and in building a purer and loftier civilization in our own land? 'Can any one deny such a possibility?   Missionaries in their preaching tours, by the use of tracts, papers, and books supplied by the Tract Society, disseminate truth, scatter seeds of eternal life that will ultimate in a rich harvest of souls, and produce changes in the thought life of the people that will aid in overturning hoary and colossal systems of error and forming a purer and grander social fabric.   This is no imaginary idea, as the work is now going on.

And when we stop long enough to think of the almost numberless opportunities that the Church has for doing good at home, and of her vast organized agencies, we are ready to ask, What could she *not* do if those agencies were baptized with the Spirit of Christ, and wisely directed along needed lines of action?   Think of her pulpits, press, Sabbath-schools, and her social means of grace.   What, if these were all used, in addition to a well-organized system of tract distribution in the circulation of our " tract literature," what might not be accomplished toward reaching the thousands of non-church-goers, and quickening the spiritual life of our membership?   Have we not tracts adapted, by their almost infinite variety of subjects, to accomplish this twofold work?   Certainly we have.   They contain truths that are suited to all conditions of life and experience—truths that antagonize every form of error and evil ; truths that expose the sophistries, worldliness, and selfishness of those who advocate a tribe of amusements that sap the very foundations of Christian life and usefulness, besides *preventing* many from becoming Christians.   We have tracts that expose the wickedness of liquor making and drinking as a beverage, as well as against other wily, subtle, persistent enemies of our civilization, who are aiming at the secularization of the Sabbath, and other enemies who are attacking the sanctity of marriage and seeking the destruction of our Christian homes. We have also tracts that defend, as well as explain, the distinctive doctrines of Methodism and its unique and unequaled economy, besides those that lift up their voice of warning against the sins of covetousness, indifference, selfishness, inactivity, and love of worldly pleasures and amusements that are so prevalent in the Church and so fatal to its spiritual life and progress. Let me ask, Can any thoughtful minister or layman doubt that a judicious distribution of such tracts would render substantial aid in giving to the Church an inspiration after a purer and more aggressive life? Would not such labor help to solve the yet unsolved problem, "*How can the thousands who never attend Church be brought under the saving influence of the Gospel of Christ?*" And would it not furnish "labor in the Lord" for thousands who are anxiously waiting for some field of usefulness, and are *wishing* that the ministers would open one for them? Brother ministers, you *know* that in all our charges there are those whose souls are being shriveled by a marvelous inactivity; and are not we at fault for this lamentable fact? How many, during the past quarter of a century, have abandoned the path of duty, fallen into the meshes of doubt, or lost themselves in the endless mazes of infidelity, if not in the deep, dark waters of vice and sensuality, simply because their pastors failed to give wise direction to their thoughts and energies! They perished in the ways of unrighteousness, because they were not given something to think about and something to do. They were left under the direction of skeptical thought and vicious influences, when a few well-chosen tracts would have met their mental wants, and a little work of tract distribution would have settled their doubts and developed their spiritual life, and thus saved most of them, at least, to Christ and his cause.

In looking, therefore, at the work to be done and at the agencies for its accomplishment, is it not time for our Church to take on a new life, and occupy a broader field of usefulness? The necessities of the times demand that she should "take a new departure," or she can not "preach the Gospel to *every* creature." Some systematic labor of the membership of our Church is demanded; for, talk and write as we may about ministers "visiting from house to house," there stands before us the palpable fact that such are the conditions of the world of labor and commerce that it is utterly impossible (even if they had the time and energy) for them to come into personal contact with half of those who are seldom or never seen at divine service. Then, there is the fact that *spoken* words are often evanescent in their influence. The varied conditions and the multitudinous temptations and forces in society soon blot out the impressions made by an occasional visit of the minister. This is the rule. The power of the printed page can do a much more extensive and permanent work; therefore, the Church is under the most solemn obligation to use this power.

What shall be the history of the Methodist Episcopal Church in the future? It is for us to determine. The Tract Society has made it possible for the Church to fulfill its mission, and it is in our power to move it along lines of action that shall develop its life and increase its aggressive and regenerating power as the years come and go. The possibilities of this Society, if properly developed, are almost infinite. Surely, if Romanists, skeptics, spiritualists, Adventists, and other organizations use the tract so skillfully, zealously, and with such amazing effect, we should not fail to use it for higher ends and diviner purposes. "If, under the adornments of rhetoric," the tract is used to circulate the poison of infidelity, sensuality, and an emasculating sentimentalism through the life-currents of society, we shall use it to stem those currents by circu-

lating a pure and an ennobling literature. We are already
fighting Romanism all over the world, Mormonism in the
far West, Buddhism, Brahminism, Hindooism, and Confucianism in the East, and materialism in Germany and
France, in Europe, by the use of the tract. Why, then,
should we not develop the grand possibilities of the Tract
Society by a systematic and persistent use of the little
messenger of truth, for evangelistic purposes, in every place
where it is practicable? What the Church needs is light
on this department of her work; then she will furnish the
money and energy needed for its accomplishment. The
circulation of a living, energetic, sanctified tract literature
would make many wildernesses of sin and deserts of religious ignorance bloom like Eden, and become fruitful as
the Garden of the Lord. Souls are perishing for lack of
knowledge within the sound of our church-bells, but they
will not come to our Church services. What shall be
done? The answer is, The people must be instructed with
regard to the necessity and feasibility of tract distribution,
then urged to organized effort, so as to utilize the forces
of the Church under a system of pastoral direction. If
this was done, we would soon see a marked change both
in the spiritual condition of the Church and in the size
and composition of our congregations. Sabbath desecra-
tion would be greatly diminished, and the number of
worldly, non-spiritual, dance-loving and theater-going members of the Church would grow far less. Only let there
be prompt, extensive, and energetic action, action upon a
scale commensurate with our abilities and opportunities,
then money would flow into the treasury of the Society,
and its possibilities for good be multiplied to an amazing
extent.

Much, however, will depend on *how* tracts are distributed. There should not, as a rule, be any sly or cowardly
dropping of them in saloons or anywhere else. The work
is *Christian* work; therefore, let it be done openly, bravely,

and prayerfully. A tract, to some, may seem an insignificant thing; but, when given with a warm heart and loving hands in the name of Jesus, it will be a messenger of life and salvation to the thoughtful. Howard visited the prisons, and Florence Nightingale ministered to wounded soldiers with her *own* loving hands, and Christ laid *his hands* upon the sick and suffering, and healed them. Let, therefore, Christian workers visit from house to house, and go among the lost everywhere, and carry them words of comfort, hope, and salvation. Let them seek to bless their neighbors and friends by "*leading them to the place where Christ is*" preached. Then let our Sabbath-schools, prayer-meetings, business-men, as well as ministers, aid in this blessed work. Let there be auxiliary societies organized wherever practicable, for the purpose of sending out men and women constantly to circulate a pure and elevated literature among the poor, the sick, and unsaved; then God will crown their efforts with abundant success, and the world will be lifted nearer God and heaven. What is needed is the *utilization* of existing agencies, and it will be done. May God help both ministers and people to do their duty!

THOMAS STALKER.

XVI.

OUR SUNDAY-SCHOOL LESSON HELPS.

THE present phases of the Sunday-school movement are eminently characteristic of the times.

I. The sanctity of learning is a vanished dream. The voice of the people, and doubtless the voice of God, is, that there shall no longer be a mysterious sacredness walling in knowledge from the people. Community of knowledge, if not of goods, is the doctrine of the day. The popularization of knowledge is, above all things else, the greatest secular achievement of this century. The sovereign people demand that all knowledge shall be for all the people; all that is known to the learned is required for common use by the masses of the unlearned. The ignorant and the penniless claim, at least for their children, the dissemination of all science through the free common school. This communistic spirit is pre-eminently exhibited in the latest developments of the Sunday-school work. The clergy no longer hold a monopoly of religious learning, to be meagerly and circumspectly dispensed to the laity, but laymen seek and are granted free range through all the long secluded paths of religious inquiry. All Biblical and theological and ecclesiastical knowledge, accumulated through ages of devout research and reflection, is now offered to the children of the poorest without charge or stint. The utmost meaning of Greek or Hebrew root is opened to the merest child. The profoundest reflection of the most learned father is communicated to a street Arab in the mission-school. The latest result of Biblical criticism is laid before a bevy of smiling girls. The stores of history and travel and science and art are ravished to illuminate and adorn the lesson for infants. Every thing that is known or has ever been conceived is rehearsed to the pauper's child.

II. International comity, coming into the place of perpetual war, is evidencing the power of Him through whose power, also, sectarian bigotry and exclusiveness are giving place to harmonious combinations of the Churches against unbelief, ungodliness, and heathenism. The extreme doctrine of the day is pseudo-liberalism, creedless, formless, indefinite, void; but the Church is not going over into that absurdity and suicide. The Churches are emphasizing to-day their points of agreement, and making secondary their points of difference. The spirit of unity is becoming prevalent in Christendom, and harmonious organization against Antichrist is the ecclesiastical achievement of the age. The great Bible societies, composed of all the Churches consenting to distribute throughout the world the Word of God, "without note or comment," as nearly as possible unadulterated by any admixture of human opinion or doctrine, remarkably illustrate this spirit of unity. Even more strikingly is this spirit of the age exhibited in the adoption of an international series of uniform lessons for the Sunday-school. The Churches agreeing together to study and teach simultaneously the same portions of Scripture, seem, now as never before, to see eye to eye. This is not merely an outward, formal combination for mutual defense, for common attack in the face of a common foe, but an inward, ingenuous, hearty agreement that the thought and heart of Christ's Church shall take a common rhythmic movement harmonized by the Master's voice. So now the intellectual resources of all the Churches are made a common stock for the enrichment of the common mind; and all that men know or think upon any portion of God's Word is simultaneously disseminated to every part of Christ's Church. The essential unity of the Christian faith and purpose is coming forth as the brightness of the sun before the delighted Church and the astonished world.

III. As the industry of the day is marked by an economy of power secured in the skilled division of labor, so religious and intellectual activity economizes power by systematizing work and organizing workers; and this, too, appears in the latest Sunday-school methods. The common schools are now graded in separate departments, according to the age and capacity of the pupils, conducted by teachers trained each for his special department, and using books, apparatus, and methods adapted to the peculiar wants of his work. In the Sunday-school will be found the same gradation of scholars and the same adaptation of teachers and teaching to special departments. We find normal classes, adult classes, young people's classes, intermediate classes, and primary or infant classes; we shall find also, we trust, teachers qualified to succeed in these several departments.

These considerations show that the question of Lesson Helps involves in their preparation a broad Christian scholarship, a spirit of catholicity in harmony with the prevalent spirit of unity among Christians, and a clear view of the varied wants of the several departments of Sunday-school instruction. These demands are certainly kept in view in the preparation of our Lesson Helps. The management of our Sunday-school literature is known for its catholicity as much as for its Methodism. The founder of Chautauqua is the chief spirit in the production of our Lesson Helps, and every part of the series exhibits his genius for Sunday-school work. In the Lesson Commentary we have for pastors, superintendents, teachers, adult scholars, and studious young people a compendious compilation of the choicest thoughts in all literature bearing upon the particular passages in hand, all fused and illuminated by the glowing spirit of a prince among teachers.

Again, in the *Sunday-school Journal* will be found every needed explanation, together with invaluable hints guiding to the most effective teaching of the lesson. The *Lesson Leaf*, for intermediate scholars, presents an astonishing amount of helpful direction for profitable home study and successful class recitation. The infant classes are, if possible, even better provided for in the artistic *Picture Lesson Paper*, and the *Leaf Cluster* supplementing the Hints to Primary Teachers in the *Sunday-school Journal*.

If, now, we add *The Study*—a quarterly magazine for superintendents, primary-class teachers, the Bible class, and normal class—a magazine *packed* with hints, facts, suggestions, outlines, and concise papers on needed topics, we have a series of Lesson Helps intended to meet the wants of all our Sunday-school workers. And what is lacking may almost certainly be found in the *Normal Guide*.

Our Lesson Helps are equal in matter, arrangement, convenience of handling, beauty of appearance, to the very best in the field. They will meet the wants of Methodist Sunday-schools incomparably better than any others. They are *our* helps. They present the catholic faith from *our* Methodistic stand-point. They familiarize our Sunday-school scholars with our statements of Christian doctrine. They recognize the Methodistic method of saving souls. They inculcate the Methodistic definitions of religious belief, experience, and duty. They are none the less Christian and catholic for being positively Methodistic; for Methodism is an insistance not so much upon non-essentials of creed as upon the essentials of Christian life. In our helps we need not so much to dogmatize upon our doctrines as to assume them and apply them in the teaching to save the scholars from sin.

There is much current sentimentalism concerning undenominational lesson helps. However, few are more taken by this sentiment than such as have these undenominational wares for sale. It requires little astuteness to discover that even undenominational lesson helps must have a bias of their own. Dr. Whedon once wrote, "None but an idiot's brain can approach a subject blank of prepossessions." Even an undenominational writer must approach his theme from some point of view. Undenominational notes on Scripture must either be confined to threadbare truisms, or allowed to run into the absurdities of liberalism, of all dogmatisms the baldest, or they must fail to maintain the undenominational character. No man holds the Catholic faith completely and purely; we have not yet attained that perfection of knowledge; infallibility is not yet apparent among us; and while we are "compassed with infirmities," it is safer, it is wiser, it is more honest to avow each his stand-point, that all may know the limitations of his view by which his thought and doctrine are determined to be thus and thus. True undenominationalism is an impossible attainment for any positively Christian man, and is not found in any human production. As Methodists, exercising our undoubted right to be Methodists, granting to all others equal liberty in perfect charity, we may and we ought to use our own Lesson Helps. Our denominationalism should not degenerate into sectarianism; denominationalism, truly so called, is the charitable exercise of denominational beliefs and methods for the saving of souls; undenominationalism is not unity, but confusion; not agreement, but disorderly commingling of ill-adjusted elements. Using our Lesson Helps, we shall strengthen ourselves and our children in the doctrinal beliefs of our fathers, we shall accept their positive convictions of religious truth, and we shall, we trust, enter into their definite experience of salvation.

N. S. ALBRIGHT.

XVII.

THE IDEAL SUNDAY-SCHOOL LIBRARY.

In the Sunday-school libraries of the Methodist Episcopal Church there are about two millions of volumes. These books are kept in unceasing circulation, and are constantly read by certainly not less than three million souls. Most of their readers are children and youth. In not a few instances, as in sparse country populations, they furnish nearly all the reading of the families to which the children and youth of the Sunday-school belong. Hence, if it be true that every book which has sufficient life in it to command readers is a sower of good or evil seed, of noble or ignoble sentiments, of true or false conceptions of life and duty, then the fact that these libraries are active forces incessantly working good or ill in a field which contains the hope of Methodism, is not to be treated lightly, thoughtlessly, or indifferently, but is of grave importance, demanding the serious consideration, not only of Sunday-school administrators, but also of Church officers, pastors, and bishops.

It can not be truthfully affirmed that the Methodist Episcopal Church has been inattentive to this question. True to her Wesleyan lineage she has made large, even liberal, provision through her Book Concerns and official editors, for supplying her Sunday-school libraries with such books as are best suited to their legitimate purposes. Her publications in this department may safely challenge both examination and comparison with those of any other American or European Church. Were her libraries generally composed of these issues there would be small occasion for anxiety. Unfortunately it is far otherwise. There is a spirit abroad which, especially since our late war, demands.a lighter, less serious, less instructive, more exciting, and more miscellaneous literature for children and youth than is either healthy for young minds or fitting for a Church press to produce. Very naturally such productions, like sweetmeats and richly seasoned food, are more relished by the young than healthy mental food. And, very foolishly in a vast number of schools, their false taste finds sympathy among the youthful librarians and teachers to whose management the library is too often consigned. These parties, no doubt, mean well; but being governed more by the clamor of the scholars for what they call "interesting books" than by the high considerations which ought to control the selection of books, and which the Church herself is bound to respect, they have become, in this matter, a power greater than the Church. They scout her authority by rejecting her publications, rush to the general book-market, and fill their libraries with works, many of which, though sweet to the taste of the unrenewed heart, are, like the prophet's roll, productive of bitter results in the hearts of their readers.

This state of things is, to quote a passage from a speech by the profound Milton, " of greatest concernment in the Church.   For books are not absolutely dead things, but do contain a potency of life in them to be as active as that soul whose progeny they are; nay, they do preserve as in a vial the purest efficacy and extraction of that living intellect that bred them. I know they are as lively and as vigorously productive as those fabulous dragon's teeth; and, being sown up and down, may chance to spring up armed men." Granting the truth of these weighty words— and who will dispute it?—the Church is bound by her obligations to the Christ, and by her hope of continued life and purity, to do what she rightly can to curb the spirit which is filling her school libraries with books that do not make either for righteousness or for Methodism, but which do make, if not for positive wickedness, yet for the strengthening of that disrelish for a pure ethical and spiritual life which is the bane of human nature.

But what can the Church do? Under a system of pure voluntaryism like ours, she can not regulate this or any other question touching the laity by compulsory authority. But she can speak with a persuasive authority that every loyal Methodist will feel bound to respect. She can so place the question before the brethren who manage her Sunday-school libraries as to induce them to regulate their purchases of books, not by a desire to gratify the senseless clamor of unreflective minds, but by the only sound principle on which a Sunday-school library can be properly founded and maintained. What is that principle? What is the true idea of the Sunday-school library?

The Sunday-school as an institution is *sui generis.* There is nothing like it on earth. Born of that divine love which finds delight in feeding the lambs of the flock of Christ, it is the organism, the sphere, in which the Church seeks to impart a religious education to the young. Its text-book is the Word of God. To make the meaning of that Holy Book clear to the understanding, to impress its precepts on the conscience, and so to present the ever-living Christ to the affections as to awaken love to his person and submission to his will are the leading points included in its conception of the religious education it aims to impart. Thus the end it seeks for each of its pupils is his intelligent Christian discipleship, and through that discipleship to train him up to the highest type of manhood.

Now, the ideal Sunday-school library, being of and for this institution, must also be *sui generis.* Unlike the common-school library, the public circulating library, or even the college library, it must not be secular and miscellaneous, but *religious.* It *has no right to be in a Sunday-school except as an auxiliary for promoting its great end.* Every book on its shelves not conceived and written in the spirit of Christ, but in the spirit of the world, is an intruder, because antagonistic to the spirit which animates, or should animate, the school. Every volume that breathes a tainted ethical tone, or suggests rationalistic doubts, or gives distorted portrayal to virtuous character, or a favorable aspect to wrong action, or presents the spiritual life as an unreal and superstitious fancy, is utterly out of place in it, because every such book is hostile to the principle on which it is founded. Nor have strictly secular books any right in it, inasmuch as they can not subserve the religious ends sought by the school. The strictly secular volume, even though moral and truthful, is as much out of place in the library as secular studies would be in the class. In short, the auxiliary relationship of the library to the school excludes from it every book which is not in harmony with the purpose of the Church to make her Sunday-schools the places in which she strives to give religious education to her youth.

On the other hand, the Sunday-school library should be composed of books which may be properly called religious, and of no others. By religious, however, we do not mean books on experimental godliness only. We use the term in its broader sense as including every topic which relates to the interpretation of the Word of God, to the explanation and enforcement of its doctrines, precepts, and experience, to the history of the Church of Christ, to the deeds of the great leaders, the faithful confessors, the heroic martyrs, the courageous reformers, the devoted missionaries, and the saintly souls who have kept and spread the faith through the ages. Thus an ideal Sunday-school library would include books on history, geography, biography, travels, moral science, the conduct of life, Christian civilization, poetry, art, and natural science, so far as these topics have relations to the divine Word and to the Church of Christ. Books on those topics are germane to an institution organized for the promotion of Christian education, provided they are written in a Christian spirit and with a clearly defined purpose to commend revealed truth to the faith and affection of their readers.

This latter point can not be too strongly emphasized by every purveyor for the Sunday-school library, inasmuch as the world is deluged with books on the above-named topics, which, though ably, eloquently, attractively written, are adulterated with the poison of skepticism, worldliness, and hostility to spiritual religion. Happily for the Churches, their authors and presses during the last half-century have brought forth an abundant supply of books on those themes, which, for the purposes of religious education, are equally able, and are imbued with the spirit of Christianity. So that they who place poisonous books in the Sunday-school library are without excuse. "They have no cloak for their sin."

Does this theory exclude fiction from the ideal library? Not all fiction absolutely. To exclude every thing that may be included under the word fictitious would shut out those portions of Holy Writ which, though true in substance, are fictitious in *form*. The sublime book of Job, though true in substance, is dramatic, and therefore, fictitious, in *form*. So are the allegories and parables and some of the poetical books of Scripture. Yet they are pregnant with inspired truths, and consequently very full of authoritative instruction. Bunyan's inimitable "Pilgrim's Progress" is fictitious in the same qualified sense. So are, by no means all, but very many of the religious stories written for children and youth by modern Christian writers. Hence, fiction in *form*, which in *substance* is not fiction, but substantial truth aiming to elucidate and enforce moral precepts, and to impart high ideals of character, is not to be wholly rejected.

But fiction not written to instruct, to awaken noble impulses and aspirations, to promote reflection on the duties and true ends of human existence, but merely to amuse, should be sternly rejected. The Sunday-school is not a playground. Its administrators, while bound to make its instruction attractive, dare not, if intelligent and conscientious, make the amusement of its pupils one of its objects, either in teaching, in addresses or by means of books which are only amusing fictions. Such books injure the intellect, because they require no effort of attention, and beget the enervating habit of reading, not for self-improvement, but only for amusement. This habit dwarfs the mind, is fatal to mental growth, because it creates disinclination to that concentration of thought which is essential to the acquisition of knowledge. Hence, such fictions beget distaste for solid reading. Most of them contain false pictures of life, monstrous improbabilities, highly wrought incidents, that aim simply to excite emotion. The effect of such excitation is necessarily injurious to character in that, not being caused by real objects, and not being made the stimulus to right action, it produces nothing better than a sickly sentimentality, which substitutes the heaving of a sigh or the shedding of a tear for the practice of real virtue. Surely, to place books so injurious both to brain and heart in a Sunday-school library is to pervert it, to make it the instrument, not of religious, but of irreligious education. It is profanation.

But children and youth demand such books, it is said. This is no doubt true of most who have been permitted to taste such poisoned fruit. But are such demands to be accepted by the Sunday-school as substitutes for the grand principles on which it is based? Rather is not the correction of such vicious taste one of the purposes of the religious education it professes to impart? It is true, as Wordsworth remarks, that "delight and liberty is the simple creed of childhood." But why are the young gathered into the school but to be taught that their creed is misleading, that their "liberty" is not to become licensed like the colts of wild asses, but a gift from God, which they are required to regulate with the bridle of duty? and also that their "delight," to be real and lasting, must be derived, not from sipping poisoned sweets, but from drinking rich draughts of the fountain of life? No; the library must not be governed by the children's creed of liberty and delight, but by the obligation of the Church to use it as an instrument of religious education.

Still it may be urged that if exciting fictions are excluded, and none but substantially truthful books admitted, the library will be neglected, that pupils will refuse the latter class of books. If this were true, it would be better to place a seal on the door of the library or to banish it forever from the school, than to give books tainted with moral or spiritual poison to the young. But is it true? May not much of this demand for exciting fictions be traced, as suggested above, to the sympathy with such works felt by the young men who usually act as librarians, by many Sunday-school teachers, and even by some worldly minded or unthinking pastors? Instead of correcting the false ideas and tastes of the scholars, too many such parties have supported their demand by saying of useful books, "Yes, they are dry and uninteresting;" or, "They are goody goody books." Had they attempted with intelligent kindness to point out the value and healthful attractiveness of such works, would they not have silenced this clamor and induced their pupils to read with pleasure and profit books they now reject because their teachers and others have unwisely censured them? Such is our opinion; and we estimate that teacher very low who can not, by a few decisive words, set an entire class to reading any properly written, useful book. Any right-minded superintendent, worthy of his responsible office, can, in like manner, move a whole school to ask for any such volume by a few judicious words spoken from his desk. Still more influential are the words of pastors commending religious books in weighty words to the parents of his Sunday scholars.

Let the Church, therefore, zealously set herself to the task of banishing all unwholesome fiction from her Sunday-schools. Let her also set her face against the excessive use of even such qualified, and in themselves unobjectionable, fictions as, in response to the demands of public opinion, her presses have already produced. A dinner should not be all dessert; neither should stories, however excellent, constitute the staple of any one's reading. The body of our libraries should be composed of books that contain living words, truths that " perish never." O blessed books,

> "That combine in one
> All ages past, and make one live with all:
>   By you we do confer with who are gone,
> And the dead-living into council call;
>   By you the unborn shall have communion
> Of what we feel and what doth us befall."

In the ideal library of a *Methodist* Sunday-school there will be a selection of the books pertaining to our Church history and to the lives of our Church fathers sufficient to make our young people not bigots, but familiar with the devout spirit and successful zeal which gave birth and growth to Methodism. It may be truthfully said of our Church that

> "Great men have been among us; hands that penned,
> And tongues that uttered wisdom—better none."

Therefore, though we should not glory in men, yet we may rejoice in the fact that we have in our history a record eminently honorable, filled with glorious achievements, attractive to the imagination, and full of spiritual inspiration. As Bishop Jewel said of the deeds of the Reformers, who were Methodists in spirit though not in name, so may we properly say of the works of our Church fathers, " Let these never be forgotten; let your children remember them forever." To secure that remembrance, and to aid in transmitting their spirit to posterity, a goodly number of our Church biographies and Church histories should be constantly kept in our libraries. And may it be truthfully said that no *Methodist* Sunday-school library possesses ideal completeness unless a liberal number of such works is on its shelves!

It scarcely needs saying that in an ideal Sunday-school library the books should be properly classified. The extent of such classification, like the size of the library itself, must be determined by the magnitude of the school. Hence, no rule can be given applicable alike to the school of twenty children on the frontiers and to the highly organized city school of a thousand or more pupils, ranging from the infant class to adult students of Holy Writ. It must suffice here, therefore, to say that there should be departments in the library for the simple literature of childhood; for books written down to the newly awakened intellectual capacities of boys and girls; for the partially developed minds of young people; and for the more thoughtful readers of the adult classes. But the principles already stated respecting the religious character of the Sunday-school book should be as rigidly applied to the adult as to the infant department. From all, not merely the anti-religious but also the irreligious volume should be conscientiously excluded.

This fidelity to the principle and aims of the Sunday-school in the higher department of the library will be objected to by those who think it desirable for the Church to furnish its adherents with books sufficient to meet all their intellectual requirements. But whoever views the question broadly and practically will see that this theory is Utopian. It is not clear that its object is even desirable, because there will always be unnumbered books needed by professional men, by artists, by mechanics, by men of special culture and of marked idiosyncrasies, which the

Church could not supply for lack of means, and ought not to furnish if she could. To attempt it would be idle, if for no other reason than the unwillingness of the people to submit to any such curtailment of their intellectual liberty. The sphere of the Church is limited to men's spiritual nature and moral action. And when her libraries are well furnished with literature which is ample to meet the demands of the higher nature of her adherents, to excite and gratify a taste for solid, useful reading, with a corresponding distaste for sensational and corrupt reading, she has reached the limit of her obligations in this direction. She has then performed the high duty of providing an antidote to the vile books which, like the frogs in Egypt, come from the Satanic press, seeking admission into every unguarded household in the land.

DANIEL WISE.

XVIII.

RELIGIOUS NEWSPAPERS.

THIS is justly called the age of the printing-press. The dissemination of printed matter is a growing wonder. It can not, however, be taken for granted that the reading public demands printed matter in the permanent form of books, or even in the comparatively durable form of magazines. It is but rarely that a book reaches a sale of even one hundred thousand in our population of fifty millions. Making a large estimate for the private circulation of a book once sold, it will be seen at once that even a popular author is not actually read by one in a hundred of his fellow-countrymen. The people read but few books, and those few not books of reflection, of science, of history, or of devotion, but rather books of travel, of adventure, of romance, and the lighter forms of fiction—books affording to the occasional thoughtful reader needed diversion and recreation, but actually dissipating mental and moral power in the habitual reader. So of the better class of literary and scientific magazines; their limited circulation proves that they are practically unknown to the common people, and are not habitually read by the majority of even intelligent people, so called. Scholars, professional men, and the exceptionally thoughtful, read valuable substantial books and magazines; but the common people—indeed, all the people—are informed, if at all, through the newspaper. The reflective, the originative, the inventive, the scholarly, write books of value, thus permanently preserving knowledge for the world's use. But in books alone this knowledge would never be popularly disseminated. It is not the author of books, but the paragraphist, writing often second-hand matter, who finally brings knowledge to the people. The people are not acquainted with books; they regard books as luxuries, the last things to be procured (unless almost forced upon them by agents personally pushing the circulation); they are not accustomed to read books, they tire at it; they find the chapters too long and the book too large, and defer the reading to days of leisure that never come.

The people are, nevertheless, not content to be ignorant. The great middle class, the vast majority of the people, is resolutely bent upon informing itself by reading; but the reading, to be acceptable, must be attractive, stimulating, even sensational, and, above all things else, it must be fresh. In cities and towns reached by the telegraph and daily mail news of yesterday is no news, discoveries of last month or last week are old, opinions of last season are stale; and this craze for novelties invades the rural districts—many a farmer insists upon having a daily newspaper. No doubt there is much in all this that is unhealthful. This constant and irrepressible demand for the newest news, the very latest novelties in science and opinion, all to be served to the public in sensational head-lines, is evident sign of a feverish and fickle public taste, and can not become the permanent mental habit of a truly great people. However, while it lasts, the Church, in no way responsible for its existence or its evil results, must not regard it with imbecile laments and denunciations, but must wisely make the best of it. In the order of Providence this has become a newspaper age; and it is not of faith to lament it, but to acknowledge it, and to utilize it for the saving of the world.

The secular newspaper is at best secular in spirit; it is well if it be not atheistic or immoral. The province of the secular newspaper is to publish the news in which its constituency is interested, and to disseminate such information as will serve the purposes of its reading patrons. Every thing is published from the secular stand-point, certainly not the Christian stand-point—well if it be not anti-Christian! Unless the popular mind is to be thoroughly secularized and de-Christianized, if not anti-Christianized, the Church must undertake the work of informing the public of passing events and current opinion from the Christian point of view. This, the Christian assumes, is the true stand-point whence to observe men, their deeds, and their doctrines. If one is a Christian at all, he holds that there is a divine origin and control of nature; a divine hand in the government of human society, and a divine purpose and meaning in human history; and it is neither bigotry nor superstition to demand the recognition of God and his Christ in the treatment of current history and opinion. The spirit of the times is eminently secular, though the reaction from materialism and false liberalism is fast setting in. The religious newspaper is a necessity in an age of secular newspapers, as much as the Sunday, or Bible, or religious school is a necessity in an age of common-schools, as much as the religious book is a necessity in an age of infidel books, as much as the religious oration or sermon is a necessity in all the ages of secular eloquence. The Church can not dispense with this powerful arm of offense and defense. The Christian needs it for his own armament in a secular age; he needs it for the defense of those he is providentially set to guard from the evils of the world; he needs it for urging the truth of Christianity in a practicable form upon the indifferent or the inimical.

As there is no adequate estimate to be put upon the influence of the secular newspaper, so widely disseminated, so eagerly read, so it is impossible to overstate the urgency of the requirement laid upon the Church to carry the religious newspaper into all Christian homes, into *all* homes. Even where the Bible is left unread by a worldly and indifferent or infidel household, the religious newspaper may find a reading; for its news is as reliable and ought to be as fresh and as concisely stated as in the secular paper.

The Church, however, can not push her papers any more than her books upon the people. The Christian public ought to demand the Christian newspaper, the religious family ought to require a religious information. No man of the world can afford to be without his secular paper, giving the state of the market in his particular line, furnishing the information needed in the prosecution of his public or private aims, and bringing from all over the world the news interesting him. No Christian, awake to the providential character of the age, alive to his duty in an age of Christian missions and charities, engaged in the urgent prosecution of the Gospel publication throughout the world, can afford to be without his religious newspaper, informing him of the current tendencies of religious life and doctrine, of the current events of religious enterprise and benevolence and evangelization, of the current news of the Church at home and abroad. The secular newspaper is indispensable to the business man, to the politician, to the well-informed man of every rank and calling; so indispensable is the religious newspaper to every Christian who has an interest in the coming of Christ's kingdom and would gladly know of its progress through the world.

19

EDITOR.

XIX.

THE CHURCH LYCEUM.

I BELIEVE the Methodist Episcopal Church is the only one that has the plan of a Lyceum, and the means of its successful inauguration and maintenance incorporated into its Book of Discipline.   This Church has ever been considerate of the temporal and intellectual condition of its members.   Beginning among the poor, the broken-hearted, the captives, the blind and bruised, it began at once to consider how physical evils could be abated, and then how ignorance could be enlightened.   The vast literature of the Church shows how faithfully it has wrought for this end.

The Lyceum meets a real want.   The mind yields the best results to training.   The body gets strength to lift two thousand pounds, the voice ability to give all the fifths between two adjacent notes, the eye clearness to discern $\frac{1}{115000}$ of an inch, and the hand skill to measure $\frac{1}{35000000}$ of an inch, but the mind is the best field for careful culture.   The Lyceum is one of the gymnasia for its exercise.

The mind especially needs to be trained to quickness of action, so that all its treasures shall be at any instant under control.   It was one of the secrets of Napoleon's power that he could instantly form new combinations to meet sudden emergencies.   As the fencer must have an eye quick as light, and a hand for defense quick as a thrust, so must the man in the quicker realm of thought be instantly ready.   How provoking is that habit of mind that gives only what the French call *esprit d'escalier*—the bright replies one thinks of after he has left the company and is on the stairs going home. Many of our possible Miltons are mute and inglorious for want of training.

The Lyceum is admirably adapted to develop this quickness of mind. It has been so used in all ages. The Greeks taught by the Socratic method. In the earlier English universities the first scholars were called wranglers because of their discussions. They have since degenerated into contestants for mathematical prizes. Henry Clay said, "I owe my success in life to one single fact, namely, that I commenced and continued for years the process of daily speaking, not unfrequently in some distant barn, with the ox or horse for my auditors. It is to this practice of the great art of all arts, that I am indebted for the leading impulses that shaped my entire destiny."

Some preaching has degenerated into orations and essays; not so was Christ's, but word answering word until men could no longer dissent, nor even ask questions.

There is no country that demands ability to speak like America. Every man is a sovereign, and may utter his decrees; every man is a citizen, and may influence every one in the city to adopt his views. The best positions await the man able to speak wisely and well. Encyclopedia wisdom may rest in the brain of a man, and be as useless as the unmined gold in the Black Hills. The owner of millions starves. But the man able to utter his wisdom, be it ever so little, in persuasive speech, has the useful coin that supplies his every want.

It is the privilege of many Americans to say with Mrs. Browning—

"I have known the pregnant thinkers of this time,
And stood by breathless, hanging on their lips,
When some chromatic sequence of fine thought
In learned modulation phrased itself
To an unconjectured harmony of truth."

This is the age of ideas, and every man should seek a forceful utterance of them. Especially should the Church see to it that the young have every advantage of training.

The Church is the school of all schools, teaching health, cleanliness, temperance, hardihood, wisdom, holiness—that is, perfect manhood. The perfect man approximates the unity of thinking, speaking, and embodiment that God has. Sin separates feeling from action, so that men may see peril and weep, but not move to safety. Christianity makes speech and deed to be instantly responsive to feeling and thought. The very instincts find quick expression in a character so pure that it has nothing to conceal. All the right instincts of youth should find full gratification under the sanction of the Church. Childhood inclines to abundant—some may say superabundant—speech; youth is the time to associate it with wisdom, so that it shall not always be a babbling brook, but a broad river, freighted with the intellectual wealth of all ages.

A full discussion of the Lyceum, its origin, aim, objections, value, disciplinary methods, course of study, etc., may be found in an admirable work, "The Church Lyceum," by Rev. T. B. Neeley.

H. W. WARREN.

XX.

RELATION OF OUR CHURCH LITERATURE TO THE TEMPERANCE WORK.

THE literature of an organization is its voice; and it is through her literature that the Church speaks to the million, in a manner more persuasive and convincing than even through her pulpit.

The ministry of the consecrated pen is second to none; not even the clergy can present a commission more directly from God than that which endows the hand and brain which fashions the literature of his Church.

The Church is known better through this medium than any other. It does not matter so much what her pulpit utters as what her press scatters abroad; and it is reserved for her pen to indorse or condemn every word which falls from the preacher in the pulpit or the minister at the altar.

The position of the Methodist Episcopal Church on the temperance question does not need to be defined, at this day, by any living man or woman. She has already gone upon record in terms which can not be mistaken. The temperance law of the Church regulates the sentiment of her people and ministry, and speaks through her tongue and pen, so that her pulpit everywhere, and every page of her literature, utters the one truth that the Gospel of the Lord Jesus Christ antagonizes not only sin in general, but in particular, and counts the drink traffic and use in every form as among the works of the devil which He came to destroy.

The Methodist Church is a unit on this question. She may be divided into branches on many other points: but on the temperance question she stands as one, and always in the vanguard. Among the first principles laid down for the guidance of those who would walk with her people is this, namely: "It is therefore expected of all who continue therein that they should continue to evidence their desire of salvation   by avoiding evil of every kind   such as   drunkenness, buying or selling spirituous liquors; or drinking them, unless in cases of extreme necessity."

As early as 1787 personal habits of temperance (which was interpreted to mean "using only that kind and degree of food" and "drink which is best for both body and soul," using "water for common drink," and wine only "medicinally or sacramentally") were strictly enjoined upon all ministers. In 1792 members were prohibited from treating, and in 1796 the following was placed upon the records and became a part of the law of the Church: "If any member of our society retail or give spirituous liquors, and any thing disorderly be transacted under his roof on this account, the preacher who has the oversight of the circuit shall proceed against him as in the case of other immoralities; and the person accused shall be cleared, censured, suspended, or excluded, according to his conduct, as in other charges of immorality. N. B. Far be it from us to wish or endeavor to intrude upon the proper religious or civil liberty of any of our people; but the retailing of drams to customers when they call at the stores are such prevalent customs at present, and are productive of so many evils, that we judge it our indispensable duty to form a regulation against them. The cause of God, which we prefer to any other consideration under heaven, absolutely requires us to step forth with humble boldness in this respect."

In 1828 the Rev. Wilbur Fisk presented to the General Conference a preamble and resolutions, which were adopted, expressing the strongest sentiments against the

use of and traffic in strong drink, and in favor of reform
in every respect; and these resolutions have been added
to by every General Conference, and nearly every annual
and district conference, from that day to this. In 1832 a
conference committee on temperance was appointed, and
has since become one of the regular committees appointed
as a matter of course at the opening of every Methodist
conference, and its report is annually added to the literature of the Church, and is, like a voice, constantly reiter-
ating the truth that there can be no fellowship between us
and the demon of rum.

A temperance address, delivered before the General
Conference of that year, was ordered to be printed in a
tract for circulation; and in 1836 the preachers and members were recommended by the General Conference to procure a copy of a volume which had been prepared by the
Rev. Dr. Edwards, secretary of the American Temperance
Society, consisting of a compilation of facts concerning the
rum traffic, and effects of total abstinence.

We might glean from all the journals of the Church,
and occupy the entire space allotted to this article with
extracts from the utterances of the men who laid broad
and deep the foundations of our Church literature in the
truth of God, as revealed in the human body and in his
law, as well as in the Gospel of Jesus.

We will content ourselves, however, with the record
of the General Conference at Cincinnati, May, 1880. Action was taken concerning the sacramental wine as follows,
"Let none but the pure unfermented juice of the grape
be used in administering the Lord's-supper, whenever practicable;" and to be inserted in the Discipline the following
as "expressive of the general sentiment of the Church on
the temperance question:" "Temperance, in its broader
meaning, is distinctively a Christian virtue, Scripturally
enjoined. It implies subordination of all the emotions,
passions, and appetites to the control of reason and con-

science. Dietetically, it means a wise use of useful articles of food and drink, with entire abstinence from such as are known to be hurtful. Both science and human experience unite with the Holy Scriptures in condemning all alcoholic beverages as being neither useful nor safe. The business of manufacturing and vending such liquors is also against the principles of morality, political economy, and the public welfare. We therefore regard voluntary total abstinence from all intoxicants as the true ground of personal temperance, and complete legal prohibition of the traffic in alcoholic drinks as the duty of civil government. We heartily approve of all lawful and Christian efforts to save society from the manifold and grievous evils resulting from intemperance, and earnestly advise our people to co-operate in all such measures as may seem to them wisely adapted to secure that end. We refer to our General Rule on this subject, and affectionately urge its strict observance upon all our members. Finally, we are fully persuaded that, under God, hope for the ultimate success of the temperance reform rests chiefly upon the combined and sanctified influence of the family, the Church, and the State."

This body further resolved:

" 1. That we recommend the organization of juvenile temperance societies in all congregations and Sunday-schools.

" 2. That we recognize the necessity of healthy temperance literature, and therefore recommend the publications of the National Temperance Association, of New York, to the patronage of our people and Sunday-schools.

" 3. That we gratefully recognize and heartily commend the ministry of the gifted and godly women of the Churches in the work of temperance, and in their crusade against the liquor traffic."

But the fathers of the Church have not stopped here in their teaching. As ever, they plant their standard on the outposts; and they have dared to speak against a vice even more widely spread and more insidious than that of drink. And to-day every candidate for the ministry of the Methodist Episcopal Church is expected to answer in the affirmative the following question, " Will you wholly abstain from the use of tobacco ?"

I have dwelt thus at some length on the teaching of the fathers, and have given this bit of Church history, because these principles have been built, like precious stones, into the foundation of our literature, and fastened, like nails in a sure place, beyond the reach of even Church legislation. It is from such root as this that all the branches of our wide-spreading system of books, papers, periodicals—books of poetry, history, essay, and story— text-books, and leaflet, and pictured page—all the foliage, blossom, and fruit of our literature, and its seed for future sowing, have sprung.

As is the Church, so is her literature; and as the relation of the Church to the temperance reform, so is the relation of her literature to the temperance work. The Church is radically opposed to the liquor traffic; therefore, the nature of the literature of the Church is to help the work of temperance reform everywhere, in the home and state, as well as in the hearts and lives of men; and I believe fully that if the press of the Church could reach the masses with its influence, if this continent could be " sown knee-deep" with the pages written with her truth, that the days of the drink traffic would be numbered.

All that has been done thus far in furnishing the people with correct temperance information, scientific, political, statistical, as well as moral, has been done, directly or indirectly, by the Churches, and a large share has passed over our own denominational lines.

Let us look for a moment at the extent of our Church literature, and from this estimate compute, if we can, its value, and consider its relation to the temperance work.

We publish, of weekly newspapers, annually, more than two hundred thousand copies; of monthly periodicals, about two hundred thousand; of Sunday-school helps, at least two millions; and have thirteen hundred and seventy-five books in our catalogue.

Look at this vast agency, whose lines of communication seem to extend to the uttermost parts of the earth, and estimate, if you can, its power, if properly applied.

In the work of reform the pen is surely mightier than the sword, and possesses a power in molding the morals of the masses such as can be claimed by no other. It is because the popular literature of the age has been corrupt that vice has so strong a foothold among the people. It is because the literature of the Church has not been taken out, sent out, crowded out, scattered every-where, that her principles of purity and truth have not as yet prevailed among the majorities; because her seed-corn has been kept too much in the barn, that the harvest does not yet meet the need of a hungry world.

We are painfully conscious of a need, not that the Church should speak more truly, more positively, more convincingly, but that her words should be carried out to those who have never yet heard her voice or language; and, also, that she should speak in a tongue that will be comprehended by those who know only the dialect of vice. It is often needful that the Church should expound to the men of the world the text of the truth, which is like household words to those whom she has brought up, so that the careless, the profane, the drunken, and the illiterate shall not be able to misunderstand her meaning. "Temperance" should never be left with an ambiguous signification, which may or may not be "license" or "prohibition," moderate self-indulgence or total abstinence. Every term employed needs to be clear cut, comprehending *all of truth*, antagonizing *all of error*. To some of those for whom the temperance work of to-day is done, the whole scheme of the Gospel needs to be translated, as into a foreign tongue.

The importance of meeting this need will be understood when we remember the influence of the Church in the world. She is recognized, even by the unthinking and the impure, as the representative of God; and she speaks with an authority that has been awarded to no other. That which she unloosens is unloosed; that which she binds is bound in the consciences of men. That which she or one of her teachers sanctions is quoted as lawful, even by the unbelieving. Her teachings are the foundation of all governments; it is the sentiment of her votaries that makes or unmakes the law of the land. Hence the absolute necessity that the sword of her written word, than which no weapon is more mighty in this battle with rum, should be charged into every hiding-place of the power of her foe. It is essential to the success of the temperance reform that her literature should meet the needs of the *whole people;* not simply those who come to her for instruction, who buy her books and take her periodicals, but those upon whom they must be thrust in the haunts of sin. She must prepare to meet all shades of thought and *unthought,* all classes and grades of intellect, all degrees of ignorance, with the clear aggressive force of well selected and plainly spoken truth, which shall be, in its influence, like the constant shining of a light that grows into the cloudless glory of perfected day.

There are places where the voice of the Church is not yet heard; and, wherever she is silent, there vice and unbelief are heard, tainting the air with the decaying fruit of corrupt thought. There are such places even in our own land, under the shadow of our own temples; such places in our own pews, and in the garden-spot of our Sunday-schools; places where her voice for prohibition and total abstinence has not been heard or understood, because the truth was not translated into the language they knew.

And to-day the real relation of Church literature to the temperance work must be that of a missionary, going out into fields that might at first seem altogether foreign; learning languages which she had not known before—the language of utter need, hopeless, helpless need, of souls bound in the prison of vice with strong chains of depraved appetites and fiery passions; not the appetites and passions of the human body simply, but those planted therein by the demon of rum, and which so far outrank all others that the same terms do not seem to apply to both, and so that it almost seems that the same Gospel remedy which meets the one can not touch the other. This need found expression one day on the lips of a man in these terms: "You talk about God being able to save folks; but I tell you it's one thing for him to be able to save you and the ladies of the Temperance Union, and it's another thing for him to be able to save a fellow like me. I guess if I'm ever saved he'll have to invent some new way." A woman said to me, "But I'm *such a low down sinner* God'll find it a dirty job to do any thing for me, I reckon."

The Gospel teaching which reaches the understanding of such men and women must be such as takes cognizance of burned-out nerves, vitiated blood, cooked brains, all in the leading of overgrown passions and of appetites of monstrous proportions; of a fettered soul in a poisoned body, which must wait the slow processes of elimination and up-building, through natural functions, for deliverance. The devil of rum has taken his work, on the human body, outside the region where God's grace, as commonly taught, operates. He will do his work in spite of God's grace, *if he can get the chance;* and this fact renders necessary a line of Gospel exposition for the victims of vice such as we have never had, which shall emphasize the doctrine of the "redemption of the body" even in this life, which shall reveal Christ as him who cleansed the *defiled temple,* as well as raised the dead.

A minister once said to me: "I am learning, in this work for these men, that the most of what I had learned for use in my ministry has to be entirely laid aside, or translated to meet the necessities of the case. I have nothing in my library, outside my Bible, that is of any practical use—absolutely nothing that I could hand to such a man as F———, with any faith that it would meet the want, unless I should sit beside him and expound as I read."

We find this often true; and we need a literature in which the most common terms of our religion shall be simplified, in which the most familiar doctrines and the plainest truths of salvation shall be so illuminated that the most darkened mind shall comprehend, and the most degraded shall find room for hope.

We need especially to double our forces along the lines of our Sunday-school work; for it is here that our great enemy makes his most persistent atteak. "Line upon line, line upon line, precept upon precept, precept upon precept, here a little and there a little," something with every Sunday-school lesson, something in every leaflet and book, which shall plead for purity, and reason of righteousness and temperance. Let the boys and girls of our Sunday-school know every thing that science, or philosophy, or political economy, or the law, or religion—every thing that polite culture, or beauty of face and form, or success in life—can teach or require concerning the drink use and traffic. Compel them to enter the path of vice, if at all, in such a blaze of light and knowledge that no responsibility shall remain with any tongue or pen for unrevealed truth.

One thing we must never forget. But for the Church there would have been no temperance reform. Nobly has she thus far met her obligation to the world of letters and the reformers of every age; and the past and present are auguries for the future. Her literature has been like good seed sown beside many waters; sown early and late; sown, often, without hope of any increase for her own reaping, but only that God's kingdom might be enriched. Her literature has been the nursing mother, the faithful guide with staff and lantern, to the temperance reform. It was because her pen had written, in learned treatise, in history and song and story, keeping God's truth always before us like an angel in the way, and ringing in the air above us like a clear-toned bell, that the women of the Church had the courage and faith to march and pray and organize against the saloon.

And if the day ever dawns when the power of the demon is broken, and home and state are free, it will be because the Church has been faithful to her trust as the representative of Him who was "manifested to destroy the work of the devil."

S. M. I. HENRY.

XXI.

LITERATURE AND ITS RELATION TO THE MORAL NATURE.

LITERATURE and the moral nature have in their history evinced a very intimate relationship; but the thinking world is divided upon the question as to which is the cause and which the effect. The Christian occupies a point of view from which he feels justified in affirming that the brightest culture is favored and developed by the highest moral attainments, while the opposer insists upon it that "ignorance is the mother of devotion." The inductive process of reasoning should here be considered satisfactory and convincing. If in different ages and in widely separated parts of the world the same plant be found growing in a soil with identical chemical constituents, we should be warranted in concluding that the soil was indispensable to the plant. So we find that the best civilization is identical with the highest moral culture on both sides of the ocean and in the isles of the sea, and, at the expense of vast treasure and many cultured and precious lives, the Church has demonstrated that the shades of ignorance recede before the widening horizon of Bible light.

Nor is this result contradicted by the distinction of classic lands in ancient times; for while it is freely admitted that in poetry and art they excelled, it will be insisted that the highest civilization consists not so much in faithful imitations as in noble and elevating ideals; not in art creations, but in the sacredness with which human life is regarded. No civilization is worthy the name which does not protect the life. Herein is a crowning glory of ours.

It stands by the cradle of infancy and steadies the steps of age, while for the sick and orphaned it founds the hospital and the asylum. These and kindred humanitarian institutions were unknown to Roman senator and Grecian philosopher. On the other hand, life with them was without value. Self-destruction and gladiatorial combat were the legitimate results of their one-sided culture.

But we are answered that the pre-eminence of our civilization is attributable to the increase of the centuries. But we have only to point to China for the fallacy of this assertion. The unchanging current of its national life appears to issue from the very portals of Noah's ark—if we credit their pretensions, though none will dispute the claim to a very high antiquity—and yet its thousands of years have not been able to relieve its waters of their slimy impurities. It demands something more than time, and that something is a proper culture of the moral nature.

No clearer proof of any proposition can be adduced than is afforded of this in the mission of Luther. It was to unchain the Bible, and open its pages; it was to swing conscience on the highest pivot of the soul—a conscience enforcing a judgment enlightened by the truth of God's Word. Now, what was the result to literature. Take Germany alone: in six years from the promulgation of the ninety-five theses at Wittenberg the number of annual publications increased twelvefold. The dark ages were past, and the morning had come.

We have said that literary and moral relations are interactive, and while deep-seated and enlightened moral convictions are agencies by which the race is lifted up to higher planes, these same convictions are susceptible of strengthening and culture.

Ours is a day when every idea has its literature. The press stands at the center of thought and influence. Its impressions may well be called leaves, since they are scarce excelled in number by the decorations which Spring hangs upon our trees. These are classified by certain moral qualities. Some are religious, some agnostic, and others infidel. It is worthy of emphasis that every system has its press, and that its activity and the sacrifice and consecration by which it is run are not always proportioned to the purity of the system or its direct contribution to the welfare of the race.

Our Christianity is thus thrown upon the defensive. It must use enlightened natural means, and not depend exclusively or generally upon its supernatural origin. A cool and discriminating age will listen to and weigh the asserted claim very much as it would form an opinion concerning any temporal enterprise, without considering the claim to a divine origin. True, the appeal must be finally made to the conscience; but the heart can not be reached while obstructions crowd the head. It will be remembered we do not claim that all Christian literature should be apologetic and on the defensive; for after it has taken the parapet it will advance and plant the cross in the very citadel, the heart. Thus we find that a religious literature is a necessity. Our people will read and be impressed, and one of the most important of all questions is, What shall they read? This depends upon the answer to another question, namely, Why should they read? Our reply is, Read for discipline, information, and culture. In each of these departments are two general classes of books, similar, it may be, in intellectual strength and facility of expression, but widely different in reference to their moral spirit. One will ignore all reference to the agency, and even the name, of God. These books abound with compliments to nature; nature is their deity. Its affinities are omniscience, its force is omnipotence, and its law is justice. Nature builds the world, educates its animals, and furnishes its men. These opinions are paraded by men who have observed widely and thoughtfully. They are skilled in the laboratory, and are all the more insidious because of their familiarity with the elements, forces, and organisms of nature. Their facts can not be denied, their brilliant discoveries must be recognized, and still the problem remains as to the best means of counteractiug their implied and intended disrespect to religion. There are a half-dozen men who, because of their brilliant endowments and bold championship, make the impression that they are vastly more numerous and important than they are, while the truth is that for every one of them there is a score of patient and skillful observers, who become equally familiar with nature, and twine their most brilliant discoveries into garlands for the Savior's cross. Isaac Newton, who lifted a ladder to the stars upon which the latest astronomer mounts to observe, was a devout Christian. Tyndall tells us that Faraday, the acknowledged high-priest in the temple of nature, who was at home in the most intricate labyrinths, and was familiar with her most profound chemical mysteries, with the simplicity of childhood, asked the Father's blessing on the food as the guest and he were seated at the table. Then, if it be true that Christian scientists are morc numerous and equally well informed, we are not under the necessity of drinking from these godless sources; for, though clear as icicles, the latter will be found unnaturally cold. How fortunate if the realm of truth can have the sheen of God's glory resting upon it; if, with our geology, we can have Dana's faith; if by the author of "Ecce Cœlum" the heavens be flooded with a brilliancy unequaled since the day of Chalmers, unless we except our own Bishop Warren, whose study of the sky is but pleasing "Recreations in Astronomy!" We can not write a catalogue, but insist that works of this spirit should displace such as are manifestly unfriendly to the higher wants of the soul.

It is a matter of glad surprise that books of this class are daily multiplying, and proposing to supplement the absence of early educational opportunities. Scieuce and art

have been popularized ; they have been relieved of technicalities and tedious repetitions, and yet left intact so far
as essentials for a general acquaintance with the truth is
concerned. They are adjusted to all years and every capacity. They broaden the outlook of age, and sharpen the
curiosity of youth for a closer intimacy with the priests in
nature's wonderful temple.

Another important purpose to be served by our literature is the culture of the faith. We refer to faith in its
widest and also in its usual significance as the soul's accept-
ance of Christ.

. The swirls of conflict are about centers of religious
dogma. Matter or spirit, immortality or annihilation, happiness for all or retribution for sin, inspiration of the Scriptures or a low plane of Bible origin, are live questions.
Their discussions fill the magazines and the more evanescent periodicals. Our young people become more or less
infected by the heresies. They appear to be called to pass
through a period in life when a false pride and strange
confidence tend presumptuously to discard the old beliefs.
They forget that many experiments have demonstrated
that there can be no morality without a religion. They
fail to remember that these old convictions are intuitive,
and not simply the result of education. It is well for the
Christian world to stop and ask what is to be done. The
danger is not imaginary. The air is full of the spirit of
skepticism. It is boastful and threatening, and because
of its thoughtfulness is deserving of attention. Older persons acquainted with history know that these vaunts have
stood on the coins of the old Roman Empire, were expressed by Celsus, Porphyry, Julian, and in recent times
by Hume, Paine, and the latter's faithful shadow; and
that each in its turn has failed to materialize, and so
should have at least become more modest, though they
have never been more obtrusive and clamorous than now.
This field has not been neglected by sanctified learning.

It has traveled amid the ruins of fallen empires, and delved among the foundations of buried cities. It has scanned the prophetic, and hearkened attentively for the historic echo. It has unearthed the leaves of earth's buried tablet, and traced its ancient history in the light of the Mosaic revelation. It has waited patiently for a light from scientific discovery to shine upon "the wheel broken at the cistern," "the sweet influences of the Pleiades," the weight of the winds. The patient waiting has been rewarded; for comparatively recent discoveries make clear the anticipations of those oldest Scriptures. Daniel waited long for the vindication of his history, but in 1854 it was unearthed at Ur of the Chaldees. The same testimony explained why he took the third instead of the second chariot. Thus we find an abundance of truth with which to counteract the tendency to unbelief. There is Bishop Newton, with his satisfactory testimony to the spirit of prophecy; and Bishop Watson, with his clear refutation of the coarse cavilings of Thomas Paine, which are equally forcible as a reply to his faithful shadow. There is a modern work by Chancellor Dawson, which, with a very wealth of learning, establishes the beautiful harmony between the earth and Genesis. We fearlessly affirm that he who has mastered the contents of these three books will have the modern skeptic at his mercy, since they furnish his quiver from the armory of God's Word, and show him how skillfully to use the same. But who sees these volumes? On what shelves are they found? What young people have so much as read their titles? And why not? for not only are they convincing in the realm of the spiritual, but they add largely to one's fund of general information. In them Herodotus tells us what occurred beyond the realm of Bible lands; the explorer lifts the veil from buried cities, while scientists give us the clearest interpretation of the wonders which belong equally to nature and revelation. We need to go back to a more solid literature, something which will challenge the powers of mind, and contribute toward that intellectual store in which is true imperial dignity. The volumes we name are only typical. I would not stop with them, but others should add their treasures to mind, and so sway the heart before the power of truth. No person disposed to work the mines of truth need be at the mercy of inflated skepticism.

But judicious selections may greatly strengthen the hand which grasps the cross. Many persons neglect their faith as though it was necessarily an evergreen whose nature would endure the fiercest blasts of sarcasm and ridicule. Why any Christian professor should pay a brilliant rhetorician to abuse him is mysterious, and specially when we remember that the faith is a delicate exotic, which can not thrive short of the care one bestows on a rose or geranium. The faith must be cultured. And here again the response to our persistent need will lead us to the library; always remembering, however, to "pray without ceasing." Religious biography is of incalculable advantage in this regard. The Church of Christ has a marvelous history, extending through the ages, into all climes, and among people of every tongue. Every feature of history interlinks with this. Its leading characters have towered into the heights of influence and power, and made a valuable contribution to the world's imperishable records. But it is not of valor in 'directing the energies of sanctified will to which we now so specially refer as conveying the lesson through which the faith may be cultivated. The world may challenge even these in comparison with its proud achievements. But when we touch the conflicts and struggles of the spiritual life we survey an uninvaded province. Here we find the impulses of a hidden life, a path of conquest marked out and trodden by faith. Take the history of Huguenot and Puritan. See them in the mountain passes, trustful and rejoicing, and catch from their sublime faith a new enthusiasm. Come to the New World, and suffer yourself to be borne along on the pioneer fringe of advancing civilization, and you will find the grandest exhibitions of faith as spiritual foes fall, one after another, before the weapons which are "mighty through God to the pulling down of strongholds."

Repentance and conversion presented sharply outlined characteristics. For some reason convictions were intensely deep, and often protracted. It was like the gloom of the night, unrelieved by "a spark of glimmering day." The soul was in no condition to be deceived. Pain is the best judge of the efficacy of pretended solace. But as we linger near, faith has its triumph, gray tints announce the dawn, the brooding shadows flee away; for the Sun of righteousness has arisen with healing in his wings. These supernatural transformations have ever had a strong attraction for the masses; they flock to see and to hear, as on the day of Pentecost. These scenes are now matters of history. Like unfading pictures, they will adorn the walls of the mighty temple with spiritual beauty, for the delight and culture of the Church through the ages. This is

> "A faith that shines more bright and clear
> When tempests rage without,
> That when in danger knows no fear,
> In darkness feels no doubt."

God's Church of to-day needs such a faith as this; for the soul and repentance and conversion are ever the same. There are other means for the quickening of this faith; but I am of opinion that our literature must be an important factor in the largest results. Take a beautiful and renowned life, and trace it back to its beginning, and see its glory bursting forth under the touch of faith with more than the wonder of magic wand, and the desire for such a faith, with its wonderful results, becomes intense. In China the priests say, "When ye pray, think of Bhuda [Buddha?], and you will be transformed into

Bhuda [Buddha?]." So we think it impossible to read of the rills of experience which flow from the touch of faith, without becoming more spiritual and devoted. Why is the eleventh chapter of Hebrews one of the most attractive of the Bible? Because it is a cluster of trophies. The noblest and best names of history are there—men made great by their faith in God and in the power of his might. Read the record, and feel the inspiration. I imagine the Grecian warrior as he casts his eye over his shield embossed with the glorious deeds of his fathers, is reminded of what valor has done, as he plunges into the fight to prove himself worthy of such sires. Let the Church to-day take the shield of faith, the burnished shield, and while the beams of the Spirit's favor kindle upon it, read its pictured record of those " who, through faith, subdued kingdoms, wrought righteousness, and attained the promises." The Church and the individual life needs to be called away from false notions of this conflict. We have followed the enemy of rationalism and science, falsely so called, into an ambush, and have lost the coveted advantage. We have forgotten to distinguish between the reason and the emotions; in fact, we have allowed contempt to be expressed for the emotions without a protest. We have read of force till we have failed to remember that "it was not by might nor by power, but by my Spirit, saith the Lord." We have crowded miracles into the smallest corner of a shrinking credulity. We have substituted an external propriety for the mysteries of godliness. And while, in spite of such numerous and general concessions, there is still some progress, it is not a tithe of what the appliances of the God-given and heaven-endowed machinery are capable of. What is the remedy? More spiritual associations; in the flesh, if possible. " Forsake not the assembling of yourselves together;" and since we are the result of the intellectual food of which we partake, again we advise, Read books of religious experience.

Benjamin Franklin says his thought and conduct received their direction from some tattered leaves of Cotton Mather's "Essay to Do Good." Christians, there is an upper department in your spiritual nature. It demands moral and spiritual culture. Will you seek it? A literature has been provided. It abounds in the most wonderful phases of history, ancient or modern. Magic wand never caused shrub to bud and flower more promptly than have the Sandwich Islands with Sharon's beautiful rose. Aladdin's lamp never beamed its bright light with more power or greater wonder than has our Lord's religion in India and China. Never has the Lord's going marked a plainer path than in the movement called Methodism. Read its history, become familiar with its pioneer characters, trace its development, and remember that its present proportions are largely the result of the permanent record of the devotion of its departed heroes. But do not forget the Bible. For all the purposes mentioned we find a wonderful adaptation in the Holy Scriptures, ranging as they do between the eternities, embellished with the most beautiful lives, the purest sympathies, and to the soul's most anxious inquiries offering the most satisfactory answers. Here is poetry in the rhythm of the skies, history that goes back further than the first human footprint, prophecies that, going before and perching on the summit of a future century, await the certain coming of the slow-moving foot of human history. "Search the Scriptures, for in them ye think ye have eternal life," and they are they which testify of Christ.

Our subject has another important bearing in view of the floods of pernicious literature which threaten to ingulf and destroy the young and impressible minds of our homes and society. This is the day of objectionable fiction, published in every variety and at any price. It adjusts itself to every state, and promises not to burden the mind with thought. Much of it is weak and silly, the variety Bishop

Thomson had in mind when he framed the following recipe:

"Take of words one hogshead,
  Of understanding one drop,
  Of human depravity and coloring matter sufficient quantity;
  Mix, and filter through green or yellow paper."

Much of this trash is shamelessly obscene, and is without higher aim than to pander to the depraved taste of the ignorant and sensual. These will debase the manners, inflame the passions, and send young people, dissatisfied with the staid ways of home and society, on the restless search of an ideal happiness, which has no existence outside the disgusting scenes of its own disordered imagination. Authors may be divided into three classes,—irreproachable, doubtful, and dangerous. The last revels in base creations, the second introduces an occasional decoy, while the first has written no line that will fail to stand the delicate test of the most cultivated and chaste home circle. You must avoid suspicious characters, or be contaminated by the association. They become to the enfeebled mind the veriest realities. They leap from the paper, take shape, and become living beings. Who will wonder at their influence, especially upon the inexperienced and unsuspecting? If these imaginary characters are evil, they lose no moment, opportune or otherwise, in honey-combing virtue and anticipating its fall. And if, on the other hand, they are good and noble, we may expect the reader to go forth breathing a magnanimous and pure spirit. We are asked, May we not read for recreation? I answer, How few know any thing of mental weariness! But even though hour after hour has felt the impress of patient thought creeping slowly over a tired brain, all this is no excuse for poisonous stimulus. If a weary body is an apology for the feverish quickening of alcohol, then we may rekindle the fires of thought with the blue blazes of objectionable fiction. Not that we indiscriminately condemn all fiction; for certainly he is healthier and stronger whose brow is cooled by the ocean breezes of Virgil and the mountain air of Knowles, who has reveled in the Palestine imagery of Willis or the wonderful creations of Milton, Young, Bunyan, Shakespeare, Tennyson, and Longfellow. We would suggest a wider latitude than we can here define; but it must be determined carefully by those who are older and more experienced. Parents should supervise the reading of their children, and furnish the library as carefully as the larder and dining-room. It will cost something to do so; it will cost more to neglect it. If books were simply a superficial luxury, we might applaud his wisdom who filled his library with painted blocks in imitation of costly volumes, or the inexpensive Patent-office Reports. Books are the teachers of the home and a principal factor in its happiness or misery. By them irrepressible activities may be wisely directed; hours of idleness, which are always fruitful with temptations, sweep by only too rapidly on the wings of cheerfulness, when employed in useful reading. There are books for the children. They abound in adventure, describe the traits of animals, and repeat the events of the past. There are books of biography, and others where a few marvels of science may impart a taste for that which is stranger than fiction. These are the teachers who will make the wisest and happiest impress on character. Parents must not excuse themselves for want of time, expense, or taste. The necessity is imperious, like that for bread. To neglect it is to dwarf mind and enfeeble the moral powers. To refuse to supervise the books and reading of young people is to license the devil in his worst and deadliest work.

We close by emphasizing our suggestion. Books are the sources and channels of knowledge, and the inspiration and encouragement to virtue. They are the best aid to parents in the effort to quicken the intelligence, restrain the passions, and culture the emotions.   Thus humanity, regenerated and informed comes to its highest possibilities, and the home becomes the shrine of all that is good in the heart and worthy and great in the life.

W. W. RAMSAY.

XXII.

OUR LITERATURE AS A SOCIAL FORCE IN THE CHURCH.

WHAT should we be without society? Life would indeed be a dreary isolation. God has shown his goodness to man by providing that he shall not be alone. "He setteth the solitary in families." When we come into the world welcoming arms receive us. Throughout infancy smiling faces, beaming with tender love, meet our gaze, and voices musical with gladness sing to us the soothing and sweet lyrics of the heart. Home is the dearest and happiest place on earth, because it is the realm in which the social nature reigns. Home would not be home were its lips dumb, its faces immobile, its sympathies frozen. It is the blissful place it is because there the heart, unrestrained, pours out its best treasures in speech, in smiles, in laughter, and in tears.

As our duties begin but do not end at home, so our social life projects itself beyond the hearthstone. They who neglect home for the sake of outside society are recreant to sacred obligations; they who give all their thought and time to the home circle, to the exclusion of all other social interests, are selfish. Some of the most intimate and tender friendships of Jesus were beyond the circle of his relatives. Religion does not stifle the social instinct, but strengthens it. Christianity is in harmony with man's nature, and develops and adorns that nature, instead of crushing it. It makes society pure, elevating, and helpful. It makes social life, by excluding from it the base passions, together with deceit and tale-bearing, a source of perennial enjoyment. Were Christ's religion universally diffused, and society completely under its dominance, our social fellowship would indeed be a high source of pleasure, even "like to that above."

I once heard a Christian of advanced years say in a meeting that a sanctified person never or rarely laughs. He was no doubt sincere, but sadly ignorant. His representation of Christian piety in its highest stage was a most abhorrent caricature. A sanctified Christian never laugh! Then why did God give us the power to laugh? The very fact that our Maker made us with a capacity for laughter is evidence positive and certain that he intended us to laugh. The trouble is not with the laughing, but with the occasion or cause of the laughter. A Christian can not innocently laugh in derision. He may not laugh at the expense of another's rights or feelings. He must not laugh at sin, however ludicrous may be the shapes it assumes. But in the enjoyment of the gladness of a true, healthful nature, in the circle of friends, amidst "the feast of reason and the flow of soul," he may smile—aye, he may laugh—and be the better for it. It is a sad pity that people, however pious, but who are afflicted with jaundice, should ever attempt to depict religion. It is brilliant with every bright and celestial hue; but to their eyes it is altogether yellow, and they think that the people who say it is not yellow, but aglow with more than diamond splendors, are ignorant of the genuine thing. The world is full of heartache; religion brings to it good cheer. It is full of frowns; religion illumines it with smiles. It is full of groans; religion gives it notes of joy. God means that we shall be happy; sin has made us miserable. He has given to us a religion whose office it is to restore to us the bliss of vanished Eden. Let us receive it as the beautiful, glorious, glad thing that it is, and rejoice in its blessedness.

As religion is adapted to our social nature, so it en-encourages and promotes the exercise and gratification of the social feelings. It bids us not to forsake the assembling of ourselves together. It requires us to visit the widow and the fatherless. It enjoins us to rejoice with those who do rejoice, and to weep with them that weep. It charges us to be kindly affectioned one to another with brotherly love. No man can be a healthy Christian and be morose, and shut up all the good he gets within himself. Christians, on the contrary, are "given to hospitality."

This explains why some ministers, whose gifts are ordinary, are notably popular. They are social. In other words, they pour out the kind and generous sympathies of their hearts in smiles that are like sunshine breaking through the clouds that hang over the hearts of their people. They have a gentle, soothing, appreciative, helpful word for every one. They haste to the chamber of sickness and to the abode of sorrow. And while they have no special attraction as preachers, they are walking benedictions among their people all through the week. Hence they are loved, and the Churches clamor for them as pastors.

The same is true of many laymen. The people love them, and they are very influential in the Church. It is not because of their wealth or talents, but because they help and comfort many by kind words and pleasant attentions. And when in a town there is a Church whose members are largely of that kind, that Church will not lack for adherents, but it will be " the people's Church."

The Church ought to be the most pleasant place. Its society ought to be the most agreeable. In a good degree, this is the case. The most delightful people, the most engaging and helpful associations on earth, are found in the Christian Church. But wherever it is possible to make the Church more attractive and useful, by improving and enlarging its social facilities, it should be done.

An efficient means of doing this is the enlisting of the members of the Church in the work of mental improvement by means of pure and profitable reading. The man or woman who never reads will never be able to exercise a wide social influence. There will, first of all, be a lack of the power of expression. He who does not habitually read will have a deficient vocabulary, and, therefore, will not be ready in speech. Words are to thoughts what the setting is to the jewel. However good, or even brilliant, the thought may be, if it is not presented in fitting language its beauty is obscured. Words fitly chosen can alone set it off at its best. Reading familiarizes us with such words, and enables us to use them with readiness and skill.

Every intelligent person has felt the difficulty of conversing with some people. They have so little knowledge of any thing beyond the daily range of their routine lives that they are unable to enter into any conversation that reaches at all outside of it. Hence a brief chat exhausts their resources. And this is not uncommon. A very intelligent lady remarked to me that very few gentlemen whom she meets in society ever say any thing to her that has any sense in it. She thought that men in social gatherings indulge in only vapid talk to women, and reserve all their weighty speech for their own sex. But the fact is that they do not find railroads and stocks and business affairs generally suitable for the staple of conversation with ladies; and, as too often they know but little about any thing else, they are not able to entertain a lady of intelligence in the drawing-room. Speak to a lady of some notable character of either sex of whom you have read; or of some piquant article or striking fact contained in the magazine or newspaper; of a beautiful poem whose sentiment and rhythm gave you pleasure; of a fresh and pleasing line of thought you have been pursuing as the result of the last new book you have read; and she will be interested and gratified, and never will she say that your conversation was futile.

Speech is a great faculty. Man is the only being on earth that God has gifted with it. What man would be without it we can infer from seeing those whose lips are dumb. They can think, and convey their thoughts rudely by motions, and even by writing, but they can not pour them forth in words. The mind is the fountain of ideas. Speech is the stream that gushes from it, carrying blessing or blight wheresoever it flows.

By the right use of speech our social natures are gratified, our religious affections are improved, and our influence for good increased. The man or woman who in a Church can converse sensibly, attractively, and instructively is, if consistent in conduct, a living power and blessing in that Church. The social gatherings which every Church ought to have from time to time, may be made, by the skillful use of conversation, a means of promoting its interests.

That which we need to make our conversation what it ought to be, is something to talk about. A very eloquent preacher, now deceased, who had a marvelously fine voice and a superior presence, once told me that after one of his first efforts in public, if not his very first, the brother at whose house he stayed told him that he had a good voice, and that the thing he needed now was something to say. And he assured me that he never forgot that significant suggestion. Many and many a time that preacher held and charmed audiences of thousands, and moved numbers to God; but he never forgot the necessity of having something to say.

What every Church needs is not only ministers, but also members, who have something to say, and something worth the saying; something to say in the prayer-meeting and class-meeting; and also something to say in the multifarious occasions of social intercourse. And an important and essential means of making sure of this is habitually to read good books—religious books—and the periodicals, at least the weekly paper, published by the Church. In no other way can he know any thing of the great enterprises carried on by the Church for the conversion of the world.

The social force of the Church would, I think, be much increased were every congregation provided with a library and a reading-room. Let the latter be open every evening for the men who are at work during the day, and for the women every afternoon. Let the religious papers be provided in abundance. Let all our Book Room volumes be in the library. In this way our people will be drawn to books and to reading. Their minds, hearts, and manners will be improved thereby. Their conversation will be suited to minister grace to the hearer. At the same time the Book Concern will become an auxiliary to the pulpit in a larger degree. Then, instead of vapid nonsense, which too often drivels from silly lips in our social gatherings, the conversation will be charming, refreshing, improving, because it will flow forth from minds stored with profitable thoughts and instructive facts. Then new converts will be helped, rather than hindered, by the society of older members, and the Church will enjoy a genial, winning, intelligent piety.

JOHN ATKINSON.

XXIII.

LITERATURE OF THE HIGHER CHRISTIAN LIFE.

THIS is an age of books. In material with which to make them, in facilities for their rapid and extended multiplication, in means for their easy and wide distribution, and in the opportunities afforded for their composition, no age ever equaled our own.

In such a time it is but part of the logic of events that literature shall assume, to a large extent, the form of monographs. Accordingly, we find nearly every possible theme known to our day worked up in this form. Books, ably written, on single topics is a prominent feature, as it is also one of the most satisfactory characteristics of the literature of the day.

It is well that religious literature is rapidly assuming this form. It may thus hope for better treatment, wider circulation, and a more profitable reading.

There is a literature of the higher Christian life. I need scarcely say that in this department Methodism is exceedingly rich, or that the Methodist Episcopal Church has upon the shelves of her great publishing-houses works upon this important subject which, for thoroughness of treatment, variety of style, and richness of experience by which they are illustrated, are not anywhere excelled. And we have not only good books which treat this subject directly, so that, in the language of Bishop Merrill, "the literature is exceedingly rich, and in it are found ample vindications of the doctrine and clear and worthy representations of every aspect of the experience," but the higher life in its teachings and experiences is found in the biographies of such precious characters as Bramwell, Carvosso, Mrs. Fletcher, Lady Maxwell, Hester Ann Rogers, Madame Guyon, Fisk, Olin, Hamline, Cookman, and others. And in the published journals of such as Wesley and Asbury do we find it, while our theological standards teach and defend it, our denominational histories record its struggles and victories, our periodicals never fail to give it place in their columns, and our hymns are fairly aglow with the glory of this exalted experience. What a hymn is the "Wrestling Jacob" of Charles Wesley—a very epic of the higher life!

It should be no matter for surprise that we, as a Church, possess such a literature, or that we make it so prominent. Did we not we would be untrue to our history and untrue to our birthright; for while all the Churches now practically admit this experience, each using its own language, it has to us a peculiar relation.

There is not and never has been a form of faith, whether Christian or heathen, which does not teach the necessity of purity in order to heaven. But Methodism seemed to have for her distinctive mission the bringing to light anew the old Gospel truth that man may be "holy in heart in this life."

The embryo of Methodism was the Holy Club of Oxford. The aim of those struggling souls was purity of heart and life, and the avowed purpose of the Wesleys was "to spread Scripture holiness." Methodism was not an ecclesiastical movement, not a contention for doctrinal formulæ, but a restoration of spiritual life and a revival of religious experience. And Methodism went out upon her mission with this one purpose, and this alone, to lead men to a holy life; and her whole economy was developed about this one idea. Her Church polity, her symbols of faith, her various prudential regulations, her peculiar means of grace, the matter and manner of her pulpit ministrations are in general harmony with this thought. It is well for us as a people that all through our history we have kept in such prominence the "only one condition previously required of those who desire admission into these societies"—"a desire to flee the wrath to come and to be saved from their sins." Just as we depart from the spirit of this "one condition" shall we be in danger of schism and fierce contention. Here at least must we stand, whatever may be the questions which are now upon us, or which may arise in the future.

Methodism must hold her people, and hold a common Protestantism, up to the standard which, under God, she had the honor to raise anew,—"Holiness unto the Lord." All other questions are incidental to this; all polity is worthless which does not work to this end. She must hold to this against the misrepresentations of her enemies and against the false representations of this glorious experience among those supposed to be her friends. She must hold to it against the strong current of worldliness which sets upon her; nor must she be ashamed of it in the midst of an idolatry of culture, an idolatry of intellect, or an idolatry of mammon. This culture of the higher life, this science of salvation, this treasure of the kingdom, must be held as needing apology to nothing earthly and as man's noblest pursuit and choicest possession. If the "signs of the times" may be read, do they not indicate a better day for the doctrine of the higher life? There is unusual and wide-spread interest in it among all the Churches. A healthy reaction has already begun from what must historically stand in the records of our Church as a period of decline with reference to this phase of doctrine—a decline brought about by the sad handling it has received at the hands of those whose zeal was disproportionate to their knowledge and prudence. We hail this reaction, and firmly trust that, baptized with new life and clothed with new power, the doctrine and experience of the higher Christian life may be exalted in the Church and by all who serve at her altars or thereon lay the consecrated offerings of their hearts.

But it becomes a question of vital moment as to what agencies are best able to promote the true and clear understanding of this doctrine, and stimulate its experiences. Among the chief must ever be the preaching of the Gospel. What is not taught and honored in the pulpit will not long remain in the pew; nor can the pew long remain unaffected by the earnest, Scriptural, and judicious presentation of truth. The ordinary channels of grace may each be made an agent in this work. The testimonies of those who have attained, and especially their consistent lives, are not least of these agencies for teaching men that there is an upward path, and in leading them to seek it.

And literature has its power. There are few more potent agencies than books, good or bad, silently yet surely to form character and lead to action. Among the publications of our denominational press we find ample assurance that there has not been left to ephemeral articles in our periodicals or to outside and somewhat irresponsible publications the care of an interest which deserves the best treatment. We have a standard literature of the higher Christian life, one carefully written, and which deserves the highest commendation, largest confidence, and widest patronage. This literature deserves to be in the homes of all the people. It should be read and re-read, until the sentiments and aspirations contained permeate the thoughts and feelings.

What untold results for good might follow the perusal of these books by all the people! What problems of ministerial inefficiency, of discouragement in Church work, of spiritual weakness, of want of revival power, and want of faith, and want of means to carry on the work of the kingdom, would such reading solve! How the Church would be energized, and how her spiritual life would be kindled anew! It is doubtful whether it is generally known, even among Methodists themselves, to what extent the Church is ready to supply works on this subject. With Wesley's "Christian Perfection" and Fletcher's works the Methodists of half a century ago were quite familiar; but it is to be feared that even these invaluable little volumes are known to few outside the ministry. To these standards have been added others, some of which deserve special mention that they may be brought to the attention of the people.

A valuable contribution is the work entitled "Saving Faith," by that sturdy logician, Dr. Israel Chamberlayne, which, while it does not deal directly with the theme of holiness, lays a foundation for its more intelligent understanding. "Walking in the Light," by D. D. Buck, D. D., is a convenient little volume, which develops in a manner at once attractive and practical that choice saying of John, "If we walk in the light as he is in the light, we have fellowship one with another, and the blood of Jesus Christ his Son cleanseth us from all sin." It will repay a close perusal.

The great duty and high privilege of entire consecration to Christ is most fully treated in Dr. Thomas Carter's volume entitled, "All for Christ." It is a book to stir the soul, and cause it to desire harmony with God. See how the author himself pleads for the use of this literature and for the verity of this experience: "What shall we say of Fletcher, Bramwell, Abbott, Carvosso, Nelson, Hester Ann Rogers, Mrs. Fletcher, Lady Maxwell, and a thousand others? Were they all mistaken, and did they perpetuate a base falsehood when they said they enjoyed the blessing of perfect love? Who can read that noble monument of untiring research and literary talent, Stevens's 'History of Methodism,' without being convinced that herein lay the strength of the founders of our Church? If every family would possess themselves of these volumes and read them, we have no doubt the result would be a grand revival throughout all the Church. How few of us in these modern times have allowed our souls to be quickened and inspired by the perusal of the lives of Fletcher, Bramwell, and the other heroes of faith to whom we have referred! If the apostle Paul, in the eleventh chapter of Hebrews, cited the worthies who preceded the era in which he lived to inflame the zeal and strengthen the faith of the early Christians, how appropriate it is that we should seek incentives to a closer walk with God by an acquaintance with the courage, the struggles, the sufferings of those to whom we owe the institutions under which we dwell! And then, as we look farther back upon the era of the great Reformation, and behold Luther, Knox, Cobham, Savonarola, Huss, Lefevre, Gustavus Adolphus, and the great army of reformers and martyrs in England, Scotland, France, Germany, and Italy, giving all for Christ, many of them dying at the stake, on the block, in the dungeon, as they laid the foundations of the religious liberty which we now enjoy, who can count up the numbers who served God with a perfect heart?"

"The Believer's Victory over Satan's Devices," although from the pen of a Calvinist, contains much that is invaluable on the higher life. Who can afford to omit the reading of a book which samples like this?—"Take, again, the simple fact of God's loving and abiding presence, sweetly manifested as a reality to the soul's inner consciousness. The result is, that we know and feel that we live and move and have our being in him, as the body lives and moves and has its being in the atmosphere which surrounds it. The soul communes with him as with an intimate, present friend. Prayer is no longer an effort to address God in the distant heavens, but is as natural and easy and spontaneous as the communion, face to face, of loving friends. It is not limited to particular hours and forms, but goes on very much as two kindred and loving minds dwelling together will, by the laws of want and suggestion, and by the very tendency of love to communicate, be always expressing themselves to each other. This presence of God may sometimes dazzle and almost blind the soul with its effulgence, as with Moses when God showed him something of his glory; but, generally, the Lord will so manifest his presence that it will be to the soul what the air is to the body, the natural, healthy, life-giving, and most satisfying element in which it is possible to live. When by this manifestation the believer's heart becomes the Shekinah wherein Jehovah dwells, it must have a life rich with all heavenly elements."

"Holiness the Birthright of All God's Children," by Dr. J. T. Crane is a valuable and very readable production.

A vigorous little volume is "The Satisfactory Portion," by A. C. George, D. D. A paragraph must suffice: "No possessions, honors, friendships, or pleasures can fill the 'aching void' in a poor sinner's soul. The 'dearest idol' of a blindly loving heart is not to be compared with Jesus enthroned in the affections. And if our heavenly Father shall lead us to taste the emptiness of the world, and prove of how little worth are its applause, its dignities, and its glories, it is that our longing desires may go out after the imperishable good which blossoms in the promises of the Gospel, and drops in precious fruit from the tree of life in the soul's paradise, at the right-hand of God."

The works of Rev. L. R. Dunn seem to be written out of rich experience. From "Holiness to the Lord" I take the following: "All systems of philosophy and ethics have labored to reform and purify the outward character and life; to make the stream sweet, the fruit good; to cleanse the outside of the cup or platter, or to whiten the sepulcher. But the Christian system looks first of all to the utter eradication of all roots of bitterness from the heart, to the purification of the fountain, to making the tree good, to bursting the cerements of the spiritual grave, and giving a resurrection from the moral death which has reigned within. This system teaches us that there can be no outward holiness in the life, in the conduct, and in the habit, unless the inward principle be implanted within, and dominating over all the powers of the soul." His work entitled "Mission of the Spirit" is a grand work on that noble theme. How rich is that chapter on "The Comforter as the Sanctifier!"

This literature of the higher life has been honored by the pens of some of the bishops, among whom we mention Peck, Foster, and Merrill. In "Aspects of Christian Experience," by the latter, the author thus writes: "Methodism teaches the doctrine of Christian perfection, and attaches importance to it as a distinctive feature to be insisted upon in public and private; and because of this peculiarity she has encountered no little opposition, and has been compelled to vindicate her faith by earnest and continued discussions. Some progress has been made in the work of impressing her views upon the minds of other Christian people, so that but few of the old forms of disputation are required; but the time has not yet come for silence, for many yet fail to appreciate the ground she occupies or the spirit in which this faith is held." What ringing words are these, and how they should sound through the aisles of our temples and in our homes: "The promotion of holiness is the mission of the Church. This was the life-work of the Son of God and the design of his death. 'He gave himself for us, that he might redeem us from all iniquity, and purify unto himself a peculiar people zealous of good works.' Then, as the work of the Church is to carry out to completion the mission of Christ, its chief calling is to establish holiness in the earth. This is particularly the providential allotment of Methodism. Mr. Wesley never felt that he was called of God to found a denomination; but he continually proclaimed that God had thrust him out to raise up a holy people. The Methodist Discipline announces that our calling is to spread 'Scriptural holiness over these lands.' Every minister ordained in the connection believes in the doctrine, expects to be made perfect in love in this life, groans after full redemption, and pledges fidelity to this calling. How, then, with any consistency, can this topic be made a specialty or an exceptional thing in the Church? It is the common duty and privilege of all the thousands of our Israel, the aim of all our services, the end of all our preaching, praying, singing, and evangelizing. It is too late to say that we are unscriptural. The Gospel is full of the thing we mean. It pervades the law and the prophets, the types and promises, the songs and sermons, the narratives and epistles of the Old and New Testaments. It thunders from Sinai, and shines from the Mount of Beatitudes. It comes down to us through the ages, attested by the testimony of martyrs and saints, and we hail it as the heritage of the Church till time shall end. Technicalities are of little value. Freedom from sin is the great thing."

"The Central Idea of Christianity," by Bishop Peck, is a standard on this theme, one of our classics. Written a quarter of a century ago, it has lived and worked along with its author. In a masterly manner the writer reveals the crystalline center of our faith, the "Idea" about which the Gospel forms itself. The venerable bishop thus closes his volume: "But these are not our appeals. They rise directly out of the fact that holiness is the central idea of Christianity. This fact, sustained by various indubitable evidences founded upon the Word of God, is before us. With what views and feelings is it contemplated? What disposition is to be made of it? Let the reader answer on his knees. Before the Searcher of hearts let him renounce the world and all carnal indulgence forever. Let him seek to secure permanent reformation by the purification of the heart through the blood of Christ, by the power of

the Holy Ghost; and having proved, by a living, triumphant faith, the blessedness of perfect love, let him obey till
he dies the great command, 'Grow in grace, and in the
knowledge of our Lord and Savior Jesus Christ,' and in a
heaven of unsullied holiness he will prove the fullness of
the Savior's beatitude, 'Blessed are the pure in heart, for
they shall see God.'"

Another of our Christian classics is the very scholarly
and thorough work of Dr. George Peck entitled, "Christian Perfection," a volume which must always occupy a
high place in our literature. The author handles his great
theme with the strength of a giant, yet with the tenderness
of a loving Christian heart. This is certainly one of the
best and most judicious books on this subject ever penned.

Bishop Foster laid the Church under obligation in the
writing of his "Christian Purity." It is a work abounding
and fairly overflowing with choice paragraphs on the
higher life. It is full of meat, a book hard to lay down,
one stimulating to holy meditation and to pious feeling,
and inspiring to the experience of heart purity. I can
give but few of these gems: "The believer is under obligation to possess all, to the last degree, of that which he
may possess in Christ. Present possibility of holiness de-
termines present duty of holiness." "What the Gospel
proposes as the privilege of man, what it promises to do
for him, particularly as it respects moral and spiritual elevation, must become the question which, by force of irresistible attraction, will yet draw all minds and sway all
hearts." "The physical man has had his day—a day
of darkness and debasement, of sensualism and crime; the
intellectual man is enjoying his—a day of refulgence and
splendor; the spiritual man must have his, and of as superior brightness as the interests pertaining to the soul are
superior to those pertaining to the perishable body."
What a trumpet blast does the good bishop sound in this:
"If there be one want of Christendom, at this time, greater

than all others, it is this: There is learning, there is piety, there is zeal; in our belief there never was more, perhaps never so much; but there is still something more wanted than extraordinary learning, piety, and zeal. It is that entire consecration, that higher development of the Christian life throughout the entire Church which can never take place until she sees the fullness of her privilege and the terribleness of her obligations. With low, or even medium views on these points, she can never pass into that higher life, that 'fullness of the blessing of the Gospel,' that 'unity of the faith,' that dwelling in God, which she must attain before the world becomes regenerate through her instrumentality." What an earnest appeal the author here makes!—such an appeal, surely, as ought to move any person in whose soul is the faintest spark of the new life of Christ: "Taking the twin lamps of truth, the Bible and conscience, with sincere prayers for the guidance of the Holy Ghost, make that diligent search which the importance of the case requires. Be candid with yourself. Make no extenuation, no apology; use no tenderness. Ferret every recess thoroughly; probe to the bottom; pass through every chamber of your soul; search it through and through with a determination to know your case, to look at yourself stripped of every disguise. What do you find? Are there no idols in the sacred temple? no 'images of gold?' no 'Babylonish garments?' no concealed 'spies?' no pride, no envy, no jealousy, no anger, no malice, no undue love of the world, no undue desire for the praise of men, no improper ambition? Does God possess your heart without a rival? Are you wholly the Lord's? O for faithfulness! Would you attain to holiness? Linger at this point. Have no mercy on yourself; be resolved to know the worst. You may have such discoveries as will astonish and distress you. Still make diligent search. What is your example? Is it all that a Christian's ought to be? Do you daily exhibit, in the family, in the social circle, in your business, everywhere, those tempers which should adorn the Christian character? What is your influence? Is it, so far as it is under your control, always decidedly and undividedly for Christ? With these and such questions closely investigate your condition, praying for light and guidance and conviction. What is the result? Do you find great want? Are there sins remaining within that need to be cast out? What now? Do you feel your need? If not, dwell upon it, in earnest prayer for the enlightening agency of the Spirit, until you do feel."

One of the latest contributions to the literature of the higher Christian life is "Love Enthroned"—a royal title, and one fitting the product of the gifted and learned author, Rev. Daniel Steele, D. D. It is a carefully, beautifully, and earnestly written work, made the more valuable and practical by the introduction of the writer's own experience, and the design of which is, "in true Pauline style, to testify unto you the Gospel of the grace of God." The volume is thoroughly Scriptural, and, of course, must therefore be Methodistic. It seems like a work inspired by the love of the author's heart. It was certainly born of gratitude for experiences possessed and desire to make known the high privileges of the Christian life to others. Every chapter is a jewel. It is a misfortune to any Christian earnestly desiring nearness to God to pass it by unread. How true are these words: "To how many Christian souls is God veiled! They have need to pray, 'Hide not thy face from me.' Many of these do not know that God is pleased to make communications of grace which shall be like the removal of a veil from the face of one beloved and adored. Such manifestations of grace to others are believed to be exceptional, that only a few persons of a peculiar and delicate spiritual organization can receive of Christ's love; whereas we are living in a dispensation in which more glorious unveilings of God to every believing soul are possible than was ever enjoyed by Enoch,

Abraham, Isaiah, or Daniel. 'The light of the moon has become as the light of the sun, and the light of the sun shall be sevenfold.' How shall not the ministration of the Spirit be rather glorious?" How well would it be if all who enjoy not this experience were to heed this counsel!— "Faith is the only door through which God enters the soul. Cease philosophizing, and take up the work of believing. No sinner would ever find Jesus if he should stubbornly seek him with the lamp of reason, refusing the lamp of faith. No imperfect believer can grasp Jesus as the complete Savior so long as he relies upon speculative reason as a supplement of his defective faith. Pride of intellect, the subtilest form of pride, is keeping thousands of Christians from that higher knowledge of God which is obtained only by climbing up the ladder of faith. It is not necessary for any soul to discriminate intellectually between regeneration and entire sanctification, or between the stream of love shed abroad by the Spirit of adoption and the ocean of love which the abiding Comforter pours around the purified soul, in order to enter upon this great salvation. As it is enough for the penitent to know that he is guilty and Jesus can pardon, so it is enough for the longing Christian to know that he is hungry, and there must be perfect satisfaction somewhere in the universe correlated to that intense and painful appetency."

Such is a view of the literature of the higher Christian life as that literature is provided by the press of the Methodist Episcopal Church.

J. ALABASTER.

XXIV

OUR LITERATURE AS AN EVANGELISTIC AGENCY

METHODISM is a synonym for evangelism. Its genius is revivalistic. A "passion for souls" is inherent to its life. This spirit has pervaded its history, and permeated all its agencies; it has gone into its polity, its ministry, its literature. Methodism has a literature that is both evangelical and evangelistic—a literature that is not only sound in doctrine, Scriptural in spirit, and emphatic respecting the vital and saving truths of the Gospel, but which exalts the conversion of souls, teaches the personal qualifications for it, and inspires a holy, intense enthusiasm in its prosecution. While our literature is wide in its range of Biblical and theological discussions, rich and crudite in its doctrinal and ecclesiastical treatises, ample in its historical and biographical material, deep and spiritual in its devotional productions; yet had it not a distinctively evangelistic tendency all its other excellencies would fail to impart the knowledge and inspiration indispensable to the aggressive work of Christianity.

The evangelistic power is a thing *sui generis.* It is a gift of the Holy Ghost. It is more than personal salvation or earnest piety; it is that help of the Holy Spirit in the experience of the child of God which makes his personality and powers effective, and imparts to him a sustained, quenchless impulse in soul-saving.

This evangelistic power has been the divine pillar of cloud by day and the pillar of fire by night, leading on the Church in its uninterrupted march of holy triumphs for eighteen centuries. It is the secret of the rapid growth and grand achievements of early Methodism. Whatever, therefore, in the agencies of our Church, tends to cultivate its spiritual power should be known, appreciated, and utilized by its ministry and membership. Our evangelistic literature is so full and varied in its character that every man of God among us, whether in pulpit or pew, may become thoroughly furnished unto the work of saving souls. The shelves of our Book Concerns are loaded with volumes, every chapter of which is like a live coal; books which, if even casually perused, kindle a warmth that is uncommon to the heart. To exhume all the wealth and exhibit all the power of our evangelistic literature would require the compass of a volume, rather than the dimensions of a chapter. Only a view of the general outlines, together with a few of the choicest features, can here be given.

The wealth of our evangelistic literature is to be found in three mines—our books, our periodicals, and our tracts.

1. *Our Books.* Among these a large number are evangelistic in design, treating of the nature, attainment, and application of revival power. There are also others, not distinctively evangelistic in title or contents, which contain incidental passages, paragraphs, and chapters pregnant with spiritual thought. Many of our historical, biographical, homiletic, periodical, and general works disseminate a revival influence; for a little leaven of spiritual power can leaven the whole lump of an otherwise lifeless and fruitless religious book. The Biblical, theological, and doctrinal works of Methodism are grand repositories of evangelistic thought. Our Commentaries, such as Clarke's Benson's, Watson's, Wesley's, Nast's, and Whedon's, abound in expositions and homiletical suggestions so quickening as to transform the devout student of them from a passive, pietistic life into an aggressive, soul-saving force. There is inherent in our commentaries that soul-

quickening power which belongs to Luther's expositions. It was while listening to the reading of Luther's "Preface to the Romans" that John Wesley "felt his heart strangely warmed."

The doctrinal books of Methodism are many, and, as a class, they are able, safe, and Scriptural, while some are so pronounced in the evangelistic power as never to be read without drawing the soul nearer to the source of power. Fletcher's works stand foremost in this class of books. No one can read his matchless defense and comprehensive statements of spiritual truth without seeing how doctrinal theology may become a living power in soul saving, and without coveting the gift of effectiveness, and without being instructed in the way to its attainment. Our theologies, Watson's, Raymond's, and Pope's, are not wanting in evangelistic vigor, though this is not their distinctive temper.

The works on different phases of doctrine are numerous: "Atonement," by Miley; "Justification," by Davies; "Freedom of the Will," by Whedon; "Love Enthroned," by Steele, a fresh and scholarly discussion of evangelical perfection; "Mission of the Holy Spirit," by Dunn, a masterly presentation of the personality, work, and dispensation of the Holy Spirit; "The Doctrine of the Holy Spirit," by Walker, emphasizing some of the operations of the Holy Spirit in respect to human personality and prevailing prayer. "Aspects of Christian Experience," by Bishop Merrill, needs only to be read to discover its spiritual as well as its intellectual worth; "The Philosophy of the Plan of Salvation," by Walker, is a book belonging to the category of evidences rather than that of doctrine. It is written in a philosophical style, and is an adopted rather than original book in Methodism.

The sermonic literature of Methodism is a stream of living waters. Its fountain-head is *Wesley's Sermons.* It is a misfortune to any of our ministers not to have saturated themselves with them. Our preachers read South, Taylor, Spurgeon, Bushnell, and Beecher; but Wesley transcends them all in that which nourishes "able ministers of the New Testament." "Watson's Sermons" are in the spirit and power of the Elijah that came before him. "Bishop Hamline's Sermons" are freighted with revivalistic power. They are as saintly as Fletcher's "Checks," and as finished as Punshon's "Lectures." "Sermons on Consecration," by A. C. George, have heart-power in them. "Simpson's Yale Lectures on Preaching" burn with the holy flame that has clothed his long and effective ministry. Many other volumes of sermons, and some single sermons, deserve mention, but space forbids.

The devotional books issued from our presses are numerous. The Christian classics, "Imitation of Christ," Mrs. Rowe's "Devout Exercises of the Heart," Baxter's "Saints' Everlasting Rest," Law's "Serious Call," Alleinc's "Alarm," "Extracts from Rutherford," and "Meditations of Madame Guyon," are well known. "All for Christ," by T. Carter; "Consecration," by A. C. George; "Mile-stone Papers," by D. Steele; "Triumphing over Death," by Hall; "Death-bed Scenes," by Bishop Clark, are later books, but not inferior in evangelistic power. These devotional works, together with "Perfect Love," by J. A. Wood, and "New Testament Piety," by W McDonald, are adapted to nourish the Christian graces.

There are also many other special books, which are devoted to the promotion of evangelism. "The Winning Worker," "Revivals of Religion," and "Camp-meetings," by Porter, are a whole curriculum of themselves in the line of Christian endeavor. "The Gift of Power," by Platt; "God's Method with Man," by Gorham; "Faith and its Effects," by Phœbe Palmer; and the "Tongue of Fire," by Arthur, form a library which would make its student, like Barnabas, a man full of faith and of the Holy Ghost.

2. *Our Periodical Literature.* The great family of our

"Advocates" contain currently such inspiring religious intelligence, ample reports of revivals, thrilling narratives of dying triumphs, interesting descriptions of heroic labors for souls, refreshing discussions of methods, and earnest presentations of spiritual truth as to exert a wonderful influence upon the soul. One of these, by the accurate and elaborate account it gave weekly of the great revival in Cincinnati, Ohio, under the labors of Rev. Thomas Harrison, scattered its fire throughout its patronizing territory. He who reads regularly one of our Church papers will have a sustained interest in and sympathy for the revivalistic work of Methodism. There are also some special periodicals, not all of them issued from our own presses, that are recognized forces in Church work. These we can not name here.

Our Berean Lesson publications are entitled to take rank among our evangelistic forces. They are not only safe, but saving in their influence. It has been noticeable of late how largely the fruit of revivals has been gathered from among those attendant upon our Sabbath-schools. The Berean sowing of nine years past is now yielding a precious harvest in souls. "The Sunday-school Journal" is no doubt raising up many of the wise who shall shine as the brightness of the firmament, and multiplying the number of those who shall turn many to righteousness and shine as the stars for ever. The "Lesson Leaves" are in like manner proving themselves efficacious for the spiritual redemption and health of 'our children and youth.

3. *Our Tract Literature.* A careful examination of the tract publications of the Methodist Episcopal Church will reveal the fact that in them we have a wide range of works, able in literary excellence, largely spiritual, and systematized in convenient series. The number adapted to awakening sinners, encouraging penitents, instructing converts, perfecting believers, and increasing the working power of the Church, is very large. Its "Pocket

Series" is concise and entertaining, and so available in form as to enable every Christian business, professional, traveling, or laboring man to be a daily evangelistic colporteur, doing good as they have opportunity. The "Leaflet Series" is serviceable for scattering far and wide the seeds of spiritual truth; and these are re-enforced by the "New Series," the "Revised Series," the "Selected Series," and the "Tract Book Series."

Testimonials are not wanting attesting the usefulness of tracts. One alone in our list, the "Dairyman's Daughter," has been instrumental in scores, if not hundreds, of conversions. The consecrated workers of Methodism will find our tracts a healthful arm of power in enhancing their evangelistic usefulness. Tracts are appreciated by those who are spiritual and aglow with love for souls. Such do not despise the day of small things. They have learned how pebbles, hurled in faith, slay giants. A scholarly and successful minister said, "Never until I received 'the baptism of fire' did I know the worth of tracts."

Our *résumé* of the evangelistic resources of the literature of Methodism is not exhaustive, yet it shows how prolific it is in productions adapted to beget, increase, and apply evangelistic power.

If the Church should decline in revival power, it will be no fault of her literature; for it is abundant, and there lives in it the baptism of fire which crowned the head of its tireless and successful founder.

S. A. KEEN.

XXV.

A PLAN FOR ORGANIZING A CHURCH LIBRARY.

IF John Wesley can be called the father of cheap religious literature he can also be called the father of the Church library idea. At London, Bristol, and Newcastle he established libraries for himself and his assistants, in each of which the nucleus consisted of fifty well-selected volumes. It is curious, as well as instructive, to note the distribution of the subjects and the proportionate number of books given to each by the conference in these libraries. They consisted of eleven books on divinity, four on physic, two on natural philosophy, one (Whiston) on astronomy, one (the Universal) on history, two (Spenser and Milton) on poetry, sixteen in Latin, twelve in Greek, and one (Buxtorf's Bible) in Hebrew.

What was done by Methodism in 1745, in a circumscribed way, is now proposed to be done throughout the whole Church, for the benefit and culture of all the membership. The multiplication of libraries of a somewhat doubtful character, the pestiferous streams of moral polluted literature which are flowing from the press, and the insatiable thirst of the present generation for reading matter require that the Church, as a matter of self-defense, shall counteract the evil by furnishing mental food for her membership, and especially for the young, that shall not only stimulate, but edify, confirm, instruct, and elevate, morally and spiritually.

This object is met in the establishment of the Church library. The literature adapted to this purpose is so varied, rich, and inexpensive, that the humblest Church organization can afford to form the nucleus of a library, which will, in course of time, not only increase in volume, but will also contribute to the intellectual growth and influence of the Church. If thought advisable, there might be a combination of the Sunday-school and Church library, and it is possible that some of the evils heretofore complained of in the Sunday-school library, by the greater diligence and scrutiny that would be imparted, would thus be avoided. The lax manner in which many of these juvenile libraries were formerly selected would give place to greater care, and the increased interest in literature would tend to make the Church the intellectual and moral, as well as religious, center of the community.

In the beginning the library should be *founded.* It is the glory of such men as Astor, Peabody, and Carnegie, that after the death of these men, their works do follow them. The library remains not only a monument to their memory, but a constantly augmenting power for good. Now, although our people may not be able to give what these wealthy men have done, they can do something toward the founding of a library. In every congregation, however obscure, may be found a few men who can furnish the youth of their community with more books than Horace Greeley had access to in his young manhood, and they may thus become the unconscious formers of habits and cultivators of intellects that otherwise might lie dormant. In the work of forming these libraries liberal-minded men, desirous of benefiting the young, and who themselves were deprived of such advantages in their youth, have already given large sums to this work.

But if no men of means should be found ready to step into the breach, let not the humblest Church despair. Membership at a dollar a year will enable such a Church to lay a good foundation for a library. Let the matter be pressed upon the attention of all; let it be shown that by combining the resources the general good will be effected; let the books be valuable and well chosen, and the library must grow, and grow to such proportions that the sacrifices that may be necessary for its implantation will be amply compensated by its usefulness and success.

The Church evidently contemplates that the subject of general education shall be made prominent. It has already made provision in its ecclesiastical councils for committees on the subject. A committee on education is annually elected in every Church, and it would be a great furtherance of the cause, if, at the time of their election, the presiding elder should explain that this work of founding libraries legitimately comes under their supervision.. In the constitution governing library associations in the Methodist Episcopal Church, it will be seen that cognizance has been taken of this committee, and that it is a constitutional factor in all such associations.

The work of organizing libraries has been in progress for a few years past, and the enterprise is meeting with a large measure of success. In those places where libraries have been established longest the interest continues unabated. Let every Church make provision for the intellectual development of its own congregation. Let the beautiful membership certificates of shares, which have been so neatly and artistically prepared, be distributed throughout all the membership as insignia of progress and wisdom, and let the work of circulating our literature by this process engage the thought and co-operation of all the office-bearers and well-wishers of the Church. So shall we contribute to the moral and intellectual advancement of the race, and harvests shall go on blooming in the long years of the future.

We append a copy of the "Constitution and By-laws governing Library Associations of the Methodist Episcopal Church," from which will be seen the practicability and feasibility of the movement. They are as follows:

CONSTITUTION.

ARTICLE I.—NAME.

This Association shall be called the Library Association of the Methodist Episcopal Church of ——.

ARTICLE II.—OBJECT.

The object of this Association shall be to provide its members with pure, instructive, and religious reading.

ARTICLE III.—QUARTERLY CONFERENCE COMMITTEE.

The Quarterly Conference Committee on Education, as provided for in the Book of Discipline of the Methodist Episcopal Church, shall be *ex-officio* members of this Association, and also of the Board of Control, with right to speak and vote upon all questions.

ARTICLE IV.—MEMBERSHIP.

Membership in this Association shall be represented by shares of one dollar each, and shall be renewed annually by the additional payment of one dollar. And any shareholder shall be entitled to all the privileges of the Association.

ARTICLE V.—LIFE MEMBERS.

Any person donating at one time the sum of twenty-five dollars to this Library Association shall be constituted a life member of the Association, and shall be entitled to all its privileges.

ARTICLE VI.—HONORARY MEMBERS.

Any person donating at one time the sum of one hundred dollars to this Library Association shall be constituted an honorary member of this Association, and shall be entitled to all the privileges of regular membership for life; shall also have the privilege of meeting with the Board of Control, and speaking upon all questions pertaining to the management of this Association; and also of designating each year five persons, who shall thereupon be entitled to receive certificates of membership for that calendar year.

ARTICLE VII.

Any person purchasing one or more shares may transfer the same, or any number thereof, to any person or persons whom he may elect, and said persons shall become members of the Association and entitled to all its privileges.

ARTICLE VIII.—OFFICERS.

The officers of this Association shall be a President, Vice-president, Treasurer, and Librarian, who shall act as Secretary; each performing the duties pertaining to the respective office.

ARTICLE IX.—BOARD OF CONTROL.

There shall be a Board of Control composed of the officers of the Association, the Quarterly Conference Committee on Education, and five members of the Association, to be elected annually at the regular election of officers; provided that two-thirds of said Board of Control shall be members of the Methodist Episcopal Church.

ARTICLE X.—GENERAL MANAGEMENT.

The Board of Control shall have general management of all the affairs of the Association, shall fill any vacancy which may occur in the board of officers, shall appoint a committee of three members of the Association, of which the pastor of the Church shall be chairman, whose duty it shall be to determine what books shall be placed in the library; this committee being authorized to purchase such books at any time, provided there are sufficient funds in the treasury.

ARTICLE XI.—ELECTION OF OFFICERS.

Section 1. The pastor of the Church shall be *ex-officio* President of this Association.

Sec. 2. The other officers of this Association shall be elected annually, on the first Tuesday of January; notice of such election being previously given in the public congregation.

Sec. 3. All elections shall be by ballot, and a majority of the votes cast shall constitute an election.

ARTICLE XII.—APPLICATION FOR MEMBERSHIP.

Application for membership shall be received at any time, and certificates of shares issued by the President, provided such membership shall date with the beginning of the current year.

BY-LAWS.

1. The President shall sign all shares issued by the Association.

2. None but members of the Association shall have access to the Library.

3. No member shall retain a book in his possession for a longer period than two weeks, nor have more than one book at the same time.

4. Any member retaining a book for a longer period than two weeks without renewal shall be fined ten cents for each week, or fractional part of a week, he retains such book thereafter, and shall not be allowed to draw another book from the library until such fine is paid.

5. Members shall be held responsible for the proper care of books in their possession.

6. No member drawing books will be allowed, under any condition, to exchange books with other members.

7. At the instance of three members of the Board of Control the President may call a special meeting of the Board of Control, or of the Association, for the transaction of business.

8. Five members of the Board of Control shall constitute a quorum for the transaction of business.

9. Fifteen members of the Association shall constitute a quorum for the transaction of business in meetings of the Association.

10. No member of the Association shall have more than one vote upon any question, or in the election of officers.

11. The Constitution and By-laws of this Association can be altered or amended only by a two-thirds majority of all members of the Association.

EDITOR.

SELECT BOOKS

FOR

THE HOME, THE CHURCH,

AND THE

SUNDAY-SCHOOL.

PREFATORY NOTE.

IN the preparation of the subjoined catalogue, the editor acknowledges his indebtedness for assistance and for favors received to the following-named publishers: Houghton, Mifflin & Co.; D. Lothrop & Co.; Henry A. Sumner & Co.; Macmillan & Co.; Porter & Coates; E. Claxton & Co.; E. P. Dutton & Co.; G. P. Putman's Sons; Harper & Brothers; D. Appleton & Co.; Anson D. F. Randolph & Co.; Presbyterian Board of Publications; Lee & Shepard; A. C. Armstrong & Sons; National Temperance Society and Publication House; Dodd, Mead & Co.; J. R. Osgood & Co.; Jansen, McClurg & Co.; Robert Clarke & Co.

The catalogue is copious and varied, but a careful examination has been made·of the works named, and they are believed to be well adapted to the purposes designed. It would have been easy to select five hundred of the choicest rather than one thousand, or to name one thousand rather than five thousand; but as tastes and wants differ, a smaller number would not have answered our purpose. We have aimed to include no books of a doubtful character, and to make choice of those only which are valuable for reading. Had we selected books for reference or consultation alone, many hundreds more might well have found a place here; but as these volumes are intended for circulation in homes, and to be read in the parlor and by the fireside, the selection was limited by the end and purpose intended to be attained. Nor have we included all adapted to meet this want; but we have given those which, in the judgment of good critics, will serve to instruct the mind, enlarge the heart, and sweeten and beautify the life.

CATALOGUE OF BOOKS.

. IN the following Catalogue the volumes are to be understood as bound in cloth, except where otherwise designated. *e* or *ea*, where it is prefixed to the price, denotes *each;* and *n* denotes *net.* Books for youths are marked *.

ABODE of Snow [Himalaya]. Wilson (Andrew).	8°	$2 00
Abroad Again; or, Fresh Forays in Foreign Fields. Guild (Curtis).	8°	2 50
Across the Desert. A Life of Moses. Campbell (S. M.) Illust.	12°	1 50
Acts and Monuments of the Church. Book of Martyrs. Fox (John).	4°	5 00
Same.	12°	2 00
Adam, Noah, and Abraham. Expository Readings on the Book of Genesis. Parker (Joseph).	16°	1 25
Adams. Familiar Letters of John Adams and his Wife, Abigail Adams, during the Revolution. Edited by Charles Francis Adams.	8°	2 00
Admiral Coligny; and the Rise of the Huguenots. Blackburn (Wm. M.) 2 vols.	12°	3 00
Admonitory Counsels to a Methodist. Bakewell (John).	18°	40
*Adventures in Canada. Geike (John C.) Illust.	16°	1 00
Adventures in Patagonia. A Missionary Exploring Trip. Coan (Titus).	12°	1 25
*Adventures of a Young Naturalist. Blant (Lucien). Illust.	12°	1 75
*Adventures of Telemachus. Fénélon (Archbishop). Illust.	8°	2 00
*Adventures on the Great Hunting Grounds. Meunier (V.) Illust.	12°	1 25
Advice to One who Meets in Class. Newstead (Robert).	72°	15
*Æsop's Fables. Illust.	12°	1 25
*Æsop's Fables. With Life of the Author, and Croxall's Applications. Illust.	12°	1 50

Æneids of Virgil, The.   Morris (William).   8° $2 50

Æneids of Virgil, The.   Rendered into English oc-
tasyllabic verse.   Conington (John).   8°   *n* 1 50

Afflicted, Companion for the.   Walker (Thos. H.)   12°   90

Africa, Diamond Fields of South.   1 50

Africa.   Through the Dark Continent.   Stanley
(H. M.)   Illust.   2 vols.   8°   *e* 5 00

Africa.   Livingstone's Last Journals.   Waller (H.)   8°   2 50

Africa, Hunting Scenes in the Wilds of.   Illust.   12°   1 75

*Africa, Livingstone in.   Jewett (S. A. W.)   Illust.   16°   1 00

*African Adventure and Adventurers.   An epitome
of the elaborate works of Bruce, Speke and
Grant, Baker and Livingstone.   Edited by G. T.
Day.   Illust.   16°   1 50

African Hunting from Natal to the Zambesi.   Baldwin (W C.)   Illust.   12°   1 50

*Afternoons with Grandma.   From the French of
Madame Garraud.   Kinmont (Mrs. Mary).
Illust.   16°   1 00

*After the Truth.   Henry (Mrs. Sarepta M. I.) Part
I—Finding; Part II—Teaching; Part III—
Using; Part IV—Husbandman—Plowing.   4
vols.   16°   *e* 1 00

*Against the Stream.   The story of an heroic age in
England.   By the author of "The Schönberg-
Cotta Family."   12°   1 00

Age, Temptation of American Christians, and
Christ's own Method of Gaining the Victory
and the Kingdom.   12°   1 25

Ages Before Moses, The.   A Series of Lectures on
the Book of Genesis.   Gibson (John M.)   12°   1 25

*Agnes and Her Neighbors.   Pratt (Frances Lee).   16°   1 50

Agnes and the Little Key; or, Bereaved Parents
Instructed and Comforted.   Adams (Nehemiah).   12°   1 00

*Agnes Morton's Trial; and the Young Governess.
Janvier (E. N.)   16°   1 00

Agreement of Science and Revelation.   Wythe
(Joseph H.)   12°   1 75

Aids to Faith.   A Series of Theological Essays by
Several Writers.   12°   2 00

Alaska, Travels and Adventures in.   Whymper (F.)
Illust.   8°   2 50

Alaska and Missions on the North Pacific Coast.
Jackson (Sheldon). Illust. 12° $1 50
Alchemy and the Alchemists. 12° 1 00
Alcohol and the State. A Discussion of the Prob-
lem of Law as Applied to the Liquor-traffic.
Pitman (Robert C.) 12° 1 50
Alfred the Great. Hughes (Thomas). 12° 1 75
Alhambra and the Kremlin. A Journey from Mad-
rid to Moscow, including Spain, Switzerland,
Russia, Finland, Norway, Sweden, Poland, and
Denmark. Prime (S. I.) Illust. 8° 2 00
Alhambra. Irving (Washington). 16° 1 25
*Alice and Adolphus; or, Worlds not Realized.
Gatty (Mrs. Alfred). 16° 85
*Alice Benson's Trials. Her Fidelity brings her
a Noble Victory at last. Illust. 18° 75
*Alice Sutherland. Bristol (Mrs. Mary C.) Illust. 16° 1 25
All About Jesus. Dickson (Alex.) 12° 2 00
*All Aboard for the Sunrise Lands. Rand (Ed-
ward A.) Illust. 4° 2 25
All Around the House; or, How to Make Homes
Happy. Beecher (Mrs. H. W.) 12° 1 50
All Around the Year. Verses from the Sky Farm.
Goodale (Elaine and Dora R.) Illust. 16° 1 25
All for Christ; or, How a Christian may Obtain,
by a Renewed Consecration of his Heart, the
Fullness of Joy Referred to by the Savior Just
Previous to his Crucifixion. With Illustrations
from the Lives of those who have made this
Consecration. Carter (Thomas). 16° 65
All True. Records of Peril and Adventure; Es-
capes and Deliverances; of Missionary Enter-
prises, etc. Macaulay (T. B.) 12° 1 50
All Quiet Along the Potomac, and Other Poems.
Beers (Ethel Lynn). 12° 1 50
Alleine's Alarm and Baxter's Call. 18° 45
*Allie's Mistake. A Christmas Story. Beach (Re-
becca G.) 16° 1 25
*All's not Gold that Glitters. 12° 1 00
Almost a Nun. Wright (Mrs. Julia McNair).
Illust. 16° 1 00
*Almost too Late. Paull (Mrs. H. H. B.) Illust. 16° 1 00

*Alypius of Tagaste. Webb (Mrs.) Illust.   16°　$1 50

*American Biographical Series. Hill (G. Canning).
Illust. 5 vols.   16°　5 00

    Captain John Smith.   Benedict Arnold, the Traitor.
    General Israel Putnam.   Daniel Boone, the Pioneer.
    Benjamin Franklin.

    Sold separately.   *e* 1 00

*American Conflict, The. A Household Story.
Robinson (Mary S.) Illust. 3 vols.   16°　3 00

American Eloquence, Cyclopædia of. Moore
(Frank). Steel Portraits. 2 vols.   8°　*e* 3 50

*American Explorers, Young Folks' Book of. Hig-
ginson (T. W.)   16°　1 50

*American Family Robinson. Belisle (D. W.)   16°　1 00

*American Fathers, True Stories of the. McConkey
(Miss Rebecca). Illust.   16°　1 25

American Gardener's Assistant. Containing Practical Directions, etc. Bridgman (Thos.) Illust.   12°　2 00

American Literature, A Primer of. Richardson
(Charles F.)   18°　50

American Note-book. Hawthorne (N). 2 vols.   16°　*e* 1 50

American Poems. Selected from Best American
Authors.   16°　1 25

American Prose. Selected from Best American
Authors.   16°　1 25

American Republic in Prophecy. Phillips (G. S.)   12°　1 25

American Woman in China, An; and her Mission-
sionary Work there. Jeter (J. B.)   12°　1 25

*Amid the Shadows [Temperance]. Martin (Mrs.
M. F.)   12°　1 25

Among my Books. Lowell (J. R.) First and Second Series. 2 vols.   12°　*e* 2 00

Among the Isles and Shoals. Thaxter (Celia).   18°　1 25

Among the Turks. Hamlin (Cyrus).   12°　1 50

Amoor Regions. Atkinson (T. W.) Illust.   8°　3 50

*Amy and Marion's Voyage Around the World.
Adams (Sarah B.) Illust.   12°　1 25

*Amy and the Birds, and Other Stories. Illust.   18°　40

*Amy's Probation; or, Six Months at a Convent
School. An Answer to the Question, Shall
Protestant Girls be Sent to Roman Catholic
Schools? Leslie (Emma). Illust.   16°　85

*Amy's Temptation. Sells (S. E.) . Illust. 16° $1 00
Analogy of Natural and Revealed Religion. But-
    ler (Jos.) Edited by Joseph Cummings. 12° 1 50
Analysis of Watson's Institutes. McClintock
    (John). 18° 45
Ancient America, in Notes on American Archæ-
    ology. Baldwin (Jno. D.) 12° 2 00
Ancient Cities and Empires. Their Prophetic
    Doom. Gillett (E. H.) 12° 1 25
Ancient History and Antiquities, Essays in. De
    Quincey (Thos.) 8° 1 75
Ancient History, Manual of. Thalheimer (M. E.)
    Illust. 8° n 1 60
Ancient History, Manual of. From the Earliest
    Times to the Fall of the Western Empire.
    Rawlinson (George). 12° 1 25
Ancient Monarchies. The Five Great Monarchies
    of the Ancient Eastern World. Rawlinson
    (George). Illust. 3 vols. 8° 9 00
    The Sixth Great Monarchy. 8° 3 00
Andes and the Amazon. Orton (James). Illust. 8° 3 00
*Andy Luttrell. Vance (Clara). Illust. 12° 1 50
Anecdotes for the Fireside. Smith (Daniel). 18° 65
*Anecdotes for the Young. Smith (Daniel). 18° 65
Anecdotes, Ladies' Book of. Smith (Daniel). 18° 65
Anecdotes of the Christian Ministry. Smith (D.) 18° 65
Angels, Nature and Ministry of. Rawson (James). 18° 30
Angels of God, The. Dunn (Lewis R.) 16° 1 25
Angélique Arnauld, Abbess of Port Royal. Martin
    (Francis). 12° 1 75
*Animal Life, Curiosities of, as Developed by the
    Recent Discoveries of the Microscope. Illust. 16° 65
*Anna Lavater. A Picture of Swiss Pastoral Life
    in the last Century. Ziethe (W.) Translated
    from the German by Catherine E. Hurst. 16° 85
*Anna Maylie. A Story of Faithful, Resolute Work
    in the Sunday-school, and in the Field of the
    Western Religious Pioneer. Farman (Ella). 16° 1 50
*Anna Ross. Kennedy (Grace). 18° 50
*Annals of Christian Martyrdom. Relating to the
    Martyrs of Pagan Rome and of the Middle
    Ages. 16° 1 00

Annals of the Christian Church. Designed to
    Fortify the Youthful Mind against Jesuitism.
    Parker (Mrs.)   18° $0 45
Annals of the Poor.   Containing the Dairyman's
    Daughter, the Young Cottager, the Negro Serv-
    ant, Cottage Conversation, Visit to the Infirm-
    ary, and the African Widow. Richmond (Legh). 18°   45
Annals of a Quiet Neighborhood.   MacDonald
    (George). Illust.   16°   1 75
*Annetta; or the Story of a Life. Hughes (M. S.)
    Illust.   16°   1 00
Annihilation of the Wicked, Scripturally Consid-
    ered. McDonald (W.)   12°   45
Antislavery Struggle and Triumph in the Methodist
    Episcopal Church. Matlack (L. C.) With an
    Introduction by D. D. Whedon.   12°   1 50
Aonio Paleario and his Friends. Blackburn (Will-
    iam M.)   16°   1 25
Apocalypse, Key to the; or Revelation of Jesus
    Christ to St. John in the Isle of Patmos.
    Brunson (Alfred).   16°   1 00
Apologetics. A Course of Lectures. Smith (Henry
    B.) Edited by William S. Karr.   12°   1 25
Apology for the Bible. A Powerful Antidote to
    Infidelity. Watson (Richard).   18°   40
Apostolic Era; or, the Early Years of Christianity.
    De Pressensé (E.)   12°   1 50
Apostolical Succession, An Essay on. Powell (Thos). 12°   90
Apostles of Mediæval Europe. Maclear (G. F.) 12°   1 75
Appeal to Matter of Fact and Common Sense.
    Fletcher (J.)   18°   45
*Apple-blossoms. Poems of Two Children. Goodale
    (Elaine and Dora R.)   16°   1 25
*Apron Strings, and which Way They Pulled.   Fell
    (Archie).   16°   1 00
Arctic Experiences: containing Captain George E.
    Tyson's Wonderful Drift on the Ice-floe, a His-
    tory of the Polaris Expedition, the Cruise of
    the Tigress, and Rescue of the Polaris Survivors.
    To which is added a General Arctic Chronol-
    ogy. Edited by E. Vale Blake. With Map and
    Illustrations.   8°   4 00

*Arctic Heroes. Facts and Incidents of Arctic Explorations. From the Earliest Voyages to the Discoveries of Sir John Franklin, embracing Sketches of Commercial and Religious Results. Mudge (Z. A.) Illust.   16° $1 00

Arctic Researches and Life among the Esquimaux: being the Narrative of an Expedition in Search of Sir John Franklin, in the Years 1860, 1861, and 1862. Hall (Charles Francis). Maps and Illustrations.   8°   5 00

Arena and Throne, The. Townsend (L. T.)   16°   75

Arizona and Sonora. The Geography, History, and Resources of the Silver Regions of North America. Mowry (S.)   12°   1 50

Arms and Armor in Antiquity and the Middle Ages. Also a Descriptive Notice of Modern Weapons. Lacombe (M. P.) Illust.   12°   1 50

*Arnold Family, The. Miller (Mary C.) Illust.   16°   1 25

Around the World. A Book of Travels. Prime (E. D. G.)   8°   3 00

*Arthur and Bessie in Egypt.   16°   65

Arthur in America. Addresses delivered in New York by Rev. William Arthur, of London.   12°   60

Art at Home. A Collection of Papers on House Decoration. Garrett (Rhoda and Agnes). Illust.   12°   1 50

Art, Literature, and Science, Reviews and Essays on. Phelps (Mrs. A. L.)   12°   1 50

Artist Biographies. Sweetser (M. F.) Illust. with 12 Heliotypes in each volume. 5 vols.   16°   e1 50

     Vol. 1. Raphael, Leonardo, Angelo.
     Vol. 2. Titian, Guido, Claude.
     Vol. 3. Reynolds, Turner, Landseer.
     Vol. 4. Dürer, Rembrandt, Van Dyck.
     Vol. 5. Angelico, Murillo, Alston.

The same are also published in smaller volumes, one biography in each. 15 vols.   18°   e50

Artists of the Nineteenth Century, and their Works. Clements (Clara E.) 2 vols.   8°   e2 50

Art of Speech. Townsend (L. T.)   18°   e 60

     Vol. 1. Studies in Poetry and Prose.
     Vol. 2. Oratory and Logic.

Arts of Intoxication. The Aim and the Results. Crane (J. T.)   16°   1 00

Art Text-books. Edited by Poynter (E. J.) Illust.　8° *e*$2 00
> 1. Architecture, Gothic and Renaissance.
> 2. German, Flemish, and Dutch Painting.
> 3. Italian Painting.
> 4. Sculpture, Antique: Egyptian and Greek.

A-saddle in the Wild West. A Glimpse of Travel among the Mountains, Lava-beds, etc., of Southern Colorado, New Mexico, and Arizona. Rideing (W H.)　18°　60
Asbury, Francis, Character and Career of. Janes (Edwin L.)　12°　1 70
Asbury and his Co-laborers. Larrabee (W. C.) 2 vols. 12°　2 00
Asbury, Life and Times of; or, The Pioneer Bishop. Strickland (W P.)　12°　1 50
Asbury's Journals. 3 vols.　12°　4 25
*Ashcliffe Hall. A Tale of the Last Century. Holt (Emily S.)　16°　1 25
Asked of God. Shipton (Anna).　16°　75
Aspects of Christian Experience. Merrill (S. M.)　16°　1 00
Aspect of German Culture. Hall (G. Stanley).　12°　1 50
Astoria. Irving (Washington).　16°　1 25
Astronomy without Mathematics. Denison (E. B.) 12°　1 50
Astronomy. Ball (R. S.)　12°　2 25
Astronomy of the Bible. Mitchel (O. M.)　12°　1 75
At Eventide. Discourses. Adams (Nehemiah).　12°　1 25
At Home in Fiji. Cumming (C. F. Gordon).　8°
Atheism to Christianity, From. Porter (Geo. P.) 16°　50
*Athens: Its Grandeur and Decay. Illust.　16°　65
Atlas of Scripture Geography. With Maps and Questions, etc.　8°　75
Atonement in Christ. Miley (John).　12°　1 25
*At the Threshold. Familiar Talks with Young Christians Concerning Doctrines and Duties. Houghton (Ross C.)　16°　60
*Aunt Agnes, A Visit to. Illust.　12°　85
*Aunt Dolly's School-room Stories. Each Story teaches a Lesson to both Teacher and Pupil. Illust.　16°　60
*Aunt Hattie's Library for Small Boys. Illust. In box. 6 vols.　18°　3 00

Lying Jim.	Factory Boy.
Golden Rule.	Chest of Tools.
Frankie's Dog Tony.	Apple Boy.

*Aunt Hattie's Library for Small Girls. Illust. In
   box. 6 vols.   18° $3 00

Maggie and the Mice	The Lost Kitty.
Lily's Birthday.	Ida's New Shoes.
The Sheep and Lambs.	Little Miss Fret.

*Aunt Jane's Hero. Prentiss (Mrs. E.)   12° 1 50
*Aunt Judy's Tales. Gatty (Mrs. Alfred). Illust. 16°   85
*Aunt Mattie. Story of Domestic Life and Experi-
   ences. Hazelton (Mabel). Illust.   12° 1 50
*Aunt Saidee's Cow. Prichard (Miss S. J.)   16° 1 25
*Avis Benson; or, Mine and Thine. With Other
   Sketches. Prentiss (Mrs. E.)   16° 1 25
*Ayesha. A Tale of the Times of Mohammed.
   Leslie (Emma). Illust.   12° 1 25

*Babies in the Basket; or, Daph and her Charge.
   Illust.   16°   57
Babylon and Nineveh. The Thrones and Palaces
   of Babylon and Nineveh. From Sea to Sea.
   A Thousand Miles on Horseback. Newman
   (J. P.) Illust.   8° 5 00
Bacchus Dethroned. Powell (Frederick).   12° 1 00
Back-log Studies. Warner (Charles Dudley). Illust. 4° 1 50
Backsliding, Antidote to.   18°   35
Bacon's Essays and Colors of Good and Evil.
   Wright (W A.)   18° 1 25
Balaustion's Adventure. Including a Transcript
   from Euripides.   16° 1 50
*Balboa, Cortez, and Pizarro, Lives of.   18°   75
Ballads and Lyrics. Selected and Arranged by
   Henry C. Lodge. With Biographical Sketches
   of Authors.   16° 1 25
Ballads of Bravery. Forty full-page illust.   4° 2 50
Ballads of Home. Beautifully Illust.   4° 2 50
*Ballads for Little Folks. Cary (Alice and Phœbe). 4° 1 50
Bangs, Rev. Dr. Nathan, Life and Times of. Ste-
   vens (Abel).   12° 1 50
Baptism, Christian. Its Subjects and Mode. Mer-
   rill (S. M.)   16° 1 00
Baptism, Hibbard on. Its Subjects, Mode, Obliga-
   tion, Import, and Relative Order. Hibbard
   (F. G.)   12° 1 50

Baptism, Obligation, Subjects, and Mode. Slicer (H.) 18° $0 45
Baptism, Obligation, Subject, and Mode. In Two
    Parts. Part 1—Infant Baptism; Part 2—The
    Mode. Shaffer (H. M.) 18° 45
*Barbara. Illust. 16° 1 50
*Bark Cabin on Kearsarge. Rand (Edward A.)
    Illust. 16° 1 00
Bascom, Bishop, Life of. Henkle (M. M.) 12° 1 25
Bascom's Lectures. 3 vols. 12° e1 50
*Bashie's Service; or, Where's a Will, There's a
    Way. Alden (Mariam). Illust. 16° 1 00
*Battles Lost and Won. Merrill (Geo. E.) Illust. 16° 1 50
Battle of Calvary; or, Universalism and Cognate
    Theories against Jesus of Nazareth. Chaffin
    (J. W.) 12° 1 00
Battles of the Republic by Sea and Land. Harri-
    son (Henry W.) 12° 1 25
*Battles Worth Fighting. Illust. 16° 1 25
*Bayard Taylor: His Life, Travels, and Literary
    Career. Conwell (Russell H.) Illust. 12° 1 50
Bazar Book of Decorum, The. 16° 1 00
Bazar Book of Health, The. 16° 1 00
Bazar Book of the Household. 16° 1 00
Beaconsfield. A Sketch of the Literary and Politi-
    cal Career of Benjamin Disraeli, Late Earl of
    Beaconsfield. Towle (George M.) 18° 60
*Bear-hunters of the Rocky Mountains. Bowman
    (Anna). Illust. 16° 1 00
*Bears' Den, The. Miller (Emily Huntington).
    Illust. 16° 85
Beaten Paths; or, A Woman's Vacation. Thomp-
    son (Mrs. Ella W.) 16° 1 50
Beatitudes, Lectures on the. Crum (G. C.) 12° 1 00
Beauties Selected from the Writings of De Quincey. 8° 1 50
*Bede's Charity. Stretton (Hesba). 12° 1 00
*Beggars of Holland: And the Grandees of Spain.
    History of the Reformation in the Netherlands.
    Mears (John W.) Illust. 16° 1 50
*Beginning Life. Chapters for Young Men on Re-
    ligion, Study, and Business. Tulloch. 16° 1 00
Believer's Victory, The, over Satan's Devices. Par-
    sons (W. L.) 12° 1 00

*Ben and Bentie Series. 2 vols.   18° e$0 75
    School Life of Ben and Bentie.
    Camp Tabor.

Benedicite. Illustrative of the Power, Wisdom,
    and Goodness of God as Manifested in his
    Works. Child (G. Chaplin).   12°   2 00
Ben-Hur. A Tale of the Christ. Wallace (Lew). 16°   1 00
Benjamin Franklin; and The Struggles of the In-
    fant Nation. Abbott (John S. C.) Illust.   12°   1 25
*Ben's Boyhood; and Trusted and Tried. Illust.   16°   75
Benson, Joseph, Life of. Treffry (R.)   12°   60
Benton's (T. H.) Thirty Years' View; or, a His-
    tory of the Working of the American Govern-
    ment for Thirty Years, from 1820 to 1850.
    2 vols.   8°   6 00
*Bernie's White Chicken. Alden (Mrs. G. R.
    [Pansy]).   16°   75
*Bessie and Her Spanish Friends.   16°   75
*Bessie Harrington's Venture. Mathews (Julia A.) 16°   1 25
*Bessie, the Cash Girl. Brine (Mrs. Mary D.)   18°   45
*Bessie Hartwell; or, Charity. Illust.   16°   1 00
*Bessie's Trials at Boarding-school. Perry (Nora).
    Illust.   16°   1 25
*Best Fellow in the World, The. [Temperance.]
    Wright (Mrs. J. McNair).   12°   1 25
Best Reading, The. Hints on the Selection of
    Books, a Classified List, etc. Perkins (F. B.) 12°   1 75
*Between the Clifts; or, Hal Forrester's Anchor.
    Marshall (Emma).   16°   1 00
Beyond the Grave. Being three Lectures before
    Chautauqua Assembly in 1878, with Papers on
    Recognition in the Future State, and other
    Addenda. Foster (Randolph S.)   12°   1 25
Bible and Modern Thought. Birks (T. R.)   12°   1 50
Bible and Slavery. Elliott (Charles).   12°   1 25
Bible Dictionary. Covel's. For Sunday-schools
    and Families. With Maps and Engravings.   85
Bible Dictionary, The Westminster. Shepherd
    (Thomas J.) Illust.   8°   1 50
*Bible, English, A Short History of the. With
    Brief Notices of the Translators. Freeman
    (James M.)   12°   n 50

Bible Geography, Hand-book of. (New and Revised Edition.) Containing the Name, Pronunciation, and Meaning of every Place, Nation, and Tribe mentioned in both the Canonical and Apocryphal Scriptures. Whitney (George H.) Illustrated by One Hundred Engravings and Forty Maps and Plans. 12° $2 25

Bible Hand-book. Theologically Arranged. Holliday (F. C.) 12° 1 25

Bible History, Outlines of. Hurst (John F.) Four Maps. 12° *n* 50

Bible History, the Chronology of, and How to Remember it. Munger (C.) 12° *n* 50

Bible, Horne's Introduction to the. Abridged. 12° 1 25

*Bible Images. A Book for the Young. Wells (James). Illust. 12° 1 25

Bible, Index and Dictionary of the. A Complete Index and Concise Dictionary of the Holy Bible. Barr (John). 12° 85

Bible in the Public Schools, The. Records, Arguments, etc., in the Case of Minor *vs.* Board of Education of Cincinnati. 8° 2 00

Bible Lands. Their Modern Customs and Manners Illustrative of Scripture. Van Lennep (Henry J.) Illust., and Colored Maps. 8° 5 00

Bible Lore. Chapters on the Rare Manuscripts, Various Translations, and Notable Characteristics of the Bible. Gray (James Comper). 16° 90

Bible Manners and Customs, Hand-book of. Containing Descriptions of the Ancient Manners and Customs mentioned in the Bible, and explaining over three thousand Scripture Texts. Freeman (James M.) Illust. by 168 Engravings, and accompanied by an Analytical Index, a Textual Index, and a Topical Index. 12° 2 25

*Bible Steps for Little Pilgrims. Stories from the Old and New Testaments. Illust. 12° 1 50

Bible Teachings in Nature. Macmillan (Hugh). 12° 1 75

Bible Thoughts and Themes. Bonar (Horatius). 12° *e* 2 00

Vol. 1. Genesis.　　Vol. 4. Acts.
Vol. 2. Old Testament.　　Vol. 5. Lesser Epistles.
Vol. 3. The Gospels.　　Vol. 6. Revelation.

Biblical Biography. Containing a full History of
Bible Men and Women. Beharrell (T. G.)   8° $3 00

Biblical Chronology, Introduction to. From Adam
to the Resurrection of Christ. Akers.   8° 2 00

Biblical Museum, The. Collection of Notes, Explanatory, Homiletical, and Illustrative, on the
Holy Scriptures. Gray (J. Comper).   12° e1 25

> Vol. 1. Matthew and Mark.
> Vol. 2. Luke and John.
> Vol. 3. Acts and Romans.
> Vol. 4. Corinthians to Philemon.
> Vol. 5. Hebrews to the End of New Testament.

Old Testament.

> Vol. 1. Genesis and Exodus.
> Vol. 2. Leviticus to Deuteronomy.
> Vol. 3. Joshua to Samuel.
> Vol. 4. Kings and Chronicles.
> Vol. 5. Ezra to Job.
> Vol. 6. Psalms.
> Vol. 7. Proverbs to Solomon's Song.

Bible Work in Bible Lands; or, Events in the History of the Syria Mission. Bird (Isaac). Illust. 12° 1 50

Biblical Literature, Illustrations of. Townley (Jas.)
2 vols.   8° 5 00

Biblical Literature, Manual of. Strickland (W P.) 12° 1 50

*Big Brother Series, The. Illust. 4 vols.   12° e1 25

> The Big Brother. A Story of Indian War. Eggleston (Geo. Cary).
> Captain Sam; or, The Scouts of 1814. Eggleston (Geo. Cary).
> The Signal Boys; or, Captain Sam's Company. Eggleston (Geo. Cary).
> Boys of Other Countries. Taylor (Bayard).

Biographical Series. Cabinet Edition of Choice
Biography. By Distinguished Authors. Sold
separately or in sets.   16° e 60

> Vol. 1. Robert Burns. Carlyle (Thomas).
> Vol. 2. William Pitt. Macaulay (T. B.)
> Vol. 3. Frederick the Great. Macaulay (T. B.)
> Vol. 4. Julius Cæsar. Liddell (Henry G.)
> Vol. 5. Columbus. Lamartine.
> Vol. 6. Martin Luther. Bunsen (Chevalier).
> Vol. 7. Hannibal. Arnold (Thomas).
> Vol. 8. Joan of Arc. Michelet (Jules).
> Vol. 9. Mahomet. Gibbon (Edward).
> Vol. 10. Oliver Cromwell. Lamartine.
> Vol. 11. Vittoria Colonna. Trollope (T. A.)
> Vol. 12. Mary Stuart. Lamartine.

*Biographical Histories. Abbott (Jacob and John S. C.) Illust. Set in box, 32 vols. 16° $32 00

Cyrus the Great.	Mary Queen of Scots.
Darius the Great.	Queen Elizabeth.
Xerxes.	Charles I.
Alexander the Great.	Charles II.
Romulus.	Hernando Cortez.
Hannibal.	Henry IV.
Pyrrhus.	Louis XIV.
Julius Cæsar.	Maria Antoinette.
Cleopatra.	Madame Roland.
Nero.	Josephine.
Alfred the Great.	Joseph Bonaparte.
William the Conqueror.	Hortense.
Richard I.	Louis Philippe.
Richard II.	Genghis Khan.
Richard III.	King Philip.
Margaret of Anjou.	Peter the Great.

Sold separately. *ea* 1 00

Biographical and Historical Essays. De Quincey (Thomas). 8° 1 75

Biology. Cook (Joseph). 12° 1 50

*Bird Book, Boys' and Girls'. Colman (Julia). Illust. Colored engravings. 12° 80

Birds of the United States. Bailey (L.) 12° 1 25

Birds and Poets. With Other Papers. Burroughs (John). 16° 1 50

*Birthday, The. A Sequel to "The Well-spent Hour." Follen (Mrs.) 16° 1 00

Bitter Sweet. A Poem. Holland (J. G.) 12° 1 50

Black Horse and Carryall; or, Outdoor Sights and Indoor Thoughts. McCarty (J. H.) 16° 1 00

Blessed Hope; or, The Glorious Coming of our Lord. Lord (Willis). 12° 1 25

*Bloomfield. A Story exhibiting Piety in its Unobtrusive Aspects, as "steady, calm, meditative, and trustful," and which does not overlook Home Work in its devotion to that abroad. Warner (Elizabeth). Illust. 16° 1 50

*Blind Man's Holiday; or, Short Tales for the Nursery. Illust. 16° 85

*Blount Family, The; or, A Widow's Toil, Trust, and Triumph. Brown (Theron). Illust. 16° 1 50

*Blue-eyed Jimmy; or, The Good Boy. Illust. Homespun (Sophia). 16° 1 00

*Blue Flag and Cloth of Gold. Warner (Miss Anna). 16° $1 25
*Boardman Library, The. Boardman (Mrs. W E.)
    Illust. 4 vols.   16° 5 00

> Haps and Mishaps of the Brown Family.
> The Sister's Triumph.
> Nellie Gates and the Little Missionary.
> The Mother-in-law.

*Boat-builders' Family, The. A Story of the Sea,
    for Boys. Mudge (Z. A.) Illust.   16° 1 25
Boat-life in Egypt and Nubia. Prime (Wm. C.) 12° 2 00
*Bobbie and Rosie; or, A Summer in the Life of
    Two Children.   12° 1 00
Bodily Strength and Skill. Depping (G.) Illust. 12° 1 25
*Bodley Abroad, Mr. Scudder (Horace E). Illust.
    Boards.   4° 1 50
*Bodleys Afoot, The. Scudder (Horace E.) Illust.
    Boards.   4° 1 50
*Bodleys on Wheels, The. Scudder (Horace E.)
    Illust. Boards.   4° 1 50
*Bodleys Telling Stories, The. Scudder (Horace E.)
    Illust. Boards.   4° 1 50
Boehm's Reminiscences. Historical and Biograph-
    ical. Wakeley (J. B.)   12° 1 50
Bold Frontier Preacher. A Portraiture of Rev.
    William Cravens. Wakeley (J. B.) 18° 40
Bonneville. Irving (Washington).   16° 1 25
*Bonnie Ærie. Illust.   16° 1 50
*Book and its Story, The. Ranyard (L. N.) 12° 1 50
Book of Ballads, The. Including Firmilian. Aytoun
    (W. E.)   16° 1 50
Book of the Farm. A Book of Husbandry. War-
    ing (George E.) Illust.   12° 2 00
*Book of the Worthies, A. Gathered from Old His-
    tories, and now Written Anew. Yonge (C. M.) 18° 1 25
*Book-stall Boy of Batherton, The. Hodder (Ed-
    win.) Illust.   ·16° 75
*Books about Boys who Fought and Won. Illust.
    4 vols.   18° 2 00
*Books about Wonderful and Curious Things. 4 vols. 16° 2 75
Borderland of Science, The. A Series of Familiar
    Dissertations on Stars, Planets, and Meteors,
    etc. Proctor (R. A.)   12° 4 00

*Bourdaloue and Louis XIV. From the French of
    Bungener (L. L. F.)   12° $1 50

Bow in the Cloud, The; and The First Bereave-
    ment. Macduff (J. R.)   18° 50

*Boyhood of Great Men. (Edgar (J. G.)   16° 1 00

*Boyhood of Martin Luther. Mayhew (H.) Illust. 16° 1 25

*Boys and Girls of Beech Hill, The. Greenough
    (A. J.)   16° 1 00

*Boys at Eastwick. Griffith (M. E.) Illust.   16° 1 00

*Boy, The, with an Idea Series. Illust. 4 vols.   8° e1 62½

> The Boy with an Idea.
> Young Mechanic; containing Directions for using all kinds
>   of Tools, etc.
> Amongst Machines; a Description of Various Mechanical
>   Appliances used in the Manufacture of Wood, etc.
> Boy Engineers. What they Did, and How they Did it.

Boys and Girls in Biology; or, Simple Studies of
    the Lower Forms of Life, based upon the latest
    Lectures of Prof. T. H. Huxley. Stevenson
    (Sarah H.) Illust.   12° 1 50

*Boys and Girls Playing; and Other Addresses to
    Children. Ryle (John C.)   16° 75

*Boys of Brimstone Court, The. With Other Stories
    by Favorite Authors. Phelps (Elizabeth Stu-
    art).   16° 75

*Boys of "76," The. A History of the Battles of
    the Revolution. Coffin (C. C.) Illust.   8° 3 00

*Boy Travelers in the Far East, The.   Knox
    (Thomas W.) Illust. 3 vols.   8° e3 00

> Part 1. Adventures of Two Youths in a Journey to Japan
>   and China.
> Part 2. Adventures of Two Youths in a Journey to Siam
>   and Java. With Descriptions of Cochin-China, Cam-
>   bodia, Sumatra, and the Malay Archipelago.
> Part 3. Adventures of Two Youths in a Journey to Ceylon
>   and India. With Descriptions of Borneo, the Philip-
>   pine Islands, and Burmah.

Bracebridge Hall. Irving (Washington).   16° 1 25

*Braid of Cords, A. A. L. O. E. Illust.   18° 75

*Brainards, The, at the Rocky Mountains. Slicer
    (Adeline E. H.) Illustrated.   16° 85

Bramwell, William, Memoir of the Life and Minis-
    try of. Sigston (James).   18° 40

*Branches of Palm. By the Author of " Evening
    Rest." Illust.   16° 1 50

Brand of Dominic. History of the Inquisition.
Rule (W. H.)　　　　　　　　　　　　　12°　$1 00
Brazil, Life in. Ewbanks (T.)　　　　　　8°　3 00
*Breakfast for Two. Mathews (Joanna.)　　16°　1 25
Breathings of the Better Life. Edited by Larcom
(Lucy.)　　　　　　　　　　　　　　18°　1 25
*Brewer's Fortune, The. [Temperance.] Chellis
(Mary D.)　　　　　　　　　　　　　12°　1 50
Bricks without Straw. Tourgee (A. W.)　　16°　1 50
Bride and Bridegroom; or Letters to a Young Mar-
ried Couple. Dorr (Julia C. R.)　　　　16°　1 00
Bride of the Rhine, The. Two Hundred Miles in
a Mosel Row-boat. Waring (Geo. E.) Illust.　16°　1 50
*Bright Days. Looking at Things from the Child's
Point of View. Howitt (Mary). Illust.　12°　1 25
*Brighter than the Sun; or, Christ the Light of the
World. A Life of our Lord for the Young.
Macduff (J. R.) Illust.　　　　　　　8°　2 00
British Poets. A New and Revised Edition, on the
Basis of Dr. Aiken's Work. Beginning with
Chaucer, and brought down to date. Johnson
(Rossiter). Portraits on Steel of the Different
Authors. 3 vols.　　　　　　　　　8°　15 00
British Poets. Red-line Edition.　　　　12°　e 1 25

Browning (Mrs).	Hemans (Mrs).	Proctor.
Chaucer.	Jean Ingelow.	Religious Poems.
Cowper.	Lucile.	Tennyson.
Coleridge.	Macaulay.	White (Kirke).
Dante.	Milton.	Wordsworth.
Dryden.	Owen Meredith.	Tupper.
Goldsmith.		

British Poets, Selections from. Woodworth (Eliza).
Illust.　　　　　　　　　　　　　12°　1 25
British Reformers, Lives and Writings of. 12 vols. 12°　e 1 25

Wickliffe to Bilney.—Tyndale, Frith, and Barnes.—Edward
VI, Parr, Balnaves, etc.—Latimer.—Hooper.—Bradford.—Ridley and Philpot.—Cranmer, Rogers, Careless, etc.—Knox.—Becon.—Jewell.—Fox, Bale, and
Coverdale.

Broadcast. A Collection of Choice Original
Thoughts on Various Topics. Adams (Nehemiah).　　　　　　　　　　　　　12°　1 00
*Broken Looking-glass, The. Sequel to the Old Look-
ing-glass. Charlesworth (Maria L.)　　16°　1 00

*Broken Fetters. Illust. 16° $1 50
*Brookside Series, The. Baker (Mrs. Harriet W.)
    Illust. In box, 4 vols. 16° 4 00
      Hole in the Pocket.   Lost but Found.
      Stopping the Leak.   Fashion and Folly.
*Brought Home. A Temperance Tale. Stretton
    (Hesba). 16° 75
*Brother and Sister; or, the Way of Peace. 16° 85
*Bruey: Little Workers for Christ. Havergal (F. R.) 12° 1 10
Bryant's Poetical Works. Household Edition. 12° 2 00
*Building Stones. Ballard (Mrs. Julia P.) Illust. 16° 1 25
Buried Cities of Campania. Adams (W. H. D.) 12° 1 50
Burnet on the Thirty-nine Articles. Edited by Page. 8° 2 50
Burnett, Peter H., the First Governor of the State
    of California. Recollections and Opinions of
    an old Pioneer. 12° 1 75
*Byrne Ransom's Building. Pardoe (Hiles C.) Illust. 16° 90

CALVINISM as It Is, Objections to. Foster (R. S.) 12° 1 00
Calvinistic Controversy. Embracing a Sermon on
    Predestination and Election. Fisk (Wilbur). 12° 85
Camp-fires of Napoleon. Watson (Henry C.) 12° 1 25
Camps in the Caribbees. Adventures and Discov-
    eries of a Naturalist in the Lesser Antilles.
    Ober (F. A.) Illust. 8° 2 50
Camp-meetings: Their Origin, History, and Utility,
    also their Perversion and How to Correct it.
    Swallow (S. C.) 12° 30
*Captain Christie's Granddaughter. Illust. 16° 1 00
Captain Waltham: A Tale of Southern India.
    Scudder (Mrs. Joseph). Illust. 16° 1 10
*Captivity of Judah, The. Illust. 18° 60
Carlyle, Thomas. His Life—His Books—His Theo-
    ries. Guernsey (A. H.) 18° 60
Carlyle, Sketch of Thomas. Conway (M. D.) 12° 1 00
*Carolina, the Hotel-keeper's Daughter. Berry
    (Mrs. M. E.) Illust. 16° 1 25
*Carrie Ellsworth; or, Seed-sowing. Johnson (M. O.)
    Illust. 16° 1 25
*Carrots: Just a Little Boy. Molesworth (Mrs.) 16° 1 50
Cartwright, Peter. Autobiography of. Edited by
    Strickland (W. P.) 12° 1 50

Carvosso, William. A Biographical Study. Wise
(Daniel.)   16° $1 00

Carvosso, William, a Memoir of: Sixty Years a
Class-leader in the Wesleyan Connection.
Written by Himself, and edited by his Son.   18°   50

*Casella. A Story of the Waldenses. Finley (Martha F.)   16°   90

*Cash-boy's Trust, The. Payne (Annie Mitchell).   16°   1 00

Castilian Days. Hay (John).   12°   2 00

Catacombs of Rome, and their Testimony Relative
to Primitive Christianity. Withrow (W H.)
Illust.   12°   2 50

*Catacombs, The Martyr of the. A Tale of Ancient
Rome. Illust.   16°   75

*Catechism, Pictorial, of the Methodist Episcopal
Church.   12°   80

*Catharine. Adams (Nehemiah).   12°   1 00

Catherine II, Empress of Russia, Memoirs of the
Court and Reign of. Smucker (Samuel M.)   12°   1 25

*Cecily: A Tale of the English Reformation. Leslie
(Emma). Illust.   12°   1 25

Cedar Christians. Cuyler (T. L.)   16°   90

Celebrated Female Sovereigns. Jameson (Mrs.)   8°   2 50

*Celesta Stories, The. Berry (Mrs. M. E.) Illust.
3 vols.   *e* 1 00

     Celesta.   Crooked and Straight.
       The Crook Straightened.

Century of Dishonor, A. A Sketch of the Dealings
of the United States Government with the
Indian Tribes. H. H.   12°   1 50

Chaff and Wheat. Willing (Jennie Fowler.)   16°   1 00

'Chalmers, Thomas, a Biographical Study. Dodds
(James).   16°   1 25

Chambers's Encyclopædia. A Dictionary of Universal Knowledge for the People. Household
Edition. Illust. 10 vols. Cloth, $15.00. Sheep,   8°   20 00

Changed Cross, The. Hobart (Mrs. Charles).   24°   50

Charity, Sweet Charity. Porter (Rose).   16°   75

Character. Smiles (S.)   12°   1 50

*Charley Laurel. An Interesting Story of Sea
Life. Kingston (W. H. G.) Illust.   16°   1 25

*Charley Hope's Testament. Illust,   18°   75

*Chart of Life. Porter (James). 16° $0 80
*Chauncey Judd; or, The Stolen Boy. A Tale of
    the Revolution. Warren (Israel P.) 16° 1 25
*Cheerful Words. From the Writings of George
    MacDonald. Edited by E. E. Brown. With a
    Biography. Introduction by James T. Fields. 16° 1 00
*Chautauqua Girls at Home, The. By Pansy (Mrs.
    G. R. Alden). Illust. 12° 1 50
CHAUTAUQUA LIBRARY OF ENGLISH HISTORY AND
    LITERATURE.
    Vol. 1. From the Earliest Times to the Later
      Norman Period. 8° n 80
    Vol. 2. The Period of the Early Plantagenets. 12° n 50
    Vol. 3. The War of the Roses. 8° n 50
CHAUTAUQUA TEXT-BOOKS, THE.
    No. 1. Biblical Exploration. A Condensed
      Manual on How to Study the Bible. Vin-
      cent (J. H.) n 10
    No. 2. Studies of the Stars. A Pocket Guide
      to the Science of Astronomy. Warren (H.W.) n 10
    *No. 3. Bible Studies for Little People. Vin-
      cent (B. T.) n 10
    No. 4. English History. Vincent (J. H.) n 10
    No. 5. Greek History. Vincent (J. H.) n 10
    No. 6. Greek Literature. Vail (A. D.) n 20
    No. 7. Memorial Days of the Chautauqua Lit-
      erary and Scientific Circle. n 10
    No. 8. What Noted Men Think of the Bible.
      Townsend (L. T.) n 10
    No. 9. William Cullen Bryant. n 10
    No. 10. What is Education? Phelps (Wm. F.) n 10
    No. 11. Socrates. Phelps (Wm. F.) n 10
    No. 12. Pestalozzi. Phelps (Wm. F.) n 10
    No. 13. Anglo-Saxon. Cook (Albert S.) n 20
    No. 14. Horace Mann. Phelps (Wm. F.) n 10
    No. 15. Frœbel. Phelps (Wm. F.) n 10
    No. 16. Roman History. Vincent (J. H.) n 10
    No. 17. Roger Ascham and John Sturm.
    . Glimpses of Education in the Sixteenth Cen-
      tury. Phelps (Wm. F.) n 10
    No. 18. Christian Evidences. Vincent (J. H.) n 10
    No. 19. The Book of Books. Freeman (J. M.) n 10

CHAUTAUQUA TEXT-BOOKS (*Continued*).

No. 20. The Chautauqua Hand-book. Vincent (J. H.)   *n* $0 10

No. 21. American History. Hurlbut (J. L.)   *n* 10

No. 22. Biblical Biology. Wythe (J. H.)   *n* 10

No. 23. English Literature. Gilmore (J. H.)   *n* 20

No. 24. Canadian History. Hughes (Jas. L.)   *n* 10

No. 25. Self-Education. Alden (Joseph).   *n* 10

No. 26. The Tabernacle. Hill (John C.)   *n* 10

No. 27. Readings from Ancient Classics.   *n* 10

No. 28. Manners and Customs of Bible Times. Freeman (J. M.)   *n* 10

No. 29. Man's Antiquity and Language. Terry (M. S.)   *n* 10

No. 30. The World of Missions. Carroll (H. K.)   *n* 10

No. 31. What Noted Men Think of Christ. Townsend (L. T.)   *n* 10

No. 32. A Brief Outline of the History of Art. De Forest (Julia B.)   *n* 10

No. 33. Elihu Burritt: the Learned Blacksmith. Northend (Charles).   *n* 10

No. 34. Asiatic History—China, Corea, Japan. Griffis (Wm. E.)   *n* 10

No. 35. Outlines of General History. Vincent (J. H.)   *n* 10

No. 36. Assembly Bible Outlines. Vincent (J. H.)   *n* 10

No. 37. Assembly Normal Outlines. Vincent (J. H.)   *n* 10

Childhood of Religion. A Simple Account of the Birth and Growth of Myths and Legends. Clodd (E.)   12°   1 25

Childhood of the English Nation; or, The Beginnings of English History. Armitage (Ella S.)   16°   1 25

*Child's History of England. Dickens (Charles).   12°   1 00

*Child's History of Greece. Bonner. 2 vols.   18°   *e* 1 25

*Child-life. A Collection of Poems for and about Children. Whittier (J. G.)   16°   2 25

*Child-life, in Prose. A Volume of Stories, Fancies, and Memories of Child-Life. Whittier (J. G.)   16°   2 25

*Child-life in Many Lands. Strong (J. D.) Illustrated.   16°   1 00

*Child Toilers of Boston Streets. Brown (Emma E.)
    With 12 Pictures drawn from Life by Kather-
    ine Pierson. Illuminated board covers.   4° $0 50
*Child World Stories. Loring (Laurie).   4° 1 25
*Child's Sabbath-day Book.   16° 40
*Children's Crusades in the Thirteenth Century.
    Gray (G. Z.)   12° 1 00
*Children and the Lion, and other Sunday Stories.
    Wilberforce (Bishop). Illust.   12° 1 00
*Children, Government of. Gere (J.)   18° 30
*Children, Ministering. Charlesworth (Maria L.)
    Illust.   16° 1 25
*Children of Lake Huron; or, the Cousins at Clo-
    verly. Illust.   16° 1 00
*Children of the Great King, The. Illust.   16° 1 00
*Children's Book of Poetry. Coates (H. T.) Illust. 8° 3 00
*Children s Treasury of Bible Stories. Gaskoin
    (Mrs. Herman). 3 parts.   e 30
        Part 1. Old Testament.
        Part 2. New Testament.
        Part 3. The Apostles, St. James, St. Paul, St. John.

China and the Chinese. General Description of
    the Country, its Inhabitants, its Civilization
    and Form of Government, its Religious and
    Social Institutions. Nevins (J. L.) Illust.   12° 1 75
China and Japan. A Record of Observations made
    during a Residence of Several years in China,
    and a Tour of Official Visitation to the Mis-
    sions of both Countries, in 1877–1878. Wiley
    (I. W.) Illust.   16° 1 25
Chinese Buddhism. Eskins (Joseph).   8° 4 50
Chinese Classics. Containing the Works of Con-
    fucius and Mencius. Legge (J.)   8° 3 50
Chinese, The: Their Education, Philosophy, and
    Letters. Martin (W. A. P.)   12° 1 75
*Chinks of Clannyford. Hamilton (Kate W.) Illust. 16° 1 40
*Chips from the White House; or, Selections from
    the Speeches, Conversations, Diaries, and Let-
    ters of all the Presidents of the United States.
    Prepared by J. Chaplin.   12° 1 50
Choctaw Indians, Life Among the, and Sketches of
    the South-west. Benson (H. C.)   12° 1 50

Choice Readings for Public and Private Entertainment. Edited by Cumnock (Robert McLain). 12° $1 75

Christ a Friend. Adams (Nehemiah). 12° 1 00

Christ Bearing Witness to Himself. Chadwick (George A.) 12° 1 25

Christ and Christianity. A Vindication of the Divine Authority of the Christian Religion, grounded on the Historical verity of the Life of Christ. Alexander (William L.) 12° 85

Christ Crucified. [Divinity of Christ.] Clarke (George W.) 18° 50

Christ: His Nature and Work. A Series of Sermons Preached by Eminent Ministers. 12° 1 50

Christ His Own Witness. All that Jesus said Concerning Himself Topically Arranged and Studied. Ballantine (E.) 12° 1 25

Christ in Modern Life. [Sermons.] Brooke (Stopford A.) 12° 2 00

Christ in Song. Selected from All Ages. Schaff (P.) 4° 2 50

Christ of History, The. Young (John). 12° 1 25

Christ, Life of. Farrar (F. W.) With Notes. 2 vols. 8° *e*2 00

Christ, Life of. Hanna (William). 3 vols. 12° *e*1 50

Christ, Life of. Stalker (James). 16° 60

Christ of the Gospels. Tullock. 12° 1 00

Christ the Consolator. A Book of Comfort for the Sick. Hopkins (E.) 16° 1 25

Christ the Light of the World. Vaughan (C. J.) 16° 1 50

Christ, The Second Coming of, Considered in its Relation to the Millennium, the Resurrection, and the Judgment. Merrill (S. M.) 16° 1 00

Christian Altar, The; or, Offices of Devotion for the Use of Persons receiving the Lord's Supper, together with a Treatise relating to that Sacrament, and Directions for the Communicants' Daily Walk with God. Wyatt (W. E.) 4° 50

Christian Believing and Living. Sermons. Huntington (F. D.) 12° 1 00

Christian Daily Treasury. Temple. 12° 1 50

Christian Effort. Facts and Incidents. Baker (Sarah). 18° 45

Christian Ethics. Wuttke (Adolph). Translated by J. P. Lacroix. 2 vols. 12° 3 00

Christian Ethics, Outlines of. Lacroix (J. P.)	12°	*n* $0 50
Christian Evidences, Outlines of. Alden (Joseph).	12°	*n* 40
Christian Exertion Explained and Enforced; or, The Duty of Private Members of the Church of Christ to Labor for the Souls of Men.	18°	30
Christian Institutious: Essays on Ecclesiastical Subjects. Stanley (Arthur P.)	12°	50
Christian Laborer, the Christian Hero. Memoirs of a Useful Man.	18°	25
Christian Lawyer, The. Being a Portraiture of the Life and Character of William George Baker.	12°	1 25
Christian Love; or, Charity an Essential Element of True Christian Character. Wise (Daniel).	24°	35
*Christian Maiden, Memorials of Eliza Hessel. Priestley (Joshua). 1 illust.	16°	1 00
Christian's Manual. A Treatise on Christian Perfection. Merritt (Timothy).	24°	30
*Christian Panoply. Containing Ned Franks and Red Cross Knight. A. L. O. E.	18°	75
Christian Pastorate: Its Character, Responsibilities, and Duties. Kidder (Daniel P.)	12°	1 50
Christian Perfection. Fletcher (J.)	24°	25
Christian Perfection, An Account of. Wesley (John).	24°	30
Christian Perfection, Scripture Doctrine of. Peck (George).	12°	1 50
Christian Philosopher. The Connection of Science and Philosophy with Religion. Dick (Thos.)	18°	45
Christian Purity; or, the Heritage of Faith. Foster (R. S.)	12°	1 50
Christian Singers of Germany. Winkworth (C.)	12°	1 75
*Christian Statesmen. A Portraiture of Sir Thomas Fowell Buxton. Mudge (Z. A.)	16°	1 00
Christian Student. Otheman (Edward).	18°	40
Christians and the Theater. Buckley (J. M.)	12°	70
Christian Theism. Testimony of Reason and Revelation to the Existence of a Supreme Being. Thompson (R. A.)	12°	1 50
Christian Theology. Clarke (A.)	12°	1 00
Christian Theology, Outlines of. Townsend (L. T.)	12°	*n* 40
Christianity, An Introduction to. Sutcliffe (J.)	18°	45

Christianity and Greek Philosophy; or the Relation
between Spontaneous and Reflective Thought
in Greece and the Positive Teaching of Christ
and His Apostles.   Cocker (B. F.)   8° $2 75
Christianity, Aspects of. Foote (A. L. R.)   16°   50
Christianity, Central Idea of. Peck (J. T.)   12°   1 25
Christianity, Early Years of. De Pressensé (E.) 12°   e1 50

> The Apostolic Era.
> The Martyrs and Apologists.
> Heresy and Christian Doctrine.
> Christian Life and Practice in the Early Church.

Christianity Tested by Eminent Men : Being Brief
Sketches of Christian Biography.   Caldwell
(Merritt).   16°   50
*Christmas Child, A. Sketch of a Boy-life. Moles-
worth (Mrs.) Illust.   16°   1 50
Christmas Chimes. Edited by Mrs. E. J. Knowles.
Illust.   12°   2 25
*Christie's Old Organ, Saved at Sea, and Little Faith.
Walton (Mrs. O. F.) In 1 vol.   16°   1 00
*Christmas Pie. Baker (Ella M.) Illust.   16°   1 25
Christus Consolator ; or, the Pulpit in Relation to
Social Life. Macleod (Alex.)   12°   1 75
Christus: A Mystery. Comprising The Divine
Tragedy, The Golden Legend, and The New
England Tragedies, etc. Longfellow (H. W.) 8°   3 00
Chronicles of an Old Manor-house. Sargent (G. E.)
Illust.   16°   1 50
Church History: Ancient and Modern, from the
Birth of Christ to the Year 1826.   Mosheim
(J. L. Von).   4°   5 00
Church Polity. Essay on. Stevens (A.)   12°   85
Church History, Outlines of. Hurst (John F.) Il-
lustrated with Maps.   12°   n 50
*Church History, Stories and Pictures from. For
Young People. Illust.   16°   1 00
Church School and Its Officers. Vincent (J. H.) 16°   65
*Cicely Brown's Trials. How she got into them,
How she got out of them, and What they did
for her. Prosser (Mrs.) Illust.   16°   1 00
Cicero, The Life of. Trollope (Anthony). 2 vols. 12°   3 00
Circumstantial Evidence of Christianity. Carey (D.) 16°   1 00

City and Ragged Schools, The. Guthrie (Thomas).	12°	$1 50
City of Sin, The, and its Capture by Immanuel's		
Army. An Allegory. Remington (E. F.)	12°	1 00
Clarke, Dr. Adam. Life of. Etheridge (J. W.)	12°	1 50
Class-leader, The. His Work, and How to Do it.		
With Illustrations of Principles, Needs, Meth-		
ods, and Results. Atkinson (John).	12°	1 25
Class-leaders, Address to. Janes (Bishop).	12°	20
Class-leader's Manual. Keys (Charles C.)	18°	40
Class Meetings. Miley (John).	18°	60
Classic Preachers of the English Church.	12°	1 50
Classical Writers. Edited by Green (J. R.)	16°	e 60

> Milton. Brooke (Stopford A.)　Virgil. Nettleship (H.)
> Euripides. Mahaffy (J. P.)　　Sophocles. Campbell (Lewis).
> 　　　　　Livy. Capes (W. W.)

*Clem and Joyce; or, the Prairie School. Smith		
(Mrs. F. B.) Illust.	18°	75
Clerical Library, The. Especially Adapted to the		
Use of Clergymen. 3 vols.	8°	e1 50

> Series 1. Three Hundred Outlines of Sermons on the New
> 　Testament.
> Series 2. Three Hundred Outlines of Sermons on the old
> 　Testament.
> Series 3. Outline Sermons to Children, with Numerous
> 　Anecdotes.

Club Essays. Swing (David).	16°	1 00
*Clover Beach. For Boys and Girls. Vandegrift		
(Margaret). Illust.	4°	1 25
*Cloverly. Higham (Mary R.)	12°	1 50
Coke, Rev. Dr. Life and Missionary Labors of.		
Drew (Samuel).	12°	80
Colenso, Fallacies of, Reviewed. Fowler (C. H.)	12°	60
*Columbus; or, the Discovery of America. Edited		
by Allen (Fred H.) Illust.	12°	1 00
*Columbus and the Discovery of America. Abbott		
(John S. C.) Illust.	12°	1 25
*Coming to the Light. Baker (S.)	16°	60
*Coming to the Light. Newbury (Mrs. F. E.) Illust.	16°	1 50
Commentaries. Bush (George). 4 vols.	12°	4 00

> Exodus.　Leviticus.　Numbers.　Joshua and Judges.

Commentary, Bible. Benson (Joseph). 5 vols. Cf.	8°	20 00
Commentary, Bible. Clarke (Adam). 6 vols. Cf.	8°	24 00

Commentary, Bible. Intended for Popular Use.
Edited by Whedon (D. D.)

    New Testament. 5 vols.   12° e$1 50

    Old Testament. 6 vols.   12°   e2 25

Commentary on the Book of Ecclesiastes. Young
(Royal).   8°   2 50

Commentary, The People's: Including Brief Notes
on the New Testament, with Copious References to Parallel and Illustrative Scripture
Passages, designed to assist Bible Students
and Common Readers to Understand the Meaning of the Inspired Word. Binney (Amos)
and Steele (Daniel). Revised with Topical
Index.   12°   3 00

Commentary on the Lord's Prayer. Denton (W.)   12°   85

*Communion Sabbath, The. Adams (Nehemiah). 12°   1 25

Companions for the Devout Life. A Series of Lectures on Well-known Devotional Works.   12°   1 50

Comparative Geography of Palestine and the Sina-
itic Peninsula, The. Adapted to the Use of
Biblical Students. Ritten (Carl). 4 vols.   8°   14 00

Comparative History of Religions. Moffat (Jas. C.)
2 vols. in one.   12°   2 50

    Part 1. Ancient Scriptures.   Part 2. Later Scriptures.

Comparative Zoölogy. Orton (James). Illust.   8°   3 00

Comprehensive Speaker, A: with Selections from
Best Authors.   12°   1 50

Concordance to the Hymnal of the Methodist Episcopal Church: To which are added Several
Important Indexes. Codville (Wm.)   12°   1 50

Concordance of the Holy Scriptures. Coles (Geo.) 18°   1 25

Concordance of the Bible, Young's Analytical.   4°   n3 65

Conduct of Life, The. Emerson (Ralph Waldo). 16°   1 50

Confessions of an English Opium-eater, and Kindred Papers. De Quincey (Thomas).   8°   1 75

Confucius: His Life and Teaching. Legge (James). 8°   4 00

*Conquering and to Conquer. By the Author of
"The Schönberg-Cotta Family."   12°   1 00

*Conrad: A Tale of Wiclif and Bohemia. Leslie
(Emma). Illust.   12°   1 25

Conscience. Cook (Joseph).   12°   1 50

*Consecrated. [Temperance.] Gilmore (Ernest). 12°   1 50

*Consecrated Life, A; or, Portraiture of Rev. Edwin Delmont Kelley, Missionary to Burmah. By His Wife. 12° $1 25

Consecration, Short Sermons on, and Kindred Themes. George (A. C.) 12° 1 00

*Consequences; or, A Bowl of Punch, and What Came of It. Dunning (Mrs. A. K.) 16° 1 25

Consolatio; or, Comfort for the Afflicted. Kenneway (C. C.) 16° 1 25

Constitution of the United States. Story (J.) 12° 1 05

*Contentment Better than Wealth. 12° 1 00

Concessions of "Liberalists" to Orthodoxy. The Deity of Christ, the Atonement, Endless Punishment. Dorchester (Daniel). 16° 1 25

*Contradictions; or, High Life at Edgerton. Dunning (Mrs. A. K.) Illust. 16° 1 50

Conversations for the Young: Designed to Promote the Profitable Reading of the Holy Scriptures. Watson (Richard). 12° 1 00

Conversion of the World, Suggestions for the. Young (Robert). 18° 35

Converted Collier, The. Morgan (R. C.) 18° 45

Converted Infidel. Scarlett (John). 18° 50

Convert's Guide and Preacher's Assistant. Merritt (Timothy). 18° 45

Cookman's Speeches. Speeches Delivered on Various Occasions. Cookman (George G.) 18° 30

Cooper, Mrs. Mary, Memoir of. Clarke (A.) 18° 40

*Cooper Stories. Being Narratives of Adventure Selected from the Works of J. Fenimore Cooper. Including Stories of the Prairie, Stories of the Woods, and Stories of the Sea. 3 vols. 16° e1 00

*Cortes; or, the Discovery and Conquest of Mexico. With a Brief Sketch of the More Recent History of the Country. Edited by Allen (Fred H.) Illust. 12° 1 00

Counsels to Young Men. Nott (E.) 18° 75

*Counsels to Converts. George (A. C.) 12° 1 00

*Count Raymond and the Crusade against the Albigenses. Elizabeth (Charlotte.) 16° 90

Court and Camp of Bonaparte, The. 18° 75

Cowper's Poems. Riverside Edition. 2 vols. 8° e1 75

*Craythorns of Stony Hallow. Hildeburn (Mary J.)
  Illust. 16° $1 15
Crayon Miscellany. Irving (Washington). 16° 1 25
Creation, The, and the Early Developments of So-
  ciety. Chapin (James H.) 12° 1 75
Credo. Townsend (L. T.) 16° 75
*Cripple Dan. Whitgift (A.) 18° 75
*Cripple of Antioch, and Other Scenes from Chris-
  tian Life in Early Times. Charles (E.) 16° 1 00
Critical and Miscellaneous Essays. Carlyle (T.)
  4 vols. 8° 7 50
Cromwell, Oliver. Carlyle (T.) 2 vols. 12° 3 50
*Cromwell, Oliver, Life of. Adams (Charles). Illust. 16° 1 00
*Cross in the Cell, The. The Way of Salvation Ex-
  plained to a Prisoner awaiting Execution.
  Adams (Nehemiah). 12° 1 00
*Cross in the Heart. Taylor (T.) 16° 65
Cruden, Alexander. Cruden's Complete Concord-
  ance. A Dictionary and Alphabetical Index to
  the Bible. (The Unabridged Edition.) 4° 2 75
*Crusade of the Children in the Thirteenth Century.
  Gray (George Z.) 12° 1 50
Crusades, The. Cox (G. W.) 16° 1 00
*Crystal River Turned into the Black Valley Rail-
  road Country, The. A Temperance Allegory.
  Hanks (S. W.) Illust. 16° 1 00
*Cuckoo Clock, The. Molesworth (Mrs.) Illust. 16° 1 50
Culture and Religion in Some of their Relations.
  Shairp (J. C.) 16° 1 25
*Cunning Workmen. A Story of Special Interest to
  Sunday-school Workers. Alden (Mrs. G. R.
  [Pansy].) Illust. 16° 1 25
*Curious Facts for Little People about Animals.
  Illust. 16° 85
*Curious Schools. Very fully illustrated from Orig-
  inal Drawings. 12° 1 00
Cyclopædia of Biblical, Theological, and Ecclesias-
  tical Literature, A. McClintock (John) and
  Strong (James). 10 vols. Cloth. 8° 50 00
  Sheep. 8° 60 00
Cyclopædia of British and American Poetry. Edited
  by Sargent (Epes.) 8° 4 50

Cyclopædia of Poetical Illustrations. Foster (Elon).
   First and Second Series.   8° *c*$5 00

Cyclopædia of Prose Illustrations. Foster (Elon).
   First and Second Series.   8° *c*5 00

Cyclopædia of United States History, Popular.
   From the Aboriginal Period to 1876. Containing Brief Sketches of Important Events and
   Conspicuous Actors. Lossing (Benson J.) Illustrated by two Steel-plate Portraits and over
   1,000 Engravings. 2 vols.   8°   12 00

Cyrus and Alexander. Abbott (Jacob).   16°   1 00

DAILY Walk with Wise Men; or, Religious Exercises for Every Day in the Year. Head
   (Nelson).   12°   1 75

*Daisy Seymour. L. A. F. Illust.   16°   1 25

Dance of Modern Society, The. Wilkinson (W. C.) 18°   60

Dancing, Essay on, Crane (J. T.)   18°   30

Dan'el Quorm and His Religious Notions. Pearse
   (Mark Guy). Illust.   12°   80

Dangerous Tendencies. Certain Dangerous Tendencies in American Life, and Other Papers.   16°   1 25

Dan Young, Autobiography of. Strickland (W. P.) 12°   1 50

*Daniel Boone, Life of. Bogart (W. H,) Illust.   12°   1 25

Daniel the Beloved. Taylor (Wm. M.)   12°   1 50

Daring Deeds of American Heroes. Brayman
   (J. G.)   12°   1 25

David, King of Israel: His Life and its Lessons.
   Taylor (Wm. M.)   12°   2 00

David, the King of Israel: A Portrait Drawn from
   Bible History and the Book of Psalms. Krum-
   macher (Frederick William). Translated by
   M. G. Easton.   12°   1 75

*Davy's Jacket. Inner and Outer Phases of Young
   Life. Ward (Hetta L. H.) Illust.   18°   75

Days of Bruce. A Story from Scottish History.
   Aguilar (Grace). Illust.   12°   1 00

Day with Christ, A. Cox (Samuel).   16°   1 00

*Deacon Gibbs's Enemy. Dunning (Mrs. A. K.)
   Illust.   16°   1 25

Death-bed Scenes. Dying with and without Religion. Clark (D. W.)   12°   1 50

Declamations and Dialogues. Adapted to Sunday-
school Occasions. Gilmore (J. H.)   16° $0 50

Deephaven. Jewett (Sarah O.)   18°   1 25

Defense of Jesus. From the French of Menard St.
Martin. Cobden (Paul).   12°   1 00

Defense of Our Fathers. Emory (Bishop).   8°   85

Demonstration of the Truth of the Christian Religion. Keith (Alex.) Illust.   12°   1 50

De Quincey. Mason (David).   12°   75

De Stael, Madame. A Study of her Life and
Times. The First Revolution and the First
Empire. Stevens (Abel). 2 vols.   12°   3 00

*Devil's Chain, The. A Temperance Story. Jenk-
ins (Edward).   16°   75

*Dewdrops and Sunshine. A Collection of Poems
about Little Children. Edited by Mrs. J. P.
Newman.   18°   1 25

Dialogues of Plato, The. Jowett (B.) 4 vols.   8°   e 2 00

Diamond Dust. Willing (Jennie Fowler).   16°   1 00

Diamonds. Unpolished and Polished. Richmond
(J. F.) Illust.   12°   1 00

Diana. Warner (Susan).   12°   1 75

Diary of a Country Pastor, Extracts from. Gardner (Mrs. H. C.)   12°   85

*Diary of Kitty Trevylyan. A Story of the Times
of Whitefield and the Wesleys. By the Author of "The Schönberg-Cotta Family."   12°   1 00

Dictionary of Dates. Haydn (Jos.)`   8°   5 00

Dictionary of Roman and Greek Antiquities, A.
With nearly 2,000 Engravings on Wood, from
Ancient Originals, Illustrative of the Industrial
Arts and Social Life of Greeks and Romans.
Rich (Anthony).   8°   4 00

Dio the Athenian; or, From Olympus to Calvary.
Burr (E. F.) Illust.   12°   2 00

Discipline, Baker on the. A Guide in the Administration of the Discipline of the Methodist
Episcopal Church. Baker (Bishop).   12°   1 00

Discipline, History of the Revisions of. Sherman
(David).   12°   2 25

*Discontent, and Other Stories. Gardner (Mrs. H. C.) 16°   1 00

Discovery of America, The. Abbott (J.) 3 vols.   16°   c 75

Discovery and Adventures in Polar Regions. 18° $0 75

Discoveries in North and Central Africa. Barth
    (Henry). Illust. 3 vols. 8° 12 00

*Distinguished Females. Written for Girls, with a
    View to their Mental and Moral Improvement. 12° 75

Divina Commedia of Dante. Translated by Long-
    fellow (H. W.) 8° 3 00

Divine Law as to Wines, The. Sampson (Geo. W.) 12° 1 00

Divine Mysteries. The Divine Treatment of Sin,
    and the Divine Mystery of Peace. Brown
    (J. Baldwin). 12° 1 50

*Docia's Journal; or, God is Love. Alden (Mrs.
    G. R. [Pansy].) 16° 75

Doctrinal Tracts. Revised. Wesley (J.) 18° 60

*Doings of the Bodley Family in Town and Country.
    Scudder (Horace E.) Illust. Boards. 4° 1 50

Dolliver Romance, The, and Other Pieces. Haw-
    thorne (N.) 16° 1 50

Domestic Piety and Family Government. Power
    (J. H.) 18° 40

*Domestic Problems. Work and Culture in the
    Household. Illust. 16° 1 00

*Donald Fraser. 16° 1 00

*Dora Hamilton; or, Sunshine and Shadow. Illust. 16° 75

*Dora's Boy. Ross (Mrs. Ellen). Illust. 16° 1 00

*Draytons and the Davenants, The. A Story of the
    Civil Wars. By the Author of "The Schön-
    berg-Cotta Family." 12° 1 00

*Dr. Deane's Way, and Other Stories. Faye Hunt-
    ington and Alden (Mrs. G. R. [Pansy].) Illust. 16° 1 25

Dr. Grant and the Mountain Nestorians. Laurie
    (Thomas). Maps and Illust. 16° 1 50

*Dr. Plassid's Patients. Bailey (Una Locke). Illust. 16° 1 25

*Dreams and Deeds. 16° 50

*Drifting Anchor. Religion in Daily Life Illustrated.
    Winton (Nelson W.) Illust. 16° 1 25

*Drifting and Anchored. Richmond (E. J.) Illust. 16° 1 00

Dryden. Saintsbury (G.) 12° 75

*Duncan Matheson, the Scottish Evangelist, Life
    and Labors of. MacPherson (John). 16° 1 25

Dutch Republic, The Rise of. Motley (John L.)
    3 vols. 8° 6 00

Duchess of Orleans, Memoir of. 12° $1 25
*Duties and Duties. Giberne (Agnes). 16° 1 25
Duty: With Illustrations of Courage, Patience, and
    Endurance. Smiles (S.) 12° 1 00
*Dying Savior and the Gipsy Girl. Sibee (Marie). 18° 45

EAGLE Nest. Ruskin. 12° 1 50
Early Christian Literature Primers. Edited by
    Fisher (George Park). 2 vols. 18° e 60

    Vol. 1. Containing the Apostolic Fathers, and The Apolo-
      gists of the Second Century, A. D. 95-180. Jackson
      (G. A.)
    Vol. 2. Containing the Fathers of the Third Century.

*Early Choice, The. A Book for Daughters. Tweedie
-   (W. K.) Illust. 16° 1 00
*Early Crowned. A Memoir of Mary E. North. 16° 1 00
*Early Dawn, The; or, Sketches of Christian Life in
    England in the Early Time. By the Author
    of "The Schonberg-Cotta Family." 12° 1 00
Early Kings of Norway, The. Carlyle (T.) 12° 1 50
Earnest Christian's Library. 4 vols. 16° e 1 00

    Plain Words on Christian Living. Sure Words of Promise.
    The Cross of Jesus.   The Soul-gatherer.

*Earnest Men, Life and Works of. Tweedie (W K.) 12° 1 50
*Earth and its Wonders. Adams (Charles). Illust. 16° 1 00
Ecce Deus. Parker (Jos.) 18° 1 50
Ecce Deus Homo; or, The Work and Kingdom of
    the Christ of Scripture. 12° 1 50
Ecce Homo. A Survey of the Life and Work of
    Jesus Christ. Seeley (J. R.) 12° 1 50
Ecce Unitas. A Plea for Christian Unity, in which
    its True Principles and Basis are Considered. 12° 60
*Echoing and Re-echoing. The Great Truths
    Spoken by the Minister Echoed and Re-echoed
    by the People. Character, as affected by truth,
    vividly and delightfully Portrayed. Hunting-
    ton (Faye). Illust. 12° 1 50
Eddy, Rev. Thomas M., D. D., Life of. Sims
    (Charles N.) 12° 1 50
*Edith Prescott; or, Lessons of Love. Marshall
    (Mrs. Emma). Illust. 16° 1 25
*Edith Vernon's Life-work. Illust. 16° 1 00
Education as a Science. Bain (Alex.) 12° 1 75

Egypt: From the Earliest Times to B. C. 300 Years.
Birch (S.)   Illust.   12° $1 00

Eighteenth Century in Literature and Scholarship.
De Quincey (Thomas).   8°   1 75

Eighteen Christian Centuries.   White (James).   12°   2 00

*Eleanor's Three Birthdays.   McKeever (Harriet B.) 16°   1 00

*Electa: A Story of a Minister's Daughter.   Conk-
lin (Mrs. N.)   12°   1 50

Elements of Intellectual Science.   Porter (Noah). 8°   3 00

*Elfreda.   A Sequel to Leofwine.   Leslie (Emma).
Illust.   12°   1 25

Elijah the Favored Man.   A Life and its Lessons
for to-day.   Patterson (R. M.)   16°   1 00

Elijah the Prophet.   Taylor (Wm. M.)   12°   1 50

*Elizabeth Christine, Wife of Frederick the Great.
From German and Other Sources.   Hurst (Cath-
erine E.)   5 Illust.   16°   1 25

*Elizabeth Tudor.   The Queen and the Woman.
Townsend (Virginia F.)   Illust.   16°   1 25

*Ellerslie House Library.   Illust.   4 vols.   16°   4 00

    Ellerslie House.   Kate and Her Cousins.
    Alice Thorne.   Wreck of the Osprey.

Elocution, The Science of.   With Exercises and
Selections Arranged for Acquiring the Art of
Reading and Speaking.   Hamill (S. S.)   12°   1 50

*Elsie Dinsmore.   Finley (Martha).   16°   1 25

*Elsie's Girlhood.   Finley (Martha).   16°   1 25

*Elsie's Holiday at Roselands.   Finley (Martha). 16°   1 25

*Elsie's Womanhood.   Finley (Martha).   16°   1 25

*Elsie's Motherhood.   Finley (Martha).   16°   1 25

*Elsie's Children.   Finley (Martha).   16°   1 25

*Elsie's Widowhood.   Finley (Martha).   16°   1 25

Elsie Venner.   Holmes (O. W.)   12°   2 00

*Emigrant Children; or, Learning to Follow Jesus. 16°   1 25

*Emily Douglas; or, A Year with the Camerons.   16°   1 00

*Emily Vernon; or, Filial Piety Exemplified.   Drum-
mond (Mrs.)   16°   85

Eminent English Liberals.   Davidson (J. Morrison). 16°   1 00

Emory, Bishop, Life of.   Emory (R.)   8°   1 75

Emotions of the Will, The.   Bain (Alex.)   8°   5 00

Encyclopedia of Religious Knowledge.   Edited by
J. Newton Brown.   Sheep.   8°   5 00

*End of a Coil, The. Warner (Miss Anna). 12° $1 75

Endless Punishment. Adams (Nehemiah). 12° 1 00

England's Antiphon. MacDonald (George). 12° 1 75

*England Two Hundred Years Ago. Gillett (E. H.) 16° 1 50

*England's Yeomen. From Life in the Nineteenth
Century. Charlesworth (Maria L.) 12° 1 50

English Colonies in America. A Short History of
the English Colonies in America. Lodge
(Henry Cabot). Half-leather. 8° 3 00

English Governess at the Siamese Court. Leonowens (Anna H.) 12° 1 25

English Literature, History of. Taine (H. A.)
2 vols. in one. 16° 1 50

English Literature in the Reign of Victoria. With
a Glance at the Past. Morley (Henry). 8° 2 00

English Men of Letters. Edited by Morley (John). 12° e 75

Johnson. Stephen (Leslie).	Milton. Pattison (Mark).
Gibbon. Morrison (Jas. C.)	Southey. Dowden (Edward).
Scott. Hutton (R. H.)	Bunyan. Froude (J. A.)
Shelley. Symonds (Jno. A.)	Chaucer. Ward (A. W.)
Goldsmith. Black (Wm.)	Cowper. Smith (Goldwin).
Hume. Huxley (Prof.)	Pope. Stephen (Leslie).
DeFoe. Minto (Wm.)	Byron. Nichol (John).
Burns. Shairp (Principal).	Locke. Fowler (Thomas).
Spenser. Church (R. W.)	Wordsworth. Myers (F.)
Thackeray. Trollope (Ant'y).	Dryden. Saintsbury (G.)
Burke. Morley (John).	Landor. Colvin (Prof. S.)
De Quincey. Masson (D.)	Hawthorne. James (Henry).

*English Alice. Illust. 16° 75

English Men of Science: Their Nature and Nurture. Galton (Francis). 12° 1 00

English Note-book. Hawthorne (N.) 2 vols. 16° e 1 50

English Poets, The. Student's Edition. 12° e 1 00

> Vol. 1. Chaucer to Donne.
> Vol. 2. Ben Jonson to Dryden.
> Vol. 3. Addison to Blake.
> Vol. 4. Wordsworth to Sidney Dobell.

*Entertainments. For Concerts, Exhibitions, Parlor
Gatherings, Church Festivals, etc. Champney
(Lizzie W.) Illust. 16° 1 00

*Envelope, The Full; or, Gleanings for Youthful
Readers. Donkersley (Richard). 1 illust. 16° 85

Ephphatha; or, the Amelioration of the World.
Farrar (F. W.) 12° 1 50

Episcopal Controversy and Defense. Emory
   (Bishop). 1 vol.   8° $1 20
Episcopal Controversy Reviewed. Emory (Bishop).   8°   90
Episcopius, The Life of. Calder (Frederic).   12°   1 00
Epworth Singers, The; and Other Poets of Meth-
   odism. Christopher (S. W.)   12°   3 00
Era of the Protestant Revolution, The. Seebohm (F.) 16°   1 00
Essays on Educational Reformers, The. Quick
   (R. H.)   12°   1 50
Essays: Historical and Miscellaneous. Macaulay.
   3 vols.   3 75
The same, in 1 vol.   1 50
Essays in Biography and Criticism. Bayne (Peter).
   2 vols.   12°   2 00
Essays in Philosophy. De Quincey (Thomas).   8°   1 75
Essays, Educational. Thomson (E.)   12°   1 25
Essays, Moral and Religious. Thomson (E.)   12°   1 25
*Ester Ried. Showing the Actual Struggles through
   which Victorious Souls must go to their Suc-
   cessive and Loftier Heights, and to their Final
   Coronation. Alden (Mrs. G. R. [Pansy].)
   Illust.   12°   1 50
*Ethel Linton; or, The Feversham Temper.   16°   1 00
Eternal Hope. Farrar (F. W.)   12°   2 00
Eucharist, Nature and Design of the. Clarke
   (Adam).   18°   30
Europe, Letters from. Thomson (E.)   12°   1 25
*Europe, Scenes in; or, Observations by an Amateur
   Artist. Post (Loretta J.)   12°   1 00
*Evening Rest. Under the Shadow of the Great
   Shepherd. Illust.   16°   1 50
*Evenings with the Children; or, Travels in South
   . America. Ramsey (Mrs.) Illust.   16°   1 00
Evenings with the Doctrines. Adams (Nehemiah). 12°   1 00
*Every Man in His Place. A Story for Boys. Illust. 16°   75
Evangelical Rationalism; or, A Consideration of
   Truths Practically Related to Man's Probation.
   Knox (L. L.)   16°   1 00
Evangelist, The True. Porter (J.)   16°   50
*Every Inch a King. A Story Illustrating the Reigns
   of David and Solomon, Kings of Israel. Gard-
   ner (Celia E.)   12°   1 25

Evidence of the Christian Religion, Derived from
the Literal Fulfillment of Prophecy. Keith
(Alex.)   12° $1 50
Evidences of Christianity. Barnes (A.)   12°   1 75
Evidences of Christianity, The. Paley (Wm.)   18°   75
Evidences of Christianity. Whately (Archbishop). 18°   30
Evidences of Revealed Religion. Thomson (E.)   12°   1 25
Every-day Religion. Sermons. Talmage (T. De
Witt.)   12°   2 00
Everlasting Righteousness, The. Bonar (Horatius). 16°   1 25
*Evenings at Home. Aikin (John) and Barbauld
(Mrs. A. L.) Illust.   16°   1 00
Evenings at the Microscope; or, Researches among
the Minuter Organs and Forms of Animal Life.
Gosse (P. H.)   12°   1 50
Evenings with the Sacred Poets. Talks about Sing-
ers and their Songs. Saunders (F.)   12°   1 75
Evolution, The Doctrine of: Its Data, Principles,
Speculations, and its Theistic Bearings. Win-
chell (Alex.)   12°   1 00
Excellent Woman, The, as Described in the Book
of Proverbs. With an Introduction by Wm.
B. Sprague. Illust.   16°   1 50
Excursions in Field and Forest. Emerson (R. W.) 16°   1 50
Exeter Hall Lectures: Delivered before the Young
Men's Christian Association, London. 20 vols. 12°   20 00
*Exiles in Babylon; or, The Children of Light.
A. L. O. E. Illust.   16°   1 00
Exposition of the Epistle of St. Paul to the Colos-
sians. Daillé (Jean).   8°   2 50
Exposition of the Epistle of St. Paul to the Philip-
pians. Daillé (Jean).   8°   2 00
Exposition of the Epistle to the Ephesians. In a
Series of Discourses. Lathrop (Joseph).   8°   2 75
*Eyes and Ears; or, How I See and Hear. Illust. 16°   1 25

*FABRICS. Inculcates the Lesson of Loving and
Living for others. Illust.   16°   1 50
Facts about Wives and Mothers. Donkersley (R.) 12°   1 00
Fairbairn on Prophecy.   8°   2 50
*Fairy-land of Science, The. Buckley (A. B.) Illust. 12°   1 50
Faith and Character. Vincent (M. R.)   12°   1 50

Faith : A Poem.   Leavitt (J. M.)   12° $0 40
*Faith Gartney's Girlhood.   Whitney (Mrs. A. D. T.) 12°   1 50
*Faithful, but not Famous.   Incidents in France in
    the Days of the Protestants.   Illust.   16°   1 25
*Faithful in Little.   Story of a Carrier-dove.   16°   1 00
Faithful to the End.   The Story of Emile Cook's
    Life.   Houghton (Louise S.)   16°   1 00
Famous American Indians.   Historical Series for
    Young People.   Eggleston (Edward) and Oth-
    ers.   Illust.   5 vols.   12° e1 25

        Tecumseh and the Shawnee Prophet.
        Red Eagle and the Wars with the Creek Indians.
        Pocahontas and Powhatan.
        Brandt and Red Jacket.
        Montezuma.

Farm Ballads.   Carleton (Will).   Illust.   8°   2 00
Farm Legends.   Carleton (Will).   Illust.   8°   2 00
Fall of Man : and Other Sermons.   Farrar (F. W.) 12°   1 50
Fall of the Stuarts, The : and Western Europe from
    1678 to 1697.   Hale (E. E.)   16°   1 00
*False Shame.   Illust.   16°   1 00
*Family at Heatherdale ; or, the Influence of Chris-
    tian Principles.   Mackay (Mrs.)   Illust.   16°   75
*Familiar Talks to Boys.   Hall (John).   16°   50
Familiar talks on English Literature.   Richardson
    (Abby Sage).   12°   2 00
Famous Americans of Recent Times.   Biographical
    Sketches of Henry Clay, Daniel Webster, John
    C. Calhoun, John Randolph, Stephen Girard,
    and Many Others.   8°   2 00
Famous London Merchants.   A Book for Boys.
    Bourne (H. R. Fox).   Illust.   16°   1 00
Famous Sculptors and Sculpture.   Shedd (Mrs.
    Julia A.)   8°   3 00
*Fan's Brother ; or, An Old Head on Young Shoul-
    ders.   Marshall (Beatrice).   Illust.   16°   50
Far East, The ; or, Letters from Egypt, Palestine,
    etc.   12°   1 75
Faraday as a Discoverer.   Tyndall (John).   12°   1 00
*Farmer-boy, The ; and How he became Commander-
    in-chief.   A Life of George Washington.   Ju-
    vinell (Uncle).   16°   1 00

*Farmer Tompkins and His Bibles. Beecher (Willis J.) Illust.   16° $1 25

Fate of Republics. Townsend (L. T.)   16°   75

Father Reeves. Methodist Class-leader. Corderoy (Edward.)   18°   30

*Father's Coming Home. A Story of the Christie Family, and what they did to Welcome their Father Home. Illust.   16°   85

*Fault-finding, and Madeline Hascall's Letter. Gardner (Mrs. H. C.)   16°   1 00

Favorite Poems. A Choice Selection from English and American Authors. Red-line. Illust.   16°   1 25

Fellowship. Letters Addressed to My Sister Mourners. Farrar (F. W.)   8°   1 00

Female Biography, Gems of. Smith (D.)   18°   65

*Fern Glen; or, Lilian's Prayer. Holt (M. H.) Illust.   16°   1 25

Fernside Library, The. Illust. 6 vols .   7 50

> Ann Ash; or, Kindness Rewarded.
> Anne Dalton; or, How to be Useful.
> The Convict's Sons; and, The Two Farmers.
> Don't Say So; or, You May be Mistaken.
> The Errand-boy; or, Your Time is Your Employer's.
> The Two Firesides; or, The Mechanic and the Tradesman.

*Fiddling Freddie. Forest (Neil).   16°   1 00

Fifty Years a Presiding Elder. Cartwright (Peter).   12°   1 25

*Fifty Years with the Sabbath-school. Ballard (A. C.)   12°   1 25

*Fighting the Enemy. Miller (Emily Huntington). Illust.   16°   1 00

Finette, the Norman Maiden, and Her English Friends. Ropes (Mary E.) Illust.   16°   1 00

Finley, Rev. J. B. Autobiography of Rev. J. B. Finley.   12°   1 75

*Fireside Reading. Clark (D. W.) 5 vols.   16°   5 00

> Traits and Anecdotes of Birds and Fishes.
> Traits and Anecdotes of Animals.
> Historical Sketches.
> Travels and Adventures.
> True Tales for the Spare Hour.

Fireside Travels. Lowell (J. R.) Household Edition.   12°   2 00

First Principles of Household Management and Cookery. Parloa (Maria).   16°   75

*Fisher-boy, The; or, Michael Penguyne. Glimpses
    of Fisher Life on the Cornish Coast. Kingston
    (W. H. G.) Illust.   16° $1 00
Five Gateways of Knowledge, The. Wilson (Geo.) 16°   75
*Five Little Peppers, and How They Grew. Sidney
    (Margaret). Illust.   12°   1 50
Five Women of England. Middleton (Meade).   16°   1 40
*Flavia; or, Loyal to the End. A Tale of the Church
    in the Second Century. Leslie (Emma). Illust. 12° 1 25
*Fleda and the Voice. With Other Stories. Lath-
    bury (Mary A. [Aunt May].) Illust.   8°   1 25
Fletcher, Beauties of. Being Extracts from his
    Checks to Antinomianism. Spicer (T.)   12°   80
Fletcher, John, Life of. Benson (Joseph).   12°   1 00
Fletcher, Mrs. Mary, Life of. Moore (Henry).   12°   1 25
Fletcher, Rev. J., Works of. 4 vols. Sheep.   8° 10 00
Fletcher's Address to Seekers of Salvation.   18°   15
Fletcher's Appeal and Address.   18°   45
Fletcher's Checks to Antinomianism. 2 vols.   8°   5 00
Fletcher's Letters.   12°   1 00
*Florence Egerton; or, Sunshine and Shadow. Illust. 16°   85
*Flower by the Prison. New Five Hundred Dollar
    Prize Stories. Illust.   16°   1 25
Flowers of the Garden and Parlor. Rand (Ed-
    ward S.)   8°   2 50
*Flower of the Family, The. A Book for Girls.
    Prentiss (Mrs. E.)   16°   1 50
Flowers for the Sky. Proctor (Richard A.) Illust. 12°   1 00
Follow the Lamb. Bonar (Horatius).   18°   40
*Following the Master. Beckwith (E. L.)   16°   1 10
Food and Nutrition, Philosophy of. Sidney (E.) 16°   60
Fool's Errand, A. Tourgee (A. W.)   16°   1 00
Footprints of an Itinerant. Gaddis (M. P.)   12°   1 75
*Footprints of Famous Men. Edgar (J. G.)   16°   1 00
Footsteps of St. Paul. Macduff (John R.) Illust. 12°   1 50
Footsteps of St. Peter. Macduff (John R.) Illust. 12°   2 00
*Forest Boy, The. A Sketch of the Life of Abra-
    ham Lincoln. Mudge (Z. A.) Illust.   16°   1 00
*For Mack's Sake. Burke (S. J.) Illust.   12°   1 25
Forms of Water, The. In Clouds and Rivers, Ice
    and Glaciers. Tyndall (John). Illust.   12°   1 50
Foundations; or, Castles in the Air. Porter (Rose). 16°   1 00

Foundations of Christianity, The.   Gibson (J. Monro).   16° $1 00

Fountain Kloof, The ; or Missionary Life in South Africa. Illust.   16°   1 50

*Four Feet, Wings and Fins.   Anderson-Maskel (Mrs. A. E.) Illust.   4°   1 75

*Four Girls at Chautauqua.   Girl Life and Character Portrayed with Rare Power.   Alden (Mrs. G. R. [Pansy].) Illust.   12°   1 50

Four Happy Days, The.   Havergal (Miss F. R.)   12°   40

Four Months in a Sneak-box.   A Boat Voyage of Twenty-six Hundred Miles down the Ohio and Mississippi Rivers, and along the Gulf of Mexico.   Bishop (Nathaniel H.) Illust.   8°   2 50

Four Years Among Spanish Americans.   Hassaurek (F.)   12°   1 75

Forty Years in the Turkish Empire.   Memoirs of Rev. William Goodell, D. D.   Prime (E. D. G.)   8°   2 50

Fragments, Religious and Theological.   A Collection of Papers Relating to Various Points of Christian Life and Doctrine.   Curry (Daniel). 12°   1 50

Francis of Assisi.   Oliphant (Mrs.)   12°   1 75

*Frank Harley, Little.   Paper cover.   12°   30

*Fraulein Mina ; or, Life in an American German Family.   Norris (Miss Mary H.) Illust.   16°   1 00

Frederick the Great.   Carlyle (Thos.) 6 vols.   12°   12 00

*Fred and Jeanie.   How They Learned about God. Drinkwater (Jennie M.)   16°   1 25

*French Bessie.   18°   50

French Men of Letters.   Mauris (M.)   18°   60

French Mission Life.   Carter (Thomas).   16°   50

French Revolution, The.   Carlyle (Thos.) 2 vols.   12°   e1 75

Fresh Leaves from The Book and Its Story. Ranyard (Ellen). Illust.   12°   2 00

Friends of Christ, The.   Adams (Nehemiah).   12°   1 00

Friendships of the Bible.   Illust.   12°   75

*Fritz's Victory, and Other Stories.   A. L. O. E. Illust.   18°   75

*From Bethlehem to Calvary.   Latimer (Faith). Illust.   16°   75

From Dan to Beersheba.   The Land of Promise as it now Appears.   Newman (J. P.) Illust.   12°   1 75

*From Dawn to Dark in Italy. A Tale of the Reformation in the Sixteenth Century. Illust.   16° $1 50

*From Different Stand-points. Alden (Mrs. G. R. [Pansy].) Illust.   12°   1 50

From Egypt to Japan. Fields (H. M.)   12°   2 00

From Egypt to Palestine. Through Syria, the Wilderness, and the South Country. Bartlett (S. C.) Illust.   8°   3 50

From Exile to Overthrow. A History of the Jews, etc. Mears (John W.) Illust.   16°   1 40

*From June to June. Cooke (Carrie A.) Illust.   16°   1 50

From the Lakes of Killarney to the Golden Horn. Field (H. M.)   12°   2 00

*From Night to Light. A Story of Bible Times. Brown (E. E.) Illust.   16°   1 25

*From Seventeen to Thirty. Binney (T.)   16°   75

*Fur-clad Adventurers; or, Travels in Skin Canoes, on Dog-sledges, on Reindeer and on Snow-shoes, through Alaska, Kamtchatka, and Eastern Siberia. Mudge (Z. A.) Illust.   16°   1 00

Future Religious Policy of America. Halstead (Wm. Riley).   12°   1 50

*Gaffney's Tavern; and the Entertainment it Afforded. Hildeburn (Mary J.) Illust.   16°   1 10

Garden of Sorrows; or, The Ministry of Tears. Atkinson (John). Revised Edition.   12°   1 25

Garden of Spices. Extracts from the Religious Letters of Rev. Samuel Rutherford. Dunn (L. R.)   12°   1 50

Garland, The. A Collection of Choice Poetry. Compiled by E. P. Gurney.   12°   1 50

Garrettson, Rev. Freeborn, Life of. Bangs (N.)   12°   80

Gatch, Rev. P., Sketch of. McLean (Judge).   16°   50

Gates Ajar, The. Phelps (Elizabeth S.)   16°   1 50

Gaussen's Origin and Inspiration of the Bible.   12°   1 50

*Gayworthys, The. A Story of Threads and Thrums. Whitney (Mrs. A. D. S.)   12°   1 50

Gems from the Coral Islands. Incidents of Contrast between Savage and Christian Life of the South Sea Islanders. Gill (William). Illust.   12°   1 25

Gems from the Coral Islands. Western Polynesia.
Gill (William). Illust. 12° $1 10

Gems of Genius. Famous Painters and Their Pictures. French (H. W.) Illust. 4° 3 00

Gems of India; or, Sketches of Distinguished Hindoo and Mohammedan Women. Humphrey (Mrs. E. J.) Illust. 12° 1 00

*Geneva's Shield. A Story of the Swiss Reformation. Blackburn (Wm. M.) Illust. 16° 1 00

Gentle Measures in the Management and Training of the Young. Abbott (Jacob). 12° 1 75

Gentile Nations, History of the. Smith (G.) Sheep. 8° 3 00

*Geoffrey, the Lollard. An Historical Story. Eastwood (Frances). 16° 90

Geological Sketches. Agassiz (Louis). Illust. 16° 1 50

Geological Sketches. Second Series. Agassiz (Louis). Illust. 16° 1 50

*George Clifford's Loss and Gain. Showing Religion to be the Chief Concern. Illust. 16° 1 00

*George Washington; or, Life in America one Hundred Years Ago. Abbott (John S. C.) Illust. 12° 1 25

*Gerald. A Story of To-day. Leslie (Emma). Illust. 12° 1 25

German Home-life. 12° 1 50

*Gertrude Terry. Graham (Mary). Illust. 16° 1 35

*Getting Ahead. Alden (Mrs. G. R. [Pansy].) 16° 75

*Giant-killer; The; or, The Battle which All Must Fight: and Sequel. A. L. O. E. 18° 75

*Gilbert Harland; or, Good in Every Thing. Barwell (Mrs.) 12° 60

*Giles Oldham; or, Miracles of Heavenly Love. A. L. O. E. 18° 75

*Gipsy Books. Pollard (Josephine). Illust. 6 vols.
In a box. 16° 4 50

Gipsy's Early Days.   Gipsy's Adventures.
Gipsy in New York.   Gipsy's Quest.
Gipsy's Travels.   The Other Gipsy.

*Girl's Money, A. Farman (Ella). Illust. 16° 1 00

*Glance Gaylord Series. Gaylord (Glance). 3 vols.
In box. 16° 3 25

Mr. Pendleton's Cup.   Jimmy's Shoes.
          Miss Patience Hathaway.

*Glaucia. A Story of Athens in the First Century. Leslie (Emma). Illust. 12° 1 25

Glaucus; or, The Wonders of the Sea-shore.
Kingsley (Charles). Illust.   12° $1 75

Gleanings in the Field of Art. Cheney (Mrs. E. D.) 12°   2 50

Glencoe Parsonage. Porter (Mrs. A. E.) Illust.   16°   1 00

*Glen Elder Books. Illust. 5 vols. In a box.   16°   5 00

> The Orphans of Glen Elder.   The Lyceum Boys.
> Frances Leslie.   ˙   The Harleys of Chelsea Place.
>   Resa Lindesay.

*Glen Morris Stories. Wise (Daniel). 5 vols. In
a box. Illust.   16°   5 00

> Guy Carlton.   Jessie Carlton.
> Dick Duncan.   Walter Sherwood.
>   Kate Carlton.

*Glenwood. Bloomfield (Julia K.)   16°   1 00

*Glimpses of our Lake Region in 1863, and Other
Papers. Gardner (Mrs. H. C.)   16°   1 25

*Glimpses Through. With Noble Views of Sickness,
Death, and the Future World. Biscoe (Ellen
L.) Illust.   16°   1 50

Globe Edition of the Poets. Illust.   16°   *e* 1 25

> Campbell.   Dante.   Herbert.
> Chaucer.   Dryden.   Milton.
> Cowper.   Hemans. 2 vols.

Glory of God in Man, The. Gifford (E. H.)   8°   1 00

*God in History and in Science. Cumming (J.)   16°   65

God-Man. Search and Manifestation. Townsend
(L. T.)   16°   75

God's Word Through Preaching. ˙ Being the Yale
Lectures for 1875. Hall (John).   12°   1 25

*God's Way; or, Gaining the Better Life. Holt
(M. A.) Illust.   16°   75

*Gold and Gilt. Capron (Mary J.) Illust.   12°   1 25

Gold and the Gospel.   12°   65

Golden Gleams of Thought. From the Words of
Leading Orators, Divines, Philosophers, States-
men, and Poets. Linn (S. P.)   8°   2 50

Golden Legend, The. Longfellow (H. W.)   16°   1 00

*Golden Lines. Illust.   16°   1 50

Golden Maxims for Every Day in the Year.   24°   25

Golden Poems by British and American Authors.
Edited by Francis F. Brown.   8°   2 50

Gold of Chickaree, The. Warner (Susan and
Anna).   12°   1 75

*Gold Threads, The, and Wee Davie. Macleod (N.)
   Illust.   16° $0 75
Good English; or, Popular Errors in Language.
   Gould (Edward S.)   12°   1 25
*Good-for Nothing Polly. A Story of Boy-life. Far-
   man (Ella). Illust.   16°   1 00
Good Girl and True Woman; or, Elements of Suc-
   cess Drawn from the Life of Mary Lyon and
   Other Similar Characters. Thayer (Wm. M.)   16°   1 00
*Good Hope Series, The. Illust. 4 vols. In box.   16°   3 25
   Belle Clement's Influence.   Lulu Reed's Pup
   Sophie's Letter-book.   Edith Withington.
*Good Voices, The. A Child's Guide to the Bible.
   Illust.   8°   1 00
*Good Work. A Story of Earnest and Successful
   Effort. Chellis (Mary D.) Illust.   16°   1 50
Gospel in Ezekiel, The. Guthrie (Thomas).   12°   1 50
Gospel in the Trees. With Opinions on Common
   Things and Fraternal Methodism. Clark
   (Alex.)   12°   1 00
*Gospel Life of Jesus, The. Davis (L. A.)   16°   1 25
Gospel Miracles, The, in their Relation to Christ
   and Christianity. Taylor (Wm. M.)   12°   1 50
Gospel Records. Their Genuineness, Authenticity,
   Historic Verity, and Inspiration, with some
   Preliminary Remarks on the Gospel History.
   Nast (William).   12°   1 50
Gospel Temperance. Van Buren (J. M.)   12°   60
Gospels, Compendium of the. Strong (James).   18°   40
Gospels, Manual of. Strong (James).   16°   75
*Grace Avery's Influence. Dunning (Mrs. A. K.)
   Illust.   16°   1 50
*Grace Courtney; or, Seeking the Shepherd. Ben-
   ning (H.)   16°   1 00
Granada. Irving (Washington).   16°   1 25
*Grandma Crosby's Household. Farman (Ella).
   Illust.   16°   1 00
*Grandmamma's Recollections.   12°   1 25
*Grandmother Dear. Molesworth (Mrs.) Illust.   16°   1 50
*Grandpa's Darlings. Alden (Mrs. G. R. [Pansy].)   16°   1 25
Great Conflict, The. Christ and Antichrist. The
   Church and the Apostasy. Loomis (H.)   12°   85

Great Fur Land; or, Sketches of Life in the Hudson's Bay Territory. Robinson (H. M.) Illust. 12° $1 75

Great German Composers, The. Comprising Biographical and Anecdotical Sketches of Bach, Handel, Gluck, Haydn, Mozart, Beethoven, Schubert, Schumann, Franz, Chopin, Weber, Mendelssohn, and Wagner. Ferris (G. T.) 18° 60

Great Ice Age, The; and Its Relation to the Antiquity of Man. Geikie (J.) Illust. 12° 2 50

Great Italian and French Composers, The. Ferris (George T.) 18° 60

Great Journey. 12° 50

*Great Lights in Sculpture and Painting. A Manual for Young Students. Doremus (S. D.) 12° 1 00

Great Musicians, The. Edited by Francis Hueffer. 12° *e* 1 00

Vol. 1. Wagner.   Vol. 4. Schubert.
Vol. 2. Weber.   Vol. 5. Rossini.
Vol. 3. Mendelssohn.   Vol. 6. Marcello.
       Vol. 7. Purcell.

Great Question. Prize Essay. White (Lorenzo). 16° 40

Great Reform, The. A Prize Essay on the Duty and the Best Method of Systematic Beneficence in the Church. Stevens (Abel). 16° 35

Great Republic, The, From the Discovery of America to the Centennial, July 4, 1876. Peck (Jesse T.) 34 Steel Engravings. 8° 3 50

Great Singers: Faustina Bordoni to Henrietta Sonntag. Ferris (George T.) 18° 60

Greece and the Golden Horn. Olin. 12° 1 50

*Greek Hero Stories. Translated from the German of Prof. Niebuhr. Hoppin (Benjamin). Illust. 16° 1 00

Greycliff, and Vashti Lethby's Heritage. Hamilton (Kate W.) Illust. 16° 1 30

Gruber, Jacob, Life of. Strickland (W P.) 12° 1 50

Guardian Angel, The. Holmes (O. W.) 12° 2 00

Gurley, William, Life of. 12° 1 00

*Gustaphus Adolphus, the Hero of the Reformation. From the French of L. Abelous. Lacroix (Mrs. C. A.) Illust. 16° 85

Guthrie, Thomas. Autobiography and Life of. 2 vols. in one. 12° 2 00

*Guttenburg; or, The Art of Printing. Pearson (Emily C.) Illust. 12° 1 25

*HALF-HOUR Studies of Life. Johnson (Edwin A.) 16° $1 00
*Half-hours with Old Humphrey. Mogridge (Geo.) 16° 85
Half-hours with the Telescope. Proctor (R. A.) 16° 1 25
Half-hours with the Best Authors. Knight (Chas.)
    3 vols. 12° 4 50
*Half-hour Series, The. Illust. 4 vols. 16° *e* 90

> Half-hours in the Deep.
> Half-hours in the Far North.
> Half-hours in the Far East.
> Half-hours in the Tiny World.

Half-hours with the Stars. Proctor (R. A.) 4° 2 50
*Half-year at Bronckton. A Vigorous and Life-like
    Story of School-boy Days. Sidney (Margaret).
    Illust. 16° 1 25
*Hall in the Grove. Alden (Mrs. G. R. [Pansy].) 16° 1 25
Hamilton, R. W., D. D. His Sermons: with a
    Sketch of his Life. 12° 1 50
Hamline, Leonidas, D. D., Life and Letters of. Late
    one of the Bishops of the Methodist Episcopal
    Church. Palmer (Walter C.) With Introduc-
    tory Letters by Bishops Morris, Janes, and
    Thomson. 12° 2 00
Hamline, Rev. Leonidas L., D. D., Biography of.
    Late one of the Bishops of the Methodist Epis-
    copal Church. Hibbard (F. G.) 12° 1 50
Hamline's Works, Bishop. Edited by F. G. Hib-
    bard. 2 vols. 12° *e* 1 50

> Vol. 1. Sermons.   Vol. 2. Miscellaneous.

*Hand-book for Sunday-school Teachers. Alden
    (Joseph). 16° $0 65
Hand-book for Travelers in Europe and the East.
    Being a Guide through Great Britain and Ire-
    land, France, Belgium, Holland, Germany,
    Austria, Italy, Egypt, Syria, Turkey, Greece,
    Switzerland, Tyrol, Denmark, Norway, Sweden,
    Russia, and Spain. Fetridge (W. Pembroke).
    With Maps and Plans of Cities. Twentieth
    Year (1881). 3 vols. Leather, pocket-book form. 12° *e* 3 00

> Vol. 1. Great Britain, Ireland, France, Belgium, Holland.
> Vol. 2. Germany, Austria, Italy, Egypt, Syria, Turkey,
>   Greece.
> Vol. 3. Switzerland, Tyrol, Denmark, Norway, Sweden,
>   Russia, Spain.

Hand-book for Home Improvement. Comprising How to Write, Talk, Behave, etc.   12° $2 25

Hand-book of Legendary and Mythological Art, A. Clement (Clara E.) Illust.   12°   3 00

Hand-book, A, of Scripture Geography. Thompson (Andrew). With Maps.   16°   75

Handy Book of Quotations. A Dictionary of Common Poetical Quotations in the English Language. Boards.   16°   75

*Happy Home Stories for Small Boys. Illust. 6 vols. In box.   18°   3 00

Diligent Dick.	Cousin Willie.
Lazy Robert.	The New Buggy.
Little Fritz.	Bertie and His Sisters.

*Happy Home Stories for Small Girls. Illust. 6 vols. In box.   18°   3 00

Little Flyaway.	The Singing Girl.
The Spoiled Picture.	Molly and the Wineglass.
Fleda's Childhood.	The Twins.

*Haps and Mishaps of Childhood. Pleasing Stories of Child-life. Illust.   16°   1 00

*Happy Light. Illust.   16°   1 50

Harmony and Exposition of the Gospels. Strong (James). Maps and Engravings. Sheep.   8°   4 50

Harmony of the Divine Dispensations. Smith (G.) Sheep.   8°   2 50

*Harry Budd; or, The History of an Orphan Boy.   16°   75

*Harry Lane, and Other Stories in Verse.   12°   80

Hartz Boys, The. The Scene is laid in Germany, and shows that "as we sow, so shall we reap." Hoffman (Franz). Illust.   16°   1 25

Haven, Gilbert. A Monograph. Wentworth (E.) With Portrait. Paper.   12°   25

Health Primers. A Series of Hand-books on Personal and Public Hygiene. Edited by Eminent Medical and Scientific Men of London. 8 vols.   16°   *e* 40

Exercise and Training.
Alcohol: Its Use and Abuse.
The House and its Surroundings.
Premature Death: Its Promotion and Prevention.
Personal Appearance in Health and Disease.
Baths and Bathing.
The Skin and its Troubles.
The Heart and its Functions.

Heart of Africa, The; or, Three Years' Travels and
Adventures in the Unexplored Regions of the
Center of Africa from 1867 to 1871. Schwein-
furth (George). Translated by Ellen E. Frewer.
Illustrations and Maps. 2 vols.   8° $8 00

Heart and Church Division, Causes and Cure of.
Asbury (Bishop).   18°   40

Heart of the White Mountains, The. Drake (Samuel Adams). Illust.   8°   3 00

*Heart's Content. A Story of Child-life in a Home
named "Heart's Content." Bates (Clara Doty).   4°   1 50

Heat as a Mode of Motion. Tyndall (John).
Illust.   12°   2 00

·Heaven, The Expanse of. Essays on the Wonders
of the Firmament. Proctor (R. A.)   12°   2 00

*Heaven, Our Friends in. Killen (J. M.)   12°   1 00

*Heavenward Led; or, The Two Bequests. Som-
mers (Jane R.)   16°   1 25

Heaven, Scripture Views of. Edmondson (Jonathan).   18°   50

*Hebrew Heroes. A Story Founded on Jewish
History. (A. L. O. E.)   18°   75

Hebrew Lawgiver, The. Lawrie (John M.) 2 vols.   16°   2 50

Hebrew People, History of the. Smith (George).   8°   3 00

Hedding, Bishop, Life and Times of. Clark (D. W.)   12°   2 25

*Helen Hervey's Change; or, Out of Darkness into
Light. English (Maria). Illust.   16°   75

*Helen Lester; to which is added "Nannie's Exper-
iment." Alden (Mrs. G. R. [Pansy].) Illust.   16°   75

*Helena's Cloud with the Silver Lining. By the
Author of "How Marjorie Watched," etc.   75

*Helena's Household. A Story of Rome in the First
Century.   12°   1 50

Hell, The New Testament Idea of. Merrill (S. M.)   16°   1 00

Helm, Cross, and Sword. Lorraine (A. M.)   12°   1 50

*Help for Sunday-school Concerts. A Choice Selec-
tion of Poems. Folsom (A. P. and M. T.)   16°   1 00

*Helpful Thoughts for Young Men. Woolsey (T. D.) 12°   1 25

*Hendricks the Hunter. A Tale of Zululand.
Kingston (W. H. G.) Illust.   12°   1 50

Henry VIII and His Six Wives, Memoirs of. Herbert (Henry W.)   12°   1 25

*Henry and Bessie; or, What they Did in the
　　Country. Prentiss (Mrs. E.)　　　　　　　16°　$1 00
Herbert Spencer, Philosophy of. Being an Exam-
　　ination of the First Principles of his System.
　　Bowne (B. P.)　　　　　　　　　　　　　12°　　1 00
Heredity. Cook (Jos.)　　　　　　　　　　12°　　1 50
Heresy and Christian Doctrine. De Pressensé (E.)　　1 50
Hermits, The. Kingsley (Charles).　　　　　12°　　1 75
Heroes of Bohemia: Huss, Jerome, and Zisca.
　　Mears (John W.)　　　　　　　　　　　16°　　1 25
Heroes of Christian History. A Series of Popular
　　Biographies.　　　　　　　　　　　　　12°　　*c* 75

　　　　William Wilberforce. Stoughton (John).
　　　　Henry Martin. Bell (Charles D.)
　　　　Philip Doddridge. Stanford (Charles).
　　　　William Carey. Culross (James).
　　　　Thomas Chalmers. Fraser (Donald).
　　　　Robert Hall. Hood (E. Paxton).
　　　　John Knox. Taylor (William M.)
　　　　Jonathan Edwards. Paterson (H. Sinclair).
　　　　Richard Baxter. Boyle (G. D.)
　　　　John Wycliffe. Fleming (James).

Heroes of the Cross, The. Biographies of Saints,
　　Martyrs, and Christian Pioneers. Adams
　　(W. H. D.)　　　　　　　　　　　　　12°　　2 25
*Heroes, The; or, Greek Fairy Tales. Kingsley
　　(Charles).　　　　　　　　　　　　　　12°　　1 75
*Heroes of History. Towle (Geo. M.) Illust. 4 vols. 16°　*c* 1 25

　　　　Vasco da Gama. His Voyages and Adventures.
　　　　Pizarro. His Adventures and Conquests.
　　　　Magellan; or, The First Voyage Round the World.
　　　　Marco Polo. His Travels and Adventures.

*Heroines of History. Owen (Mrs. O. F.)　　12°　　1 00
*Heroine of the White Nile; or, What a Woman
　　Did and Dared. A Sketch of the Remarkable
　　Travels and Experience of Miss Alexina Tinne.
　　Wells (William). Illust.　　　　　　　12°　　　85
*Heroism of Christian Women of Our Own Times.
　　Darton (J. M.)　　　　　　　　　　　12°　　1 50
*Hester Trueworthy's Royalty.　　　　　　16°　　1 25
*Hidden Treasure. The Treasure of a Generous,
　　Loving Heart. Illust.　　　　　　　　16°　　1 25
*Hidden Treasure; or, The Secret of Success in Life.
　　Babcock (Sarah A.)　　　　　　　　　16°　　　85

*High Days and Holidays in Old England and New
England. Illust. 4 vols. In a box.   16° $2 50

    Vol. 1. Fourth of July in New England.
    Vol. 2. Red-letter Days in Old England and New England.
    Vol. 3. Joy Days on Both Sides of the Water.
    Vol. 4. Festal and Floral Days in New England.

Higher Christian Life, The. Boardman (W E.)   16°   1 50
*Hill Farm. Honesty and Faithfulness Rewarded.
Temple (Crona). Illust.   16°   60
Hints for Home Reading. A Series of Chapters on
Books and their Use. Abbott (Lyman), and
Others. Cloth, $1. Boards.   8°   75
Hints to Self-Educated Ministers. Including Local
Preachers, Exhorters, and Other Christians,
whose Duty it is to Speak More or Less in
Public. Porter (James).   12°   1 25
Historical Confirmation of Scripture. Blatch (W.) 18°   30
Historical Evidences of the Truth of the Bible.
Rawlinson (G.)   12°   1 75
Historical Illustrations of the Old Testament. Raw-
linson (G.)   16°   1 00
Historical Sketch of the Protestant Church of
France. Lorimer (John G.)   12°   1 30
*Historical Sketches. Myrtle (Annie). Illust.   16°   1 25
*Historical Tales for Young American Protestants. 16°   75
Historical Views of the Revolution. Green (G. W.) 12°   1 50
History of the Jews, from the Earliest Period to
Present Times. Milman (H. H.) Maps and
Illust. 3 vols.   18°   2 25
History, Ancient, A Manual of. Thalheimer (M. E.) 8°   n1 60
History and Critical Essays. De Quincey. 2 vols. 12°   3 00
*History for Boys. Edgar (J. G.)   16°   1 00
History, Modern, A Manual of. Thalheimer (M. E.) 8°   n1 60
History of American Bible Society, from its Organi-
zation in 1816 to the Present Time. Strick-
land (W. P.)   8°   2 00
History of Arabia. Crichton (Andrew). 2 vols. 18°   1 50
History of the Bible. Gleig (G. R.) 2 vols.   18°   1 50
History of Christianity. Abbott (John S. C.) Illust. 12°   2 00
History of Christianity from the Birth of Christ to
the Abolition of Paganism in the Roman Em-
pire. Milman (H. H.)   8°   2 00

History of the Christian Church. Hase (K.)	8°	$3 50
History of the Christian Church. Ruter (Martin).	8°	2 50
History of the Christian Church. From its Origin to the Present Time. Blackburn (W. M.)	8°	2 50
History of the Church. From the Earliest Ages to the Reformation. Waddington (M. A.)	8°	2 00
History of the Church in the Eighteenth and Nineteenth Centuries. Hagenbach (K.) 2 vols.	8°	6 00
History of Civilization. Guizot (F.) 2 vols.	12°	4 00
History of Civilization in England. Buckle (H. T.) 2 vols.	8°	4 00
History of the Consulate and Empire of France under Napoleon. Thiers (M. Adolphe). Translated by D. Forbes Campbell and H. W Herbert. Illust. 5 vols.	8°	12 50
History of the Crusades, The. Michaud (Joseph Francois). 3 vols.	8°	3 75
History of the Council of Trent. From the French of L. F. Bungener. Edited by Rev. John McClintock.	12°	1 50
History of the Decline and Fall of the Roman Empire. Gibbon (Edward). With Notes by the Rev. H. H. Milman. 6 vols.	12°	5 00
History of Doctrines. Hagenbach (K.) 2 vols.	8°	6 00
*History of Egypt. Clement (Clara E.) Illust.	12°	1 50
History of England, from the Fall of Wolsey to the Death of Elizabeth. Froude (J. A.) 12 vols.	12°	15 00
History of England. An Illustrated History of Society and Government from the Earliest Period to our Own Times. Knight (Charles). 8 vols.		18 00
History of England. From the Invasion of Julius Cæsar to the Abdication of James II, 1688. Hume (David). 6 vols.	12°	5 00
History of England from the Accession of James II. Macaulay (T. B.) 5 vols.	12°	5 00
History of England in the Eighteenth Century. Lecky (W E. H.) 2 vols.	8°	5 00
History of European Morals from Augustus to Charlemagne. Lecky (W E. H.) 2 vols.	12°	3 00
History of France from the Earliest Times to 1848. White (James).	8°	3 00

History of Greece, A General, from the Earliest
Period to the Death of Alexander the Great.
With a Sketch of the Subsequent History to
the Present Time. Cox (G. W.)   12° $1 50

History of the Huguenots. Marsh (Mrs.)   16°   1 25

⁰History of India. Feudge (Fanny Roper). Illust. 12°   1 50

History of the Jewish Church. Stanley (Dean).
3 vols.   8°   7 50

> Vol. 1. Abraham to Samuel.
> Vol. 2. Samuel to the Captivity.
> Vol. 3. From the Captivity to the Christian Era.

*History of the Jewish Nation, A. From the Earli-
est Times to the Present Day. Palmer (E. F.)
Illust.   16°   1 25

History of Philosophy, Schwegler's. Translated
from the Original German by J. H. Seelye.   12°   2 00

History of the Presbyterian Church in the United
States of America. Gillett (E. H.) 2 vols.   12°   5 00

History Primers. Edited by J. R. Green. 6 vols. 18°   *en* 45

> Greece. Fyffe (C. A.)
> Rome. Creighton (M.)
> Geography. Grove (George).
> Europe. Freeman (E. A.)
> Old Greek Life. Mahaffy (J. P.)
> Roman Antiquities. Wilkins (A. S.)

History of the Reformation. D'Aubigné.   8°   2 50

History of the Great Reformation. Carter (T.)   12°   1 25

History of the Reformation. Fisher (George P.)   8°   3 00

History of the Romans. Merivale (Charles). 4 vols. 12°   7 00

*History of Spain. Harrison (James Albert). Illust. 12°   1 50

*History of Switzerland. Slidell-Mackenzie (Har-
riet D.) Illust.   12°   1 50

History of the United Netherlands from the Death
of William the Silent to the Twelve Years'
Truce. Motley (J. L.) 4 vols.   8°   8 00

*History of the United States, Young Folks' Hig-
ginson (T. W.) Illust.   16°   1 50

History of the United States. Bancroft. 6 vols.   12°   *e* 2 50

History of the United States. Ridpath (John
Clark).   8°   3 00

*History of the World. Barth (C.)   12°   85

History of the Waldenses, The. Baird.   8°   2 50

*Holiday Gift, My. Illust.   12°   1 00

28

*Holiday House. A Series of Stories. Sinclair (Catherine). Illust.   16° $1 25

Holiness the Birthright of all God's Children. Crane (J. T.)   16°   85

Holiness to the Lord. Dunn (L. R.)   12°   85

Holland and its People. De Amicis (Edmondo.) Illust.   12°   2 00

Hollywood Series.   Wise (Daniel). Illustrated. 6 vols.   16°   7 50

> Stephen and His Tempter.
> Florence Baldwin's Picnic.
> Lionel's Courage; or, Clementina's Great Peril.
> Florence Rewarded; or, Priscilla the Beautiful.
> Nat and His Chum; or, The Friendly Rivals.
> Elbert's Return; or, "Foxy" at Home Again.

Holy Gospels, Thoughts on the. How they came to be in Manner and Form as they are. Upham (Francis W.)   12°   1 25

Holy Ground, On. Travels in Palestine. Hodder (Edwin).   12°   1 25

Holy Living, Rules for. Newstead (R.)   72°   15

Holy Living, The Rule and Exercises of. Taylor (Jeremy).   12°   1 25

Holy Living and Dying. Taylor (Jeremy).   12°   1 50

Holy Spirit, The Doctrine of the. Walker (J. B.) 12°   1 25

Holy War. Bunyan (John).   12°   1 25

Holy War. Bunyan (John). Illust.   8°   2 00

Home Altar, The. An Appeal in Behalf of Family Worship, with Prayers and Hymns. Deems (C. F.)   18°   1 25

Home as It Should Be. With Counsel for All. Barrows (L. D.)   18°   30

*Home Influence. Aguilar (Grace). Illust.   12°   1 00

Home Life; or, How to Make Home Happy. Illust. 16°   75

Home Life, The, in the Light of its Divine Idea. Brown (J. B.)   18°   75

Home Pictures of English Poets, for Fireside and School-room. Illust.   12°   85

*Home Scenes, and Heart Studies. Aguilar (Grace). 12°   1 00

*Home Story Series, No. 1. Larned (Augusta). 3 vols.   16°   3 50

> Country Stories.   Holiday Stories.
>   Stories for Leisure Hours.

•Home Story Series, No. 2.   Larned (Augusta).
   3 vols.   16° $3 50
     Vacation Stories.   Stories for Little People.
             Fireside Stories.

*Home Sunshine; or, Bear and Forbear. Illust. 16°   75
Homespun; or, Five and Twenty Years Ago.
   Lackland (Thomas).   16° 1 50
Home Truths. Ryle (J. C.)   16°   60
Homes without Hands; or, A Description of the
   Habitation of Animals, Classed According to
   their Principles of Construction. Wood (J. C.)
   Illust.   8° 4 50
Homer's Iliad. Derby (Edward, Earl). 2 vols in one. 12° 1 50
Homer's Iliad. W. C. Bryant's Translation. 2 vols.
   in one.   12° 3 00
Homer's Odyssey. W C. Bryant's Translation. 12° 3 00
Homiletical Index. Hand-book of Texts, Themes,
   and Authors, for the Use of Preachers and
   Bible Scholars. Pittingill (J. H.)   8° 3 00
Homiletical and Pastoral Lectures. By Archbishop
   Thompson, Bishops Goodwin, Thorold, Ryan,
   and Tilcomb; and Others..   8° 1 75
Homiletics, A Treatise on. Kidder (D. P.) 12° 1 50
Homilist, The. Sermons for Preachers and Lay-
   men. House (E.)   12° 1 50
*Honest and Earnest. Forest (Neil). 16° 1 00
*Honey Brook Library, The. Illust. 6 vols. 16° 6 00

     Julius Farley.   Boy of Mt. Rhigi.
     Larry Lockwell.   Romantic Belinda.
     True Manliness.   Blind Nellie's Boy.

*Honor, Six Steps to. Great Truths Illustrated.
   Andrews (H. P.)   16°   85
*Hope Raymond; or, What is Truth? Richmond
   (Mrs. E. J.) Illust.   16°   85
Hours of Christian Devotion. Tholuck (A.) 8° 3 00
Hours of Exercise in the Alps. Tyndall (John).
   Illust.   8° 2 00
House and Home Papers. Stowe (H. B.) 16° 1 50
*House that Jack Built, The. Hamilton (Kate W.)
   Illust.   16° 1 25
*Household Angel in Disguise, The. Leslie (Mrs.
   Madeline).   12° 1 00

Household Book of Poetry. Dana (Charles A.)
　　Illust. with Steel Engravings. 8° $3 50
Household Education. Martineau (Harriet). 18° 1 25
*Household Puzzles. A Story of Home-life. Alden
　　(Mrs. G. R. [Pansy].) Illust. 12° 1 50
*Household Stories. From the German of Madame
　　Ottilie Wildermuth. Kinmont (Eleanor). Illust.
　　4 vols. 16° 4 00
Houses of Lancaster and York, The. With the
　　Conquest and Loss of France. Gairdner (Jas.) 16° 1 00
*How a Farthing Made a Fortune; or, Honesty is
　　the Best Policy. Bowen (C. E.) 18° 50
How to Educate Yourself with or without a Master.
　　Eggleston (George Cary). Board. 16° 50
How to Get Strong and How to Stay so. Blaikie
　　(William). Illust. 16° 1 00
How to Make a Living. Eggleston (George Cary).
　　Boards. 12° 50
How to Pay Church Debts, and How to Keep
　　Churches out of Debt. Stall (S.) 12° 1 50
*Howard, John, Memoirs of. True (C. K.) 16° 1 00
Howard, Mrs. Susan, Memoir of. Chapin (Wm.) 18° 30
*How Marjorie Watched. Illust. 16° 70
*How to Conduct Prayer - meetings. Thompson
　　(Lewis O.) 12° 1 25
How Two Girls Tried Farming. A Piquant Nar-
　　rative of an Actual Experience. Shepherd
　　(Dorothea Alice). 16° 1 00
How the World was Peopled. Ethnological Lec-
　　tures. Fontaine (Edward). 12° 2 00
Huguenots, The. Smiles (S.) 8° 2 00
Huguenots, The, after the Revocation. Smiles (S.) 8° 2 00
Human Race, The: And Other Sermons. Preached
　　at Cheltenham, Oxford, and Brighton. Robert-
　　son (F. W.) 12° 1 50
*Hunting Adventures on Land and Sea: The Young
　　Nimrods in North America. A Book for Boys.
　　Knox (Thomas W.) Illust. 8° 2 50
*Huntingdon, Lady, Portrayed. Mudge (Z. A.)
　　Illust. 16° 1 00
Hymns of the Ages. First, Second, and Third
　　Series. Each in 1 vol. 12° e1 50

Hymns of Frederick William Faber. With a Sketch
of His Life. Illust. 16° $1 25
Hypatia. Kingsley (Charles). 12° 1 75
Hyperion. Longfellow (H. W.) 12° 1 50

IDLE Word, The. Short Religious Essays upon the
Gift of Speech. Goulburn (E. M.) 12° 75
I Go A-Fishing. Prime (Wm. C.) 8° 2 50
Illustrations of Scripture: Suggested by a Trip
through the Holy Land. Hackett (H. B.) Illust. 12° 1 50
Illustrated Gatherings. Bowes (G. S.) 12° 1 75
Second Series. 12° 1 75
Imitation of Christ. Kempis (Thomas à). 16° 1 00
Immortality of the Soul, and the Final Condition
of the Wicked Carefully Considered. Landis
(Robert W.) 12° 1 50
Immortality, The Bible Doctrine of. Mattison (H.)
Paper cover. 12° 25
Improvement of Society by the General Diffusion
of Knowledge. Dick (Thomas). 18° 45
In Prospect of Sunday. A Collection of Analyses,
Arguments, Applications, Counsels, Cautions,
etc., for Use of Preachers and Sunday-school
Teachers. Bowes (G. S.) 12 1 50
Insect Lives; or, Born in Prison. Ballard (Julia P.)
Illust. 12° 1 00
Insects Abroad. Being a Popular Account of For-
eign Insects, their Structure, Habits, and
Transformation. Wood (J. G.) 8° 4 00
Inquirer and New Convert. Young (Robert.) In
1 vol. 18° 25
Inside the Gates. McCarty (J. Hendrickson). 16° 1 00
Interior Life. Upham (T. C.) 12° 1 50
Intermediate World, The. Townsend (L. T.) 16° 75
*Interpreter's House, The; or, Sermons to Children.
Newton (W. W.) Illust. 16° 1 25
Introduction to the Gospel Records. Nast (Wm.) 12° 1 50
Introduction to the Study of the Holy Scriptures.
Harman (Henry M.) 8° 4 00
In the Arctic Seas. A Narrative of the Discovery
of the Fate of Sir John Franklin and His
Companions. McClintock (R. N.) Illust. 12° 1 25

In the Fields. Poems which have for their Subjects
the Objects and Thoughts of the Grassy Fields.
Hathaway (Miss M. E. N.)   16° $1 25

In the Mist. Porter (Rose).   16° 1 25

In the Days of Thy Youth. Farrar (F. W.)   12° 2 00

Indian and White Man, The; or, The Indian in
Self-defense. Right-Hand Thunder (Indian
Chief.) Edited by D. W Risher.   12° 1 50

Indian Biography. Thatcher. 2 vols.   18° 1 50

Infidelity, Best Method of Counteracting. Christlieb (Theo.)   12° 1 75

Infant Baptism Briefly Considered. Doane (N.)   16° 65

Infant Church Membership. Gregg (S.)   16° 80

*Infant Sunday-school. Knox (Mrs. and Rev. C. E.) 12° 65

*Influence. Illust.   16° 1 30

Influence of Jesus, The. Bohlen Lectures. 1879.
Brooks (Phillips).   16° 1 25

*Inglises, The; or, How the Way Opened. Rober-
son (Margaret M.)   12° 1 50

*Inventor, Trials of an; or, Life and Discoveries of
Charles Goodyear. Peirce (B. K.)   16° 1 00

*Iron Boot, The: And Other Stories.   18° 40

Irving's Belles-lettres Works. Including Alhambra,
Bracebridge Hall, Crayon Miscellany, Gold-
smith, Knickerbocker, Sketch-book, Tales of a
Traveler, Wolfert's Roost. 8 vols.   16° 12 00

*Irving, Washington. Memoir of: With Selections
from his Works and Criticisms. Adams (Chas.) 16° 1 00

Isaac, Jacob, and Joseph. [Expository Reading.]
Dods (Marcus).   16° 1 25

Island Life; or, The Phenomena of Insular Faunas
and Floras, with their Causes. Including an
entire Revision of the Problem of Geological
Climates. Wallace (Alfred Russel). Illust.
and Maps.   8° 4 00

Island of Fire, The; or, A Thousand Years of the
Old Northmen's Home, 874–1874. Headley
(P. C.) Illust.   12° 1 50

Ismailia: A Narrative of the Expedition to Central
Africa for the Suppression of the Slave-trade,
Organized by Ismail, Khedive of Egypt. Baker
(Samuel White). Maps and Illust.   8° 5 00

Israel in Egypt; or, Egypt's Place among the Ancient Monarchies. Clark (Edward L.) — 8° — $4 00

*Israel Putnam, Life of, Major-general in the Continental Army. Tarbox (I. N.) Maps and Illust. — 12° — 1 25

Israelites, Ancient, Manners of the. Fleury (Claude). — 18° — 55

Isoult Barry of Wynscote, Her Diurnal Book. A Tale of Tudor Times. Holt (Emily S.) — 16° — 1 50

Italy, Florence, and Venice. Taine. — 8° — 2 50

Itinerancy, Life in the. Davis (L. D.) — 12° — 1 25

Itinerant, Recollections of an. Smith (H.) — 16° — 85

*Itinerant Side; or, Pictures of Life in the Itinerancy. Babcock (Sarah A.) Illustrated. — 16° — 85

Itinerant's Wife: Her Qualifications, etc. Eaton (H. M.) — 18° — 25

*Ivy Fennhaven; or, Womanhood in Christ. — 12° — 1 25

*JACK the Conqueror; or, Difficulties Overcome. Bowen (C. E.) Illust. — 18° — 75

*Jack Masters; or, the Berry-pickers. Mills (Lucy A.) Illust. — 16° — 1 25

*Jack and Rosy. A True Story. Forrest (Neil). — 16° — 1 00

*Jacques Bonneval, A Tale of the Hugenots. Manning (Anna). — 16° — 75

Janet's Love and Service. Robertson (M. M.) — 12° — 1 75

*Jessie in Switzerland. Illust. — 16° — 75

*Jesse Wells; or, How to Save the Lost. Alden (Mrs. G. R. [Pansy].) Illust. — 16° — 75

Jesus Christ: His Times, Life, and Work. Abridged. Pressensé (E. De). — 12° — 1 25

Jesus of Nazareth. His Life and Teachings, Founded on the Four Gospels, and Illustrated by Reference to the Manners, Customs, Religious Beliefs, and Political Institutions of His Times. Abbott (Lyman). Illust. — 8° — 3 50

Jeweled Ministry; or, Life of Rev. Thomas Collins. Coley (Samuel). — 12° — 1 25

Jewish Church. Stanley. (A. P.) 2 vols. — 8° — 5 00

*Joan the Maid, Deliverer of France and England. A Story of the Fifteenth Century. Done into Modern English by the Author of "The Schönburg-Cotta Family." — 12° — 1 00

*Joanna; or, Learning to Follow Jesus. Haven
   (Marion). 16° $1 00
*Joe Witless. Illust. 16° 1 00
*John Bremm. His Prison Bars. A Temperance
   Story. Hopkins (A. A.) 16° 1 25
*John Carey; or, What is a Christian? A. L. O. E.
   Illust. 18° 75
John Lothrop Motley. A Memoir. With Fine
   Steel Portrait. 16° 1 50
*John Richmond; or, A Sister's Love. Taylor (T.)
   Illust. 16° 85
*John Winthrop and the Great Colony; or, Sketches
   of the Settlement of Boston and of the More
   Prominent Persons Connected with the Massa-
   chusetts Colony. True (Charles K.) Illust. 16° 85
*Johnny Jones; or, The Bad Boy. Homespun (So-
   phia). Illust. 16° 1 00
*Johnnie, the Railroad Boy. Poole (Mrs. I. E.)
   Illust. 16° 1 00
*Johnny's Vacations, and Other Stories. Hatha-
   way (Mary E. N.) Illust. 16° 1 25
Johnson's Works, Dr. Samuel. The Complete
   Works of Samuel Johnson, LL. D. With an
   Essay on his Life and Genius. Murphy
   (Arthur). 2 vols. 8° 4 00
*Jottings from Life; or, Passages from the Diary of
   an Itinerant's Wife. Cutler (Helen R.) 12° 85
Journal of the Discovery of the Source of the Nile.
   Speke (John H.) Maps and Illust. 8° 4 00
Journal of John Woolman, The. Introduction by
   John G. Whittier. 16° 1 50
Journey in Brazil, A. Agassiz (Prof. and Mrs.)
   Illust. 8° 5 00
*Judah's Lion. Elizabeth (Charlotte). 16° 90
*Judge's Sons, The. Showing the Success that fol-
   lows Pure and High Aims. Kendall (Mrs. E.
   D.) Illust. 16° 1 50
*Julia Ried. Alden (Mrs. G. R. [Pansy].) Illust. 12° 1 50
Justification, A Treatise on. Davies (R. N.) 16° 1 00
Justification, Hare on. 18° 50
Juventus Mundi. Gods and Men of the Heroic
   Age. Gladstone (W. E.) 8° 1 50

*Kangaroo Hunters. Bowman (Anna). Illust. 16° $1 00
*Katharine's Experience. Showing the Transform-
    ing Power of Grace. Biscoe (Ellen L.) Illust. 16° 1 50
*Katie Johnstone Library. Illust. 5 vols. 16° 4 75

    Katie Johnstone's Cross.   One of the Billingses.
    The Grocer's Boy.   Emily Milman.
        Cottagers of Glencarran.

Kathrina: Her Life and Mine. Holland (J. G.) 12° 1 50
Kavanagh. A Daguerreotype of New England
    Life. Longfellow (H. W.) 16° 1 50
*Kenneth and Hugh; or, Self-mastery. 16° 1 25
Kept for the Master's Use. Havergal (F. R.) 18° 25
King and Commonwealth. A History of Charles
    I and the Great Rebellion. Cordery (B. Mer-
    iton) and Phillpotts (J. S.) 12° 1 75
*King of Day. Urmy (W. S.) One illust. 16° 75
*King's Daughter, A. With Other Stories from Real
    Life. Gardner (Mrs. H. C.) One illust. 16° 1 00
*King's Daughter, The. Alden (Mrs. G. R. [Pansy].)
    Illust. 18° 1 50
*King in His Beauty, The. Newton (Richard). 16° 1 25
*Kings, Queens, and Barbarians; or, Seven Historic
    Ages. Familiar Talks about History for Young
    Folks. Gilman (Arthur). Illust. 16° 1 00
*Kitty Kent's Troubles. Eastman (Julia A.) Illust. 16° 1 50
Kitto's Bible Illustrations. Kitto (John). 8 vols. 7 00
Knickerbocker. Irving (Washington). 16° 1 25
Knights and their Days. Doran. 8° 1 75
Knights and Sea-kings; or, The Middle Ages. Ed-
    ited by S. F. Smith. Illust. 12° 1 50
*Knowing and Doing. Paull (Mrs. H. H. B.) Illus-
    trated. 16° 1 00

Labor. Cook (Joseph). 12° 1 50
Lacon; or, Many Things in Few Words. Colton
    (C. C.) 16° 1 25
Ladies' and Gentlemen's Complete Etiquette. Duf-
    fey (Mrs. E. B.) 16° 1 50
Ladies of the Covenant. Memoirs of Distinguished
    Scottish Female Characters. Anderson (Jas.) 12° 1 50
Lake Regions of Central Africa, The. A Picture
    of Explorations. Burton (Richard F.) 8° 3 50

Lake Region in 1862, Glimpses of Our. Gardner
    (Mrs. H. C.)   16° $1 25

*Lame Bessie; or, Simple Faith.   16° 1 25

*Lances of Lynwood, The. Young (M. C.) Illust. 12° 1 25

Land and the Book, The. Southern Palestine and
    Jerusalem. Thompson (Wm. M.)   8° 7 50

Land and Its Story, The; or, The Sacred Historical
    Geography of Palestine. Burt (N. C.) Illust.
    with Maps, Sketches, Charts, and Engravings. 8° 3 50

Land of Desolation, The. A Personal Narrative
    of Observations and Adventures in Greenland.
    Hayes (I. I.) Illust.   12° 1 75

Land of Israel, The, According to the Covenant with
    Abraham, with Isaac, and with Jacob. Keith
    (Alex.) Illust.   12° 1 50

Land of Moab. Travels and Discoveries on the
    East Side of the Dead Sea and the Jordan.
    Tristram (H. B.) Illust.   8° 2 50

Land of Promise. Kitto (John).   12° 1 00

Land of Shadowing Wings; or, The Empire of the
    Sea. Loomis (H.)   12° 1 00

Land of the Midnight Sun, The. Summer and
    Winter Journeys through Sweden, Norway,
    Lapland, and Northern Finland. Du Chaillu
    (Paul B.) With Map and Illust. 2 vols. 8° 7 50

Land of the Veda. Being Personal Reminiscences
    of India; its People, Castes, Thugs, and Fa-
    kirs; its Religion, Mythology, Principal Mon-
    uments, Palaces, and Mausoleums; together
    with Incidents of the Great Sepoy Rebellion,
    and its Results to Christianity and Civilization.
    With a Map of India, and Forty-two Illustra-
    tions. Also, Statistical Tables of Christian
    Missions, and a Glossary of Indian Terms used
    in this Work and in Missionary Correspond-
    ence. Butler (William).   3 50

Land of the White Elephant, The. Vincent (F.)
    Illust.   8° 3 50

*Lapsed, but not Lost. A Tale of Carthage and the
    Early Church. By the Author of the Schön-
    berg-Cotta Family."   12° 1 00

*Last Gladiatorial Show. Short (John T.) Illust. 16° 1 00

Last Witness. Dying Sayings of Christians. Baker (O. C.)	24°	$0 25
Latin Christianity. Milman (H. H.) 8 vols.	8°	e1 75
*Laura Linwood.	16°	1 25
Law, Ecclesiastical, Treatise on. Henry (W. J.) and Harris (W. L.)	8°	3 00
Laws Relating to Religious Corporations. A Compilation of the Statutes of the Several States of the United States in Relation to the Incorporation and Maintenance of Religious Societies, and to the Disturbance of Religious Meetings. Hunt (Sandford). With an Address on Laws affecting Religious Corporations in the State of New York, by E. L. Fancher. Sheep.	12°	1 25
Law of Love and Love as a Law, The; or, Christian Ethics. Hopkins (Mark).	12°	1 75
Lays of the Scottish Cavaliers. Aytoun (Wm. E.)	16°	1 00
Lay-Preacher, The. Helps for the Study, Platform, Pulpit, and Desk. Wagstaff (F.)	12°	1 50
*Leaders of Men. A Book of Biographies. Page (H. A.)	12°	1 50
*Lea's Playground. A Book for Boys. Illust.	16°	1 00
*Leaves and Fruit. Griffith (M. E.) Illust.	16°	1 25
Lectures and Addresses. Dempster (John).	12°	1 50
Lectures and Sermons. Punshon (W. M.)	12°	2 00
Lectures Delivered in America. Kingsley (Chas.)	12°	1 25
Lectures on Preaching. Delivered before the Theological Department of Yale College. Simpson (Matthew).	12°	1 50
Lectures on Preaching. Delivered before the Theological Department of Yale College. Brooks (Phillips).	16°	1 50
Lectures of a Certain Professor, The. Farrell (Jos.)	12°	1 50
Lectures on the True, the Beautiful, and the Good. Cousin.	8°	2 00
Lectures, Select London. Clark (D. W.)	12°	1 25
Lectures to Young Men. Smith (D.)	12°	65
*Lee, Alice, Discipline of. A Truthful Temperance Story. Illust.	16°	85
Legends of the Madonna, as Represented in the Fine Arts. Jameson (Anna).	18°	1 50
Legend of Thomas Didymus, The. Clarke (J. F.)	12°	1 75

Legends of the Monastic Orders, as represented in the Fine Arts. Jameson (Anna).	18°	$1 50
*Lena; or, The Stark Family. A Sketch of Real Life. From the Swedish of H. Hofston. Larsen (Carl).	16°	85
*Lenna, the Orphan. Hosmer (Margaret).	16°	1 25
*Leofwine, the Saxon. A Story of Hopes and Struggles. Leslie (Emma). Illust.	12°	1 25
*Leslie Stories, The. Leslie (Mrs. Madeline.) Illust. 4 vols.	16°	3 00
*Leslie's Scholarship; or, the Secret of Success. Illust.	16°	75
Lessons in Electricity. Tyndall (John). Illust.	12°	1 00
*Letter of Credit, The. Warner (Miss Anna).	12°	1 75
Letters and Social Aims. Emerson (R. W.)	16°	1 50
Letters from Egypt. Whately (Mary L.)	16°	75
Letters from Spain and Other Countries. Bryant (W C.)	12°	1 25
*Letters to School-girls. Mathews (J. McD.)	18°	50
*Letters to a School-boy.	16°	85
*Lettie Sterling. Illust.	16°	1 25
*Letting Down the Bars. Dunning (Mrs. A. K.) Illust.	16°	1 00
Lewis, Samuel, Biography of.	12°	1 25
Life, A, that Speaketh. A Biography of Rev. Geo. P. Wilson. Knowles (D. C.)	16°	85
Life Among the Indians. Finley (J. B.)	12°	1 75
Life and Education of Laura Dewey Bridgman. Lamson (Mary S.)	12°·	1 00
Life and Epistles of St. Paul. Conybeare and Howson. Popular Edition. Maps and Illust.	12°	1 50
*Life and Explorations of David Livingstone. Roberts (John S.) Illust.	12°	1 50
Life and Growth of Language, The. An Outline of Linguistic Science. Whitney (W. D.)	12°	1 50
Life and Letters of Rev. Stephen Olin, D. D. 2 vols.	12°	3 00
Life and Letters of Rev. F. W Robertson.	12°	1 50
Life and Letters of Washington Irving. Irving. 4 vols.	16°	c1 25
Life and Literature in the Fatherland. Hurst (John F.)	12°	2 25
Life and Times of Lord Bacon. 2 vols.	8°	5 00

Life and Religious Opinions of Madame Guyon: Together with Some Accounts of the Personal History and Religious Opinions of Archbishop Fénélon. Upham (T. C.) 2 vols.	12°	$3 00
Life and Speeches of the Right Honorable John Bright, M. P. Smith (George Barnett). 2 vols. in one.	8°	2 50
Life and Times of John Wesley, Founder of the Methodists. Tyerman (Luke). 3 vols.	8°	7 50
Life and Times of John Knox. True (C. K.)	16°	1 00
Life and Times of St. Bernard. Morison (J. C.)	12°	2 00
Life and Travels of Herodotus, in the Fifth Century before Christ. An Imaginary Biography. Founded on Fact. Wheeler (J. T.) 2 vols.	12°	3 50
Life and Words of Christ. Geikie (C.)	8°	1 50
Life and Works of Mary Carpenter. Carpenter (J. E.)	8°	2 75
Life and Works of St. Paul. Farrar (F. W.) Complete in 1 vol.	8°	3 00
*Life in Narrow Streets. Thompson (Julia Carrie). Illust.	16°	1 15
Life in the Laity. Davis (L. D.)	16°	65
Life: Its True Genesis. Wright (R. W.)	12°	1 50
Life Mosaic, The Ministry of Song, and Under the Surface. Havergal (Frances R.)	4°	4 00
Life of a Scotch Naturalist. Smiles (S.)	12°	1 50
Life of Alexander Duff, D. D. Smith (George).	8°	2 00
Life of Rev. Alfred Cookman. Ridgaway (H. B.)	12°	2 00
Life of Amos Lawrence. Lawrence (W. R.) Illust.	16°	1 50
Life of Andrew Jackson. Jenkins (John S.)	12°	1 25
Life of Beethoven. Translated by John J. Lalor.	12°	1 25
Life of Benedict Arnold. His Patriotism and his Treason. Arnold (Isaac N.)	8°	2 50
Life of Benjamin Abbott. Ffirth (John).	18°	45
Life of Bishop Roberts. Elliott (Charles).	12°	85
Life of Cicero, The. Trollope (Anthony). 2 vols.	12°	3 00
Life of Columbus. Irving (Washington). 3 vols.	16°	e 1 25
Life of Charles Dickens, A Short. Jones (C. H.)	18°	60
Life of Charles Sumner. Chaplin (J. and J. D.) Illust.	16°	1 50
Life of Daniel Webster. Banvard (J.) Illust.	16°	1 50
Life of Daniel Webster. Tefft (B. F.)	12°	1 25

Life of David, as Reflected in the Psalms. Mac-
laren (A.) 16° $1 25
Life of Edmund S. Janes. Ridgaway (H. B.) Por-
traits and Illust. 12° 1 50
Life of Edward Irving. The. Oliphant (Mrs.) 8° 3 50
Life of Edward Livingston. Hunt (C. H.) With
an Introduction by George Bancroft. Portrait. 8° 4 00
*Life of the Empress Josephine. Headley (P. C.) 12° 1 50
Life of the Empress Josephine, Wife of Napoleon
the Great. Hartley (C. B.) 12° 1 25
Life of Faith. Upham (T. C.) 12° 1 50
Life of George Washington. Bancroft (Aaron). 12° 1 25
Life of George Whitefield. Tyerman (L.) 2 vols. 8° 4 00
Life of Goldsmith. Irving (Washington). 16° 1 25
Life of Henry Clay. Sargent (Epes) and Greeley
(Horace). 12° 1 25
Life of Hester Ann Rogers. 18° 50
Life of Jabez Bunting. With Notices of Contem-
porary Persons and Events. Bunting (T. P.) 12° 1 50
Life of John Eadie, D. D., Professor of Biblical Lit-
erature and Exegesis, United Presbyterian
Church. Brown (James). 12° 2 00
Life of John James Audubon, the Naturalist. 12° 1 75
Life of John Huss. Gillett (E. H.) 2 vols. 8° e2 50
Life of John Knox: Containing Illustrations of
the History of the Reformation in Scotland.
McCrie (Thomas). 8° 2 00
Life of John Q. Adams. Seward (William H.) 12° 1 25
Life of Lady Jane Grey. Bartlett (David W.) 12° 1 25
Life of Lafayette. Headley (P. C.) 12° 1 50
Life of Lord Nelson. Southey (R.) 18° 75
Life of Madame Catharine Adorna. Including Some
Leading Facts and Traits in her Religious Ex-
perience. Upham (T. C.) 16° 75
Life of Mary, Queen of Scots. Headley (P. C.) 12° 1 50
*Life of Major André. Sargent. 8° 2 50
Life of Mozart. Translated by Lalor (John J.) 12° 1 25
Life of Napoleon Bonaparte. Headley (P. C.) 12° 1 50
Life of Napoleon Bonaparte, The. Lockhart (J. G.)
2 vols. 18° 1 50
1 vol. Edition. Illust. 12° 1 00
*Life of Oliver Cromwell. Adams (Charles). 16° 1 00

Life of Oliver Cromwell. Carlyle (T.) 2 vols.	12° *e*	$1 75
Life of Oliver Cromwell. Herbert (Henry Wm.)	12°	1 25
Life of Patrick Henry. Wirt (Wm.)	12°	1 50
Life of Samuel Johnson, The : Including a Journal of a Tour to the Hebrides. Boswell (James). With Numerous Additions and Notes by John Croker. 2 vols.	8°	4 00
4 vol. Edition.	12°	5 00
*Life of Samuel Johnson. Adams (C.) Illust.	16°	1 00
Life of Wilbur Fisk, D. D. Holdich (Jos.)	8°	2 50
Life of William E. Gladstone, A Short. Jones (C. H.)	18°	60
Life of William H. Harrison. Montgomery (II.)	12°	1 25
Life of Zachary Taylor. Montgomery (H.)	12°	1 25
Life Studies; or, How to Live. Illustrated in the Biography of Bunyan, Tersteegen, Montgomery, and Others. Baillie (John).	16°	1 00
Life Worth Living, A. Memorials of Emily Blise Gould. Bacon (Leonard W.)	12°	1 50
Life's Quiet Hours. Quiet Hints for Young and Old.	4°	1 00
Light and Electricity. Tyndall (John).	12°	1 25
*Light for the Little Ones. Compiled by Martha Van Marter. Illuminated Cover.	8°	1 00
Light in Dark Places. Neander (Augustus).	16°	50
Light in the Valley; or, Life of Mrs. Bocking. Annesley (Miss).	18°	35
*Lights of the World. Stoughton (John).	16°	85
Light on the Dark River; or, Memorials of Mrs. H. A. Hamlin. Lawrence (Mrs. Margaret W.) Steel Plate.	12°	1 50
Light on the Pathway of Holiness. McCabe (L. D.)	16°	65
Light Science for Leisure Hours. A Series of Familiar Essays on Scientific Subjects, Natural Phenomena, etc. Proctor (R. A.)	12°	1 75
*Lilian: A Story of the Days of Martyrdom in England Three Hundred Years Ago. Illust.	16°	75
*Lilian Grey. Lilian was what she prayed to be, a Blessing. Holt (G. H.) Illust.	16°	1 25
*Lilly's Travels through France to Switzerland. Illust.	16°	1 00
*Lindendale Stories, The. Wise (Daniel). 5 vols. In a box.	16°	5 00

*Lindsay Lee and His Friends. A Story for the Times.	16°	$0 65
*Links in Rebecca's Life. Alden (Mrs. G. R. [Pansy].) Illust.	12°	1 50
*Line upon Line.	16°	50
Lion-hunting in Algeria. Gerard.	12°	1 50
Literary and Historical Miscellanies. Bancroft (George).	8°	3 00
Literary Attractions of the Bible. Halsey (Le Roy J.)	12°	1 00
Literary Characteristics and Achievements of the Bible. Trail (W.)	12°	1 50
Literary Reminiscences. De Quincey. 2 vols.	12°	3 00
Literature and Life. Whipple (Edwin P.)	16°	1 50
Literature Primers. Edited by J. R. Green.	18°	e n 45

> English Grammar. Morris (R.)
> English Literature. Brooke (S.)
> Philology. Peile (J.)
> Classical Geography. Tozer (H. F.)
> Shakespeare. Dowden (E.)
> Studies in Bryant. Alden (J.)
> Greek Literature. Jebb (R. C.)
> English Grammar Exercises. Morris and Bowen.
> Homer. Gladstone. (William E.)
> English Composition. Nichol (John).

*Little and Wise; or, Sermons to Children. Newton (W. W.) Illust.	16°	1 25
*Little Ben Hadden; or, Do Right, Whatever Comes of It. Kingston (W H. G.) Illust.	16°	1 25
*Little Brothers and Sisters. Marshall (Emma).	16°	1 25
Little Classics. Edited by Rossiter Johnson.	18°	e 1 00

> Exile. Childhood.
> Life. Humanity.

*Little Door-keeper. Illust.	16°	1 00
*Little Drops of Rain.	16°	1 00
*Little Foxes. By the Author of "How Marjorie Watched." Illust.	16°	75
*Little Effie's Home.	16°	1 25
*Little Housekeeper, The, and Other Stories. Illust.	18°	40
*Little Lights Along the Shore. Cobden (Paul).	16°	1 25
*Little Mother and Her Christmas, The, and Other Stories. McKeen (Phebe). Illust.	16°	1 00
*Little People Whom the Lord Loved. Illust.	16°	1 00
*Little Lucy's Wonderful Globe. Yonge (C. M.)	16°	75

*Little Peach-blossom ; or, Rambles in the Central Park. Illust.   16° $1 00

*Little Pillows: Being Good-night Thoughts for Little Ones. Havergal (F R.)   18°   25

*Little Preacher, The. Prentiss (Mrs. E.)   16°   1 00

*Little Princess, and Other Stories. Chiefly About Christmas.   18°   55

*Little Rosie Stories. Hosmer (Margaret). Illust.   18°   e 75

> Little Rosie's Christmas Times.
> Little Rosie's First Play-days.
> Little Rosie in the Country.

*Little Three-year old. Davis (Mrs. C. E. K.)   16°   75

*Little Threads; or, Tangle Thread, Silver Thread, and Golden Thread. Prentiss (Mrs. E.)   16°   1 00

*Little Toss. A Story showing the Value of Christian Trust. Cummings (M. J.) Illust.   16°   1 25

*Little Trowel. Waddy (Edith). Illust.   16°   75

*Little Woman, A. Farman (Ella).   16°   1 00

Little Women. Alcott (Louisa M.) 2 vols.   16°   3 00

*Live Boy, The ; or, Charlie's Letters. Johnson (E. A.) Illust.   16°   85

Lives of the Leaders of our Church Universal, from the Days of the Succession of the Apostles to the Present Time. Piper (Ferdinand) and McCracken.   8°   3 00

Lives of the Apostles and Early Martyrs of the Church. Illust.   18°   75

Lives of the British Reformers. With Portraits.   12°   1 50

Lives of Celebrated Female Sovereigns. Jameson (Mrs. Anna). 2 vols.   18°   1 50

     The same, 1 vol.   12°   1 25

*Lives Made Sublime by Faith and Works. Illust.   16°   1 00

Lives of the Popes.   12°   1 50

Lives of the Queens of England from the Norman Conquest. Strickland (Agnes). Illust.   12°   1 25

Lives of the Three Mrs. Judsons—Ann, Sarah, and Emily. With Portraits. Wilson (Mrs. A. M.)   12°   1 25

Living Christianity; or, Old Truths Restated. Halsey (Le Roy J.)   12°   1 25

*Living in Earnest. A Book for Young Men. Johnson (Joseph).   16°   1 00

Living Waters for Daily Use.   24°   30

Living Way. Atkinson (J.)	16°	$0 45
Living Wesley, The. Rigg (James H.)	12°	1 00
Living Words; or, Unwritten Sermons of the Late		
John McClintock, D. D., LL. D.	12°	1 50
Locusts and Wild Honey, The Pastoral Bee, etc.		
Burroughs (John).	16°	1 50
Looking Toward Sunset. Child (Lydia Maria).	8°	2 50
Lord Herbert of Cherbury, and Thomas Ellwood.		
Howells (W. D.) "Little Classic" Style.	16°	1 25
Lord's Prayer, The. Seven Homilies. Gladden		
(Washington).	16°	1 00
Lord's Supper, The. A Treatise on. Bickersteth		
(E. H.)	18°	50
Lord's Supper. Luckey (Samuel).	18°	50
Lord's Supper, Guide to the. Smith (D.)	24°	25
Lost Blessing, The. Shipton (Anna).	16°	75
Lost Forever. Townsend (L. T.)	16°	75
*Lost and Found. Urmy (W. S.)	16°	85
*Lost Purse, The; or, Bessie Bleak. Temptation Re-		
sisted. Illust.	16°	75
*Louis XV and His Times. From the French of		
L. L. F. Bungener.	12°	1 50
Love Enthroned; or, Essays on Evangelical Perfec-		
tion. Steele (Daniel).	12°	1 25
Love in Marriage. An Historical Study. Lady		
Rachel Russell. Guizot.	16°	75
*Loved into Shape, and Osgood's Rebellion. Illust.	16°	1 00
*Loving Heart and Helping Hand Library. Illust.		
5 vols.	16°	4 75

> Nettie and Her Friends.
> Philip Moore, the Sculptor.
> An Orphan's Story.
> Carrie Williams and her Scholars.
> The Story of a Moss Rose.

Loyal Response; or, Daily Melodies for the King's		
Minstrels. Havergal (F. R.)	18°	25
*Lucien Guglieri. Lee (Mary B.)	16°	50
Lucile, and Other Poems. Meredith (Owen).	16°	1 50
*Luck of Alden Farm. Mudge (Z. A.) Illust.	16°	1 50
*Lucy Forester's Triumphs. McKeever (Harriet B.)	16°	1 00
*Lucy, the Light-bearer. Sargent (G. F.) Illust.	16°	1 00
Luther, Martin, Life of. Cubitt (George).	12°	85

*Luther Martin, Historical Souvenirs of. Hubner
    (Charles W.) Illust. 12° $0 85
*Lyntonville Library. 4 vols. 16° 4 00
> Life in Lyntonville.   Fishers of Derby Haven.
> Miss Carroll's School.   Grace's Visit.

Lyra Americana; or, Verses of Praise and Faith
    from American Poets. 12° 1 50

*Mabel Livingstone; or, Christward Led. Illust. 16° 1 25
*Mabel's Faith. A Practical Story. Illust. 16° 75
Macaulay, Lord. His Life and His Writings. Jones
    (C. H.) 18° 60
Madame De Stael. Stevens (A.) 2 vols. 12° e1 50
*Madam How and Lady Why; or, First Lessons in
    Earth Lore for Children. Kingsley (Charles).
    Illust. 12° 1 75
*Maggie's Message. A Charming Story, by the Au-
    thor of "Soldier Fritz." Illust. 75
Mahomet. Irving (Washington). 2 vols. 16° e1 25
Malacca, Indo-China, and China. Ten Years' Trav-
    els, Adventures, and Residence Abroad. Thom-
    son (J.) Illust. 8° 4 00
Malay Archipelago, The. Wallace (A. R.) Illust. 8° 2 50
Mammon. Harris (John). 18° 40
Man All Immortal; or, The Nature and Destination
    of Man as Taught by Reason and Revelation.
    Clark (D. W.) 12° 1 50
Man and Beast, Here and Hereafter. Wood (J. G.)
    Illust. 8° 1 50
Man and the Gospel; and Our Father's Business.
    Guthrie (Thomas). In 1 vol. 12° 1 50
*Man of One Book, The; or, The Life of Rev.
    William Marsh. By His Daughter. 16° 1 25
*Man with the Book; or, the Bible Among the Peo-
    ple. Waylland (John Matthias). Illust. 16° 1 00
Manliness of Christ. Hughes (Thomas). 16° 1 00
Manly Character, Formation of a. A Series of Lec-
    tures to Young Men. Peck (George). 16° 65
Manners, Book of. A Guide to Social Intercourse.
    Smith (Daniel). 24° 35
*Manuscript Man; or, The Bible in Ireland. Walshe
    (Miss E. H.) Illust. 16° 1 00

*Marble Preacher. Clark (Mrs. Henry Steele).
  Illust. 16° $1 50
*Marcella of Rome. The Fearless Christian Maiden.
  Eastwood (Frances). 16° 90
*Margaret at Home; or, The Leaven Still Working. 16° 1 00
*Margaret's Old Home. A Tale of Christian Love.
  Illust. 16° 1 25
*Margaret Worthington. A Young Girl Shows a
  Genuine Christian Purpose. Provost (Katha-
  rine). Illust. 16° 1 50
*Margarethe: A Tale of the Sixteenth Century.
  Illustrated. 12° 1 25
*Marguerite; or, The Huguenot Child. Taylor
  (Miss T.) 16° 85
*Marian's Mission; or, The Influence of Sunday-
  schools. Leslie (Emma). 16° 85
*Marion and Jessie; or, Children's Influence. Illust. 16° 85
*Marjorie's Quest. Gould (Jeanie T.) Illust. 12° 1 50
*Mark Churchill. Mark was a hero indeed, with a
  fixed purpose to do right. A noble example
  for boys to follow. Illust. 16° 1 25
*Mark Thoresby; or, The Evangelist Among the
  Indians. A Narrative of the Seventeenth
  Century. 16° 1 35
Marriage. Cook (Joseph). 12° 1 50
Marriage, A Treatise on Christian. Davie (H.) 8° 1 50
*Mary Leslie's Trials. McKeever (Harriet B). 16° 1 00
*Marsh's Help, Mrs. Dana (J. J.) Illust. 16° 1 00
Martyrs, Fox's Book of. 12° 1 25
Martyrs and Apologists. Pressensé (E. De). 1 50
*Martyrs of the Catacombs. 16° 75
*Martyrs to the Tract Cause. A Contribution to the
  History of the Reformation. Hurst (J. F.) 12° 65
Mary and I; or, Forty Years with the Sioux. Riggs
  (Stephen R.,) 12° 1 50
Mason, Mrs. Mary W., Life of. With an Introduc-
  tion by Bishop Janes. 12° 1 25
Master and Pupil. The True Work of Education
  in Public Schools. Five Hundred Dollar Prize
  Stories. Illust. 16° 1 50
Master Missionaries. Studies in Heroic Pioneer
  Work. 12° 1 50

Masterpieces of Pulpit Eloquence. Fish (Henry C.) 8° $3 00
*Mat and Sofie. 18° 35
Maternal Duty. Abbott (J. S. C.) Illust. 16° 1 00
*Matthew Frost, Carrier; or, Little Snow-drop's Mission. Marshall (Emma). 16° 1 00
*Maude Grenville Library. Illust. 5 vols. In a box. 16° 5 00

    Maude Grenville.   Enoch Roden's Training.
    Heroism of Boyhood.   Victor and Hilaria.
      The Children of the Great King.

Maxwell, Lady, Life of. Lancaster (John). 12° 1 00
*Maybee's Stepping-stones. Capron (Mary J.) 1 25
*May; or, Grandpa's Pet. Smith (Mrs. F. B.) Illust. 18° 75
*May Bell. The Devotion of a Young Girl to the Work appointed her by Filial Love and Christian Faith. Illust. 16° 1 50
*May Dundas; or, Passages in Young Life. Geldart (Mrs. Thomas). 16° 85
McClintock, John, D. D., LL. D., Life and Letters of. Crooks (George R.) 12° 1 50
Mediæval and Modern Saints and Miracles. A Sharp, Searching Analysis of Roman Catholic Pretensions. 12° 1 50
Meditations on the Actual State of Christianity. Guizot (M.) 12° 1 50
Meditations on the Essence of Christianity. Guizot (M.) 12° 1 50
*Mehetabel. A Story of the Revolution. Gardner (Mrs. H. C.) Illust. 16° 1 00
Memorable Scenes in French History. From the Era of Cardinal Richelieu to the Present Time. Smucker (Samuel M.) 12° 1 25
Memoir and Remains of the Rev. Robert Murray McCheyne. Bonar (Andrew A.) 12° 1 00
Memoir of Col. Charles S. Todd. Griffin (G. W.) 12° 1 50
Memoir of General William Francis Bartlett. Palfrey (F. W.) 16° 1 50
Memoirs of a Huguenot Family. Maury (Ann). 12° 1 75
Memories of Fifty Years. Containing Brief Biographical Notices of Distinguished Americans, and Anecdotes of Remarkable Men, etc. Sparks (W. H.) 8° 2 50

Memories of Patmos; or, Some of the Great Words
    and Visions of the Apocalypse. Macduff
    (J. R.)   12° $1 25

Memorial Hour, The; or, The Lord's Supper in its
    Relation to Doctrine and Life. Chaplin (Jer-
    emiah).   16° 1 50

Memorial Name, The. Reply to Bishop Colenso.
    MacWhorter (Alexander).   16° 1 00

Memorials of Frances Ridley Havergal. By her
    Sister.   12° 1 75

Memorials from Journals and Letters of Samuel
    Clarke. Edited by his Wife.   12° 2 00

*Men, Women, and Ghosts. Phelps (Elizabeth S.) 16° 1 50

Mendelssohn Family, The. (1729–1847.) From
    Letters and Journals. Hensel (Sebastian).
    Translated by Carl Klingemann and an Amer-
    ican Collaborator. Eight Portraits. 2 vols.   8° 5 00

Mental Discipline. Clark (D. W.)   18°   65

Mental Science, Elements of. Smith (M.)   12° 1 75

Mental Science. A Compendium of Psychology
    and History of Philosophy. Bain (Alex.)   12° 1 50

Meredith's, Owen, Poems. Household Edition. 12° 2 00

Mercy of God, Contemplations on the. Etheridge
    (J. W.)   18°   40

*Merry Times for Boys and Girls. Illust.   4° 1 25

Methodism, American, A Compendious History of.
    Abridged from the Author's History of the
    Methodist Episcopal Church. Stevens (Abel).
    Illust.   8° 3 00

Methodism, A Comprehensive History of. Em-
    bracing Origin, Progress, and Present Spiritual,
    Educational, Benevolent Status in all Lands.
    Porter (James).   12° 1 75

Methodism and its Methods. Crane (J. T.)   12° 1 25

Methodism and the Centennial of American Inde-
    pendence; or, The Loyal and Liberal Services
    of the Methodist Episcopal Church during the
    First Century of the History of the United
    States. With a Brief History of the Various
    Branches of Methodism, and Full Statistical
    Tables. Wood (E. M.)   12° 1 50

Methodism, American. Statistical History of the
    First Century. Goss (C. C.)   16° $0 85
Methodism and the Temperance Reformation.
    Wheeler (H.)   12°   1 50
Methodism, A Hundred Years of. Simpson (M.) 12°   1 50
Methodism, Centenary of American. Stevens (A.) 12°   1 50
Methodism, Compendium of. Porter (James).   12°   1 50
Methodism, Ecclesiastical Polity of. Hodgson (F.) 18°   30
Methodism Forty Years Ago and Now. Culver
    (Newell.)   12°   1 00
Methodism, Heroes of. Wakeley (J. B.)   12°   1 50
Methodism, Heroines of. Coles (G.)   12°   1 00
*Methodism, History of. For Our Young People.
   Bennett (W W.) Illust.   16°   1 25
Methodism, History of. Stevens (A.) 3 vols.   12°   4 50
Methodism, Inside Views of. Reddy (W.)   18°   40
Methodism in the Field; or, Pastor and People.
    Potts (J. H.) With an Introduction by J. M.
    Reid.   16°   1 00
Methodism in West Jersey. Raybold (G. A.)   18°   40
Methodism, Manual of; or, The Doctrines, General
    Rules, and Usages of the Methodist Episcopal
    Church. With Scripture Proofs and Explana-
    tions. Hawley (B.)   12°   85
Methodism, Women of. Stevens (A.)   12°   1 25
Methodist Episcopal Church, History of the, in the
    United States of America. Stevens (A.)
    4 vols.   12°   6 00
Methodist Episcopal Church, History of the. Bangs
    (N.) 4 vols.   12°   5 00
Methodist Episcopal Church, Responsibilities of the.
    Bangs (N.)   18°   50
Methodist Episcopal Church of the United States,
    Statistics of the. De Puy (W. H.) Paper.   12°   20
Methodist Episcopal Pulpit. A Collection of Orig-
    inal Sermons. Clark (D. W.)   12°   1 50
Methodist, Reasons for Becoming a. Smith (I.) 18°   40
Methodists Vindicated. Letter to Dr. Pusey. Jack-
    son (T.)   18°   35
Methodist? Why are You a. Peck (G.)   18°   50
Methodology. Lectures on Theological Encyclopæ-
    dia and Methodology. McClintock (John). 12°   1 25

Might of Right, The. Gladstone (W E.)	16°	$1 00
Mikado's Empire, The; History of Japan, etc. Griffis (W E.) Illust.	8°	4 00
Milestone Papers, Doctrinal, Ethical, and Experimental, on Christian Progress. Steele (Daniel).	16°	85
Mind and Body. The Theory of their Relations. Bain (Alex.)	12°	1 50
*Ministering Children. Charlesworth (M. L.) Illust.	12°	1 25
*Ministering Children, Sequel to. Charlesworth (M. L.)	12°	1 50
Minister of Christ for the Times. Adams (C.)	12°	60
Ministry of Life, The. Charlesworth (M. L.) Illust.	16°	1 00
Ministry of Song. Havergal (F. R.)		75
Miracle in Stone; or, The Great Pyramid of Egypt. Seiss (Joseph A.)	12°	1 25
*Miracles of Heavenly Love in Daily Life. Illust.	16°	1 00
Miscellany of Entertaining Tracts. Chambers. 10 vols.	12°	10 00
Misread Passages of Scripture. Second Series. Brown (J. Baldwin).	12°	85
*Missionary, Adventures of a; or, Rivers of Water in a Dry Place. Illust.	16°	1 00
*Missionary Among Cannibals. 1 Illust.	16°	85
*Missionary Concerts for the Sunday-school. A Collection of Declamations, Select Readings, and Dialogues. Smith (W T.)	16°	75
*Missionary in Many Lands. House (E.) Illust.	16°	1 00
Missionary Memorials in West Africa. Moister (W.)	12°	75
Missionary Life Among the Villages in India. Scott (T. J.)	12°	1 50
Mission of the Comforter. Hare.	12°	1 75
Mission of the Spirit; or, The Office and Work of the Comforter in Human Redemption. Dunn (L. R.)	12°	1 00
Missions and Missionary Society of the Methodist Episcopal Church. Reid (J. M.) Maps and Illust. 2 vols.		3 00
Mister Horn and His Friends; or, Givers and Giving. Pearse (Mark Guy.) Illust.	12°	80
*Miss Priscilla Hunter and My Daughter Susan. Alden (Mrs. G. R. [Pansy].) Illust.	16°	1 25

*Miss Wealthy's Hope. Davis (Mrs. C. E. K.) Illust. 16° $1 50
*Misunderstood. Intended for those who are Interested in Children. Montgomery (Florence). 16° 1 25
*Mistress of the House. Chamberlain (P. B.) 16° 1 00
Model Superintendent, The. Trumbull (H. Clay). 12° 1 00
Model for Men of Business. 18° 50
Model Preacher. Taylor (William). 12° 1 50
Modern British Essayists. Containing the Essays of Alison, Carlyle, Jeffrey, Macaulay, Mackintosh, Sydney Smith, Talfourd, Stephen, and Wilson. 6 vols. In box. 8° 12 00
Modern Classics. A reprint, in new form, of the Popular and Sterling Vest-pocket Series. Including Selections from the most celebrated Authors of England and America, and Translations of several Masterpieces by Continental Writers. *e* 75

1. Evangeline; The Courtship of Miles Standish; Favorite Poems. Longfellow.
2. Culture, Behavior, Beauty; Books, Art, Eloquence; Power, Wealth, Illusions. Emerson.
3. Nature; Love, Friendship, Domestic Life; Success, Greatness, Immortality. Emerson.
4. Snow-bound; The Tent on the Beach; Favorite Poems. Whittier.
5. The Vision of Sir Launfal; The Cathedral; Favorite Poems. Lowell.
6. In and Out of Doors with Charles Dickens. Fields. A Christmas Carol. Dickens. Barry Cornwall and some of his Friends. Fields.
7. The Ancient Mariner; Favorite Poems. Coleridge. Favorite Poems. Wordsworth.
8. Undine; Sintram. Fouque. Paul and Virginia. St. Pierre.
9. Rab and his Friends; Marjorie Fleming; Thackeray; John Leech. Dr. John Brown.
10. Enoch Arden; In Memoriam; Favorite Poems. Tennyson.
11. The Princess; Maud; Locksley Hall. Tennyson.
12. Elizabeth Barrett Browning; an Essay. Stedman (E. C.) Lady Geraldine's Courtship. Browning (Mrs.) Favorite Poems. Browning (Robert).
13. Goethe; an Essay. Carlyle. The Tale; Favorite Poems. Goethe.
14. Schiller; an Essay. Carlyle. The Lay of the Bell, and Fridolin; Favorite Poems. Schiller.
15. Burns; an Essay. Carlyle. Favorite Poems. Burns. Favorite Poems. Scott.
16. Byron; an Essay. Macaulay. Favorite Poems. Byron. Favorite Poems. Hood.

30

Modern Classics. (*Continued.*)

17. Milton; an Essay. Macaulay. L'Allegro; Il Penseroso. Milton. Elegy in a Country Church-yard, etc. Gray.
18. A Deserted Village, etc. Goldsmith. Favorite Poems. Cowper. Favorite Poems. Mrs. Hemans.
19. Characteristics. Carlyle. Favorite Poems. Shelley. The Eve of St. Agnes, etc. Keats.
20. An Essay on Man; Favorite Poems. Pope. Favorite Poems. Moore.
21. The Choice of Books. Carlyle. Essays from Elia. Lamb. Favorite Poems. Southey.
22. Spring; Summer; Autumn; Winter. Thomson.
23. The Pleasures of Hope; Favorite Poems. Campbell. Pleasures of Memory. Rogers.
24. Sonnets; Songs. Shakespeare. Favorite Poems. Leigh Hunt.
25. Favorite Poems. Herbert. Favorite Poems. Collins, Dryden, Marvell. Favorite Poems. Herrick.
26. Lays of Ancient Rome, and Other Poems. Macaulay. Lays of the Scottish Cavaliers. Aytoun.
27 Favorite Poems. Charles Kingsley. Favorite Poems. Owen Meredith. Favorite Poems. Stedman.
28. Nathaniel Hawthorne; an Essay. Fields. Tales of the White Hills; Legends of New England. Hawthorne.
29. Oliver Cromwell. Carlyle. A Virtuoso's Collection; Legends of the Province House. Hawthorne.
30. The Story of Iris; Favorite Poems. Holmes. Health. Dr. John Brown.
31. My Garden Acquaintance; A Moosehead Journal. Lowell. The Farmer's Boy. Bloomfield.
32. A Day's Pleasure; The Parlor Car. Howells. A True Story. Mark Twain.

Modern Classics. Containing Selections from Various Authors.	12°	$1 25
Modern Doubt and Christian Belief Considered. Christlieb (Theo.)	8°	3 00
Modern Genesis. Being an Inquiry into the Credibility of the Nebular Theory of the Origin of Planetary Bodies, the Structure of the Solar System, and of General Cosmical History. Slaughter (W. B.)	16°	85
*Modern Prophets. Interesting and Effective Temperance Stories for the Times. Alden (Mrs. G. R. [Pansy]), and Huntington (Faye). Illust.	12°	1 50
Modern Story-teller. A Collection of Amusing and Entertaining Anecdotes Selected from the Best Authors.	12°	1 25
Mohammed and Mohammedanism. Smith (R. B.)	12°	1 50
Monarchy, Sixth Great. Rawlinson.	8°	3 00

Moon, The. Her Motions, Aspect, Scenery, and
 Physical Conditions. Proctor (R. A.) Illust. 12° $3 50
Moore, Rev. Henry, Life of. Smith (Mrs. R.) 12° 70
*Morag. A Story of Highland Life. 12° 1 00
Moral and Political Philosophy. Paley (Wm.) 12° 1 50
Moral Science. A Compendium of Ethics. Bain
 (Alex.) 12° 1 50
*Mordecai's Tenants. Walker (Miss A. D.) Illust. 16° 65
*More Ways than One. Perry (Alice). Illust. 16° 1 50
*Morning Bells; or, Waking Thoughts for Little
 Ones. Havergal (F. R.) 18° 25
Morning, Noon, and Night; or, Christ in Every
 Page. A Manual of Devotion. 8° 2 50
Morning of Joy. Bonar (Horatius). 18° 60
*Morning Stars; or, Names of Christ for His Little
 Ones. Havergal (F. R.) 18° 25
Mormonism and the Mormons. Kidder (D. P.) 18° 45
Morocco: Its People and Places. Amicis (Ed-
 mondo De). Illust. 12° 2 00
Morris, Rev. Thomas A., D. D., Life of, Late Senior
 Bishop of the Methodist Episcopal Church.
 Marlay (John F.) 12° 1 50
Morris's Miscellany. Essays, Sketches, etc. 12° 1 25
Mortimer, Mrs. Elizabeth, Memoir of. Bulmer
 (Agnes). 18° 45
*Moss Rose Series. For Very Small Children. Illust.
 12 vols. In box. 32° 3 00

Willie's Wish.	Afraid of the Dark.
Curious Tom.	Little Minnie.
The Two Mottoes.	Birthday Present.
Little James.	A Real Victory.
Old Ben's Stockings.	Sowing Little Seed.
Little Bertie.	Milly's Doves.

*Mother Herring's Chicken. Meade (L. T.) Illust. 12° 1 00
Mother, The, At Home; or, The Principles of Ma-
 ternal Duty. Abbott (J. S. C.) Illust. 16° 1 00
Mother's Recompense, A. Aguilar (Grace). Illust. 12° 1 00
*Mother's Gift to Her Little Ones at Home. 16° 50
*Mother's Mission. Sketches from Real Life. Illust. 16° 1 00
Mother's Practical Guide. Bakewell (Mrs. J.) 18° 50
Mother, Home, and Heaven. A Collection of
 Poems. Edited by Mrs. J. P. Newman. 18° 1 25

Mother of the Wesleys. Kirk (John).	12°	$1 50
Motives of Life. Swing (David).	16°	1 00
Mrs. Deane's Way. The Value and Happiness of Trusting in God happily exemplified. Huntington (Faye). Illust.	16°	1 25
Mrs. Harry Harper's Awakening. A Missionary Story. Alden (Mrs. G. R. [Pansy].) Illust.	12°	1 00
*Mrs. Thorne's Guests; or, Salt with Savor and without. Fell (Archie). Illust.	16°	1 50
*Much Fruit. An Earnest Plea, in Story Form, to the Young, for Kind Deeds and Words for the Master's Sake. Homespun (Sophia). Illust.	16°	1 00
Music and Morals. Haweis (H. R.) Illust.	12°	1 75
Music Study in Germany. Fay (Miss Amy).	12°	1 25
*My Father and I; and Helva's Child. The two in one vol. Marsh (Katharine M.)	12°	1 00
*My Hero. Porter (Mrs. A. E.) Illust.	16°	1 50
*My Mates and I. Exhibits the Contrasted Results of Lives which are and those which are not Animated by a Christian Faith and Purpose. Illust.	16°	1 00
*Myra Sherwood's Cross, and How She Bore it. Illust.	16°	1 50
My Summer in a Garden. Warner (Charles D).	16°	1 00
Mysteries of the Head and Heart Explained. Grimes (J. Stanley). Illust.	12°	1 50
Mythology, Manual of. Murry (A. T.) Illust.	8°	2 25
*Myths and Heroes; or, The Childhood of the World. Edited by S. F. Smith. Illust.	16°	1 50
Myths and Myth-makers. Old Tales and Superstitions interpreted by Comparative Mythology. Fiske (John).	12°	2 00
NAPOLEON and His Marshals. (Headley (J. T.)	12°	2 50
Napoleon and the Marshals of the Empire. With Portraits. Complete in 1 vol.	8°	2 25
Nations Around, The. A Sketch of the Early History of the Great Eastern Empires, whose Territories surrounded, and sometimes included, Palestine: Forming a Supplement to the Jewish History in the Bible Narrative. Kary (A.)	12°	1 75

Narrative and Miscellaneous Papers. De Quincey (Thos.)	8°	$1 75
National Sermons. Haven (Gilbert).	8°	2 00
Nature and Life. Collyer (R.)	12°	1 50
Nature of Light, with a General Account of Physical Optics. Lummel (E.) Illust.	12°	2 00
Natural Goodness. Mercein (T. F. R.)	12°	85
Natural History, Popular. Wood (J. G.)	8°	1 75
Natural History of the Bible. Tristram (H. B.)	12°	1 50
Natural Science and Religion. Gray (Asa).	12°	1 00
Natural Theology. Paley (William). 2 vols.	18°	1 50
Naturalist, The, on the River Amazon. Bates.	8°	2 50
*Ned and His Engine; and Will and John. Two Interesting English Stories for Boys. Illust.	16°	1 00
*Neighbor's House, The. Two Neighboring Families Contrasted. Shaw (Jennie R.) Illust.	16°	1 50
*Neighborly Love. Illust.	16°	1 00
*Neither Rome nor Judah. Hoven (Ernest). Illust.	16°	1 10
*Nelson; or, How a Country Boy Made His Way in the City. Thayer (Wm. M.)	16°	1 25
*Nettie Nesmith; or, The Bad Girl. Showing Indian Character and Style of Life. Homespun (Sophia). Illust.	16°	1 00
*New Commandment, The; or, Ella's Ministry. Shaw (Jennie R.) Illust.	16°	1 50
New Divinity, System of, Examined. Hodgson (F.)	12°	75
New England Bird-life. A Manual of New England Ornithology. Stearns (Winifred A.)	8°	2 50
New England Divines, Sketches of. Sherman (D.)	12°	1 50
*New Graft on the Family Tree, A. Full of the Sweetness of Evangelical Religion. Alden (Mrs. G. R. [Pansy].) Illust.	12°	1 50
New Life Dawning, and Other Discourses of the Late B. N. Nadal, D. D.	12°	1 50
*Newlyn House, the Home of the Davenports. Illust.	16°	1 25
New Plutarch Series, The. Lives of Men and Women of Action. 13 vols.	12°	*e*1 00

Abraham Lincoln; the Abolition of Slavery. With a Portrait. Leland (Charles G.)

Coligny: the Failure of the French Reformation. With a Portrait. Besant (Walter).

Judas Maccabæus and the Jewish War of Independence. Conder (Claude Reignier).

New Plutarch Series. (*Continued.*)

Victor Emmanuel; the Attainment of Italian Unity.
Dicey (Edward).
Joan of Arc; the Expulsion of the English from France.
Tuckey (Janet).
Alexander the Great and His Age. Brodribb (W. J.)
The Caliph Haroun al. Raschid; Saracen Civilization.
Palmer (E. H.)
Richelieu and His Court. Pollock (Walter Herries).
Hannibal and Carthaginian Civilization. Lee (Samuel).
Harold Fair-hair and the Scandinavians. Magnússon
(Erik).
Charlemagne and His Time. Beesley (Prof.)
Gustavus Adolphus. Garnett (Richard).
Whittington, Lord Mayor of London. Rice (James).

New Puritan, The. New England Two Hundred Years Ago. Pike (Jas. S.)	12°	$1 00
New Testament Church Members. Adams (C.)	12°	75
New Testament Expounded and Illustrated. Moody (C.)	8°	3 50
New Testament History. [Abridged.] Maclear (G. F.)	18°	30
*Next Things. A Story for Little Folks. Alden (Mrs. G. R. [Pansy].) Illust.	12°	1 00
Nez Perce Joseph. An Account of His Ancestors, His Lands, His Confederates, His Enemies, His Murders, His War, His Pursuit and Capture. Howard (O. O.)	8°	2 50
*New York Bible Woman, The. Wright (Mrs. J. McNair). Illust.	16°	1 10
*New York Needle-woman, The; or, Elsie's Stars. Illust.	16°	80
Night Lessons from Scripture. Sewell (E. M.)	16°	1 00
Night of Weeping. Bonar (Horatius).	18°	50
Nile Notes of a Howadji. A Volume of Eastern Travels. Curtis (George William).	12°	1 50
Nile Tributaries of Abyssinia. Baker (S. W.)	8°	2 50
Nineteen Beautiful Years; or, Sketches of a Girl's Life. Willard (Frances E.)	16°	1 00
Nineteenth Century, The. A History. Mackenzie. (Robert). English Edition.	12°	1 50
Nineveh, Discoveries at. Layard (A. H.) Illust.	12°	1 75
*Nita's Music-lesson, and Other Stories. Illust.	18°	40
Nix's Offerings. Benning (H.) Illust.	16°	1 25
*No Such Word as Fail. Illust.	12°	1 00

Noble Deeds of American Women. Clement (F.)
Illust. 12° $1 25
*Noble Life, A; or, Hints for Living. Kingsbury
(O. A.) 16° 1 25
*Noble Printer, The, and His Adopted Daughter. A
Story of the First Printed Bible. Translated,
with additions, by Campbell Overend. Illust. 16° 1 50
*Noble Workers. Sketches of Men who have risen
to Distinction. Edited by S. F. Smith. Illust. 12° 1 50
*Nobody but Nan. 16° 85
*Nora Crena. How She Saved Her Own. Meade
(L. F.) 12° 1 25
Normans in Europe, The. Johnson (A. H.) 16° 1 00
*Norse Life, A Tale of. Boyesen (H. H.) 12° 1 25
Norse Mythology. Anderson (R. B.) 12° 2 50
*North Pole Voyages. Embracing Sketches of the
Important Facts and Incidents in the Latest
American Efforts to Reach the North Pole,
from the Second Grinnell Expedition to the
Polaris. Mudge (Z. A.) 16° 1 00
*North-west, Early History of the. Hildreth (S. P.) 16° 85
North American Antiquities, The. Short (John T.)
Illust. 8° 3 00
*Not Bread Alone; or, Miss Helen's Neighbors.
Drinkwater (Jennie M.) 16° 1 25
*Note-book of the Bertram Family. A Sequel to
Winifred Bertram. By the Author of the
Schönberg-Cotta Family. 12° 1 00
*Nothing Venture, Nothing Have. Haven (Mrs. A.B.) 12° 1 00
*Now and Forever. Leslie (Mrs. M.) 12° 1 00
Nubia and Abyssinia. Russell (M.) 18° 75

OBLIGATIONS of the World to the Bible. Spring
(Gardiner). 8° 2 00
Observations in the East. Durbin (J. P.) 2 vols. 12° 3 00
*Object of Life. Illustrating the Insufficiency of the
World and the Sufficiency of Christ. Illust. 16° 1 00
*Odd One, The. Payne (A. M. Mitchell). 16° 1 25
Odes of Horace. Translated into English Verse.
Martin (Theodore). 16° 1 00
Odyssey of Homer, The. W C. Bryant's Trans-
lation. 12° 3 00

Office of the Holy Communion in the Book of
Common Prayer. A Series of Lectures. Goulburn (E. M.)   12° $1 00

Official Guide-book to Philadelphia. Westcott
(Thompson). Illust.   16°   1 50

Official Members of the Methodist Episcopal
Church, Helps to. Porter (James).   16°   70

*Old and New Friends. The Story has Pathos and
Religious Tone. Oliver (Maria). Illust.   12°   1 50

*Old Chateau, The. McKeever (Harriet). Illust. 16°   1 50

Old England: Its Scenery, Art, and People. Hoppin (James M.)   16°   1 75

Old Friends and New. Jewett (Miss Sarah O.)   18°   1 25

*Old Humphrey, Half-hours with. Mogridge (Geo.) 16°   85

*Old Looking-glass, The. Charlesworth (Maria L.)
Illust.   16°   1 00

*Old Market-cart, The. A Pleasant Narrative of
Country Life. Smith (Mrs. F. B.) Illust.   18°   75

*Old Portmanteau. Hamilton (Kate W.) Illust.   16°   1 00

*Old Schoolfellows, and What Became of Them.
Illust.   16°   1 25

*Old Stone House, The. March (Anna). Illust.   16°   1 50

*Old Tales Retold from Grecian Mythology in Talks
Around the Fire. Larned (Augusta). Illust. 12°   1 70

Old Testament Characters Delineated and Illustrated. Floy (James).   12°   1 50

Old Testament History. Abridged. Maclear (G. F.) 18°   30

Old Testament Shadows of New Testament Truths.
Abbott (Lyman). Illust.   8°   3 00

Oldtown Folks. Stowe (H. B.)   12°   1 50

Old Wells Dug Out. Sermons of T. DeWitt Talmage.   12°   2 00

*Olio, Boys' and Girls'. An Interesting Work for
Children. Illust.   12°   80

*Olive Loring's Mission. Lawrence (Annie M.)
Illust.   12°   1 25

*Oliver of the Mill. Charlesworth (Maria L.)   12°   1 50

*On Board the Rocket. Adams (R. C.) Illust.   12°   1 50

*On Both Sides of the Sea. A Story of the Com-
monwealth and the Restoration. Being a
Sequel to "The Draytons and Davenants." By
the Author of "The Schönberg-Cotta Family." 12°   1 00

On the Parables. Guthrie (Thomas). Illust.	12°	$1 50
On the Plains and Among the Peaks; or, How Mrs. Maxwell Made Her Natural Collection. Dartt (Mary).	18°	1 00
*On the Seas. A Story for Boys. Illust.	16°	80
On the Threshold. Munger (T. T.)	16°	1 00
*Once Upon a Time. Brown (E. E.)	16°	1 25
*One Quiet Life. Colter (Mrs. J. J.) Illust.	12°	1 25
*One Year of My Life. Illust.	16°	1 25
*Only Ned; or, Grandma's Message. Drinkwater (J. M.)	16°	1 25
*Only Way Out, The. A Temperance Story of the Highest Order. Willing (Jennie F.)	12°	1 50
*Onward to the Heights of Life. Illust.	16°	1 25
*Open Letters to Primary Teachers. With Hints to Intermediate Class Teachers. Crafts (Mrs. W. F.)	12°	80
Open Polar Seas. Hayes (I. I.)	8°	3 75
Orators and Statesmen of Ancient and Modern Times, The Most Eminent. Harsha (David A.) With Portraits.	8°	2 50
Oratory and Orators. Matthews (Wm.)	12°	2 00
Oriental Missions, Our. India, China, and Bulgaria. Thomson (Edward). 2 vols.	12°	2 00
Origin of Nations, The. Rawlinson (G.)	16°	1 00
*Orphan Nieces, The; or, Duty and Inclination. Guernsey (Lucy E.)	16°	1 25
Orthodoxy. Cook (Joseph).	12°	1 50
Orthodox Theology of To-day, The. Smith (Newman).	12°	1 25
*Other House, The. Higham (Mary R.)	16°	1 00
Other Worlds than Ours. The Plurality of Worlds Studied under the Light of Recent Scientific Researches. Proctor (R. A.) Illust.	12°	2 50
*Our Captain. The Heroes of Barton School. Ridley (M. L.) Illust.	12°	1 25
Our Children. Haygood (A. G.)	12°	1 50
Our Country. Its Trial and Triumph. Peck (Geo.)	12°	1 25
Our English Bible and Its Ancestors. Walden (Treadwell).	16°	1 25
*Our Father in Heaven. The Lord's Prayer Explained and Illustrated. Wilson (J. H.) Illust.	16°	1 25

Our Homes. [Temperance.] Chellis (Mary D.) 12° $1 50
*Our King; or, The Story of our Lord's Life on
    Earth. Wise (Daniel). Illust. 12° 1 70
Our Next-door Neighbor. Sketches of Mexico.
    Haven (Gilbert). Maps and Illust. 8° 3 50
Our Old Home. A Series of English Sketches.
    Hawthorne (N.) 16° 1 50
Our Place Among the Infinities. Contrasting our
    Little Abode in Space and Time with the In-
    finities Around Us. Proctor (R. A.) 12° 1 75
Our Poetical Favorites. Edited by A. C. Hendrick.
    3 vols. 12° *e* 2 00

> *First Series.* Being a Selection from the Best Minor Poems.
> *Second Series.* Being a Selection Chiefly from the Best of the
>   Longer English Poems.
> *Third Series.* Being a Selection from the Best Poems of the
>   English Language, both English and American.

*Our Streets. A Powerful Plea for Temperance.
    Clark (Mrs. S. R. Graham). Illust. 12° 1 50
Ouseley, Gideon, Life of. Arthur (Wm.) 12° 1 00
*Out in the World; or, A Selfish Life. Wolfe (H. J.) 16° 1 00
*Out of Debt, Out of Danger. Haven (Mrs. A. B.) 12° 1 00
*Out of the Dark: A Story of Experience. Illust. 16° 1 20
Out of the Deep. Wood (E. P.) 16° 1 50
Out of the Harness. Guthrie (Thomas). 12° 1 50
Outposts of Zion. Goode (W. H.) 12° 1 50
*Outside the Gate. Illust. 16° 1 25
*Outside the Walls. Payne (Mrs. A. M. M.) 12° 1 50
*Over Seas; or, Here, There, and Everywhere.
    Graphic Descriptions of Scenes in Foreign
    Lands. By Popular Authors. Illust. 12° 1 00
*Overcoming. Churchill (Mrs. E. K.) Illust. 16° 1 25
*Overhead. What Harry and Nelly Discovered in
    the Heavens. Illuminated covers. Illust. 4° 1 00
Oxford Methodists, The. Tyerman (L.) 8° 2 50

PADDOCK, Rev. Benjamin, Memoir of. Paddock (Z.) 12° 1 25
Painters, Sculptors, Architects, Engravers, and
    Their Works. Clement (Clara E.) Illust. 12° 3 00
*Palace Beautiful, The; or, Sermons to the Children.
    Newton (W. W.) 16° 1 25
Palestine, Domestic Life in. Rogers (Mary E.) 12° 1 75

Palestine, Geography and History of. Hibbard
(F. G.)   12° $1 50

*Palissy, the Huguenot Potter. Brightwell (C. L.)
Illust.   16°   1 00

*Pansy, The. Edited by Mrs. G. R. Alden (Pansy).
Bound volume, 1881.   1 00

*Pansies. Alden (Mrs. G. R. [Pansy].) Chromo
board covers.   4°   75

    Fully illustrated, library style, cloth.   16°   75

Papacy, The, and Civil Power. Thompson (R. W.)   8°   3 00

*Papa's Boy. Davis (Mrs. C. K.) Illust.   16°   1 00

*Parables for Children. Abbott (E. A.) Illust.   12°   1 00

*Parables from Nature. Gatty (Mrs. Alfred.) Illust.   16°   85

   * The same. 2 vols.   18°   *e* 1 00

Parables of Jesus. Nevin (Alfred).   12°   1 50

Parables of Our Lord Explained and Applied.
Bourdillon (Francis).   12°   1 25

Paradise Lost. Milton.   12°   1 25

Paradise: The Place and State of Saved Souls between Death and the Resurrection. Patterson
(Robert M.)   16°   1 25

Paraclete, The. Essay on the Personality and Ministry of the Holy Ghost. Parker (Jos.)   12°   1 50

Parent's Friend. Smith (D.)   18°   45

*Parsonage in the Hartz, The. McFadden (Mrs.
Cornelia).   16°   1 15

*Parsonage in India, The. Adapted from the Ger-
man. McFadden (Mrs. Cornelia).   16°   1 00

Passing Thoughts on Religion. Sewell (E. M.)   16°   1 00

Past in the Present, The. What is Civilization?
Mitchell (Arthur). Illust.   8°   3 00

Pastor and People; or, Methodism in the Field.
Potts (J. H.)   16°   1 00

Pastor's Sketches; or, Conversations with Anxious
Inquirers Respecting the Way of Salvation.
Spencer (I. S.) 2 vols.   16°   2 00

Pastoral Office in the Methodist Episcopal Church.
Wythes (J. H.)   18°   25

Pastoral Theology. The Pastor in the Various Duties of His Office. Murphy (Thomas).   8°   3 00

*Path of Life; or, Sketches of the Way to Glory
and Immortality. Wise (D.)   12°   85

*Patient Susie; or, Paying the Mortgage. Illust. 16° $1 00
*Patient Waiting No Loss. 12° 1 00
Patriarchal Age; or, The History and Religion of
    Mankind from the Creation to the Death of
    Isaac. Smith (G.) 8° 2 75
*Paul Morris. Miller (Mary C.) Illust. 16° 1 25
Paul the Missionary. Taylor (Wm. M.) Illust. 12° 1 50
Payson, Rev. Edward, D. D., Mementos of. Janes
    (Edwin L.) 12° 1 25
*Payson, the Model Boy. 18° 35
Pearls of Thought. Edited by Maturin M. Ballou. 16° 1 50
*Peasant Boy Philosopher, The. Founded on the
    Early Life of Furguson, the Shepherd Boy As-
    tronomer. Mayhew (H.) 16° 1 25
*Pebbles from the Brook. Sermons to Children.
    Newton (Richard). 16° 1 25
Peck, Rev. George, D. D., Life and Times of. Writ-
    ten by Himself. 12° 1 50
Peculiar People, A; or, Reality in Romance. Balch
    (William S.) 12° 1 25
*Peeps at our Sunday-schools. Taylor (Alfred). 12° 1 00
*Peep Behind the Scenes, A. Walton (Mrs.) Illust. 16° 1 25
*Peep of Day; or, A Series of Earliest Religious
    Instructions. Illust. 18° 50
*Percy Raydon. A Story of Self-conquest. Leslie
    (Emma). Illust. 16° 1 00
*Percys, The. Prentiss (Mrs. E.) 16° 1 25
Perfect Love. Wood (J. A.) 12° 1 25
*Perfect Man, The; or, Jesus an Example of Godly
    Life. Jones (Harry). 16° 1 00
Person of Christ, The. Schaff (Philip). 12° 1 25
Personal Effort Explained and Enforced. Wise (D.) 24° 25
Personal Life of David Livingstone. Blaikie
    (William G.) 8° 3 50
Peter the Apostle. Taylor (Wm. M.) 12° 1 50
*Peter the Apprentice. A Historical Tale of the
    Reformation in England. 16° 75
*Peter the Ship-boy. Kingston (William H. G.)
    Illust. 16° 1 00
*Peter's Strange Story. Mills (Lucy A.) Illust. 16° 1 50
*Peter Trawl; or, The Adventures of a Whaler.
    Kingston (W. H. G.) Illust. 12° 1 50

*Peterchen and Gretchen; or, Tales of Early Child-
hood. Prentiss (Mrs. E.)   16° $1 00

*Petite; or, The Story of a Child's Life. Full of
Practical Lessons. Bray (Mrs. R. M.) Illust.   16°   1 25

Philosophy of Food and Nutrition in Plants and
Animals. Sidney (E.)   12°   65

Philosophy, Principles of a System of. An Essay
toward Solving Some of the More Difficult
Questions in Metaphysics and Religion. Bier-
bower (A.)   12°   1 00

*Pictorial Catechism of the Methodist Episcopal
Church.   12°   80

*Pictorial Gatherings.   8°   80

*Pictures from our Portfolio. Arranged by Annie
Myrtle. 100 illust.   16°   1 25

Pictures from Italy. Dickens (Charles).   12°   1 50

Pictures of Country Life. Cary (Alice).   8°   2 00

Pilgrim's Progress. Bunyan (J.) With Notes by
Thomas Scott, D. D. Illust.   8°   2 50

Pilgrim's Progress. Bunyan (J.) With Life of
Author by Robert Southey. Illust.   12°   1 50

Pilgrim's Progress.   18°   75

Pilgrim's Progress. Bunyan (J.)   12°   1 00

Pilgrim Fathers of New England. Martyn (W.)   12°   1 25

Pillar of Fire. Ingraham (J. H.)   12°   2 00

Pillars in the Temple; or, Lives of Deceased Laymen of the Methodist Episcopal Church Distinguished for their Piety and Usefulness.
Smith (W. C.)   12°   1 00

Pillars of Truth. A Series of Sermons on the Decalogue. Haven (E. O.)   12°   1 00

Pioneer, Autobiography of a. Young (Jacob).   12°   1 50

Pioneer Library, The. Thayer (Wm. M.) Illust.
3 vols,   16°   3 75

> Stories of the Creation.   Soldiers of the Bible.
> Stories of the Patriarchs.

Pioneers and Founders; or, Recent Workers in
the Mission-field. Yonge (C. M.)   8°   1 75

*Pioneers of the New World. With an Account of
the Old French War. Banvard (Joseph).   16°   1 25

Pioneers of the West. Strickland (W P.)   12°   1 50

Pioneer Women of the West, The. Ellet (Eliza-
    beth F.)   12° $1 25

*Pizarro ; or, the Conquest of Peru. A Concise and
    Interesting History. Edited by Fred. H.
    Allen. Illust.   12° 1 00

*Place for Every Thing, A. Haven (Mrs. A. B.)   16° 1 00

Platform Papers: Addresses, Discussions, and Es-
    says on Social, Moral, and Religious Subjects.
    Curry (Daniel).   12° 1 50

Plato's Best Thoughts. Compiled from Prof. Jow-
    ett's Translation of the Dialogues of Plato.
    Buckley (C. H. A.)   8° 2 50

*Play-days. Stories for Children. Jewett (Sarah O.) 16° 1 50

*Pleasant Pathways. Persuasives to Early Piety.
    Wise (Daniel).   12° 1 00

Pledge and the Cross, The. [Temperance.] Henry
    (Mrs. S. M. I.)   12° 1 00

*Plus and Minus ; or, The Briaridge Problem. Fell
    (Archie). Illust.   16° 1 50

Plutarch's Lives. Langhorne (John and William.) 8° 2 00

*Plymouth and the Pilgrims ; or, Incidents and Ad-
    ventures of the First Settlers. Banvard (Jo-
    seph). Illust.   16° 1 25

*Plymouth Rock, Views from. Mudge (Z. A.)
    Illust.   16° 1 25

*Pocket Measure, The. Alden (Mrs. G. R. [Pansy].) 12° 1 50

Poems. Herbert and Vaughan. Riverside Edition. 8° 1 75

*Poems in Company with Children. Piatt (Mrs.
    S. M. B.) Illust.   16° 1 25

Poems. Larcom (Lucy).   16° 1 25

Poems. Havergal (Frances Ridley). Complete. 16° 1 75

Poems of Faith. Cary (Phœbe).   8° 1 50

Poems, Complete. Whittier (J. G.) Household
    Edition.   12° 2 00

Poems. Young (Edward). Riverside Edition. 8° 1 75

Poems on Moral and Religious Subjects. Lutton
    (Anne).   12° 50

Poetical Works of O. W. Holmes. Household
    Edition.   12° 2 00

*Poet Preacher. A Brief Memorial of Charles Wes-
    ley, the Eminent Preacher and Poet. Adams
    (C.) Illustrated.   16° 85

Poetic Interpretations of Nature. Shairp (J. C.) 16° $1 25
Poetical Works of Alice and Phœbe Cary. Red-
    line Edition. 8° 3 50
Poetical Quotations, Dictionary of. Watson (J. T.) 12° 1 50
Poetical Works of J. R. Lowell. Household Edition. 12° 2 00
Poetical Works of H. W. Longfellow. Household
    Edition. 12° 2 00
Poetical Works of Chaucer. Edited by Gilman.
    3 vols. 8° 5 25
Poetical Works of Owen Meredith. Household
    Edition. 12° 2 00
Poetical Works of John G. Saxe. 16° 1 50
Poetical Works of Alfred Tennyson. Household
    Edition. 12° 2 00
Poetical Works of Bayard Taylor. Household
    Edition. 12° 2 00
*Poetry for Children. Edited by Samuel Elliott. 16° 75
Poetry for Home and School. Edited by Anna C.
    Brackett and Ida M. Eliot. 16° 1 25
Poets, Quotations from the, Moral and Religious.
    Rice (Wm.) 8° 2 50
Pointed Papers. For the Christian Life. Cuyler
    (T. L.) 12° 1 50
Politics for Young Americans. Nordhoff (Charles). 16° 75
Political Romanism. Hughey (G. W.) 12° 1 25
*Pomponia; or, the Gospel in Cæsar's Household.
    Webb (Mrs.) Illust. 16° 1 50
*Poor Boy, The, and the Merchant Prince; or, Ele-
    ments of Success drawn from the Life of Amos
    Lawrence and Other Similar Characters.
    Thayer (Wm. M.) 16° 1 00
Pope, Temporal Power of the. McClintock (J.) 12° 50
Popery and its Aims. Moody (Granville). 12° 40
Popery, Dialogues on. Stanley (J.) 18° 45
*Poplar Row, A Year at. Ellenwood (March). 16° 1 00
Popular Amusements. Crane (J. T.) 12° 85
Popular Antiquities. Brand (John). 3 vols. 12° 7 50
Popular Astronomy. Mitchel (O. M.) 12° 1 75
*Popular Library of History for Young People. Illust.
    4 vols. In a box. 16° 3 75

    Stories of Old England.   Count Ulrich of Lindburg.
    History of the Crusades.   The Hero of Brittany.

Popular Science Library, The. A Series of Popular Books on Science. 5 vols.   12° *e* $1 00

> Health. Smith (Edward).
> The Natural History of Man. Quatrefages (A. de). Translated from the French by Eliza A. Youmans.
> The Science of Music. Taylor (Sedley).
> Outline of the Evolution Philosophy. Cazelles (E.) Translated from the French by O. B. Frothingham.
> English Men of Science, their Nature and Nurture. Galton (Francis).

*Posie, the Minister's Daughter. Illust.   16°   1 00

Positive Theology. Lowrey (A.)   12°   1 25

Potiphar Papers. Curtis (G. W.)   12°   1 50

Power of Prayer, The. Illustrated in Wonderful Displays of Divine Grace at Fulton Street and Other Meetings in New York and Elsewhere. Prime (S. I.)   12°   1 50

Power, The Gift of. Platt (S. H.)   12°   1 00

Practical Christianity. Designed Especially for Young Men. Abbott (John S. C.)   16°   1 00

Prayer and its Remarkable Answers. Patton (W. W.)   12°   2 00

Prayer and the Prayer Gauge. Hopkins (Mark).   16°   75

Prayer, Helps to. A Manual Designed to Aid Christian Believers in Acquiring the Gift, and in Maintaining the Practice of Prayer, in the Closet, the Family, the Social Gatherings, and the Public Congregations. Kidder (D. P.)   12°   1 50

Prayer-meeting and its Improvement, The. Thompson (Lewis O.)   16°   1 25

Prayer-meetings, Importance of. Young (R.)   18°   25

Prayers of the Ages. Compiled by Caroline S. Whitmarsh.   12°   1 50

Prayer of Faith. Judd (Carrie F.)   18°   50

Prayer, Secret and Social. Treffry (R.)   18°   40

Praying and Working. What Men Can do When in Earnest. Stevenson (Wm. F.)   16°   1 00

Preachers' Manual. Including Clavis Biblica, and A Letter to a Methodist Preacher. Clarke (A.) and Coke.   12°   85

Preaching Required by the Times. Stevens (Abel).   12°   85

*Precept upon Precept. Peep-of-day Series.   16°   50

*Precious Gems for the Savior's Diadem. Shipton
(Anna). . 16° $0 75
Pre-historic World, The. Berthet (Elie). 12° 1 50
Pre-historic Nations. Baldwin (J. D.) 12° 1 75
Pre-historic Times. As Illustrated by Ancient
Remains and the Manners and Customs of
Modern Savages. Lubbock (Sir John). Illust. 8° 5 00
Preparing to Teach. For Sunday-school Teachers,
etc. Hall (John) and Others. Illust. 12° 1 75
Primary Truths of Religion. Clark (Thos. M.) 12° 1 00
Primitive Church, Constitution of. King (Lord). 12° 85
*Prince and the Page, The. A Story of the Last
Crusade. Yonge (C. M.) Illust. 12° 1 25
Prince of Good Fellows, The. [Temperance.] Wil-
mer (Margaret E.) 12° 1 25
Prince of the House of David. Ingraham (J. H.) 12° 2 00
Princes of Art, The. Engravers, Painters, Sculp-
tors, and Architects. Urbino (Mrs. S. R.)
Illust. 12° 2 00
*Prince of Pulpit Orators. A Portraiture of Rev.
George Whitefield, M. A. Illustrated by An-
ecdotes and Incidents. Wakeley (J. B.) 16° 1 00
Principles of Education, Drawn from Nature and
Revelation and Applied to Female Education
in the Upper Classes. Sewell (E. M.) 12° 2 00
Principles of Geology; or, The Modern Changes of
the Earth and its Inhabitants Considered as
Illustrative of Geology. Lyell (C.) Illust. with
Maps, Plates, etc. 2 vols. 8° 8 00
Prison Life. Memorials of. Finley (J. B.) 12° 1 25
*Pro and Con. A Story for Boys and Girls. Swift
(Maggie). Illust. 16° 1 25
Probationers' Manual. Bass (E. C.) 18° 30
Problem of Evil. Translated from the French of
M. Ernest Naville. Lacroix (John P.) 12° 1 25
Problem of Religious Progress, The. Dorches-
ter (D.) 12° 2 00
Prodigal Son. Four Discourses. Punshon (W. M.) 12° 25
*Progress of Science, The. A Short History of
Natural Science for Schools and Young People.
Buckley (A. B.) 12° 2 00
Prohibitionists' Text-book, The. 12° 1 00

Promise and Promiser, The. Shipton (Anna).   16° $0 75
Property, Consecrated. Prize Essay.   16°   50
Prophecy Viewed in Respect to its Distinctive Na-
    ture, Special Function, and Proper Interpreta-
    tion. Fairbairn (P.)   8°   2 50
Prophet of Fire, The; or, The Life and Times of
    Elijah. Macduff (J. R.)   12°   1 50
Proverbs of Solomon. Illustrated by Historical
    Parallels from Drawings by John Gilbert.
    Illust.   12°   2 50
Proverbial Philosophy, and Other Poems. Tupper
    (M. F.)   12°   1 25
Proverbs, and their Lessons. Trench (R. C.)   1 00
Psychology; or, The Science of the Mind. Mun-
    sell (O. S.)   12°   1 70
Public Speaking and Debate, Rudiments of. Bar-
    rows (L. D.)   12°   1 25
Pulpit Eloquence of the Nineteenth Century. Fish
    (Henry C.)   8°   3 00
Pupils of St. John the Divine. Yonge (C. M.)   8°   1 75
Puritan Revolution, The. Gardiner (S. R.)   16°   1 00
Pursuit of Holiness. A Sequel to "Thoughts on
    Personal Religion." Goulburn (E. M.)   12°   75
Pursuit of Knowledge Under Difficulties: Its Pleas-
    ures and Rewards. Illustrated by Memoirs of
    Eminent Men. Craik (George L.) 2 vols.   12°   3 00
*Pushing Ahead; or, Big Brother Dave. Rand (Ed-
    ward A.) Illust.   16°   1 25

*QUADRATUS. A Tale of the World in the Church.
    Leslie (Emma). Illust.   12°   1 25
Queens of England, Lives of, from the Norman
    Conquest. Parker (Caroline G.)   12°   1 25
*Queen of Navarre, The Protestant. The Mother of
    the Bourbons. Townsend (Virginia F.) 4 Il-
    lust.   16°   1 25
*Queen Louisa of Prussia; or, Goodness in a Palace.
    From German Sources. Hurst (Catherine E.)
    Illust.   16°   85
*Queer Lesson, A, and Other Stories. Illust.   18°   40
*Queer People. Illust. Bennett (Mrs. M. A.)   16°   1 00
Quinn, Rev. J., Life and Labors of. Wright (J. F.) 12°   75

*Rabaut and Bridaine. From the French of L. L. F. Bungener. A Continuation of the Fascinating Story of "Louis XV and His Times." Illust.   12° $1 50

Races of European Turkey, The. Their History, Condition, and Future Prospects. Clark (Edson L.)   8°   3 00

Races of the Old World, The.   8°   2 50

Rachel Weeping for Her Children. Vansant (N.) Introduction by C. N. Sims.   18°   65

*Rainbow Side. Edwards (Mrs. C. M.) Illust.   16°   1 00

*Raleigh, Sir Walter, Life and Times of, Pioneer of Anglo-American Colonization. True (C. K.)   16°   1 00

*Ralph and Dick. A Sea Story. Kingston (W H. G.) Illust.   16°   1 00

*Ralph's Possessions. A Revelation of the Deeper, Heartfelt Life. Hopkins (George). Illust.   16°   1 50

Rambles Among Insects. Findley (Samuel). Illust.   16°   1 25

Rambles in Wonder-land; or, Up the Yellowstone and Among the Geysers. Stanley (Edwin J.) Illust.   12°   1 25

Randolphs, The. The Characters so interesting in "Household Puzzles" appear again. Alden (Mrs. G. R. [Pansy].)   12°   1 50

Raphael and Michael Angelo. Duppa (R.)   12°   2 50

*Rare Piece of Work, A. Chamberlain (P. B.)   16°   1 00

Rationalism, Evangelical; or, A Consideration of Truths Practically Related to Man's Probation. Knox (L. L.)   16°   1 25

Rationalism, History of. Hurst (J. F.)   8°   3 00

*Rays from the Sun of Righteousness. Newton (Richard). Illust.   16°   1 25

Real and Pretended Christianity. Townsend (L. T.)   16°   50

*Real Folks. Whitney (Mrs. A. D. T.) Illust.   12°   1 50

Reconciliation of Science and Religion. Winchell (Alex.)   12°   2 00

Recovery of Jerusalem, The. A Narrative of Exploration, and Discovery of the City and the Holy Land. Wilson (Capt.) Illust.   8°   3 50

Recreations in Astronomy. With Directions for Practical Experiments and Telescopic Work. Warren (W. H.) Illust.   12°   1 75

*Red Apple, The, and Other Stories. Illust.	18°	$0 40
Reformed Pastor. Baxter (Richard).	12°	65
Reindeer, Dogs, and Snow-shoes. A Journal of Siberian Travel and Explorations, made in the Years 1865-7. Bush (R. J.)	8°	3 00
Relation of Civil Law to Ecclesiastical Polity, Property, and Discipline. Strong (Wm.)	12°	1 25
Relation of Science and Religion. Calderwood (H.)	12°	1 75
Religion of Childhood. Hibbard (Freeborn G.)	12°	1 50
Religion in China. Edkins (Joseph).	8°	2 50
Religions of China, The. Legge (Jas.)	12°	1 50
Religion and the Reign of Terror ; or, The Church during the French Revolution. Prepared from the French of M. Edmond De Pressensé. Lacroix (J. P.)	12°	1 50
Religion of the Family. Wiley (I. W.)	16°	90
Religion, Philosophy of. Dick (T.)	18°	45
*Religion Recommended to Youth. Thayer (Mrs.)	24°	25
Religion the Weal and Need of the Church. Steward (G.)	12°	75
Religious Training of Children. Olin (S.)	18°	20
Religions of the World, The, and Their Relations to Christianity. Maurice (F. D.)	12°	1 75
Remains of Lost Empires. Sketches of the Ruins of Palmyra, Nineveh, Babylon, and Persepolis. With Some Notes on India and the Cashmerian Himalayas. Myers (P. V. N.) Illust.	8°	3 50
Remarkable Events in the World's History. Young (L. H.)	12°	1 25
Remarkable Examples of Moral Recovery.	18°	40
Remarkable Providences, Illustrating the Divine Government.	12°	⚹1 75
Reminiscences by Thomas Carlyle. Edited by Jas. A. Froude. (Illust.)	16°	50
*Renata of Este. From the German of Rev. Carl Strack. Hurst (Catherine E.)	16°	1 00
Rent Vail, The. Bonar (Horatius).	16°	1 25
Resurgit. A Collection of Hymns and Songs of the Resurrection. Edited with Biographical and Historical Notes. Foxcroft (Frank).	12°	2 00
Resurrection of the Dead. Kingsley (C.)	18°	35
Revivals, Promotion of, Helps to the. Watson (J. V.)	12°	85

Revivals of Religion. Showing their Theory, Means,
Obstructions, Importations, and Perversions,
with the Duty of Christians in Regard to
Them. Revised and Enlarged Edition. Por-
ter (James).   12° $1 00
Revolt of the Netherlands, The. Trial and Execu-
tion of Counts Egmont and Horn, and the
Siege of Antwerp. Schiller (Frederick).   12°   1 00
*Rhoda's Corner. Payne (Mrs. A. M. Mitchell).   16°   1 25
Richards, Lucy, Memoir of.   18°   40
*Riches without Wings. Illustrated by Lessons from
Life. Illust.   12°   1 50
Ride through Palestine. Dulles (John W.) Illust.   12°   2 00
Right Way. Lectures on the Decalogue. Crane
(J. T.)   12°   80
Rivers and Lakes of Scripture. Tweedie (W. K.)
Illust.   16°   1 00
*Riverside Farm, A Year at. Miller (Emily Hunt-
ington). Illust.   16°   85
*Rob and Mag; or, A Little Light in a Dark Corner.
Marston (L.) Illust.   16°   75
Rob Roy, The, on the Jordan, Nile, Red Sea, and
Gennesareth, etc. A Canoe Cruise in Palestine
and Egypt and the Waters of Damascus. Mac-
gregor (J.) Maps and Illust.   8°   2 50
*Robbie Meredith. Cotter (Mrs. J. J.) Illust.   16°   1 00
Robert Dick, Baker of Thurso, Geologist and Bota-
nist. Smiles (S.) Illust.   12°   1 50
*Robin Tremayne: A Tale of the Marian Persecu-
tion. Holt (Emily S.)   12°   1 50
Robinsons, The. Bissell (Mary L.) Illust.   16°   1 25
Rocky Mountains. History of the Expeditions
under the command of Captains Lewis and
Clarke, etc., during the Years 1804, 1805, 1806.
2 vols.   18°   1 50
Roddy's Ideal. Johnson (Helen K.)   16°   1 00
Roddy's Reality. Johnson (Helen K.)   16°   1 00
Roddy's Romance. Johnson (Helen K.)   16°   1 00
Rogers, Hester Ann, Journal of.   16°   60
Rollins's Ancient History. 2 vols.   8°   4 50
Romance of American History. De Vere (M. S.)   12°   1 50
Romance of the Harem. Leonowens (Mrs. Anna H.)   12°   1 25

Romance of M. Rénan and the Christ of the Gospels. Schaff (P.) and Roussel (M.)   12° $1 00

Romance of the Revolution. Being True Stories
of Heroic Exploits of the Days of '76. Bunce
(Oliver B.)   12°   1 25

*Romance without Fiction ; or, Sketches from the
Portfolio of an Old Missionary. Bleby (Henry).
1 Illust.   16°   1 50

Romanism, Delineation of. Elliott (C.) 2 vols.   8°   5 00

Rome and Italy at the Opening of the Œcumenical
Council. Depicted in Twelve Letters written
from Rome to a Gentleman in America. Pressensé (Edmond De).   12°   1 25

*Romneys of Ridgemont, The. Eastman (Julia A.)
Illust.   16°   1 50

*Rosa Leighton ; or, In His Strength. [Temper-
ance.] Martin (Mrs. M. F.)   12°   75

*Rosamond Dayton. Gardner (Mrs. H. C.)   16°   1 25

*Rose and Millie. By the Author of "Hester's
Happy Summer." Illust.   16°   1 25

*Rosedale. A Story of Self-denial. Gardner (Mrs.
H. C.)   12°   1 50

Rosedale Library, The. Illust. 6 vols.   16°   6 00

> Henry Arden; or, It is Only a Pin.
> Honest Gabriel ; or, The Reward of Perseverance.
> Joe Fulwood; or, Honesty and Perseverance Triumphant.
> Kate Kemp and the Swan's Egg.
> Little Jane ; or, The Reward of Well-doing.
> The Little German Drummer-Boy.

*Rose Marbury. Pritchard (S. J.)   16°   1 25

*Rosy Dawn Stories, The. For Small Children.
Illust. 6 vols. In a box.   18°   3 60

> The Picnic Party.   The Twin Brothers.
> The Water-cress Girl.   The Violet Girls.
> The Little Indian.   The Two Birthdays.

Round the World. A Series of Letters. Kingsley
(Calvin). 2 vols.   12°   2 00

Royal Bounty ; or, Evening Thoughts for the King's
Guests. Havergal (F. R.)   18°   25

Royal Commandments; or, Morning Thoughts for
the King's Servants. Havergal (F. R.)   18°   25

Royal Invitation ; or, Daily Thoughts on Coming
to Christ. Havergal (F. R.)   18°   25

*Royal Preacher. Lectures on Ecclesiastes. Hamilton (James). 16° $1 25

Royal Responses; or, Daily Melodies for the King's Minstrels. Havergal (F. R.) 18° 25

*Royal Road to Fortune. Miller (Emily H.) Illust. 16° 1 25

*Roy's Dory at the Sea-shore. A Sequel to " Pushing Ahead." Rand (Edward A.) Illust. 16° 1 25

*Ruby Hamilton. Full of Stirring Incident and Earnest Christian Lessons. Oliver (Marie). Illust. 16° 1 50

*Rue's Helps. Drinkwater (Jennie M.) 12° 1 50

*Rufus the Unready. Farquharson (Martha). Illust. 16° 1 25

*Rule and Exercises of Holy Living. Taylor (Jeremy). 18° 75

Rule and Exercises of Holy Dying. Taylor (Jeremy). 18° 75

Rule of Faith. Appeal from Tradition. Peck (G.) 12° 1 00

Ruskin on Painting. With a Biographical Sketch. 18° 60

*Ruth and Her Friends. A Story for Girls. Illust. 16° 1 00

*Ruth Erskine's Crosses. Showing the Power of the Word of God to Teach and Comfort. Alden (Mrs. G. R. [Pansy].) Illust. 12° 1 50

*Ruth Hawthorne; or, Led to the Rock. Illust. 16° 1 25

Ruth the Moabitess, the Ancestress of Our Lord. Houghton (Ross C.) Illust. 12° 1 50

*Rutherford Frown, The. Illust. 16° 75

*Ruthie Shaw; or, The Good Girl. A Collection of Well-drawn Portraits. Homespun (Sophia). Illust. 16° 1 00

Sabbath Chimes. Punshon (W. M.) 12° 1 70

Sabbath, Christian, Practical Considerations on the. McOwan (P.) 18° 50

*Sabbath-day Book, Child's. 16° 40

*Sabbath-school and Bible Teaching. Inglis (J.) 12° 85

Sabbaths, The Two. Fuller (E. Q.) 12° 60

*Sabrina Hackett. Illust. 16° 1 50

Sacraments of the New Testament, The, as Instituted by our Lord Jesus Christ. Armstrong (George D.) 8° 2 50

Sacred Mountains. Characters and Scenes in the Holy Land. Headley (J. T.) 8° 2 00

Sacred and Legendary Art.   Jameson (Anna).
   2 vols.   18° *e*$1 50

> The first containing Legends of the Angels and Archangels,
> the Evangelists, the Apostles, the Doctors of the
> Church, and St. Mary Magdalene;
> The second, the Legends of the Patron Saints, the Martyrs,
> the Early Bishops, the Hermits, and the Warrior
> Saints of Christendom, as represented in the Fine
> Arts.

Sacred Annals.   Smith (G.)   4 vols.   Sheep.   8°   11 25

> The Patriarchal Age.   The Gentile Nations.
> The Hebrew People.   Harmony of Divine Dispensations.

Sacred Hour.   Gaddis (M. P.)   12°   1 00
Sacred Memories; or, Annals of Deceased Preach-
   ers of the New York and New York East Con-
   ferences.   Smith (W. C.)   16°   1 00
Sacred Tabernacle of the Hebrews, The.   Atwater
   (E. E.)   Illust.   8°   2 50
St. Anselm.   Church (R. W.)   12°   1 75
Saint's Inheritance, The.   Guthrie (Thomas).   12°   1 50
Saint Louis and Calvin.   Great Christians of France.
   Guizot (M.)   12°   1 75
Saintly Workers.   Farrar (F. W.)   12°   1 25
Saintly and Successful Worker; or, Sixty Years a
   Class-leader.   A Biographical Study.   Includ-
   ing Incidental Discussions of the Theory and
   Experience of Perfect Love of the Class and
   Class-meeting, and of the Art of Winning
   Souls, suggested by the Experience and La-
   bors of William Carvosso.   Wise (Daniel).   12°   1 00
Saints' Everlasting Rest.   Baxter (Richard).   12°   1 25
Salmagundi.   Irving (Washington).   16°   1 25
Salvation, Philosophy of the Plan of.   A Book for
   the Times.   Walker (James B.)   12°   1 25
*Sanford and Merton.   Day (Thomas).   16°   1 00
Satisfactory Portion.   George (A. C.)   12°   50
Saving Faith: Its Rationale.   Chamberlayne (I.)   12°   1 00
*Saxby.   A Tale of Old and New England.   Leslie
   (Emma).   Illust.   12°   1 25
*Say and Do Series, The.   Warner (Miss Anna).
   6 vols.   In a box.   16°   *e*1 25

> Little Camp on Eagle Hill.   A Flag of Truce.
> Willow Brook.   Bread and Oranges.
> Scepters and Crowns.   Rapids of Niagara.

Sayings of Sages. Converse (C. C.)	12°	$1 25
*Scattered. Dunning (Mrs. A. K.) Illust.	16°	1 00
Scenes in My Life, occurring during a Ministry of Nearly Half a Century in the Methodist Episcopal Church. Trafton (Mark).	12°	1 25
Schönberg-Cotta Family, Chronicles of the, as Told by Two of Themselves. A History of Luther and His Times. Charles (Mrs. Andrew).	12°	.1 00
Schools and School-masters, My; or, The Story of My Education. Miller (Hugh.)	12°	1 50
*School-days of Beulah Romney. Eastman (Julia A.) Illust.	16°	1 50
Science and Revelation. Wythe (J. H.)	12°	1 75
*Science for the Young. Abbott (J.) Illust. 4 vols.	12°	e1 50

Heat.   Light.   Water and Land.   Force.

Science of Law, The. Sheldon (Amos).	12°	1 75
Science of Life; or, Animal and Vegetable Biology. Wythe (J. H.) Illust.	12°	1 50
Science, Philosophy, and Religion. Bascom (J.)	12°	1 75
Science Primers. Edited by Profs. Huxley, Roscoe, and Balfour Stewart.	18°	e n 45

Introductory. Huxley (T. H.)
Chemistry. Roscoe (H. E.)
Physics. Stewart (Balfour.)
Physical Geography. Geikie (Archibald.)
Geology. Geikie (Archibald).
Physiology. Foster (M.)
Astronomy. Lockyer (J. Norman).
Botany. Hooker (J. D.)
Logic. Jevons (W. S.)
Inventional Geometry. Spencer (W. G.)
Piano-forte Playing. Taylor (Franklin).
Political Economy. Jevons (W. S.)
Natural Resources of the United States. Patton (J. N.)

Scotch and Irish Seed in American Soil. The Early History of the Scotch and Irish Churches, and Their Relations to the Presbyterian Church of America. Craighead (J. G.)	16°	1 00
Scramble Among the Alps. Whymper (F.)	8°	2 50
Scripture Manual, The. Alphabetically and Systematically Arranged. Designed to Facilitate the Finding of Proof-texts. Simmons (Chas.)	12°	1 75
Scripture Promises. Clarke (Samuel).	32°	50
Scripture Cabinet. House (E.)	12°	1 50
*Sealed Orders. Phelps (Elizabeth S.)	16°	1 50

Sears, Mrs. Angeline B., Memoir of. Hamline
(Mrs. Melinda).   18° $0 50

Sea Sermons. Lorraine (Alfred M.)   16°   50

Sea-side Studies in Natural History. Agassiz (E. C.
and A.)   8°   3 00

Sea-kings and Naval Heroes. Edgar (J. G.)   16°   1 00

Second Arctic Expedition. Kane (E. K.) 2 vols.   8°   5 00

Secret of Success, The; or, How to Get On in the
World. Adams (W H. Davenport).   12°   1 50

Secret of the Lord, The. Shipton (Anna).   16°   75

*Secret of Victory. [Temperance.] Winslow (Miss
M. E.)   12°   75

Seed-thought. A Hand-book of Doctrine and Devotion. Robinson (Geo. C.)   12°   85

*Seed-time and Harvest; or, Sow Well and Reap
Well. A Book for the Young. Tweedie
(W K.) Illust.   16°   1 25

Seekers After God. The Lives of Seneca, Epic-
tetus, and Marcus Aurelius. Farrar (F. W.)   12°   1 75

Self-help. With Illustrations of Character, Conduct, and Perseverance. Smiles (S.)   12°   1 00

Self-culture: Intellectual, Physical, and Moral.
Blackie (J. S.)   16°   1 00

Self-culture. Clarke (James Freeman).   12°   1 50

Self-government, Concise System of. Edmondson (J.)   18°   40

Self-knowledge, Treatise on. Mason (J.)   18°   45

Senses and the Intellect, The. Bain (Alex.)   8°   5 00

*Sequel to "Peep of Day," A. Illust.   18°   60

Sermons Preached at Brighton. Robertson (F W.) 12°   2 00

Sermons and Essays on the Apostolic Age. Stanley (A. P.)   12°   2 25

Sermons. Chalmers (Thomas). 2 vols. in one.   8°   3 00

Sermons. Brooks (Phillips).   12°   1 75

Sermons. Clark (D. W.)   12°   1 50

Sermons. Hamilton (R. Winter). With a Sketch
of his Life by Bishop Simpson.   12°   1 50

Sermons, Fraternal Camp-meeting. Preached by
Ministers of the Various Branches of Methodism at the Round-lake Camp-meeting.   12°   1 50

Sermons, Occasional, and Reviews and Essays.
Floy (James).   12°   1 50

Sermons on Miscellaneous Subjects. By the Bishops of the Methodist Episcopal Church and Others. 12° $1 50

Sermons on Various Subjects. Morris (T. A.) 12° 1 25

Sermons Preached on Various Occasions. Goulburn (E. M.) 12° 1 00

Sermons and Travels in the East. Stanley (Arthur P.) 12° 1 50

Sermons on Nature's Testimony to Nature's God. Newton (Wm.) 12° 1 00

Sermons, Speeches, and Letters. Haven (Gilbert.) 8° 3 00

Serpent-charmer, The. Rousselet (L.) Illust. 8° 2 50

Seven Lamps of Architecture. Ruskin. 12° 1 75

*Seven Little People and Their Friends. Scudder (Horace E.) Illust. 16° 75

*Seven Wonders of the World. Illust. 16° 1 00

*Seven Words from the Cross, The. Meditations on the Last Sayings of Christ. Adams (W H.) 12° 1 00

*Shawny and the Light-house. Pritchard (Miss S. J.) Illust. 16° 60

*Sheer Off. A. L. O. E. Illust. 18° 75

*Shell Cove. A Story of the Sea-shore and of the Sea. Mudge (Z. A.) Illust. 16° 1 50

*Shepherd King. A. L. O. E. Illust. 16° 1 00

Shield of Faith; or, Articles of Religion, General Rules, Baptismal and Church Covenants, and Methodist Episcopacy. With Scripture Proofs. Hawley (Bostwick). 16° 25

*Shining Hours. Moraine (Paul). Illust. 16° 1 50

*Shoe-binders, The, of New York; or, The Fields White to the Harvest. Wright (Mrs. J. McNair). Illust. 16° 80

*Shore and Ocean, A Tale of the. Kingston (W. H. G.) Illust. 12° 1 50

*Short-comings and Long-goings. Lessons of Duty and Religion. Eastman (Julia A.) Illust. 16° 1 25

Short History of Art. DeForest (Julia B.) Illust. 8° 2 00

Short History of English Colonies in America. Lodge (H. C.) 8° 3 00

Short History of English People. Green (J. R.) 8° 1 50

*Short History of France for Young People, A. Kirkland (Miss E. S.) 12° 1 50

Short Sermon on Consecration and Kindred Themes.
George (A. C.)   12° $1 00

Siberia. Atkinson (T. W.) Illust.   8°   3 50

*Sights and Insights; or, Knowledge by Travel.
Warren (Henry W.) Illust.   16°   1 00

*Signal Lights.   12°   1 25

*Signet Ring, and Other Gems. Liefde (I. De).   16°   1 25

*Silas Gower's Daughters. Noble (Annette L.)
Illust.   16°   1 25

Silence and Voices, The. Farrar (F. W.)   12°   1 00

*Silent Tom. A Picture of the Life of Our Times.
Edson (N. I.) Illust.   16°   1 75

*Silent Partner, The. Phelps (Elizabeth S.)   16°   1 50

Silver Casket; or, The World and its Wiles.
A. L. O. E. Illust.   16°   85

Silver Keys, The. A. L. O. E. Illust.   18°   75

*Silver Sands; or, Pennie's Romance. A Bright
and Beautiful Story for Girls. Crampton
(G. E. E.) Illust.   16°   1 50

Similarities of Physical and Religious Knowledge.
Bixby (J. T.)   12°   1 50

*Simple Stories with Odd Pictures; or, Evening
Amusements for the Little Ones. Konewka
(Paul). Illust.   16°   65

*Sinner and Saint. A Story of the Woman's Cru-
sade. Hopkins (A. A.)   12°   1 25

*Sister Eleanor's Brood. Phelps (Mrs. S. B.) Illust. 16°   1 50

*Sister Margaret, My. Edwards (Mrs. C. M.) Illust. 16°   1 00

*Six Little Girls. Alden (Mrs. G. R. [Pansy].)
Illust.   16°   75

*Six Months at Mrs. Prior's. A Story of Womanly
Tact Combined with Christian Trust. Adams
(Emily). Illust.   16°   1 25

Six Months in Italy. Hillard (George S.)   16°   2 00

*Six Years in India; or, Sketches of India and its
People, as Seen by a Lady Missionary: Given
in a Series of Letters to Her Mother. Humphrey (Mrs. E. J.) 8 Illust.   12°   1 00

Sketch-book; or, Miscellaneous Anecdotes. Smith
(W C.)   12°   1 00

Sketch-book. Irving (Washington). People's Edition.   16°   1 25

Spain in Profile. A Summer Among Olives and
    Aloes. Harrison (Jas. A.) "Little Classic"
    Style. 18° $1 50
Spanish Conquests in America. Helps (Arthur).
    4 vols. 12° 6 00
Spanish Papers. Irving (Washington). 16° 1 25
Speaking to the Heart. Guthrie (Thomas). 12° 1 50
Specimens of German Romance. Carlyle (T.) 12° 1 25
Spectacle Series, The. 16° *e*1 00
    1. The House with Spectacles. Robinson (Leora B.)
    2. Patsy. Robinson (Leora B.)
    3. Six Sinners. Wheaton (Campbell).

Speeches of Daniel Webster. Tefft (B. F.) 12° 1 25
Spiritualism: With the Testimony of God and Man
    Against It. McDonald (W.) 12° 1 00
Spiritualism and Necromancy. Morrison (A. B.) 12° 1 00
Spiritual Struggles of a Roman Catholic. An Au-
    tobiographical Sketch. Beaudry (Louis N.) 12° 1 00
Spirit of Life. Bickersteth (E. H.) 12° 1 25
Spiritual Letters to Men. Fénélon (Archbishop). 12° 1 25
Spiritual Letters to Women. Fénélon (Archbishop). 12° 1 25
Spiritual Progress; or, Instructions in the Divine
    Life of the Soul. Fénélon (Archbishop).
    Including " Christian Counsel and Spiritual
    Letters," and Madame Guyon's "Short and
    Easy Method of Prayer." 12° 1 50
Sports that Kill. Sermons by T. DeWitt Talmage. 12° 1 25
Spur of Monmouth, The; or, Washington in
    Arms. A Historical and Centennial Romance
    of the Revolution, etc. 12° 1 75
*Squire of Walton Hall, The; or, Sketches and In-
    cidents from the Life of Charles Waterton,
    Esq., the Adventurous Traveler and Daring
    Naturalist. Wise (Daniel). Illust. 16° 1 00
Standard Series of Temperance Tales, The. Chellis
    (Mary Dwinell). Illust. 4 vols. In box. 16° 5 00
    Bill Drock's Investment.   Mark Dunning's Enemy.
    The Old Doctor's Son.   Gray Heads on Green Shoulders.
*Stanifords of Staniford's Folly, The. Full of Fine
    Feeling and Sound Teaching. Kendall (Mrs.
    E. D.) Illust. 16° 1 50
*St. Augustine's Ladder. Noble (Annette L.) Illust. 16° 1 50

Star of our Lord; or, Christ Jesus, King of all
    Worlds, both of Time or Space. With
    Thoughts on Inspiration and the Astronomic
    Doubt as to Christianity. Upham (Francis W.) 12° $1 50
Stars and the Earth, The; or, Thoughts upon
    Space, Time, and Eternity. 16° 40
*Stella and the Priest; or, the Star of Rockburn.
    Loring (Laurie). Illust. 16° 1 50
*Stellafont Abbey. Marshall (Emma). 16° 1 00
Stepping Heavenward. Prentiss (Mrs. E.) 12° 1 75
*Stepping-Stones. A Story of Our Inner Life. Doud-
    ney (Sarah). 16° 1 00
Stewards and the People. Porter (J.) Paper. Per
    dozen. 18° 60
Sier, Rudolf, Life of. From German Sources. La-
    croix (John P.) 12° 1 25
Still Hour; or, Communion with God. Phelps
    (Austin). 16° 60
Stoner, David, Life of. 18° 40
*Stony Road. A Scottish Story from Real Life. 16° 75
*Storehouse of Stories, A. Yonge (C. M.) 2 vols. 16° *e* 1 00
*Story of the Apostles. Illust. 18° 60
Story of the Battle of Waterloo, A True. Gleig
    (G. R.) 12° 1 50
Story of Aunt Lizzie Aiken, The. Anderson (Mrs.
    Galusha). With Portrait. 16° 1 00
*Story of the Christians and the Moors of Spain.
    Yonge (C. M.) 18° 1 25
Story of the Earth and Man, The. Dawson (J. W.)
    Illust. 12° 1 50
*Story of English Literature for Young Readers,
    The. White (Lucy Cecil). Illust. 12° 1 25
*Story of the Faith in Hungary. Illust. 16° 85
*Story of a Fellow-soldier. The Life of Bishop Pat-
    terson. Narrated for the Young. Awdry (F.)
    Illust. 16° 1 00
Story of the Great March. Diary of General Sher-
    man's Campaign through Georgia and the Car-
    olinas. Nichols (George W.) Illust. 12° 2 00
*Story of Four Lives, A. Four Young Ladies Just
    Leaving School. Dunning (Mrs. A. K.) Illust. 16° 1 50
*Story of Liberty, The. Coffin (C. C.) Illust. 8° 3 00

*Story of Madagascar. Mears (John W.) Illust. 16° $1 25
Story of Manuscripts. With Fac-simile Illustrations
   of Various New Testament Manuscripts. Mer-
   rill (George). 12° 1 00
*Story of a Pocket Bible. Illust. 16° 1 00'
Story of the Prayers of Christian History. Illust. 12° 1 50
*Stories and Romances. Scudder (Horace E.) 16° 1 25
*Stories from Ancient History. Strickland (Agnes).
   Illust. 16° 1 25
*Stories from English History. Strickland (Agnes).
   Illust. 16° 1 25
*Stories from History. Strickland (Agnes). Illust. 16° 1 25
*Stories from Modern History. Strickland (Agnes).
   Illust. 16° 1 25
*Stories from My Attic. Scudder (Horace E.) 16° 1 00
*Stories from the Histories of Rome. Beesly (Mrs.) 16° 90
*Stories from the Moorland. A Story of the Scotch
   Covenanters. Bates (Elizabeth). Illust. 16° 1 25
*Stories of Christ the Lord. Cave (Harriet). 12° 75
*Stories of the Old Dominion. From the Settlement
   to the End of the Revolution. Cooke (John E.) 12° 1 50
*Stories of the Saints. Chenoweth (Mrs. C. Van D.)
   Illust. 12° 2 00
*Stories of Success. Edited by S. F. Smith. Illust. 12° 1 50
Storms: Their Nature, Classification, and Laws.
   Blasius (William). Illust. 12° 2 50
*Strawberry Hill. Vance (Clara). Illust. 16° 1 50
Stray Moments with Thackeray. Rideing (W. H.) 18° ·60
Stray Studies from England and Italy. Green
   (J. R.) 8° 1 75
Streets and Lanes of a City, The. Being the Rem-
   iniscence of Amy Dutton. Stokes (H. P.) 16° 1 00
*Strength and Beauty. Discussions for Young Men.
   Hopkins (Mark.) 12° 1 25
*Striking for the Right. Eastman (Julia A.) Illust. 16° 1 75
Student's Classical Dictionary of Biography, My-
   thology, and Geography. Smith (William).
   Illust. 12° 1 25
Student's Historical Series. Uniform in Style. 12°
   Ancient History of the East. From the Earliest
     Times to the Conquest by Alexander the
     Great. Smith (Philip). 1 25

Student's Historical Series. (*Continued.*)

Students' Ecclesiastical History. A History of the Christian Church from the Times of the of Apostles to the Full Establishment of the Papal Power. Smith (P.) Illust. 12° $1 50

Student's Elements of Geology. Lyell (Sir Charles). Illust. 12° 1 25

Studies and Stories. Jameson (Anna). 18° 1 50

Studies in Literature. Griffin (G. W.) 12° 1 75

Studies in the Creative Week. Boardman (G. D.) 12° 1 25

Studies in the Model Prayer. Boardman (G. D.) 12° 1 25

Studies of Character. Guthrie (Thomas). 12° 1 50

Studies in Poetry and Philosophy. Shairp (J. C.) 16° 1 50

Studio, Field, and Gallery. A Manual of Painting for the Student and Amateur, with Information for the General Reader. Rollin (H. J.) 12° 1 50

Sub-tropical Rambles. Pike (N.) 8° 3 50

Success and Its Conditions. Whipple (Edwin P.) 16° 1 50

Successful Merchant. Arthur (W.) 16° 80

Sunday Half-hours with the Great Preachers. Simons (M. L.) With Portraits. 8° 3 75

*Summer Days at Kirkwood. Miller (Emily Huntington). Illust. 16° 1 00

*Summer Days on the Hudson. The Story of a Pleasure Tour from Sandy Hook to the Saranac Lakes: Including Incidents of Travel, Legends, Historical Anecdotes, Sketches of Scenery, etc. Wise (Daniel). Illust. with 109 Engravings. 12° 1 70

*Summer Driftwood for Winter Fire. Porter (Rose). 16° 1 00

*Summer in Leslie Goldthwaite's Life. Whitney (Mrs. A. D. T.) Illust. 12° 1 50

Summer in Norway, A. With Notes on the Industries, Habits, etc., of the People, the History of the Country, the Climate and Productions, and of the Red Deer, Reindeer, and Elk. Caton (J. D.) Illust. 8° 1 75

Summer in Scotland. Abbott (J.) Illust. 12° 1 75

Summer Rambles in Europe. A Series of Sketches of Life and Travels in Great Britain and upon the Continent. Clark (Alex.) 12° 1 00

*Sun, Moon, and Stars, The. A Book for Beginners. Giberne (Agnes). Illust. 12° 1 50

*Sunday Afternoons. A Book for Little People.
    Burr (E. F.)   16° $0 65

Sunday-school Concerts, Ten Complete. With
    Thirty Additional Concert Pieces, Dialogues,
    and Addresses. Reade (T. C.)   16   65

Sunday - school Concerts, Monthly. Containing
    Twelve New Concert Exercises. Butterworth
    (Hezekiah).   16°   50

*Sunday-school Hand-book. House (Erwin).   12°   1 00

*Sunday-School Institutes and Normal Classes. Vin-
    cent (J. H.) With an Introduction by Alfred
    Taylor.   16°   65

*Sunday-school Teachers' Guide.   12°   1 00

*Sunday-school Teachers, Hand-book for. Alden
    (Joseph).   16°   65

*Sunlight Through the Mist. Lessons from the
    Lives of Great and Good Men.   16°   75

*Sunny Skies; or, Adventures in Italy. Channing
    (Barbara H.) Illust.   16°   1 25

Sunrise Kingdom; or, Life and Scenes in Japan,
    and Woman's Work for Women There. Car-
    rothers (Julia D.) Illust.   12°   2 00

*Sunshine of Blackpool. Leslie (Emma).   16°   85

*Sunset Mountain. Christian Faith Permeating
    Character and Beautifying Life. Porter (Mrs.
    A. E.) Illust.   16°   1 50

Superannuate, Sketches of a. Lewis (D.)   16°   1 25

Supernatural Factor in Religious Revivals, The.
    Townsend (L. T.)   12°   75

Suplée's Trench on Words.   12°   1 25

*Sure; or, It Pays. Ministers to What is Highest in
    Social Morals and Vital in Religion. Illust.   16°   1 50

Sure Mercies of David; or, God's Dealings in the
    Sanctuary. Shipton (Anna).   16°   75

*Susie's Spectacles. For the Eyes of the Mind.   16°   1 25

*Suzanne De L'Orme. A Story of Huguenot Times. 16°   1 00

*Sweet Story of Old; or, Tell Me About Jesus.
    Illust.   16°   65

*Swiss Family Robinson. Edited and Revised by
    Cecil Hartley.   16°   1 00

Sword and Garment; or, Ministerial Culture.
    Townsend (L. T.)   16°   75

*Sybil's Way. Underlaid with a Christian Purpose.
    Illust.   16° $1 25

*Sylvan Glen Stories, The. Illust. 4 vols. In box. 16°   4 00

> Breaking the Rules.   Jamie Noble.
> Charley Wheeler's Reward.   Great Success.

Syrian Home Life. Jessup (H. H.) Illust.   16°   90

Systematic Beneficence. Comprising The Great
    Reform, The Great Question, and Property
    Consecrated.   16°   85

Systematic Theology. Raymond (Miner). 3 vols. 12°   5 00

Tait. Memoir of Catharine and Craufurd Tait,
    Wife and Son of the Archbishop of Canter-
    bury. Edited by W Benham.   12°   1 50

*Take Care of Number One. Power (P. B.) Illust. 16°   1 00

*Talbury Girls, The. Vance (Clara). Illust.   16°   1 50

Tales and Takings. Watson (J. V.)   12°   1 50

*Tales from Alsace; or, Scenes and Portraits from
    Life in the Days of the Reformation.   16°   1 50

*Tales from Shakespeare. Lamb (Charles and Mary).
    Illust.   16°   1 00

*Tales from the Norse Grandmother. Larned (Au-
    gusta).   12°   1 50

*Tales of a Grandfather. Scott (Walter). Globe
    Edition. 4 vols.   16°   c1 00

Tales of Ancient Greece. Cox (G. W.)   12°   1 50

*Tales of the Family; or, Home Life Illustrated. 16°   1 50

*Tales of the Persecuted. Illust.   16°   1 50

Talks on Temperance. Farrar (F. W.)   12°   60

*Talks with Girls. Larned (Augusta).   16°   1 25

Talmud Miscellany. Hershon (P. I.)   8°   4 50

Tanglewood Tales. Hawthorne (N.)   16°   1 25

*Tapestry Room, The. Molesworth (Mrs.) Illust. 16°   1 50

Tatham, Mrs. Mary, Memoir of. Beaumont (J.) 12°   55

Taylor, Rev. Edward T., Incidents and Anecdotes
    of. Over Forty Years Pastor of the Seamen's
    Bethel, Boston. Haven (Gilbert) and Russell
    (Thomas).   12°   1 50

Teachers' Helper, The. Alden (Mrs. G. R. [Pansy).]
    Illust.   16°   1 00

Teacher, The. Moral Influence Employed in the

Instruction and Government of the Young. Abbott (Jacob). Illust.	12°	$1 75
Teaching, Outlines on. Alden (Jos.)	12°	40
Tears for the Little Ones. A Collection of Poems and Passages inspired by the Loss of Children. Edited by Helen K. Johnson.	12°	1 50
*Tell Jesus. Recollections of Emily Gosse. Shipton (Anna).	16°	75
*Tell me a Story. Graham (Ennis). Illust.	16°	1 50
Telephone: An Account of the Phenomena of Electricity, Magnetism, and Sound, as Involved in Its Action. Dolbear (A. E.)	4°	75
Telephone, the Microphone, and the Phonograph, The. Moncel (Count Du). Illust.	12°	1 25
*Temptation and Triumph. Townsend (Virginia F.)	16°	1 25
*Tempter Behind, The. A Temperance Story. Saunders (John). Illust.	12°	1 25
Ten Lectures on Alcohol. Richardson (B. W.)	12°	1 00
Tennesseean in Persia and Koordistan, The. Scenes and Incidents in the Life of Samuel Audley Rhea. Marsh (Dwight W.) Illust.	12°	2 00
Tennyson's (Alfred) Poems. Household Edition. Illust.	12°	2 00
*Tent in the Notch, The. Rand (Edward A.)	16°	1 00
Tent-life in the Holy Land. Prime (W. C.) Illust.	12°	2 00
Ten Great Religions. An Essay in Comparative Theology. Clarke (J. F.)	8°	3 00
*Tessa Wadsworth's Discipline. Drinkwater (Jennie M.)	12°	1 50
Text-book of Temperance. Lees (F R.)	12°	1 25
*That Boy Bob. Huntington (Faye) and Alden (Mrs. G. R. [Pansy].) Illust.	16°	75
*That Boy of Newkirk's. Bates (L.) Illust.	16°	1 25
*That Boy. Who Shall Have Him? Daniels (W H.) Illust.	12°	1 50
*Theban Legion, The. A Story of the Times of Diocletian. Blackburn (Wm. M.) Illust.	16°	1 00
*Their Children. Clarke (Mrs. S. H.) Illust.	16°	1 50
Theistic Argument, The, as Effected by Recent Theories. Diman (J. Lewis).	8°	2 00
Theistic Conception of the World. Cocker (B. F.)	8°	2 50
Theism, Studies in. Bowne (Borden P.)	12°	1 50

Theodicy ; or, Vindication of the Divine Glory as
Manifested in the Constitution and Government
of the Moral World. Bledsoe (A. T.) Half
Morocco. 8° $2 50

Theological Compend Improved. Containing a
Synopsis of the Evidences, Doctrines, Morals,
and Institutions of Christianity. Designed for
Bible Classes, Theological Students, and Young
Preachers. Binney (Amos) and Steele (Daniel). 12° 75

Théology, Christian, A Compendium of. Being
Analytical Outlines of a Course of Theological
Study, Biblical, Dogmatic, Historical. Pope
(William Burt). 3 vols. 8° 7 50

Theology of the English Poets. Brooke (S. A.) 12° 2 00

Theology, Christian, A Complete System of; or, a
Concise, Comprehensive, and Systematic View
of the Evidences, Doctrines, Morals, and Institutions of Christianity. Wakefield (Samuel). 2 50

Theology, General and Christian, Elements of.
Townsend (L. T.) 12° 45

Theology of the New Testament. A Hand-book for
Bible Students. Van Oosterzee (J. J.) Translated by Maurice J. Evans. 12° 1 50

Thirty Years. Being Poems, New and Old. Mulock
(Dinah M.) 16° 1 50

Thirty Years' War, The, History of. 1618–1648.
Schiller (F.) Translated from the German by
A. J. W. Morrison. 16° 1 00

*Thirty Years' War. True (Charles K.) 12° 1 00

*This One Thing I Do. Porter (Mrs. A. E.) Illust. 16° 1 50

*Thornton Hall ; or, Old Questions in Young Lives.
McKeen (Phebe F.) 12° 1 50

*Those Boys. Book for the Older Boys. Hunting-
ton (Faye). Illust. 16° 1 50

*Those Dark Days ; or, the Diaries of Two Nether-
land Girls. Chapman (Helen C). Illust. 16° 1 00

Thoughts for a Young Man. Mann (Horace). 16° 75

Thought-hives. Cuyler (T. L.) 12° 1 50

Thoughts, Letters, and Opuscules of Blaise Pascal,
The. Translated from the French by O. W.
Wight. 8° 2 25

Thoughts on Religion. Pascal (Blaise). 12° 2 25

Thoughts on Personal Religion. Being a Treatise on the Christian Life in its Two Chief Elements, Devotion and Practice. Goulburn (E. M.) 12° $1 00

Thoughts on the Religious Life. Alden (Joseph). With Introduction by W. C. Bryant. 16° 1 00

Thoughts Selected from the Writings of Horace Mann. 16° 1 25

Thoughts that Breathe. From the Writings of Dean Stanley. Edited by E. E. Brown. Introduction by Phillips Brooks. 16° 1 00

*Three Christmas Eves. By the Author of "The Parsonage in the Hartz." Adapted from the German. McFadden (Mrs. Cornelia). 16° 1 25

Three Gardens, The. Eden, Gethsemane, and Paradise; or, Man's Ruin, Redemption, and Restoration. Adams (Wm.) 12° 2 00

*Three Judges, The. Story of the Men Who Beheaded their King. Warren (I. P.) Illust. 16° 1 25

*Three of Us. Story of Three Girls Won to a Religious Life. Illust. 12° 1 00

*Three People. A Temperance Story. Alden (Mrs. G. R. [Pansy].) Illust. 12° 1 50

Threescore Years and Beyond; or, Experiences of the Aged. A Book for Old People, describing the Labors, Habits, Home-life, and Closing Experiences of a Large Number of Aged Representative Men and Women of the Earlier and Later Times. De Puy (W. H.) Illust. 8° 3 00

Three Visits to Madagascar during the Years 1853, 1854, 1856. Including a Journey to the Capital, with Notices of the Natural History of the Country and the Present Civilization of the People. Ellis (Wm.) Maps, Illust., etc. 8° 3 50

Three Years in Arizona, the Marvelous Country. Cozzens (S. W.) Illust. 8° 2 50

Thrift. Smiles (S.) 12° 1 00

Thrilling Adventures by Sea and Land: Being Remarkable Historical Facts, gathered from Authentic Sources. Edited by James O. Brayman. Illust. 12° 1 25

Throne of David. Ingraham (J. H.) 12° 2 00

Through and Through the Tropics. Vincent (F.) 12° 1 50

Through the Dark Continent. Stanley (H. M.)
    Illust. 2 vols.   8° $10 00
Through Nature to Christ.   8° 3 00
Through Normandy. Macquoid (K. S.) Illust. 12° 1 50
Through Persia by Caravan. Arnold (Arthur). 12° 1 50
*Through Struggle to Victory. Helpful to All Who
    are Struggling for Knowledge. Meservy (A.) 16°   80
*Through the Eye to the Heart; or, Eye-teaching
    in the Sunday-school. Crafts (W. F.)   12°   80
*Through the Dark to the Day. A Story. Willing
    (Mrs. Jennie F.)   16° 1 00
*Through the Wilderness. Willard (Mary E.) Illust. 16° 1 00
*Through Trials to Triumph. A Story of Boy's
    School Life. Putnam (Miss H. A.) Illust. 16° 1 00
*Tip Lewis and His Lamp. Alden (Mrs. G. R.
    [Pansy].) Illust.   16° 1 50
To Cuba and Back. Dana (R. H.)   16° 1 25
*Together; or, Life on the Circuit. Boyd (Mrs. E. E.)
    Illust.   16°   75
*Tom Brown at Oxford. Hughes (Thomas). Illust. 16° 1 25
*Tom Brown's School-days at Rugby. Hughes
    (Thomas). Illust.   16° 1 00
Tonga and Feejee, Missions in. Lawry (W.) 12° 1 25
Tongue of Fire, The. Arthur (Wm.)   12° 1 25
*Topics for Teachers. A New and Valuable Work
    for Ministers, Sunday-school Teachers, and
    Others. On an Entirely New Plan. Gray
    (J. Comper.) Illust.; also 6 Maps. 2 vols. 12° 2 50
*Torch-bearers, The. Examples of Love and Self-
    denial. Bates (Elizabeth). Illust.   16° 1 25
*Torn and Mended. "God's Love Shineth through
    all," is its Motto. Round (Wm. M. F.) 16° 1 00
Tower of Constancy, The; or, Bearing the Cross.
    From the French of L. L. F. Bungener. Illust. 12° 1 50
Tracts. From Nos. 1 to 455 inclusive. 9 vols. 12° *e* 1 25
Transcendentalism. Cook (Joseph).   12° 1 50
*Trapper's Niece, The. Story of Western Life.
    Illust.   16° 1 25
Travels Around the World. Seward (William H.)
    Edited by Olive Risley Seward. Illust.   8° 5 00
Travels in Central America. Stephens (J. L.)
    Illust. 2 vols.   8° 6 00

Travels in Egypt. Stephens (J. L.) Illust. 2 vols. 12° $3 00
Travels in Greece. Stephens (J. L.) Illust. 2 vols. 12° 3 00
Travels in Yucatan. Stephens (J. L.) Illust. 2 vols. 8° 6 00
Travels in Europe and the East. Prime (S. I.)
    Illust. 2 vols. 12° 3 00
Travels in the East Indian Archipelago. Beck-
    more (A. S.) Illust. 8° 3 50
Traveler's Prayer. Clarke (A.) 24° 20
Traveler, The. Irving (Washington). 16° 1 25
Travelers in Africa. Narratives and Adventures
    of Charles Williams. Illust. 12° 1 25
Tregenoweth, John, His Mark. Pearse (Mark
    Guy). 12° 50
*Trials of an Inventor. Life and Discoveries of
    Charles Goodyear. Peirce (B. K.) 16° 1 00
*Tried in the Fire. Treating of Struggles with Skep-
    tics and Skeptical Tendencies. Blanchard
    (Leone). Illust. 16° 1 25
*Trifles. Showing the Influence Exerted upon Char-
    acter by what are often Deemed Little and
    Unimportant Things. Dunning (Mrs. A. K.)
    Illust. 16° 1 25
Trip to England, The. Winter (Wm.) Photo.
    Illust. 16° 2 00
Trip up the Volga. Munro-Butler-Johnstone (H. A.)
    Illust. 12° 1 25
Triumph Over Death. A Narrative of the Closing
    Scenes of the Life of William Gordon, M. D.,
    F. L. S., of Kingston-upon-Hull. Hall (New-
    man). 12° 1 00
*Triumph Over Midian, The. A. L. O. E. Illust. 18° 75
*Tropics, The. Conversations Portraying Life in the
    Tropical Regions. Illust. 16° 1 25
*Trotty Book, The. Phelps (Elizabeth S.) Illust. 4° 1 25
True and Beautiful, The. Ruskin. 12° 2 00
True Manliness. From the Writings of Thomas
    Hughes. Edited by E. E. Brown. Introduc-
    tion by James Russell Lowell. 16° 1 00
True Order of Studies, The. Hill (Thomas). 16° 1 25
*True Stories About Pets. Illust. Boards, 60c. Cloth. 16° 1 00
True Stories from History and Biography. Haw-
    thorne (N.) 16° 1 25

*True Stories of Real Pets; or, Friends in Fur and
    Feathers. Illust. 16° $1 00
True Story of the Exodus, The: Together with a
    Brief View of the History of Monumental
    Egypt. Compiled from the work of Dr. Henry
    Brugsch-Bey. Edited, with an Introduction
    and Notes, by Francis H. Underwood. 12° 1 50
*Truffle Nephews: And How They Commenced a
    New Charity. Power (P. B.) 16° 1 00
*Trust in God; or, Three Days in the Life of Gellert. 18° 35
*Truth is Always Best; or, the Fatal Necklace. 18° 35
Trye's Year Among the Hindoos. Thompson
    (Julia C.) Illust. 16° 1 35
Turning-points in Life. Arnold (Frederick). 12° 1 75
Twelve Lectures to Young Men on Various Import-
    ant Subjects. Beecher (H. W.) 12° 1 50
*Two Boys. Alden (Mrs. G. R. [Pansy].) Illust. 16° 75
Two Circuits, The. A Story of Pioneer Life. Crane
    (J. L.) Illust. 12° 1 00
*Two Families and Two Aims in Life. Illust. 16° 1 25
*Two Miss Jean Dawsons, The. Robertson (M. M.) 16° 1 50
*Two Paths, The. Richmond (Mrs. E. J.) Illust. 16° 85
*Two Voyages, The; or, Midnight and Daylight.
    Illust. 16° 1 50
*Two Years Before the Mast. New and Enlarged
    Edition. Dana (Richard H.) 12° 1 50
*Two Young Homesteaders. Jenness (Mrs. Theo-
    dora R.) Illust. 12° 1 50

Ulrich Zwingli, the Patriotic Reformer. Black-
    burn (Wm. M.) 12° 1 50
Unbeaten Tracks in Japan. An Account of Travels
    on Horseback in the Interior. Including Visits
    to the Aborigines of Yezo and the Shrines of
    Nikkô and Isé. Bird (Isabella L.) Illust. 8° 3 00
Unbelief in the Eighteenth Century, as Contrasted
    with its Earlier and Later History. Cairns
    (John). 12° 60
*Uncle Anthony. Cummings (M. J.) Illust. 16° 1 25
*Uncle Dick's Legacy. Miller (Emily Huntington.)
    Illust. 16° 85
*Uncle Gilbert. Miller (Mary C.) Illust. 16° 1 00

*Uncle Toby, My. His Table-talks and Reflections. By an Attorney-at-law. 16° $1 00

Uncle Tom's Cabin. Stowe (Mrs. H. B.) 12° 2 00

*Uncrowned Kings; or, Sketches of Some Men of Mark who rose from Obscurity to Renown. Wise (Daniel). Illust. 16° 1 00

Underbrush. Fields (James T.) 8° 1 25

*Under the Holly. A Book for Girls. Hosmer (Margaret). 16° 1 25

Under the Trees. Prime (S. I.) 8° 2 00

Undiscovered Country, The. Howells (W. D.) 12° 1 50

Unity of the New Testament, The. Maurice (F. D.) 12° 2 00

Universalism not of the Bible. Being an Examination of more than One Hundred Texts of Scripture in Controversy between Evangelical Christians and Universalists. Comprising a Refutation of Universalist Theology, and an Exposure of the Sophistical Arguments and Other Means by which it is Propagated: With a General and Scripture Index. George (N. D.) 12° 1 50

Universe, The; or, The Infinitely Great and the Infinitely Little. Pouchet (F. A.) Illust. 8° 3 75

*Unselfish Freddy, and Other Stories. 18° 40

*Uplands and Lowlands; or, Three Chapters in Life. Porter (Rose). 16° 1 25

*Urbané and His Friends. Prentiss (Mrs. E.) 12° 1 50

*VAGABOND and Victor. The Story of David Sheldon. Hamilton (Kate W.) Illust. 16° 1 25

Vale of Cedars; or, The Martyrs. Aguilar (Grace). Illust. 12° 1 00

*Vanquished Victors; or, Sketches of Distinguished Men who Overcame the Obstacles in their Way to Fame, but Failed to Gain that Self-mastery which is the Greatest and Grandest of all Conquests. Wise (Daniel). Illust. 16° 1 00

Vaudois Church, History of the. From its Origin, and of the Vaudois of Piedmont to the Present Day. Monastier (A.) 12° 1 00

*Veil on the Heart, The. Phelps (Miss L. L.) Illust. 16° 1 25

Venetian Life. Including Commercial, Social, Historical, and Artistic Notes of Venice. 12° 1 50

*Vesper, and Other Stories. Translated from the
    French. Booth (Mary L.)   16° $0 85
Vicar of Wakefield, The. Riverside Classic. Illust. 16°   1 00
Victoria: With Other Poems. Henry (S. I.)   12°   85
Victorian Poets. A Complete Guide-book to the
    Poetry of the Victorian Era.   8°   2 50
*Victory of the Vanquished, The. A Story of the
    First Century. By the Author of "The Schön-
    berg-Cotta Family."   12°   1 00
Views Afoot; or, Europe Seen with Knapsack and
    Staff. Taylor (Bayard).   12°   1 50
Village Blacksmith, The: A Memoir of Samuel
    Hicks. Everett (James).   18°   60
Village Improvements and Farm Villages. Waring
    (George E.) Illust.   18°   75
Villages and Village Life. With Hints for their
    Improvement. Egleston (N. H.)   8°   1 75
*Violet and Daisy; or, The Picture with Two Sides.
    Illust.   16°   1 00
*Violet Douglas; or, The Problems of Life. Mar-
    shall (Emma). Illust.   16°   1 50
*Virginia. Story of Adventure in the Early History
    of Our Country. Kingston (W H. G.) Illust. 16°   1 25
Visions of Heaven, for the Life on Earth. Patter-
    son (Robert M.)   16°   1 50
*Vivian and His Friends; or, Two Hundred Years
    Ago. Illust.   16°   1 10
Voice of the Home, A. Henry (Mrs. S. M. I.)   12°   1 25
Voices from Babylon; or, the Records of Daniel
    the Prophet. Seiss (Joseph A.)   12°   1 50
Voyage of the Paper Canoe. A Geographical
    Journey of Twenty-five Hundred Miles from
    Quebec to the Gulf of Mexico. Bishop (Na-
    thaniel H.) Illust.   8°   2 50
*Voyage of the Steadfast. Kingston (W. H. G.)
    Illust.   16°   1 00
Voyage, Thy; or, A Song of the Sea, and Other
    Poems. Burr (E. F.)   8°   3 00

*WADSWORTH Boys, The. Erickson (D. S.) Illust. 16°   1 50
Waiting at the Cross. A Collection of Prose and
    Poetry, Original and Selected. Eddy (D. C.) 18°   1 50

Waiting Hours with the Hungry and Weary and
    Thirsty in the Wilderness. Shipton (Anna). 16° $0 75
Wake Robin. Burroughs (John). Illust. 16° 1 50
Waldenses. Sketches of the Evangelical Christians
    of the Valleys of Piedmont. Illust. 16° 1 25
Walker, Rev. G. W., Recollections of. Gaddis
    (M. P.) 12° 1 75
Walks to Emmaus. Adams (Nehemiah). 12° 1 00
Walking in the Light. Buck (D. D.) 12° 50
*Wallingford's Mistake, Mr. Dunning (Mrs. A. K.)
    Illust. 16° 1 00
Wall's End Miner; or, A Brief Memoir of the Life
    of William Crister. Everett (J.) 18° 40
*Walter: A Tale of the Times of Wesley. Leslie
    (Emma). Illust. 12° 1 25
*Walter Macdonald; or, Aunt Kitty's Legacy. Illust. 16° 1 50
*Walter Neal's Example. Story with Incidents from
    Real Life. Brown (Theron). Illust. 16° 1 25
*Wanderings Over Bible Lands. By the Author of
    "The Schönberg-Cotta Family." 1 00
Ware, Rev. Thomas, Life of. Written by Himself.
    With a Portrait. 12° 90
Warfare of Science, The. White (Andrew D.) 12° 1 00
*Warlock o' Glenwarlock. MacDonald (Geo.) Illust. 12° 1 75
*Was I Right? Walton (Mrs. O. F.) 16° 1 00
Washington and His Generals. Headley (J. T.) 12° 2 50
Washington, George, Life of. Irving (Washington).
    5 vols. 16° e 1 25
*Wat Adams, the Young Machinist. Boyd (Mary
    D. R.) Illust. 16° 1 00
Watch-tower, The, in the Wilderness. Shipton
    (Anna). 16° 75
*Waterton's Wanderings in South America. Edited
    by J. G. Wood. Illust. 12° 2 00
Watson's Apology for the Bible. Watson (Bishop). 18° 40
Watson's Biblical and Theological Dictionary. With
    5 Maps. 8° 4 50
Watson's Conversations on the Bible. 12° 1 00
Watson, Rev. Richard, Life of. Jackson (T.) With
    a Portrait. 8° 2 25
Watson's Sermons and Sketches. 2 vols. 8° 5 00
Watson's Theological Institutes. 2 vols. 8° 5 00

*Watson's Woods; or, Margaret Huntington's Ex-
    periment.   16° $1 25
*Way Lost and Found, The. Tuttle (Joseph F.)
    Illust.   16° 1 15
Way of Life, The. Guthrie (Thomas.) 12° 1 50
Wayside Service; or, The Day of Small Things.
    Shipton (Anna).   16° 75
*We Got Agate of Singing.   18° 35
*We Three. Hamilton (Kate W.) Illust. 16° 1 10
*Weaver Boy, The, who Became a Missionary. Story
    of the Life and Labors of David Livingstone.
    Adams (H. G.) Illust.   16° 1 25
Week-day Religion. Miller (J. R.)   16° 1 00
*Well in the Desert, The. An Old Legend of the
    House of Arundel. Holt (Emily S.) 16° 1 25
*Well-spent Hour, The. Follen (Mrs. E. L.) Illust. 16° 1 00
*Wentworths, The. A Story of College Life. Pin-
    dar (Susan Cooper). Illust.   16° 1 25
Wesley and His Coadjutors. Larrabee (W. C.)
    2 vols.   16° e1 00
Wesley and Methodism. Taylor (I.) 12° 1 50
Wesleyana. A System of Wesleyan Theology. 12° 75
Wesleyan Preachers, Memoirs of. West (R. A.) 12° 75
Wesleyan Student. Life of A. H. Hurd. Holdich
    (Joseph).   18° 45
Wesleyan Demosthenes, The. Wakeley (J. B.) 16° 1 00
Wesley Family, Memoirs of the. Clarke (A.) 12° 1 50
Wesley Family, Memorials of. Including Bio-
    graphical and Historical Sketches of all the
    Members of the Family for Two Hundred and
    Fifty Years: Together with a Genealogical
    Table of the Wesleys, with Historical Notes,
    for more than Nine Hundred Years. 8° 3 50
Wesley His Own Historian. Illustrations of His
    Character, Labors, and Achievements. From
    His Own Diaries. Janes (Edwin L.) 12° 1 25
Wesley, Rev. Charles, Life of. Jackson (T.) With
    a Portrait.   8° 2 70
Wesley, Rev. John, Life of. Watson (R.) 12° 1 00
Wesley, Rev. John, Works of. 7 vols. 8° e2 50
    Full set, Plain, or Half Calf.   24 50
Wesleys, Anecdotes of the. Wakeley (J. B.) 12° 1 00

Wesley's Letters. Select Letters, Chiefly on Personal Religion. 12° $0 65
Wesley's Missionaries to America. Sandford (P. P.) 12° 75
Wesley's Notes on the New Testament. 12° 1 50
Wesley's Journal. 2 vols. 8° e2 50
Western Pioneer; or, Incidents of the Life and Times of Rev. Alfred Brunson, D. D. 2 vols. 12° e1 50
'Westward. A Tale of American Emigrant Life. Wright (Mrs. J. McNair). Illust. 16° 1 10
What Mr. Darwin Saw in His Voyage Around the World. Illust. 8° 3 00
*What God Does is Well Done. From the German of C. G. Salzmann. Disosway (Miss E. T.) 16° 1 00
*What is a Child? or, the Properties and Laws of Child-nature Stated and Illustrated. Groser (W. H.) 15
What Must I Do to be Saved? Peck (J. T.) 18° 50
*What Shall I Read? A Confidential Chat on Books. 16° 65
*What She Said. Alden (Mrs. G. R. [Pansy].) The two stories, "What She Said: and What She Meant," and "People Who Have n't Time and Can't Afford It," in 1 vol. Illust. 16° 1 25
*When I was a Little Girl. Stories for Children. Illust. 16° 1 00
*Where there's a Will, there's a Way. 12° 1 00
*White Chrysanthemum, The. A Story. 16° 1 25
Why Four Gospels? or, The Gospel for all the World. A Manual Designed to Aid Christians in a Study of the Scriptures, and to a Better Understanding of the Gospels. Gregory (D. S.) 12° 1 25
*Wicket-gate; or, Sermons to Children. Newton (W. W.) Illust. 16° 1 25
Widow's Souvenir. A Gift-book for Widows. Rose (A. C.) 24° 35
Wild North-land. Butler. (W. F.) 12° 1 75
*Wildfords in India, The. Illust. 16° 1 25
Wiley, Rev. A., Life and Times of. Holliday (F. C.) 12° 60
*Wilfred. A Story with a Happy Ending. Winthrop (A. T.) 12° 1 25
William Farel, and The Story of the Swiss Reform. 12° 1 50
Will, The Freedom of the. Whedon (D. D.) 12° 1 50

*Will Phillips. Richards (C. H.) Illust.   16°   \$1 50
Williams, Richard, Memoir of.   16°   45
*Williams, Roger, Footprints of. Mudge (Z. A.)
     Illust.   16°   1 00
*William the Silent, and the Netherland War. Bar-
     rett (Mary). With Maps and Engravings.   16°   1 50
*William the Taciturn. Translated by J. P. Lacroix.
     From the French of L. Abelous. Illust.   16°   1 00
*Willie's Money-box. Illust.   16°   1 25
*Wings of Courage. Stories for American Boys and
     Girls. Field (Marie E.) Illust.   16°   1 25
Wine in the Word. An Inquiry Concerning the
     Wine Christ Made, the Wine of the Supper,
     etc. Coles (Abraham).   12°   40
*Winifred Bertram, and the World She Lived In.
     By the Author of "The Schönberg-Cotta Fam-
     ily."   12°   1 00
*Winifred Leigh Library. Illust. 4 vols. In a box. 16°   3 50

> Winifred Leigh.
> The Captive Boy in Terra del Fuego.
> In Self and Out of Self.
> Hetty Porter.

Winter Fire, The. A Sequel to Summer Driftwood.
     Porter (Rose).   16°   1 25
*Winter at Woodlawn: or, The Armor of Light Il-
     lustrated.   16°   75
Winter in Spitzbergen. A Tale of the North-land.
     From the German of C. Hildebrandt. Trans-
     lated by E. Goodrich Smith. Illust.   16°   90
*Winwood Cliff Stories. Wise (Daniel).   16°   e1 00

> Winwood Cliff; or, Oscar, the Sailor's Son.
> Ben Blinker; or, Maggie's Golden Motto.
> Roderick Ashcourt. A Story showing how a Manly Boy and
>   Noble Girl Bravely Battled with Great Troubles.
> Thorncliffe Hall: or, Why Joel Milford Changed His
>   Opinion of Boys whom he called "Goody-goody
>   fellows."

*Wise and Otherwise. Alden (Mrs. G. R. [Pansy].)
     Illust.   12°   1 50
Wise Men. Who They Were; and How They
     Came to Jerusalem. Upham (Francis W.)   12°   1 00
Wise Words and Loving Deeds. A Book of Biog-
     raphies for Girls. Gray (E. C.)   12°   1 50

Wit and Wisdom of Sydney Smith, The: Being Se-
lections from His Writings. 8° $1 75
*Witch Hill. A History of Salem Witchcraft, in-
cluding Illustrative Sketches of Persons and
Places. Mudge (Z. A.) Illust. 16° 1 00
Witnessing Church. Harris (J.) 24° 25
Witness of the Spirit. Walton (D.) 18° 40
Witness of History to Christ. Farrar (F. W.) 8° 1 50
Witness of the Psalms to Christ. Alexander (W.) 8° 2 25
Wolfert's Roost. Irving (Washington). 16° 1 25
Womanhood. Lectures on Woman's Work in the
World. Newton (R. Heber). 16° 1 25
Woman's Experiences in Europe, A. Wallace
(Mrs. E. D.) 12° 1 50
Woman's Friendship. Aguilar (Grace). Illust. 12° 1 00
Woman's Foreign Missionary Society of the Meth-
odist Episcopal Church, First Decade of. With
Sketches of its Missionaries. Wheeler (Mary
Sparkes). 12° 1 50
Woman's Handiwork. Harrison (C. C.) Illust. 8° 2 00
Woman, The True. Peck (Jesse T.) 12° 1 50
Women of the Bible. Headley (P. C.) Illust. 12° 1 50
*Women of Christendom. Being Sketches of the
Lives of the Notable Christian Women of His-
tory. By the Author of "The Schönberg-
Cotta Family." 12° 1 00
Women of Israel, The. Aguilar (Grace). Illust. 12° 1 00
Women of the Arabs. Jessup (H. H.) Illust. 12° 1 25
*Women of the Bible. Adams (C.) 12° 85
Women of Methodism. Stevens (Abel). 12° 1 25
Women of the Orient. An Account of the Relig-
ious, Intellectual, and Social Condition of
Women in Japan, China, India, Egypt, Syria,
and Turkey. Houghton (Ross C.) Illust. 12° 1 50
*Wonder-book for Boys and Girls. Hawthorne (N.) 16° 1 25
*Wonderful Lamp, The, and Other Talks to Chil-
dren. Macleod (Alex.) Illust. 16° 1 00
*Wonderful Life, The. A Life of Christ for Young
Readers. Stretton (Hesba). 16° 90
*Wonderful Life, The Story of a; or, Pen Pictures
of the Most Interesting Incidents in the Life of
John Wesley. Wise (Daniel). Illust. 16° 1 00

*Wonderful and Curious Things, Our Library of
 Books About. Illust. 4 vols. In a box. 16° $3 00

  Wonders in the Air.
  The Wonders of Fire and Water.
  The Birthday Present.
  Elder Park Garden.

*Wonders Near Home. Houghton (W.) Illust. 16° 1 00
 Wonders of Science. Life of a Wonderful Boy.
  Written for Boys. Mayhew (H.) 16° 1 25
*Wonders of Insect Life. The Structure, Habits,
 and Instincts of Insects, as Illustrating the
 Wisdom, Power, and Goodness of God. Willet
 (I. E.) With Engravings and Colored Illust. 16° 1 75
*Wonders of the Deep. DeVere (M. Schele). Illust. 12° 1 25
*Wonders of the Plant World. Illust. 12° 1 50
*Wonder-stories Told for Children. Andersen
 (Hans Christian). Illust. 8° 1 50
*Woodlawn Series, The. For Small Children. Les-
 lie (Mrs. Madeline). 6 vols. In a box. Illust. 18° 3 60

  Bertie's Home.   Bertie and the Masons.
  Bertie and the Plumbers. Bertie and the Painters.
  Bertie and the Carpenters. Bertie and the Gardeners.

*Word of God Opened. Pierce (B. K.) 16° 1 00
*Words and Deeds; or, Watching for Opportunities. 16° 1 25
 Words of the Wise. For Every Day in the Year. 24° 30
*Words that Shook the World; or, Martin Luther
 His Own Biographer. Adams (C.) Illust. 16° 1 00
 Work Illustrated. Alcott (Louisa M.) 12° 1 75
 Works of Charles Lamb. Complete. 3 vols. 8° 3 75
 Work of God in Great Britain, The, under Messrs.
  Moody and Sankey, 1873 to 1875: Together with
  Some Discourses Preached by Mr. Moody.
  Clark (Rufus W.) 12° 1 50
 Work of the Spirit in the Human Heart. Edwards
  (Jonathan). Abridged by John Wesley. 18° 30
 Works of Francis Bacon. 2 vols. 8° 5 00
 Works of Mrs. Hannah More. Complete in 1 vol.
  Sheep.' 8° 3 00
 Works of Henry Hallam. Complete. Comprising
  The Constitutional History of England, The
  Middle Ages, and Introduction to the Litera-
  ture of Europe. 6 vols. 8° 7 50

Works of Henry Hart Milman, D. D. Complete. Comprising The History of the Jews, History of Christianity, and History of Latin Christianity. Standard Edition. 8 vols.   8° $12 00

Works of Joseph Addison : Embracing the Whole of the "Spectator." Complete in 3 vols.   8°   6 00

Works of Oliver Goldsmith. Complete. With Notes by James Prior. 4 vols.   12°   5 00

Works of Thomas Dick, LL. D. Complete. 5 vols.   12°   10 00

Works of William Jay. Complete. 3 vols.   8°   6 00

World of Wonders, A. Marvels in Animate and Inanimate Nature.   8°   2 00

World's Witness of Jesus Christ. The Power of Christianity in Developing Modern Civilization. Williams (Jno.)   8°   1 00

*Wrecked, Not Lost. A Book of Adventure for Boys. Dundas (Mrs.) Illust.   16°   1 00

Wrestling Jacob. Hannah (J.)   24°   25

*Wych Hazel. Warner (Susan and Anna).   12°   1 75

YALE Lectures on Preaching. Beecher (H. W.) 3 vols.   12°   *e* 1 25

Yale Lectures on Preaching. Hall (John).   12°   1 50

Yale Lectures on Preaching. Simpson (Matthew).   12°   1 25

*Year in the Country, A ; or, Keilei's Missionary Work. Burton (Mrs. Bella F.) Illust.   16°   1 25

*Year at Riverside Farm, A. Miller (Emily Huntington). Illust.   16°   85

Years that are Told, The. Porter (Rose).   16°   1 25

*Yensie Walton. A Story of Girl Life. Clark (Mrs. R. S. Graham). Illust.   16°   1 50

Yesterday, To-day, and Forever. Bickersteth (E. H.)   16°   1 00

Yesterdays with Authors. Fields (J. T.)   12°   2 00

York and a Lancaster Rose, A. A Book for Girls. Keary (A.)   12°   1 25

*Young Americans Abroad ; or, Vacation in Europe. Choules (John Overton) and His Pupils. Illust.   16°   1 25

*Young Benjamin Franklin ; or, The Right Road Through Life. Mayhew (H.) Illust.   16°   1 25

*Young Folks' Cyclopædia of Common Things. Champlin (J. D.) Illust.   8°   3 00

*Young Christian Series, The.   Abbott (Jacob).
    Illust.   12° *c*$1 75

  1. The Young Christian.   3. The Way to do good.
  2. The Corner-stone.   4. Hoaryhead and McDonner.

*Young Folks' Bible History.   Yonge (Charlotte M.)
    Illust.   12° 1 25

*Young Folks' History of America.   Edited by Hez-
    ekiah Butterworth, Author of "Notable Prayers
    of Christian History."   Illust.   12° 1 50

*Young Folks' History of Boston.   Butterworth
    (Hezekiah).   Illust.   1 50

*Young Folks' History of England.   Yonge (Char-
    lotte M.)   Uniform with "Germany" and
    "Greece."   12° 1 30

*Young Folks' History of Germany.   Yonge (Char-
    lotte M.)   Illust.   12° 1 30

*Young Folks' History of France.   Yonge (Char-
    lotte M.)   Illust.   12° 1 30

*Young Folks' History of Greece.   Yonge (Charlotte
    M.)   Illust.   12° 1 30

*Young Folks' History of the Netherlands.   A Con-
    cise History of Holland and Belgium, from
    Earliest Times Down to the Present.   Young
    (Alexander).   12° 1 50

*Young Folks' History of Rome.   Yonge (Charlotte
    M.)   Illust.   12° 1 30

*Young Folks' History of Russia.   Dole (Nathan
    Haskell).   Illust.   12° 1 50

*Young Folks of Renfrew.   [In the Interest of the
    Missionary Cause.]   Taneyhill (Miss Ellen).
    Illust.   16°   85

*Young Lady's Counselor.   Wise (D.)   16°   85

*Young Ladies' Friend.   Ward (Mrs. H. O.)   12° 1 50

*Young Life; or, The Boys and Girls of Pleasant
    Valley.   Mather (Mrs. Sarah A.)   Illust.   16° 1 25

*Young Life, The, Equipping Itself for God's Serv-
    ice.   Vaughan (Charles J.)   12° 1 00

*Young Man Advised; or, Illustrations and Con-
    firmations of Some of the Chief Historical
    Facts of the Bible.   Haven (E. O.)   12° 1 00

*Young Man's Counselor.   Wise (D.)   16°   85

*Young Man's Friend and Guide through Life to
    Immortality. James (J. A.)   16° $1 25
  Young Minister, S. B. Bangs. Magruder (W. H. N.) 12°   1 00
*Young People's Half-hour Series. Paper covers.   12°   *e* 20

    Keep Good Company. Smiles (Samuel).
    Daniel, the Uncompromising Young Man. Payne (C. H.)
    Ten Days in Switzerland. Ridgaway (H. B.)
    Two Weeks in the Yosemite Valley. Buckley (J. M.)

*Young Pilgrim, The. Illustrative of Pilgrim's
    Progress. A. L. O. E.   18°   75
*Young Rick. Eastman (Julia A.) Illust.   16°   1 50
*Young Shetlander and His Home. Being a Bio-
    graphical Sketch of young Thomas Edmonston,
    the Naturalist, and an Interesting Account of
    the Shetland Islands. Pierce (B. K.) Illust. 16°   1 00
*Young Whaler, The. Kingston (W. H. G.)   16°   75
*Young Woman's Friend and Guide through Life
    to Immortality. James (J. A.)   16°   1 25
  Young Workers in the Church ; or, The Training
    and Organization of Young People for Chris-
    tian Activity. Neely (T. B.)   12°   1 00

*ZINA; or, Morning Mists. Giberne (A.) Illust. 16°   1 50
  Zulu-land; or, Life Among the Zulu Kafirs of
    Natal and Zulu-land, South Africa. Grout
    (Lewis). Illust.   12°   1 50

ADDITIONAL BOOKS.

After-glow, The, of European Travel. Harrington
    (Adelaide L.) Illust.   12° $1 50
Age of Fable; or, The Beauties of Mythology.
    Bulfinch (Thomas).   8°   2 50
*Alice's Adventures in Wonderland. Carroll (Lewis). 12°   1 50
American Men of Letters. A Series of Biographies
    of Eminent American Authors. Edited by
    Charles Dudley Warner. In uniform volumes.
    The following are now ready: 16° *e*1 25

> Washington Irving. Warner (Charles Dudley).
> Noah Webster. Scudder (Horace E.)
> Henry D. Thoreau. Sanborn (Frank B.)
> Nathaniel Hawthorne. Lowell (James Russell).
> J. Fenimore Cooper. Lounsbury (T. R.)
> N. P. Willis. Aldrich (Thomas Bailey).
> William Gilmore Simms. Cable (George W.)
> Benjamin Franklin. Higginson (T. W.)

Around the Hub. A Boy's Book about Boston.
    Drake (Samuel A.) Illust.   8°   2 00
Around-the-world Tour of Christian Missions. A
    Universal Survey. Bainbridge (Wm. F.)   8°   2 00
Biographical Notes and Personal Sketches of James
    T. Fields.   8°   2 00
Civilization of the Period of the Renaissance in
    Italy. Burckhardt (Jacob). Translated by S.
    G. C. Middlemore. 2 vols.   8° *e*2 50
Constitutional History of England, The, from 1760
    to 1860. Yonge (Charles Duke).   12°   1 75
D'Israeli (I.) Complete Works. Edited by His Son,
    Lord Beaconsfield. 6 vols.   8°   7 50

> Curiosities of Literature. 3 vols.
> Calamities and Quarrels of Authors, and Memories. 1 vol.
> Literary Character; History of Men of Genius. 1 vol.
> Amenities of Literature; Sketches and Characters. 1 vol.

*Dr. Gilbert's Daughters. Mathews (Margaret Har-
    riet). Illust.   12°   1 50
Eastern Proverbs and Emblems Illustrating Old
    Truths. Long (J.)   8°   1 00

English Men of Letters. Edited by Jno. Morley. 12° $0 75

Lamb. Ainger (Alfred). Dickens. Ward (A. W.)
Bentley. Jebb (R. C.) Grey. Gosse (E. W.)

Euthanasy; or, Happy Talks Toward the End of
Life. Mountford (William). 12° 2 00

Fortunate Failure. Le Row (Caroline B.) 12° 1 25

*French History for English Children. Brook (Sarah).
With Colored Maps. 8° 2 00

Gems of Illustrations. From Sermons and Other
Writings of the Rev. Thomas Guthrie. 8° 1 50

*Golden Motto Series. Illust. 4 vols. 16° 3 00

Robert Rightheart. The Golden Motto.
Earl Whiting. The Adventurer.

Henry W Longfellow. Biography, Anecdote, Letters, Criticism. With Portrait. Kennedy (W.
Sloane). Illust. 8° 1 50

Heroic Methodists of the Olden Time. Wise
(Daniel). 1 25

History of American Literature. Tyler (Moses Coit). 8° 3 00

History of Ancient Egypt. Rawlinson (George).
2 vols. 8° e3 00

History of the Egyptian Religion. Tiele (C. P.)
Translated by James Ballingal. 8° 3 00

In the Levant. Warner (Charles Dudley). 8° 2 00

*Jessie and Ray. Studies in Natural History and
Science. Woodbridge (Miss A. E.) Illust. 16° 1 00

Knight-Banneret. Sermons. Cross (Joseph). 12° 1 50

*Lady Greensatin; or, The History of Jean Paul and
His Little Mice. Illust. 12° 1 25

Living Truths. From the Writings of Charles
Kingsley. Selected by E. E. Brown. 16° 1 00

Mission Life in Greece and Palestine. Memorials
of Mary Biscoe Baldwin. Pitman (Emma Raymond). Illust. 12° 1 50

Mrs. Solomon Smith Looking On. Alden (Mrs.
G. R. [Pansy].) 16° 1 50

My Winter on the Nile. Warner (Charles Dudley). 8° 2 00

Odyssey of Homer, The. Done into English Prose.
Butcher (S. H.) and Lang (A.) 8° 2 00

*One Winter's Work. Payne (Mrs. A. M. M.) 16° 1 00

Orations and Essays, with Selected Parish Sermons.
Diman (J. Lewis). 8° 2 50

Parent's Assistant; or, Stories for Children. Edge-
worth (Maria). Illust. 18 $1 00
Pictures and Legends from Normandy and Brittany.
Macquoid (Thomas and Katharine). 8° 2 25
Practical Microscopy. Davis (George E.) Illust. 8° 3 00
Preparatory Greek Course in English. Wilkinson
(W. C.) 1 00
Protestant Foreign Missions. Their Present State.
Christlieb (Theodore). 16° 1 00
Prudence Palfrey. Aldrich (Thomas Bailey). 16° 1 50
Prophets of Israel. Smith (W. Robertson). 8° 1 75
Republic of God, The. An Institute of Theology.
Mulford (Elisha). 8° 2 00
Saunterings in Europe. Wood (Charles). 8° 1 50
*Sea and Shore. Wright (Julia McNair). Illust. 12° 1 25
Social Equality. A Short Study in a Missing Sci-
ence. Mallock (William H.) 12° 1 00
Spare Hours. First and Second Series. Brown
(John). Illust. 2 vols. 12° *e*1 50
*Sweet Clover Series. May (Carrie L.) Illust.
4 vols. 16° 4 00

> Nellie Milton's Housekeeping. Brownie Sanford.
> Sylvia's Burden. Ruth Lovell.

*Talks to Boys and Girls about Jesus. A Life of
Christ for the Young. Crafts (W F.) 16° 75
*The Christmas Tree: A Story of German Domestic
Life. Skelton (Mrs. Henrietta). Illust. 16° 1 25
*Through the Looking-glass, and What Alice Found
There. Carroll (Lewis). Illust. 12° 1 50
Three in Norway. By Two of Them. Illust. 12° 1 75
To-days and Yesterdays. Cooke (Carrie Adelaide). 12° 1 25
*True Womanhood. Hints on the Formation of
Womanly Character. Johnson (Franklin). 16° 1 00
*Walnut Grove Series. Illust. 4 vols. 16° 4 00

> Good Measure. Making Honey.
> Carl Bartlett. Little Peanut Merchant.

*Water-babies, The. A Fairy Tale for a Land-baby.
Kingsley (Charles). Illust. 16° 1 75
*What Our Girls Ought to Know. Studley (Mary J.) 16° 1 00
*World's Foundation, The; or, Geology for Begin-
ners. Giberne (Agnes). 12° 1 50
Yesterdays with Authors. Fields (James T.) 12° 2 00

MISSIONARY LITERATURE.

THE Missionary Theme is inexhaustible, and furnishes a fruitful field for the highest manifestations of genius in presenting the work and its necessities in such a light as to draw to itself the careful consideration of not only Churches, but nations also. Nations and Churches are composed of individuals. If we shall succeed in teaching individuals, then whole nations and Churches shall be taught and inspired.

In this work, as in all other great undertakings, the printing-press has been made to serve its purpose. Missionary literature has multiplied; and much that has been written, without this purpose specially in view, has been pressed into its service, and made to do valiant work in giving us a comprehensive view of the dark places of the earth and their great need of the Gospel of our Lord Jesus Christ as an elevating and refining influence.

Christian missions are no longer subject to the blind impulses of emotions aroused by the glowing rhetoric of eloquent orators, nor is prosperity longer dependent upon the stimulated fervor of the passing hour. What Churches demand to-day is broad and comprehensive intelligence upon this subject. They would know facts, and then meet these facts with intelligent action. As this knowlege increases, the sense of responsibility intensifies, and benevolence will become a positive factor in churchly life.

In presenting the following very complete and comprehensive Catalogue of Books and Tracts, illustrating the different fields of Protestant missionary labor and the different phases of missionary work, we do so recognizing the demand of the Church for a broad and universal knowledge of this important theme.

We believe all the books and tracts here mentioned are worthy of perusal and study, and that by reading them our people will be inspired with a zeal for the divinely appointed scheme for evangelizing the entire world, and redeeming lost and perishing humanity from the darkness of superstition and thralldom of death, and bringing them to the glorious life and liberty of the children of God.

---

1. GENERAL TREATMENT OF MISSIONS.

Foreign Missionary Manual. Contains much Information. Dobbins (F. S.)	16°	$1 00
Foreign Missions. Anderson (Rufus).	12°	1 25
Foreign Protestant Missions. Christlieb (Theodor).	16°	75
Missionary Papers. Lowrie (J. C.)	12°	1 25
Proceedings of the First Interseminary Missionary Convention. Paper cover.	8°	25
Problem of Religious Progress, The. Dorchester (D.)	12°	2 00

2. GENERAL HISTORY.

Foreign Missions of the Presbyterian Church, The. Lowrie (J. C.)	12°	75
Historical Sketches of Woman's Missionary Societies. Daggett (Mrs. L. H.)	16°	75
History of the Missions of the American Board. [India, Sandwich Islands, Oriental Churches, 2 vols.] Anderson (Rufus). 4 vols.	12°	*e*1 50
Missionary Sketches. A Concise History of the Work of the American Baptist Union. Smith (S. F.)	16°	1 00
Missions and Missionary Society of the Methodist Episcopal Church. Reid (J. M.) 2 vols.	12°	3 00
Woman's Foreign Missionary Society, The, of the Methodist Episcopal Church. Wheeler (Mrs. Mary Sparkes).	12°	1 50
Woman's Medical Work in Foreign Lands. Gracey (Mrs. J. T.)	16°	30

3. BIOGRAPHY.

Heroines of the Mission Field. Pitman (Mrs. E. R.)	12°	1 50
Leaders of the Church Universal. From the German of Dr. Piper. Maccracken (H. M.)	8°	3 00
Journal and Letters of Henry Martyn. Wilberforce (S.)	12°	1 25
Life of Alexander Duff, D. D. Smith (George). 2 vols. in one.	8°	2 00

Life of Coke. Drew (Samuel).	16°	$0 80
Life of David Livingstone. Blaikie (W. G.)	8°	3 50
Life of John Scudder. Waterbury (J. B.)	12°	1 75
Life of William Carey. Belcher (Joseph).	16°	1 25
Life of William Ellis. Ellis (J. E.) Introduction by Henry Allon.	8°	4 20
Memoir of Rev. William C. Burns, Missionary to China, English Presbyterian Church. Burns (Islay).	12°	2 50
Memoirs of William Goodell, D. D.; or, Forty Years in the Turkish Empire. Prime (E. D. G.)	12°	2 50

4. INDIA.

Four Years' Campaign in India. Taylor (William).	12°	1 25
Gems of India. Humphrey (Mrs. E. J.)	12°	1 00
History of India. An Excellent Manual. Taylor (Meadows).	16°	3 50
History of Protestant Missions in India. Of Special Value. Sherring (M. A.)	8°	7 20
India. History, Description, and Illustration. Feudge (Fannie R.)	12°	1 50
Indian Missionary Directory, 1881. Badley (B. H.)	8°	1 50
Land of the Veda, The. Butler (William).	8°	3 50
Life by the Ganges. Mullens (Mrs.)	16°	80
Missionary Life among the Villages in India. Scott (T. J.)	12°	1 50
Six Years in India. Humphrey (Mrs. E. J.)	16°	1 00

5. CHINA.

China and Japan. Wiley (I. W.)	12°	1 25
China and the Chinese. Nevius (J. L.)	12°	1 75
Chinese Buddhism. Edkins (Joseph).	8°	4 50
Chinese, The, their Education, etc. Martin (W. A. P.)	12°	1 50
Foreigner in China, The. Wheeler (Rev. S. N.)	12°	1 25
Journeys in North China, Mongolia, etc. Williamson (Alexander). 2 vols.	12°	6 00
Middle Kingdom, The. Williams (S. Wells). 2 vols.	12°	4 00
Our Life in China. Nevius (Mrs. Helen S. C.)	16°	1 50
Religions in China. Edkins (Joseph).	8°	2 50
Religions of China, The. Legge (James).	12°	1 50

River of Golden Sand, The.   Travels through China,
including Western China, and Eastern Thibet to
Burmah.   Gill (William).   2 vols.   8° $12 00
Social Life of the Chinese. Doolittle (Justus). 2 vols. 12°   5 00

6. JAPAN.

China and Japan.   Wiley (I. W.)   12°   1 25
Mikado's Empire, The.   Griffis (W. E.)   8°   4 00
Unbeaten Tracks in Japan. Bird (Isabella L.) 2 vols. 8°   5 00

7. THE TURKISH EMPIRE.

Among the Turks.   Hamlin (Cyrus).   12°   1 50
Bible Work in Bible Lands.   Bird (Isaac).   12°   1 50
Forty Years in the Turkish Empire.   Memoirs of
William Goodell, D. D.   Prime (E. D. G.)   12°   2 50
Races of European Turkey.   Clark (E. L.)   8°   3 00
Romance of Missions.   Woman's Work in Asiatic
Turkey.   West (Maria A.)   12°   2 00
Ten Years on the Euphrates. A Very Useful Book.
Wheeler (C. H.)   16°   1 00

8. AFRICA.

Adventures of a Missionary.- (Moffat).   12°   1 00
Central Africa.   Long (C. Chaillé).   8°   2 50
Christian Adventures in South Africa. Taylor (W.) 12°   1 50
Colonel Gordon in Central Africa, 1874–79.   8°   8 00
Four Years in Ashantee.   Ramseyer and Kuhne
(Missionaries).   12°   1 75
Livingstone in South Africa. From 1840–1856. Jew-
ett (S. H.)   16°   1 00
Memoirs of Missionary Labors in Africa and the
West Indies.   Moister (William).   12°   75
Missionary Travels and Researches in South Africa.
Livingstone (David).   8°   4 50
To the Central African Lakes and Back.   The Nar-
rative of the Royal Geographical Society's Last
Central African Expedition, 1878–80.   Thomson
(Joseph), in command.   2 vols.   12°   6 00
Twelve Months in Madagascar. Mullens (Joseph). 12°   1 75
Western Africa.   Wilson (J. Leighton).   12° `1 25
Zulu Land.   Grout (Lewis).   12°   1 50

9. SOUTH SEAS.

Forty Years' Mission Work in Polynesia and New Guinea. Murray (H. W.)	12°	$2 50
Gems from the Coral Islands. Gill (Wm.) 2 vols.	12°	2 50
Missionary Among Cannibals, A. A Life of Rev. John Hunt in Fiji. Rowe (G. S.)	12°	85
Polynesian Researches. Ellis (W.) 4 vols.	12°	5 00

10. MEXICO.

Our Next-door Neighbor. Haven (Gilbert).	12°	3 50

11. AMERICAN INDIANS.

Life Among the Choctaws. Benson (Henry C.)	12°	1 50
Life Among the Indians. Finley (J. B.)	12°	1 50
Mission Life Among the Indians of Oregon.	16°	50

12. MISCELLANEOUS, TRAVELS, ETC.

Around the World. Hendrix (E. R.)	12°	2 00
Chinese in America, The. Gibson (O.)	12°	1 50
Christian Missions before the Reformation. Walrond (F. F.)	16°	1 25
From Egypt to Japan. Field (H. M.)	12°	2 00
Missionary Concerts for the Sunday-school. A Collection of Declamations, Select Readings, and Dialogues. Smith (W. T.)	16°	75
Missionary in Many Lands, The. House (Erwin).	12°	1 00
Mister Horn and His Friends; or, Givers and Giving. Pearse (Mark Guy.) Paper, 50c.	16°	1 00
Non-Christian Religious Systems.	18°	e 75

Hinduism. Williams (Monier). Islam. Stobart (J. W. H.). The Koran. Muir (Sir W.) Buddhism. Davids (Rys). Confucianism. Douglas (R. K.)

Orient and its People, The. Hauser (Mrs.)	12°	1 50
Our Oriental Missions. Thomson (Edward). 2 vols.	12°	2 00
Round the World. Kingsley (Calvin). 2 vols.	12°	2 00
These for Those: Our Indebtedness to Missions. Warren (William).	16°	1 50
To the East by the Way of the West. Marvin (Bishop).	12°	2 00
White Fields of France, The. Bonar (Horatius).	12°	1 25

Women of the Orient, The. Houghton (Ross C.)   12° $1 50
Young Folks of Renfrew. Beverle (Mrs. Dr. J. H.
    [Miss M. E. Taneyhill].)   16°   75

YOUTH'S LIBRARY.

Ceylonese Converts, The. Brief Memoirs of Emi-
    nent Workers in the Ceylon Missions.   30
Conversations on the Life of William Carey, D. D.,
    Founder of the Baptist Missions in the East
    Indies. Designed for Youth.   35
History of Early Missions in India, The. To which
    is added a Memoir of Mrs. Ann Hazeltine
    Judson.   45
History of the Missions in Greenland and Labra-
    dor, A. From Carne's Lives of Eminent Mis-
    sionaries.   45
Indian Missionary Reminiscences. Elliott (Chas.)   50
Life of Christian F. Swartz, The, one of the First
    Protestant Missionaries in India. Norris (W. H.)   35
Life of Rev. Henry Martyn, The, Missionary to India.
    Norris (W H.)   35
Life of Robert Morrison, The, the First Protestant
    Missionary to China. Alcott (Wm. A.)   35
Missionary Anecdotes.   16°   90
Missionary Book for the Young. A First Book on
    Missions.   40
Missionary Narrative of the Triumphs of Grace, A,
    as Seen in the Conversion of Kafirs, Hotten-
    tots, Fingoes, and Other Natives in South Africa.
    Young (Samuel), twelve years a Missionary in
    that Country.   40
Missionary Teacher, The. A Memoir and Early
    History of the Oregon Mission. Mudge (Z. A.)   45
Mission Life Among the Indians of Oregon.   50
New Zealanders, The. Abridged from the Library
    of Entertaining Knowledge. Smith (Daniel).   50
Notices of Foochow and Other Ports of China,
    with Reference to Missionary Operations.   45
South Sea Missions. No. 1. Island of Rurutu.   30
Tortola; or, The Native Missionary of the West
    India Islands.   35

MISSIONARY TRACTS.

How Much, and How. A Treatise on Systematic Giving. A Valuable Tract. Stevens (Abel). Pp. 16.

Japanese Door, The. Fowler (C. H.)

Message, The. Fowler (C. H.) Pp. 52.

> Spirit of the Gospel. Christ Necessary. Our Business and "Home Heathen." Cost. Our Field is Larger than Our Availability. Success. The Triumph in Our Day. Protestantism and Romanism. How to Raise the Money.

Missionary Office Tract, No. 3. Pp. 51.

Our Missionary Society. What is it? What is its Field? Is it Expensive? Do Missions Pay? Will we Succeed? Results. Reid (J. M.) Pp. 20.

Speedy Christianization of the World. A Sketch of the Missionary Enterprise and its Agencies. Butler (William). Pp. 20.

Support of Missions, The. How the Missionary Society is Administered. Instructions of the Discipline on Missions: Elements of Power of the Plan. Harris (Bishop). Pp. 36.

> [All the above series of Tracts may be had at the rate of one cent for 30 pages.]

Appeal on Behalf of Missions, An. Tract-book Series. Edwards (W. S.) $0 05

Appeal to Christian Workers of All Denominations, etc., An. Pocket Series, No. 83. Mahan (Asa), Lowrey (A.), Steele (Daniel), and Swan (Frederick G.) Single, 3c. Ten copies.   21

Conversion of Padre Rojana, a Mexican Priest. Carter (Thomas).   3

Developing the Missionary Spirit in Sunday-schools. Murdock (J. W.)   2

Go or Die. Kelley (Dr.)   15

Go or Send. A Plea for Missions. Prize Essay. Published by Order of the Board of Missions of the Methodist Episcopal Church, South. Haygood (A. G.)   20

Mexico: The Past and Present of the Country: Its Resources and Prospects. Ellinwood (F. F.)   10

Missionary Office Leaflets, Nos. 1-5. Gratuitous.

Missionary Outline Series—China. Extent, History, Population, Industries, and Religions of China, and Christian Missions therein. Gracey (J. T.) Maps showing Location of Missions of all Societies. $0 25

Missions. An Essay. Anderson (Dr.), Missionary to Spain.   15

Mission Work. Thrall (H. S.)   15

Principles and Facts of Missions, The. Bond (B. W.)   15

Thoughts on Missions; or, the Principles, Facts, and Obligations of Christian Missions. Cunnyngham (Dr.)   15

World of Missions, The. A General Review of the Results of Protestant Missions in 1879. Chautauqua Text-book, No. 30. Carroll (H. K.)   10

Fifty-four Four-paged Tracts, in one Package, suitable for distribution in Sunday-schools.   15

The following are the titles of the Tracts, viz.:

1. Missionary First-fruits.
2. The Lord's-day in a Heathen Land.
3. Mongolian Boy.
4. Hindu and the Tracts.
5. Self-torture.
6. New Zealand.
7. Heathens Know not the Good God.
8. Karen Converts.
9. Cherokee Indian.
10. Greenlanders.
11. Siberian Leper.
12. Tupe of Raratonga.
13. Wild Men of the Jungle.
14. Little Cornelia.
15. Heathen Prayers.
16. African Girl.
17. Orphans in the East.
18. Where shall I Go Last of All?
19. Hadara.
20. Missionary Ship.
21. Trust in God.
22. Hindu School-girls.
23. Treading the Fire.
24. Juggernaut..
25. Wild Choop.
26. Happy Hottentot.
27. All Given Up for Christ.
28. New Zealand Girl.
29. Mystery Man.
30. Old Saul.
31. Blind Bartimeus.
32. Sandwich Islander.
33. Hook-swinging.
34. Andres Stoffles, etc.

INDEX OF AUTHORS.

www.ingramcontent.com/pod-product-compliance
Lightning Source LLC
Chambersburg PA
CBHW021330110726
47900CB00005B/1418